A MATTER OF FAITH

by Duke Woodrick

Dedication

This book is dedicated to my granddaughter,
Kylee Brewer.
The only angel I know.

Foreword

This book was a pleasure to read and the story hit close to home. I lost my father when I was twenty-one-years old and this story brought me closer to him and helped me to remember our experiences together.

If you have lost loved ones and ever wanted a moment to see or speak to them again, this is your story. I hope that you enjoy reading it as much as I have.

Deneishia L. Jacobpito, MFA

Acknowledgments

I would like to thank all the people who read this novel before it was published and gave me their support: Wanda Barnett, Carol Ricci, Patti Koons, Gordon and Sandy Becker, my wife, Marjorie, and my mother, Wylda Woodrick.

A special thanks to Mary Schramski, president of the Henderson Libraries Foundation and the NEA (The National Endowment for the Arts) for sponsoring the Writers' Forum that made this publication possible. To my editor, Jami Carpenter, for making my writing more readable.

Also by Duke Woodrick

In the Beginning: Project Genesis

A fast-paced, enthralling story about the UFO crash in Roswell, New Mexico, and the lengths to which the government goes to cover it up. (A 2014 Readers' Favorite Book Award Finalist.)

Prologue

Canon City, Colorado

It was a cold night. Colder than usual, with snowdrifts three feet high on each side of the road leading into the Canon Prison parking lot. I was there to witness Jason Thomas Bradford's execution. He'd confessed to seven murders and wanted the death penalty as his punishment.

This was where I met Ella Martin. I'd seen her several times before on the witness stand and in the gallery at Jason's trial.

I was working as a freelance writer, writing mostly for a small independent newspaper called the *Denver Review*. My column focused on politics, found on the Opinion page. My opinion normally leaned left of center, so being against the death penalty wasn't unusual for me. I'd won a seat at the execution through a state lottery, designed to limit the number of reporters covering the event. Ella, on the other hand, was there at the request of the condemned man.

Originally, Jason was charged with premeditation in the cold-blooded killing of Sandra Brown, a single woman living alone, found beaten to death on her living room floor. After a lengthy trial, the charges were reduced to second-degree, with no premeditation. For his crime, he received a sentence of eighteen years to life. After serving fewer than five, he mysteriously confessed to six more murders. He'd been the prime suspect in four of those killings, but there was no direct evidence linking him to the murders—just similarities. And the other two happened many years before when Jason was a young boy, both considered accidental at the time. Jason said he wouldn't give any names of the victims or details unless he received the death penalty.

Ella Martin was the star witness for the prosecution. She was also the only so-called eyewitness to the murder of Sandra Brown. This, however, became a point of contention during the trial because Ella Martin was never physically there to witness the crime. In reality, Ella was eleven hundred miles away, lying on a gurney in an emergency room at the moment of Sandra Brown's death.

~~~

I found a place to park, then bundled up in my fur-lined Parka and stepped out onto the snow-covered ground. I headed for the bus that would transport the witnesses into the prison.

In the parking lot was a thin demarcation line drawn in the snow. Half a dozen police officers stood on one side for crowd control. On the other side of the line were roughly fifty people. All were there to protest the execution of Jason Thomas Bradford.

The crowd, in solidarity, held up lit candles and waved them back and forth in a protest vigil. One man, who looked like the spitting image of John Phillips of the Mamas and Papas folk rock band, played guitar and sang an old Bob Dylan song, "I Shall Be Released." When he finished his rendition, he sang another Dylan song, "The Times They Are A-Changin'."

As I walked toward the bus, one of the protesters spat at me and called me a bastard. Several of the protesters held up signs. One of the signs read: FREE JASON BRADFORD, HE'S AN INNOCENT MAN. Another read: ATHEISTS AGAINST CAPITAL PUNISHMENT. And still another exclaimed: LETHAL INJECTION IS INHUMANE!

When I stepped onto the bus, the driver, in a prison guard uniform, asked me for some form of identification. I showed him the pass I'd received from the state and my press card. He made a mark on his clipboard and with the eraser end of his pencil pointed sternly toward the back of the bus.

As I walked down the center aisle I recognized several familiar faces from the trial. Sandra Brown's father sat stone-faced to my left. He looked as though he had aged twenty years and put on forty pounds. His hair, as I remembered it, had been dark brown with a little gray around the temples. Now it was snow-white. He blinked with only one eye, haphazardly, which made me think he may have suffered a stroke.

Across the aisle on the opposite side was Jason Bradford's mother, a slight woman in her sixties. She had not aged a day. Seated next to her was a young man in his late teens, wearing dark-framed glasses and sporting a snake tattoo on his neck.

I made my way to the back of the bus and sat between two large women, who could have played defensive linebackers for the Denver Broncos' football team.

Once all passengers were on board, the bus driver gave us a brief history of the prison in a well-rehearsed speech: when it was built and the names of the most notorious outlaws to have occupied a cell. Then he went into how it had changed over the years. When he finished, he started the bus and headed toward the prison. Two minutes later we were passing through the front gate.

Once inside, he drove around to the back of the main building and said, "This building houses cell blocks A and B. It is also where the death row inmates live. Today, eight are awaiting execution. Tomorrow there will be seven.

"After you exit the bus, please walk up the steps onto the platform where officers will greet you and escort you into the building."

At the top of the steps, we met four uniformed officers—all carrying shotguns. Once on the platform, we were separated and reassembled into three groups. Each group under the control of one of the four officers. Then we marched into the building, single file, the fourth officer taking up the rear to make sure no one wandered off on their own or lagged too far behind.

We walked down a long corridor that seemed like it would never end. We passed an intersecting corridor, which led to cell blocks A and B, where the most violent criminals lived.

Finally, at the end of the corridor, we entered a room to our right. The room was white. The walls were made of cinderblock. A row of lockers rested against one wall. We were told to select a locker and put everything we had on us inside that wasn't clothing. A woman, who identified herself as the prison administrator, asked us to form a line as she called our names. Then we went through a metal detector, after which each journalist was handed a tablet and pencil and led to the Viewing Room.

The Viewing Room accommodated thirty witnesses. There were three rows of ten chairs on a tiered platform overlooking one another, like seating in a movie theater. The death chamber was five feet in front of the first row, separated by a large glass panel. A curtain hung inside the chamber in a closed position so the witnesses could not see the condemned man until right before his execution.

I sat two rows behind Ella Martin.

At eleven-fifty, the warden drew back the curtain. He seemed smaller than I remembered. And unusually calm for a man about to be euthanized. He lay on a padded metal table, which had two flat armrests, each extending outward, resembling a cross. Straps restrained him in place so he couldn't disrupt the procedure. A catheter was taped to his left arm through which the deadly mixture would flow.

I watched Jason's eyes desperately scanning

the Viewing Room, searching for someone. Then, finally, they locked on the person seated two rows in front of me. Ella Martin. His focus was nowhere else. Not even on his mother—only her. When he saw her, he smiled. I could see her reflection in the window smiling back, genuinely pleased to see him.

At eleven-fifty-five, the warden asked Jason if he had anything to say to the relatives of the victims or the reporters.

Jason turned his head to face the audience. "There's nothing I can say that could bring back your loved ones. If I could, I would. Having said that, I will say I am sorry for all the pain you've had to go through over the past seven years, and for some of you, even longer." He paused.

"I sincerely believe that your loved ones are now in a much better place, with his or her creator. I will soon be in His presence, and only He and He alone can judge me. I would like to thank my friend, my only friend, Ella Martin, for being here tonight." He looked over at the warden and said, "That's all."

The warden looked at his watch, wiped a hesitant tear from his eye, and silently nodded for the executioner to start the procedure. The executioner was in a booth, hidden from view of the audience.

The executioner pushed the first button, which opened a valve that started the flow of sodium pentothal, a painkiller. Calm and euphoric, Jason looked over at Ella again, and gave a thumb up. Ella did the same. The executioner pressed the second button, starting the flow of pancuronium bromide, a paralytic agent and respiration suppressant. Jason's fists compressed and eyes fluttered in spasmodic rhythm. His breathing stilled. Not minutes after, he closed them. His body was motionless. The third and final button released the flow of potassium chloride. Finally, his heart stopped and his hands relaxed.

At 12:07 a.m., on November 20, 2007, Jason Thomas Bradford was declared dead. The warden closed the curtain as the witnesses rose out of their chairs, and slowly exited the room.

From the time we left the Viewing Room until we boarded the bus, I don't remember anyone saying a word.

Back on the bus, I watched where Ella sat down, then rushed over and sat next to her. I waited until after the engine started before I got up the nerve to ask her what I hoped would be a profitable proposition, at least for me. I looked at her and asked, "Mrs. Martin?"

She immediately interrupted me. "Ms.," she said.

"Pardon?"

"It's Ms."

"Oh, I'm sorry."

"Don't be," she said. "It's by choice. I never found time to remarry after my husband died."

I told her my name was John Adams and that I was a writer, a journalist, and had followed the case from the beginning. I asked if I could set up an interview session with her.

"I don't know if that is possible," she muttered.

She stated that since her mission was complete,

her time was running out. I assumed she meant that nothing was keeping her here now that Jason was gone. Then she said, "But if you're willing, I'd be more than happy to go somewhere—like a nice warm coffee shop—where I could get a bite to eat. And you can ask me anything your heart desires."

There was no hesitation. I jumped at the chance.

After exiting the bus, we walked to my car, and I drove out of the prison parking lot looking for a place where we could talk. It was late. When I reached the main highway, she looked over at me and asked, "Are you religious?" I looked back at her and told her I wasn't, and that I considered myself a devout atheist. I asked her if that made a difference. "Yes, in a way it would. It means you'll listen to what I have to say with a certain degree of skepticism." I turned my head back to the road, still looking for a quiet place to go.

At 1:00 a.m., I pulled into a Denny's. The storm had passed and the moon was full.

We made our way to a secluded booth, away from other late-night patrons. We ordered two breakfast specials, which consisted of two eggs, two pancakes, two pieces of bacon or sausage, and hash brown potatoes. I told the server if she kept the coffee flowing there'd be a big tip when we finished. Little did I know how much later that would be.

Ella looked over at me. "You know, I do remember seeing you in the gallery at the trial."

I removed my cassette recorder from my briefcase and set it down on the table with two extra blank one-hour tapes. She asked me where she should start. I knew some of the story from the trial, but I wasn't expecting anything like I was about to hear.

I began: "Why don't you start by telling me a little bit about yourself. Then you can go into what happened the day Sandra Brown died."

After three hours, I ran out of tape. I was lucky because the Denny's restaurant we were in was next to a small mini-mall, which also had a Walgreen's Drugstore, open twenty-four hours. I was back in a flash with five more one-hour blank cassettes.

She talked without stopping until seven in the morning. Then she looked at me and said, "Well, I guess that's about it. I can't think of anything more to say."

I had planned on having maybe enough information to write a half page or so for the Opinion on the pros and cons of the death penalty— from both sides of the political spectrum. From the perspective of a prosecution witness to a friend of the condemned. At the time, I had no idea how instrumental this woman would be in Jason's decision to confess to the other murders. My half-page article was starting to blossom before my very eyes, beyond my wildest imagination.

After I gave the waitress a one-hundred-dollar bill we left the restaurant and headed back to my car. We drove back to the prison, where Ella had parked her car. She turned toward me. "Do you think you could write whatever it is you're going to write, so people won't be afraid to die? There is something waiting on the other side."

The wheels in my head were already turning. I was thinking of how I might take this information and turn it into a book. I told her I would do my best. I thanked Ella for the interview. Then she got out of my car, smiled, and as she got into to hers, she turned to me. "You know, it's all just a matter of faith; don't you think? Unless you've been there, then that word has no meaning."

I went back to the hotel where I was staying, sat down at my laptop, and began laying out a plan. Ella had mentioned some important people she thought I should talk to before I ended my investigation. One person, in particular, was the warden.

Chapter 1

Forty-two years earlier

Macon, Georgia was a sleepy Southern city back in 1966. The conflict in Vietnam had been raging for a little more than a year, and most folks in the South supported fighting communism over there rather than in our back yard.

Sally Jo Allen grew up dirt poor in a small two-bedroom bungalow with two younger sisters and an older brother. The girls all shared the same bedroom, while her brother made his bed on the living room couch. He had recently received his draft notice and would be leaving for his induction center in El Paso, Texas.

Her father worked nights as a janitor and her mother was a waitress at a small café, where she worked for minimum wage, plus tips. Sally had a tenth-grade education. She despised authority, including what little bit her parents provided. She hung out with the wrong crowd, where she learned all about drugs, alcohol, and boys. When she attended school, which wasn't often, she spent as much time in detention as she did in her regular classes. She swore she'd be out of Macon before she was sixteen.

Her prediction was pretty close. She was sixteen and four months when she made her escape.

The British invasion had already taken place several years earlier with the Beatles performing on the *Ed Sullivan Television Show*. Bob Dylan had transformed folk music into folk rock. And psychedelic music was gaining popularity in the Haight-Ashbury section of San Francisco, with groups like Jefferson Airplane and the Grateful Death leading the way.

And so, on July 17, 1966, Sally Jo Allen met and rode out of town with a group of musicians from New York. They'd just finished a two-week engagement at a club called the Island. The band called themselves Civilized Confusion and played psychedelic rock. They traveled around in an old van covered in graffiti … hippie artwork. They were headed to Denver, where they were the opening act for a well-established group known as Holy Mackerel.

Before she ran away, she took every cent her father and mother had stashed away for the following month's rent.

~~~

Sally Jo lived in Denver with the group for almost a year. She learned how to play the tambourine and had a good sense of rhythm, so to earn her keep, she started playing with the band. Then they moved to Colorado Springs, where they got a long-term contract as the house band, playing at The Corral, a hangout for the military police stationed at Fort Carson. This was where she met Jack, her future husband.

~~~

Jack Bradford was a big man with a powerful physique. He was strikingly handsome. Sally Jo was intrigued by his ability to draw women to him. She watched with curiosity as the women flocked around him as if he was a rock star. *What was it about Jack that was so appealing?* She didn't know but wanted to find out. She knew that coming onto him would probably be a mistake. She didn't want to be just another trophy or a notch on a bedpost. She developed a plan to get his attention.

Jack was an excellent pool player. Eight-ball was his game. Once he started playing, he controlled the table. The pool table was next to the bar. At the end of every set, Sally decided to spend her break at the bar where she'd order a soft drink. People asked her why she didn't drink alcohol. She told them that liquor made her lose her timing on the stage. But the truth was, she wasn't old enough to drink. And as long as she wasn't drinking, there was no reason to ask how old she was.

One night, while Jack was on the table getting ready to bank the eight ball into the corner pocket, she made her move. On his backstroke, she deliberately bumped his cue stick, causing the cue ball to scratch in the side pocket. Jack was furious. He turned around ready to fight, but when he realized Sally was the culprit, he smiled. He'd been secretly watching her for weeks, and this gave him the opportunity to talk to her. He ordered a drink, and they went outside together.

They didn't go to bed together that night, or any other night until they wed … three weeks later.

They found a small one-bedroom apartment in town, not far from the club. Jack was a jealous man, which surprised Sally. He went to the club every night so he could keep an eye on her. They'd been married about four months when Sally found out she was pregnant. She worked until she started to show and then quit the band. They moved again, this time into a small two-bedroom house on the west side of town.

Jack Bradford was a mechanic assigned to the Military Police. He had reached the rank of staff sergeant early in his career but was busted down to corporal after punching his company commander. Jack had served two tours of duty in Vietnam and hoped he wouldn't be going back.

They named the first child Prescott, and shortly after his birth, Sally was pregnant again. They named him Troy. And one year to the day after Troy was born, she gave birth to Ryan, her third child.

Jack was a violent man. He loved to fight. At 6 feet 6 inches tall, weighing roughly 250 pounds, he was solid muscle. His company commander had sent him to a psychiatrist to find out what made him tick. Buried on the last page of the report was the therapist's finding: Jack had a personality disorder, and he manifested aggressive, antisocial tendencies. The medical term for this pattern of behavior was psychopath. The report was passed to another doctor for a second opinion and possible discharge if the findings were similar. This page of the report mysteriously disappeared before it reached his company commander's desk.

Besides fighting, Jack liked to drink. And when he drank, he got mean. And when he got mean, he took out his aggression on his boys. He'd make them do stupid things for his own sadistic pleasure.

Everything went well over the next year, until the day Sally informed Jack she was pregnant ... again. All his hard work, staying out of trouble, disappeared in an instant. He took out his anger on the mess hall cook. It began with hitting him in the head with a serving tray and ended with the cook going to the emergency room for stitches.

For this, Jack got four months in the stockade and a reduction in rank, back down to private first class.

Chapter 2

The scene outside Penrose Hospital was almost as chaotic as what was taking place in the maternity ward on the fourth floor.

An electrical storm was putting on a light show that some would say was more spectacular than any Fourth of July celebration they'd ever witnessed. Bolts of lightning, like spider veins, tore through the night sky. Thunder so loud … you had to put your hands over your ears to muffle the sound.

Directly in front of the hospital, firemen scrambled to hook up their pumper truck to a nearby hydrant in an effort to supply enough water to extinguish an old elm set ablaze by the storm.

The tree was considered a landmark. It was the oldest living thing still standing inside the city limits. It had been there for decades, before anyone thought of building a town around it.

Inside, the woman in Room 403 of the maternity ward couldn't care less about the tree, or for that matter, anything else that was going on outside her room. In severe pain, she shouted obscenities at anyone and everyone—especially someone named Jack.

Finally, at precisely 11:59 p.m. on October 31, 1971, Sally Jo Bradford gave birth to her fourth son, a 4-pound, 7-ounce boy named Jason Thomas Bradford.

His father wouldn't meet the latest addition to the family for almost another month. Not until he completed his time in the stockade for simple assault.

It had been a hard birth, but so were the other three. Nothing came easy for Sally. She was a tough woman, small in stature, standing all of five feet tall, weighing 100 pounds soaking wet. The boy was two months premature. He was colicky and had a cleft lip. He looked more like his mother than his father. Jack took one look at him and swore the boy wasn't his.

Ten weeks after his birth, Jason had surgery to close the opening in his lip. The surgery closed the opening but left a noticeable scar that ran from his upper lip and disappeared somewhere inside his left nostril.

For the first four years, Jack ignored Jason … as if he didn't exist. And then, suddenly, Jack focused all his attention on his youngest child. Everything that went wrong was Jason's fault. From Jack and Sally's declining sex life to his poor performance at work. As the boy grew, so did the cruelty.

The cruelty came in the way of verbal abuse, meant to humiliate the boy. Jack called him demeaning names like Harelip or Peewee.

Of the four boys, the oldest, Prescott was the luckiest. He got the new clothes and when he could no longer fit in them, they were handed down to Troy, then Ryan, and finally to Jason. By the time Jason got them, they were well worn.

In school, Jason was a whiz, smarter by far than anyone else in his school. He excelled in all subjects, especially math and science. But this, with his looks, made him an outcast. As the years passed by, he grew more and more antisocial. He became a loner. While the other children interacted with one another at recess, he either stayed in the classroom or sat by himself on one of the blue-gray school benches outside the cafeteria.

At home, while the other three boys were outside playing, Jason stayed in the house helping his mother with household chores. And when he wasn't helping her, he was cleaning up after his three brothers.

Sally was Jason's protector. At least, that's what she considered herself.

~~~

On May 16th, 1984, Jack Bradford was found in his back yard, dead from a single gunshot wound to the chest. According to the Colorado Springs Medical Examiner, Megan Jackson, the preliminary cause of death was severe trauma to the heart muscle and surrounding major blood vessels. Namely, the right auricle, superior vena cave, pulmonary artery, and aorta, based on the location of the entrance and exit wound. The crime scene investigator's preliminary findings ruled the cause of death as accidental. Jack was laying a shotgun down on a picnic table when it discharged.

The crime scene investigator's report described how a branch of an elm tree had somehow managed to wedge itself between two of the wooden slats that made up the tabletop. The branch, over time, broke off, leaving only a stub. The stub protruded roughly one and a quarter inch above the tabletop. And according to the deceased's twelve-year-old son, who witnessed the accident, his father loaded the shotgun and was setting it down when it went off. On closer examination, it appeared that when the deceased set the shotgun down, the stub of the branch poked inside the trigger guard, causing it to accidentally discharge.

Jack was found lying on the ground in a supine position, with his feet still resting on the bench of the picnic table. After discharging, the shotgun recoiled and broke off the protruding stub, leaving what was left flush with the surface.

The investigator noted in his report that Jack's son was helpful to the investigation. He provided a timeline. He saw what happened. And he called the police.

Jason told the investigator his father almost always cleaned his hunting rifle immediately after returning home from a hunting trip. When the accident happened, Jason was in the house washing dishes and looking out the window. He had a clear view of his father, watching him clean his shotgun and put linseed oil on the stock like he always did. Then he loaded shells into the chamber and set it down with the barrel facing him. He always kept his shotgun loaded and hidden under his side of the bed where he could get to it fast if someone broke into the house.

The investigator jotted down every word Jason said. Jason told him that when the shotgun went off, he saw his father jerk backward and fall off the bench. The shotgun went sailing in the opposite direction. At first, he wasn't sure how badly his father was hurt. Not until he ran outside to see if he could help. That's when he realized the extent of his injury and ran back into the house to call the police.

At the time of the accident, Jason said his mother was working as a housekeeper for her husband's Battalion Commander, Colonel Beauregard-Jones, a.k.a., Beau Jones.

The medical examiner took a second look at the boy talking to the CSI. She was trying to recall where she'd seen him before. She knew he looked familiar, because of the cleft lip. She just didn't know from where. Then, after loading Jack's body into the wagon, she saw Jason spit. That's when it dawned on her. Like a revelation, it all came back. It was a couple of years earlier. She was picking up the body of a young boy who had died after falling from Miller's Bridge railing into the nearly dry creek bed below. Jason's house was about one hundred yards north of Miller's Bridge. He was the last person to see and talk to the young boy before the accident.

Megan recalled Jason telling the crime scene investigator that on the day of the accident he was walking home from school with the boy until he got to the road that led to his house. Then they split up and went their separate ways. He also told the CSI that on many occasions he and the other boy would 'walk the rail,' as he put it. Miller's Bridge had a span of about sixty feet and was roughly thirty feet above the creek bed, which was mostly dry during the summer months. After the winter, when the snow melted, the creek would rise to within five feet of the underside of the bridge. The boy, whose name she didn't recall, had fallen sometime in the late summer, when the water was just a trickle. He broke his neck and both radius and ulna bones in his forearm. His death was recorded as accidental.

Megan looked over at the boy one last time as he stood beside the CSI, wiping tears from his eyes. She felt sorry for him, losing his friend, and now his father, all within a couple of years. She waved goodbye to the CSI, who remained on scene and drove off, headed for the morgue.

Chapter 3

The voice of Hank Williams, Jr. broke the morning silence with a new rendition of an old song once made popular by his father, Hank Williams, Sr. The woman in the red satin pajamas rolled over, and with one hand reached out and pushed down on her snooze button, giving her an extra ten minutes to rest. But after a minute or two, she decided to get up. There was no reason to prolong the inevitable.

Before she'd gone to bed the previous night, she doubled the recommended dosage prescribed on the back of the Maalox bottle, hoping it would give her enough relief so she could fall asleep—which it had. She sat up and swung her legs over the edge of the bed. And when she did, the nagging discomfort of indigestion that had bothered her for the past couple of days suddenly returned.

For a brief second, she thought about calling in sick. But if she did, it would tarnish her perfect attendance record. She immediately dismissed the idea, turned off her alarm, and got out of bed.

Ella was a fifty-four-year-old widow, slightly

overweight. She had short blonde hair and stood 5 feet 5 inches tall.

She worked for a large law firm in Beverly Hills that concentrated on high-profile cases, mainly those of the rich and famous. After her husband died, she focused all her attention on her work. She sold their house in Long Beach and bought a two-story townhouse in Westchester, which was just north of the Los Angeles International Airport (LAX).

She headed to the kitchen where she turned on her coffeemaker. Then it was off to the shower. And then back to the kitchen for a glance at the headlines over a bowl of Cream-of-Wheat. After she finished, she dressed. She put some cat food in Gizmo's bowl, then took another big swig of Maalox and was out the door.

She inserted a CD of her favorite singer, Willie Nelson, into the built-in player, and within seconds, his voice came booming out through her newly installed custom Bose sound system.

She backed out of her garage, changed gears, and was off on her morning commute.

She took the scenic route up Sepulveda Boulevard toward Beverly Hills, her final destination. She didn't like traveling on the freeway, so she left early; with the traffic light, she had plenty of time. Willie was singing "Georgia on My Mind," her all-time number one song, written by Hoagland "Hoagy" Carmichael. She loved music and was once an aspiring musician. She had played the cello in concert with an orchestra at Carnegie Hall.

She pulled into the parking structure attached to a ten-story professional building where she worked. Riedel, Darin, and Charles, her employer, occupied the top three floors. The parking attendant knew everyone who worked in the building, so after saying, "Hello," he waved her through.

She pulled into her personal parking stall and shut off the engine. As she did, her left arm, shoulder, and jaw suddenly went numb. She opened the car door, thinking she'd pinched a nerve and if she stood up, it would go away. But when she placed her feet on the ground and tried to stand, her legs turned into rubber, and she collapsed.

When she woke up, she was lying on her side. She didn't know how long she'd been unconscious. Not long, she guessed, because no one had found her and she was in plain sight. She was feeling better now, so she stood up, brushed herself off, locked her car door, and headed for the elevator lobby twenty yards away.

Once inside she took a private car to the top floor, where her office was. Ella worked for Riedel, the founding owner's son, who also held the controlling interest in the firm.

She stepped out of the elevator car and directly onto a sea of plush red carpet that filled a large open space. All the offices were along the perimeter in a horseshoe fashion. In the center of the open space, below a large chandelier, was a round slab of marble with an engraved image of a blindfolded Lady of Justice holding two equally balanced scales.

The ninth floor housed the firm's legal team

made up of lawyers, paralegals, investigators, and the secretarial pool. The eighth floor held the law library, where most of the real work took place. At almost any time of the day, paralegals could be found combing through the large array of books and documents, looking for some historical case or information that might benefit the firm's client in a courtroom.

Ella was the first to arrive, like always. She started up the four coffee pots, watered the plants, and looked at the day's schedule.

The morning dragged on. She spent her lunch hour in an empty conference room, reading John Sanford's latest *Prey* novel. At 4 p.m., she left work and headed for the post office.

After mailing off some sensitive material, she got back on the road and headed toward her home in Westchester. She remembered Gizmo was nearly out of cat food, and she needed more antacid tablets, so she extended her commute, driving past her townhouse and into the parking lot of a nearby supermarket.

She found a place to park and hurried inside.

She headed first for the pet aisle. The food Gizmo liked was on a shelf at the far end. She managed to reach the middle of the aisle when her heartburn returned. But this time it was different. This time, it felt like someone had driven a stake through her heart. She stopped dead in her tracks and reached for her chest. That's when the ceiling lights above the aisle started to spin and she collapsed.

A man pushing a shopping cart with a young

child sitting inside watched Ella as she reached for her chest and fell to the floor. He removed a cell phone from his pocket and dialed 911. The man was in his early thirties, and once spent a summer working as a lifeguard at a local beach. He quickly checked Ella for a pulse and put his ear near her mouth while looking at her chest for signs of breathing. She was not breathing, but he felt a weak pulse. He started to give her mouth-to-mouth resuscitation.

The paramedics responded quickly, being only two aisles over shopping for groceries when the call came in. They took over for the man working on Ella and within a minute or two, she was breathing or her own again.

Using a penlight, one of the paramedics checked her eyes to see if they were equal and reactive. Another took her blood pressure. And still another placed a nasal cannula over her ears and inserted the two stubby plastic air tubes into her nostrils, giving her a constant flow of oxygen.

The first thing Ella noticed was the bright light. Next, a voice asked if she was all right. Through the bright light, she saw several fuzzy figures leaning over her. Slowly their faces came into focus. She asked, "Where am I?"

A voice replied, "You're in a supermarket on Sepulveda Boulevard."

Over the next few minutes, an exchange of words occurred between Ella and the Los Angeles Fire Department Paramedics.

They worked up a medical history on her and connected her to a portable electrocardiogram,

EKG. They checked for any variation in her heartbeat from a normal rhythm. But their equipment recorded nothing decisive. To be on the safe side, because of her reoccurring pain, they decided to transport her to a nearby hospital.

~~~

The ride down the hill into Playa Del Rey, where the Marina del Rey Hospital was, took forever. Traffic was bumper-to-bumper. No red lights or sirens were in use. She worried about Gizmo. She wondered if she had left a night-light on and given him enough food to get by.

When they removed her from the ambulance, it was dark out and she was staring straight up into the night sky. The moon was full and she could see Ursa Major—the Big Dipper. She heard the automatic sliding glass doors open, and they pushed her through the back entrance to the emergency room. Once inside, they rolled down a corridor, where they briefly stopped at a reception desk to check her in. Then they put her in a semi-private room with a white dividing curtain to provide some privacy.

Since they didn't consider her an immediate emergency, there was no reason for a doctor to rush right into her room. A nurse handed her a hospital gown to change into, after which the nurse helped her onto another gurney. It was comfortable, with an adjustable backrest. Once in place, the nurse reconnected her to a wall mounted electrocardiogram machine and blood pressure cuff. The new monitoring equipment had all the bells and whistles. It registered the number of respirations per minute, pulse rate, blood pressure, and body temperature. She looked at a clock on the wall above the equipment: 5:30 p.m. She was getting hungry. She hadn't had anything to eat since breakfast, and her stomach was growling, making embarrassing sounds.

Chapter 4

At 6:00 p.m., a man dressed in green medical scrubs entered Ella's partitioned room. She guessed he was younger than her, somewhere in his mid-to-late forties. He was short with small features. His hair, from what she could see of it extending below his surgical cap, was silver gray. His eyes were the bluest of blue, which immediately reminded her of the Toni Morrison novel she had recently read, *The Bluest Eye*. He wore his stethoscope around his neck, draped over his shoulders, like Dr. Mark Greene on the old hit TV show, *ER*.

When he introduced himself as Dr. Henderson, head surgeon in charge of the ER, his voice surprised her. She expected a voice with a much higher pitch, not the bass or low baritone she heard. He looked at the numbers lit up on the monitor. Then he picked up the clipboard at the foot of her bed and scanned the information the paramedics had provided. When finished, he looked at her and asked her how she was feeling.

She told him she was feeling much better.

Dr. Henderson moved from the foot of the bed to her side and recommended that she remain at the hospital overnight for observation. And then, if everything went as he expected, she would be released in the morning and given an ambulatory monitor to wear over the weekend. He told her the device would record her heart rate and rhythm. It was small, and she could clip it onto a waistband or belt, and continue to do regular activities, including exercise while wearing it. Then she could bring it back on Monday and one of the doctors would analyze the data.

Before leaving, Dr. Henderson decided to take one last look at her vital signs. When he did, he noticed the numbers starting to vary. Her heart rate was increasing while her blood pressure was dropping. He checked the electrodes attached to her chest, arms, and legs, then followed the wires back to the monitor, searching for a loose lead. But he couldn't find anything wrong with the equipment.

At the same time, Ella looked over his shoulder at the clock on the wall to see the time. The numbers were out of focus. She couldn't read them. She looked back at Dr. Henderson to tell him about her blurry vision when the crushing pain in her chest returned. It was so devastating, she couldn't speak. Then she heard all the bells and whistles on her monitoring equipment sound at once. The room slowly started to spin, reminding her of the teacup ride at Disneyland. Faster and faster it went. Dr. Henderson was swept up in the swirl. The room suddenly went dark and the monitoring equipment went silent.

At first, she thought the hospital had lost

power. She lay there quietly, waiting for the lights to come back on. While she waited, she realized the pain in her chest was no longer there. And she felt wonderful. She wanted to tell the doctor there was no need for her to spend the night. She couldn't remember the last time she felt like this. Maybe never.

Then the light in the room and the monitors came back to life. The equipment was no longer making the same protesting sound it was making before the power outage. Now it was more constant, a continuous even tone. Ella realized she was no longer lying on the hospital bed; she was standing up. *Funny*, she thought. *I don't remember getting out of bed.* She was standing behind Dr. Henderson, who was leaning over a bed, taking care of a patient. She heard him say, "Ella, Ella," repeatedly calling out her name. She answered, "Dr. Henderson, I'm over here. Right behind you." But he didn't hear her. Instead, he continued shouting at the person on the bed using her name.

That's impossible, she thought. No one else had her same name. At least not many. She moved in closer and peeked over his shoulder. That's when it dawned on her. It was her body on the gurney that he was talking to, not someone else.

She watched with fascination as the doctor tilted back her head to get an open airway. He checked her pulse at the carotid artery on the side of her neck. He looked back at the monitors mounted on the wall and yelled, 'V-fib, code blue, Room 10A.'

Everyone who could respond, responded. One of the nurses ran down the corridor, then seconds later, she was back, pushing a cart toward Room 10A. The cart looked like a mechanic's tool chest, with many small drawers, four lockable wheels, and a piece of equipment resting on top. Ella knew what the piece of equipment was. She also knew what code blue meant. She'd watched enough emergency room reality TV shows over the years to know the medical jargon. Someone's heart had stopped beating and that heart belonged to her.

Ella watched as Dr. Henderson climbed up on top of the gurney and straddled her. Then he began pushing down on the center of her chest. Nurses and doctors rushed into the room as he shouted out orders. She watched as they exposed her chest. It surprised her that she wasn't the least bit embarrassed. From the crash cart, they removed a couple of round paddles with handles. Then they put some lubricant or gel on the paddles and rubbed them together. Ella watched as they placed the paddles on her chest. Dr. Henderson yelled, "Clear," and everyone backed away from the bed. The doctor pressed a trigger on one of the paddles and as the equipment made a loud thumping sound, her body jerked upward.

She looked at the monitoring equipment on the wall. There were no numbers after the 'R' for respiration. The same for 'P,' pulse. She saw a flat line running across the screen that had previously registered her heart rhythm with peaks and valleys. She wondered what all the fuss was about. She felt great; the pain was gone, and she felt as light as a feather.

Ella looked down at her body, cloaked in a golden robe. She had arms and legs, but they were translucent. She could see through herself. Her body, she thought, was like a light bulb, giving off a beautiful glow, and she felt warm all over. If this was what death was like, she welcomed it.

Suddenly, she felt herself drifting away from the hospital room where her body lay dead on the gurney. She was pulled right through the wall. She could see the metal studs sandwiched in between the sheets of drywall. She hovered just below ceiling level as she floated down the corridor toward the receptionist desk. She heard a nurse tell the receptionist, a big-busted redhead, that the woman with the blonde hair in Room 10A just flat lined. She heard the receptionist say, "That's too bad. I wanted to find out where she got her hair done." Ella again felt herself being pulled away, this time up even higher.

She went through the ceiling tiles, through the concrete that separated the first and second floor. She briefly stopped inside the nursery area of the maternity ward. She read the information on the outside of the only two occupied transparent baskets in the nursery. One was a black baby named Tyrone Smith. He was a big boy, weighed 9 pounds 3 ounces. The other baby was white. His name was Fredrick Moorehouse. He weighed 6 pounds 10 ounces.

She continued up to the third floor, unable to control her movement. She was being pulled like a piece of metal toward a magnet. She drifted down a third-floor corridor to a set of double doors. A sign posted on the wall over the entrance read, 'Oncology Department.' Once through the doors, she saw several people receiving chemotherapy.

She continued down the corridor until she was outside Room 301. She didn't have to enter—she could see through the wall.

Inside this room, lying on the bed, was an elderly gentleman. People, obviously family, were gathered around him. Ella could feel the love in the room. A doctor took his vital signs and shook his head in a negative manner. The old man's eyes were closed but he was talking to someone. Then his room suddenly filled with golden mist, which took on a human form and hovered over the dying man. Nobody could see it, except Ella. She heard the doctor tell the man's relatives that he was hallucinating, which is one of the signs when someone is near death. Brighter and brighter the form grew. Then it took the old man by the hand, kissed his forehead, and they both left the room—in spirit form, together—straight up through the ceiling. The EKG mounted on the wall stopped beeping and became a continuous tone. His relatives started crying and moved closer to the body left behind.

Ella traveled up through the roof and away from the building. She looked down at the landscape as it shrunk beneath her. The cars on Lincoln Boulevard were soon the size of ants, and then she couldn't see them at all. Only their headlights, tiny specks of light, barely moving along a freeway in rush-hour traffic. As she continued to ascend, she saw the sun coming up over the Pacific Ocean, off to the west. She knew the sun rose in the east, which, at first, confused her. Then she realized the farther she moved from Earth, the less she was connected to it. Earth became a huge ball, and then, in a split second, it was reduced to the size of a marble. And then it was gone.

Ella felt herself speeding up, moving through space, heading into the unknown. But for some reason, she wasn't afraid. Realizing she had no control of where she was going, she decided to just enjoy the ride. It reminded her of *Star Trek*, looking out the window of the spaceship The Enterprise, seeing the stars sailing by at warp speed. Up ahead in the distance, she could see a point of light, brighter than any other stars, and for some unknown reason, she knew that was her destination.

The closer she got, the brighter the light became. But it didn't hurt her eyes. She felt like she was part of the light—as if they were one and the same. Like she had been away for a while and now she was back.

Ella came to a stop in front of the light. Inside the light was a human form ... or something like it. A long robe covered its body. The light entity didn't say anything, orally, yet it said everything. It told her to look at herself. She wondered what it meant. And then suddenly she was watching her mother in a hospital room giving birth. She felt a part of her light source enter the baby's body at the same time the baby took a breath. Then she was seeing the world through the baby's eyes, reliving her life. She couldn't stop what she was seeing or change anything she saw. But she could feel the effect she had on other people. If she said something hurtful, she felt the other person's pain. If she said or did something good, she could also feel their joy.

Suddenly, she realized she wasn't alone with this being. She heard the roar of a crowd in the background. She felt like she was standing in the center of a large stadium and that she was the center of their attention. Her life was like a large three-dimensional holographic image—projected for everyone to see. She saw things she wished she could erase. Embarrassing things she'd said and done. Yet, all the while, she never felt as though she was being judged, only that she was her judging herself. Things she considered bad went unnoticed or had little meaning. When she did something good … like make someone smile, or simply smile at someone, the spectators roared with approval.

As her life was reeling to an end, she began to feel warm all over. She watched as her soul left her body in the emergency room on Earth. At that moment, it was like the crescendo of an orchestra, increasing in volume to the point where she thought every soul in Heaven must be applauding. The warmth she felt was not from any heat source she was familiar with. It was coming from everywhere, all at once, filling her soul with unconditional love, accepting her.

The being of light asked her if she had any questions.

She thought for a second. "Are you … God?"

"Well, that depends on your perception. Everything you see is God or a creation of the Almighty. I guess in a way I am … and so are you."

She thought of the words of an old John Lennon song "I am the Walrus": 'I am he, as you are he, as you are me, and we are all together.' "Am I in Heaven?"

"Not exactly. But I can let you take a peek;

open your eyes."

And just like that, she was no longer hovering in space. She could see 360 degrees. She was standing in a field of flowers, beautiful flowers with colors she'd never seen before, at least, not with the human eye. A stream of crystal-clear water ran down a hillside. She saw fish swimming between the rocks, playing tag with one another. She felt their contentment, their joy. And she knew the light being was right. They were one.

Ella heard someone calling her name. She turned her head and suddenly a child with a black Labrador Retriever appeared at the top of a nearby hill. He looked down at her. "Ella, you tell my daddy I'm sorry. Tell him to look underneath the big rock." Then the boy and dog were gone.

Ella walked up the hillside and looked over the ridge. On the other side was a golden city. She started to head for it, but came to a sudden stop, realizing that was as far as she was allowed to go.

The being of light asked her if it looked familiar. She said, "Yes, it feels like I've been here before. Déjà vu!"

"You have. You were only gone for less than a blink of an eye."

"Why did I leave?"

"It was your choice! A learning experience. You may decide to go again. And if you do, you'll pick the moment of your birth. You can't select your parents or where you will live. That's just a roll of the dice, the luck of the draw. You're on your own. We are all colors or brush strokes on a canvas. How you blend in is up to you. Each time you go, you take what you have learned from past experience and build on them. If you were an accountant before, on your next trip you might be a mathematician."

"Is there a Hell?"

"Yes, if you think you belong in Hell. Hell can be many things to many souls. It's an earthbound realm. It is neither condemnation nor judgment. It's not a punishment. It has a purpose: to rid the soul of negativity before entering Heaven. Hell is where you go to purge the soul of your obsessions, fear, anger, regret, arrogance, guilt, rage, self-pity, anything that keeps you from reaching your highest level of enlightenment. If you're argumentative, you may spend time there with others who disagree with you, until you hit bottom and work your way out. Hell is what you make of it. You're there as long as you wish to be. It's up to you. You decide when you've learned from the experience and are ready to leave. This is an earthbound realm. Those who are not ready or willing to enter the light will remain until they lose their earthly desires."

Next, the being of light said, "It's time for you to return." Ella pleaded with the light source to let her stay. "You have no choice. You haven't completed your mission."

"What mission? I thought it was a learning experience, something that I willingly decided to do."

"Yes, it was your decision, but there was a clause in the agreement. There always is. The reason you're here is that you strayed from your original purpose. You wandered off track. You haven't completed your objective. If you were to leave now, three souls may not ascend to the level they should. All souls are touched and touch others, yours included. So far, you haven't met your soul mates. And they haven't met you; you must return. It's time for you to meet them."

"Will I remember this experience?" Ella asked.

"You will remember it like you would a dream. Except that you will believe it was real. You will not remember any past experience before your earthly voyage, only a sense of being somewhere else before. You will gradually become more in tune with the spiritual realm. You may call it instinct, intuition or … a sixth sense."

Chapter 5

Her descent from Heaven was instantaneous. No fooling around, traveling through space. Poof—just like that, she was back on *terra firma*. But not in her physical body. She didn't know if she was standing or floating. She couldn't feel her feet or her legs ... or anything, for that matter. Not even the cold snow going right through her.

Ella knew she wasn't near her home in Southern California. It never got cold enough to snow where she lived. It only happened once in a blue moon. She couldn't remember the last time she'd seen a blue moon.

It was dark out. She was in the street in a residential neighborhood, staring at a green, single-story house. Why she found it attractive was beyond her. It looked like all the other houses on the block, every fifth one identical—a tract home development.

The only light visible, other than those inside each house, came from a lamppost at the far end of the block. She could see like a hawk, her vision acute. The lamppost cast enough light on a nearby street sign for her to make out the letters. She was on Wildwood Road. The cross street—Hidden Valley Drive.

Ella's attention returned to the green house. With all the lights out, she guessed no one was home. *So why was she there? Who was she supposed to meet, and why wasn't she back in her own body?*

She suddenly drifted away from the street toward the house. Not by choice or will of her own.

She instinctively stopped moving when she reached the start of the driveway just as a car pulled up to the curb on the opposite side of the street. Someone stepped out.

Wearing a hooded sweatshirt drawn tightly over the head, only the person's nose and eyes were visible. The hooded figure wore blue medical booties over the shoes, which Ella thought seemed a little odd.

Walking to the back of the car, the person opened the trunk and removed a duffel bag, then moved across the street toward her.

As the person approached, she said, "Hi! I'm Ella Martin." But the person didn't notice her and continued to walk up the driveway as if she weren't even there.

Remembering the words of the light, she wondered, *how would they meet if she was invisible?*

She followed a short distance behind until they were both at the back of the house. Once there, she watched as the person set down the duffel bag and lower the hood of the sweatshirt.

The back-porch light was on, making it easy for her to see who it was. It was a male who appeared to be in his late twenties or early thirties. His hair was dark brown, medium length, combed straight back, with a tight shave on the sides in a military fashion. He had a mustache that covered his upper lip. Even with clothes on, she could see that he was thin. And short, about the same height as she was, five feet five inches.

Reaching down, he unzipped the duffel bag and procured a folded square of white material. He shook out the folds and it turned into a jumpsuit, with built-in booties and attached hood. The man removed his sweatshirt and put it in the duffel bag. Then he stepped into the jumpsuit and zipped it up. She tried to think of what he reminded her of. And then it came to her. From behind, he looked like the Pillsbury Doughboy.

The suit was not a typical jumpsuit; it was loose fitting. It was similar to the clothing lab technicians might wear, or maybe someone involved in cleaning up hazardous material. He reached into the duffel bag and removed a box labeled 'PVC gloves,' took out a pair and put them on. First the left and then the right. As he put on the right glove, she noticed a small tattoo of a happy face inked on his skin between his thumb and index finger.

He moved closer to the porch so he could read the time on his watch. As he raised his wrist to take a look, Ella peeked over his shoulder. She, too, was curious about the time.

It was 7:15 p.m. She quickly did the math. If she remembered correctly, it was 6 p.m. when Dr. Henderson first walked into her room. If she was somewhere in California, maybe Big Bear, then one hour had elapsed. If she were in a different time zone with a one-hour difference, only a few minutes had gone by. She had been here, with this person (wherever *here* was) for, she guessed, nearly fifteen minutes.

She watched the little man remove a cigarette pack from his duffel bag and pull out one cigarette. She couldn't read the brand name, but the package was green. He tore off the filter and put it in his duffel bag, along with the pack. She thought how considerate he was not wanting to litter the ground. He lit the cigarette, using a lighter that looked like one her father had. She remembered him calling it a Zippo. When he finished, he smothered the butt in the snow. Then he squeezed the tobacco from the soggy paper and put it in his duffel bag.

Next, he carried the bag over to the side of the porch and set it down out of sight, behind a hedge. When he returned, he was holding something in his hand. Ella moved closer to get a better look. It looked familiar, although she hadn't seen anything like it in years. It was about twelve to fifteen inches long, made of wood, and looked like a miniature bat, except the one she remembered was no toy. Her father had called it his fish tranquilizer. After catching a fish, he'd stun it so it wouldn't thrash around while he unhooked it. She remembered the bat weighed a ton. It had a lead weight inside, making it heavy.

She watched him carefully wrap the head of the

bat with an ace bandage.

The little man spat into the snow. Then he looked at his watch again and called out loud angrily, "Where are you, Sally? You should've been here by now!"

No sooner had he said that then a car entered the driveway. Its headlights lit up the garage door. Ella heard the crunching of snow get louder the closer it got. The little man made a mad dash for cover behind the hedge next to the back porch. He crouched down low on the ground to blend in with the snow.

Ella watched the garage door open. As the car drove in, she noticed its license plate, though both edges of the plate had snow on them, limiting what she could see. Three letters at the bottom stood out: ORA. She guessed Colorado.

A few seconds later, she saw a brown-haired woman walk out of the garage. She estimated her age to be somewhere between twenty-five and thirty-five. She was white and on the small side.

She headed straight for the back porch, but suddenly stopped abruptly before reaching it. Then, unexpectedly, she spun around and headed back toward her garage. Ella heard a click and the trunk of her car popped open. She reached in and removed what looked like a bag of groceries.

She turned around and headed back toward her porch, and he watched every step she took. As she approached, Ella heard him whisper under his breath, "Sally, you bitch. Tonight, you're going to die!"

He had done this act many times before; each

time it became more exciting. Not knowing exactly what to expect, the adrenaline rush made him feel alive. He wiped a bead of sweat from the bridge of his nose. The suit was like a sauna, holding in heat.

The woman walked up the three steps to the top of the back porch. He heard her fumbling around in her purse for something. Then he heard a 'chirp' and knew she'd temporarily disarmed her security system. As she opened the door and stepped across the threshold, she set her purse on the washing machine just inside.

He made his move. He darted out from behind the hedge toward the back porch, taking all three steps in a single bound. As he leaped into the air, Ella shouted, "Look out! He's right behind you!" But it didn't matter. Neither one of them heard her.

He landed on the wooden back porch with a thud. By the time the woman turned around to see what it was, it was too late. The bat was on its way down, only inches from her head.

He hit her once. The blow wasn't meant to kill her, at least for now. That's why he'd wrapped the bat in an ace bandage.

She felt the bat crash down on the back of her skull. Then something went wrong with her vision. She saw little flashes of light, like fireflies, blinking on and off all around her. Next, she lost all feeling in her legs and arms, dropping her groceries and falling to her knees on the laundry room floor, just inside the back door. She remained on her knees, trance-like for a second or two, before falling face first. When her head hit the floor, everything went black.

The little man punched a code into her alarm system, disabling it, then went outside and got his duffel bag. When he came back into the house, he set it down next to the woman still lying on the floor, groceries splayed around her.

He sat on the woman, straddling her thighs with authority. Excited, he reached into his duffel bag, and after a few seconds of searching, brought out a long plastic zip tie. Then he pulled her arms together, behind her back, and forcefully secured her wrists with the zip tie. With precision, he reached again and removed a roll of duct tape, ripping off two pieces, placing one firmly over her eyes and the other over her mouth.

Continuing, he removed a small flashlight from his bag, got up and quickly went through her house, closing all the blinds. As he did Ella was right behind him, watching every move. The house was small, which was good. Less space for him to clean. It had hardwood floors, which was also good, making it easy to wipe down.

Once he was sure no one could see him moving around inside the house, it was time to get down to business—to do what he came to do.

He went into her living room and turned on an overhead light. He needed some working space to lay out what he had brought with him. A colorful Persian rug was conveniently located in the middle of the living room. He pushed her couch and loveseat off the rug, got down on his hands and knees, and rolled her rug up into a tight-fitting tube, pushing it out of the way.

He went back to the laundry room to get his

bag and bring it to the living room. Opening it, he removed a folded sheet of thin, white plastic, just a little thicker than an average trash bag. He set it down in the middle of the floor and unfolded it. The white plastic made it easier for him to see any blood splatter. He'd used black material the first two times, but it was hard to tell where all the blood went. That's when he got the bright idea to use white.

He'd also learned that if he placed a towel on the back of their heads before striking them, there'd be no blood splatter, as long as he placed a new towel over the old one the minute he saw blood seeping through.

~~~

The woman woke up with the worst headache of her life. She tried to open her eyes but couldn't raise her eyelids. Something was preventing her from opening them. She tried to reach for her face, but her hands wouldn't move. They were bound together behind her back. Confused and still in a daze, she yelled for help. But all she heard was a muffled sound. Then it dawned on her what had happened; she'd been attacked. Hit from behind, knocked unconscious. Not knowing if her attacker was still around, she decided it wasn't a good idea to say anything. Instead, she lay on the floor, afraid to move … listening.

At first, she heard nothing except the beat of her own pulse pounding in her head. Once she isolated the sound, she thought she heard someone singing. It was way off in the background, barely audible. As it grew louder, she could make out some of the words, though they didn't make any sense. "Sally, Sally, your majesty. I made the bed and cleaned the head. What more can I do, that would please only you?"

The little man walked back into the laundry room. He looked down at her and said, "Sally, look what you've done. You spilled all your groceries. Now someone will have to pick them up. And I don't see anyone around here, who can do that, except me."

He reached down and put her groceries back in the bag. Then he carried the bag into the kitchen and set it down on the counter beside the sink, next to the refrigerator.

After he put the items away, he returned to the laundry room, and looked down at the woman. He knew she could hear him. By now she was awake. Would she cry? Would she beg him to take whatever his little heart desired? What he wanted wasn't her precious possessions. He was no thief. No burglar or robber.

He was the Cleaner. She'd been a bad girl! She wasn't tidy. She had to be punished. She'd left dirty dishes in the kitchen sink. When he'd first gone through the house, he'd noticed that her bed was a mess. She needed help, and that's what he was going to do. He was going to help her.

He said, "Sally, I think it's time we get this show on the road. Don't you?" He knew she couldn't say anything that would make sense, not with the duct tape over her mouth.

She continued to keep still. Afraid to move. *He must be confused*, she thought. *My name isn't Sally. It's Sandy.*

He reached down and grabbed her ankles.

She felt his cold hands against her skin, sending a chill up her spine.

She was small. All his women were small. He lifted her feet, spun her around, and dragged her through the kitchen and dining area toward the front room. Then he abruptly stopped, turned her 90 degrees, so she was parallel with the edge of the plastic sheet. Then he let go of her ankles.

After a few seconds, she felt him put his hands on her side and flip her over, not once, but several times. She wondered, terrified, *what on earth is he doing?*

Finally, he stopped rolling her and left her lying face down, in the center of the sheet.

The foreign material felt cold against her cheek. She wasn't sure what it was, but she was sure it didn't belong in her house.

Then she heard movement. He was doing something, but she didn't know what it was.

He searched through his duffel bag for another zip tie. Once he found it, he secured her ankles. "There, that ought to keep you still for a while."

~~~

Ella understood early on that she wasn't there, wherever *there* was, to intervene. What would happen would happen. She was there strictly as an observer, an eyewitness. She decided to make the best of it by taking mental notes of everything that took place.

After he'd moved the woman, he took out a CD player from his duffel bag, along with a handful of

CDs. He inserted a disk into the player, and in a couple of seconds, it was booming out a Rolling Stones song.

He cranked up the bass, giving it a more soulful sound. Ella knew the song but didn't remember its name until she heard the chorus. Mick Jagger sang, 'Pleased to meet you, hope you guess my name.' and then she remembered the title, "Sympathy for the Devil."

Ella thought back to the first time she heard that song. It was 1969. She normally listened to Country or Easy Listening and wasn't into sixties Rock music like her friends. Two of her girlfriends talked her into driving up north to see the Rolling Stones in concert at the Altamont Speedway. She remembered it well because the Stones had hired the Hell's Angels Motorcycle Club to work the event as security, or someone had designated them security. Anyway, the Hell's Angels killed a young black concertgoer. If she remembered it correctly, it happened during the song, "Sympathy for the Devil." After that night, the Stones quit playing that song at their concerts for several years.

When the music started playing, he went back to the kitchen, took off his gloves and set them beside the sink. He looked in the cabinet below the sink and found a box of dish soap and a scrubbing pad. He poured a small amount of soap into the basin and filled it with water. Next, he turned around and searched the cabinets on the wall directly behind him. He removed a glass from one of the cupboards and carried it into the dining room where he had left his duffel bag. He rummaged through the bag and pulled out a bottle of wine. "I think this calls for a celebration! Don't you, Sally?" He popped the cork and was about to fill his glass when he unexpectedly changed his mind. "No! No! This won't do! It's the wrong glass. You can't drink wine from a water glass. That's not proper."

At this point, Ella no longer thought he was talking to the woman lying on the floor a few feet from where he stood. He just rattled on, talking to himself.

Ella followed close behind him as he marched back into the kitchen, carrying the water glass in one hand and the wine bottle in the other. He put the water glass back where he found it and continued to search the cubbyholes, looking for something that resembled a wine glass. And then he said, "There you are," as if he was talking to the glass, "hiding behind a decanter." He removed the glass from the shelf and began to fill it with red wine.

As Ella watched him, she suddenly got a sharp pain in her chest. Just like that, the room momentarily went black.

Somewhere in the darkness, she heard an unfamiliar voice say, "She's ... back!" As the lights slowly came back on, she realized she was no longer in the house with the little man wearing the white lab suit. She was back in the hospital, with people all around her. The only face she recognized was that of Dr. Henderson.

He saw her blink. "Well, hello! How are you feeling?"

She couldn't answer him. Something was down her throat, preventing her from speaking. She felt terrible. That pain was back in her chest.

She was upset returning to her body when she did, missing what was taking place back at the house. She'd been content in her spirit form. No pain and no fear of death. She guessed the man was going to kill the woman, but she didn't know that for sure. He was kind-of-nutty, talking to himself. Maybe he was just going to rob her and leave her there, on the floor, tied up. But somewhere down deep inside, she knew that wasn't true. She needed to return. To go back. Otherwise, what was the *point*?

And then, just as quick as she had reentered her body—she left it again. She was back in the house where the little man was finishing the dishes. "Sympathy for the Devil" was still playing on his boom box. He was sweating profusely, looking funny in the white suit with only his eyes, nose, and mouth visible.

When he finished with the few dishes she'd left in the sink, he washed down the basin and put his medical gloves back on. Then put her dishes away and wiped his fingerprints off the soapbox, putting the box back in the cabinet beneath the sink. Carefully, he wiped off the faucet and the hot- and cold-water handles. When he was sure he'd left no telltale sign of him being there, he turned around and headed for the cabinet where he'd found the wine glass.

By now, "Sympathy for the Devil" was in its final chorus. He put the clean wine glass back on the shelf behind the decanter and wiped off the cabinet door. He did a little dance, Mick Jagger style, as he sang the words to the end of the song: "Pleased to meet you, hope you guess my name.

But what's puzzling you is the nature of my game."

~~~

Dr. Henderson heard the heart monitor switch from a beep to a solid tone and knew he'd lost his patient once more. He asked for the paddles again and everyone stood back. "Clear!" and sent another jolt of electricity through her heart. But nothing changed. All they saw was a familiar straight line, moving from left to right, horizontally across the screen.

~~~

Ella was going crazy being pulled back and forth, like she was the rope in a tug-of-war match. But this time when she'd crossed over, it had opened up a new awareness, a link between the two. She was able to hear what was said in the hospital while still in the woman's house with the little man.

She followed him back through the house, past the dining area, passed the woman on the floor, into the bathroom between the two bedrooms.

Once inside the bathroom, he turned on the light. Then he looked at himself in the mirror above the woman's vanity. He leaned in, puckered up his lips, mimicking Mick Jagger, and sang, "Well, he can't be a man 'cause he doesn't smoke the same cigarettes as me. I can't get no, Oh, no, no, no. Hey, hey, hey. That's what I say. No satisfaction..."

Ella had a better look at his face. She was right behind him, staring over his shoulder, looking at his reflection in the mirror. His eyes were small and brown. He had prominent cheekbones, making her think he was thinner than she had originally thought. His nose was narrow and straight with no hint of a bridge. It was obvious to her now why he grew such a thick, caterpillar mustache; it covered a birth defect. A deformity. If it weren't for the mustache, he might've been able to pass as a female.

He didn't want to be there all night. He inspected the room. Her small trash container was empty, which surprised him. Then he noticed that only a few sheets were left on the toilet paper roll. And the roll was put on backward.

Out loud he said, hoping the woman on the floor could hear him: "Bad girl! Didn't anyone ever teach you the proper way to put toilet paper on the sprocket? You never put the paper on the tube so the lead falls off the back. You put it on so the lead comes off the front. That way you don't have to fish around, underneath, to find it!"

He checked inside the vanity cabinet. "I found a roll. I'll replace the old one for you!" He reached in and removed a new roll and put it on the sprocket, so the paper came over the front side. He took the old near-empty cardboard tube and set it on top of her vanity in plain sight so he would remember not to leave it behind when he eventually left. And then—out of the blue—he sneezed. He didn't feel sick; it just happened. *Allergies,* he thought.

Then it happened again. He quickly scanned the room and noticed a box of Kleenex on top of the vanity to the left of the washbasin. He removed a single sheet from the box and blew his nose. Just as he was about to drop it in the toilet, he remembered something his mother once said. "Don't put Kleenex in the toilet. They don't dissolve like toilet paper. Put them in the trash." So that's what he did. He put the used tissue in the trash container on the floor beside the commode.

At that moment, Ella realized another awareness had opened up: she was able to read his mind. She knew what he was thinking the moment a thought entered his head.

~~~

She heard a female voice with a heavy Spanish accent say, "I've got an IV." Then she heard another voice, this one she recognized. It was the deep voice of Dr. Henderson, saying, "Good. Give her one milligram of epinephrine."

As the woman complied, Ella felt the familiar pain in her chest again. Again, she was back in her own body, looking up at the bright light. And once again, it didn't last long. Perhaps only a minute or two before she returned to the house.

~~~

The little man was still in the bathroom. But now he was on his knees, reaching into the bathtub, scrubbing away a soap ring that only he could see.

After he finished cleaning the shower and tub, he wiped off her mirror and sink. Then he headed down her hallway and opened a closet. There he found a dust mop and ran it over her hardwood floors. When he finished doing that, he removed a vacuum cleaner from the same closet and vacuumed the carpet in both bedrooms. Then he hung a wrinkled blouse he found on top of her unmade bed and made her bed. "There! I think that should just about do it! Don't you?"

The woman on the floor wasn't sure if he was

talking to her or to himself. He sounded as though he was a long way away. Two minutes later, she heard her floor squeak and knew exactly where he was. He was in the hallway between the two bedrooms.

Next, she heard heavy breathing above her, and then him singing out the words to one of the songs he'd previously played. "Pleased to meet you, hope you guess my name. But what's puzzling you is the nature of my game."

She couldn't keep still any longer. She was shivering from the cold air in the room and the fear of not knowing what her assailant would do next. She began to cry.

"That's right, Sally!" the little man said, "If it makes you feel any better, go ahead. Let it all out!"

The little man strolled back into the kitchen and picked up the uncorked bottle of wine. Then he returned to the dining room and set it down on her table beside his boom box and duffel bag, careful not to touch the woman's mail laying there. Mick Jagger was deep into the last song on the CD, and he wanted to hear it play out before ejecting it. Humming intently, he dug into the big green bag and removed five white towels, all nicely folded. He knew five was probably overkill. Two would surely do the trick, but just in case, it was better to be safe than sorry. He carried the towels over to where the woman was on the plastic sheet and set them down on the floor beside her shoulder.

He went back to the table and ejected The Stones CD from his player and inserted a new disc. Now he was ready to get the job done. He picked up his tiny bat and carried it over to where the woman was. Straddling her hips, he sat down on her buttock.

When she felt his weight on top of her, she knew something bad was about to happened. She started to panic, squirming like a worm, trying to wiggle away from him in a desperate attempt to break free. But it was useless to struggle. She wasn't going anywhere.

The second he sat down, he felt her come alive below him. Her whimper grew louder and louder with each passing second. He was delighted with her reaction, not being able to ask for anything more satisfying.

The little man set the miniature bat down on the plastic sheet to the woman's left as Bob Seger started singing, "Fire Down Below." Next, he straightened her head, so her nose and forehead were face down on the plastic sheet. Grabbing the top towel from the stack he'd placed next to her head, he unfolded it just once, and carefully placed it on the back of her head. She felt it and begin to cry even louder, sensing something terrible was about to happen.

He smiled. "Who's your daddy!"

She knew it wasn't a question. Not the way he said it. It was more of a rhetorical statement meant to degrade her.

He swung the bat, striking the back of the woman's head. Not hard. A love tap. A practice swing, you might say. He didn't want his fun to end quickly; he wanted to postpone the inevitable as long as he possibly could. His goal was to inflict as much pain as humanly possible, even though it could never match the pain he'd endured growing up. The pain of humiliation was much worse than any physical pain. He thought he'd ended his suffering at the age of twelve, but no, he was wrong. It simply changed hands and continued on, tearing at his soul, leaving an invisible mark that would never heal, remaining hidden deep inside to bleed and fester. The only way he could ease the pain was when he struck back and killed the source.

Ella watched the little man as he brought down the bat against the woman's skull. She couldn't feel the blow; she could only imagine what it felt like. And since she now knew the little man's thoughts, she knew it was not going to end quickly.

When he hit the woman, she stopped fidgeting. And when she stopped moving, Ella no longer watched from the sideline but was given a more active role. She saw what he saw, felt what he felt. And what he was feeling was much more disturbing than anything she could have imagined.

He waited until she'd regained consciousness, and then hit her a second time. This time, he noticed a tiny speck of blood seeping through the terrycloth towel. He placed a second towel over the first. Now that he was warmed up, he whacked her three times in rapid succession. And then he felt her carotid artery for a pulse and said aloud, "Yep, she's got one." He could see blood starting to soak through the second towel, so he added a third. He repeated the three blows and felt for a pulse again. She still had one, but barely. He knew that death was right around the corner, so he decided to remove the duct tape from her mouth. She was far too weak to scream. After all, he was no novice. This wasn't his first time. And it certainly wouldn't be the last. He was starting to enjoy getting even too much to quit now.

Ella watched as the room lit up with a golden mist, similar to the one she'd witnessed in the hospital with the dying cancer patient. The mist took on a human form, knelt next to the woman's head, and whispered something in her ear. What it said, only the woman on the floor could hear. She said, "Thank you, Lord."

The little man got a strange look on his face. "That's right, Sally! You'd better thank me. Now your house will pass inspection." Just as he swung the bat again, the woman's soul left her body. The spirit form took her by the hand and the two of them floated out of the house, through the ceiling. The little man hit the woman again and again, now in a wild and crazy rage. He screamed, "Sally, why did you let him make me wear that dress? Why did you let him put that diaper on my head? Why did you let him lock me in the basement? You bitch! I'll kill you! You were supposed to protect me from his wrath, but no, you ended up worse than him, you self-righteous bitch."

Ella was confused. A face kept flashing in front of her, but it wasn't the face of the dead woman on the floor. It was someone else. Someone who looked a lot like her. But it wasn't her. She had the same eyes and the same hair color, but older, prettier.

~~~

He reached down and felt for a pulse. There

was none.

Dr. Henderson looked at the clock on the wall and said, "Let's call it." One of the nurses wrote down the time of death at 7:01 p.m. (PST).

~~~

The killer got up and went over to his duffel bag, removing a medium size trash bag and a pair of wire cutters. He returned to the body on the floor, cut the ties that bound the woman's hands and feet, and removed the duct tape from her eyes, discarding the tools-of-his-trade in the trash bag. Then he stood up, pulling the white sheet with the woman's body on it, into the dining area.

Once the rug and her furniture were back in place, he pulled her off the plastic sheet and placed her face down in the center of her living room. He removed the three now blood-soaked towels from the back of her head and put them in the trash bag. Then he picked up the two fresh towels off the plastic sheet and put them back in his duffel bag. Checking the white plastic sheet for blood spatter, he saw none, but put it in the trash bag anyway. He couldn't afford to keep it, not with her DNA all over it.

He put the cork back in his wine bottle, turned off his battery-operated CD player, and put them away. Then he took one quick walk around the house, turning off lights after checking each room to make sure he wasn't leaving something of his behind. All the while, he had the oddest feeling he was being watched. He had that feeling from the moment he'd gotten out of his car and crossed the road. Why, he didn't know. He'd checked all the niches but found no one. He wrote it off as paranoia. He went back into her bathroom and picked up the cardboard toilet paper tube that he'd left on the vanity. Put it in the trash bag. Turned out the light and headed for the kitchen.

He was almost done. Once in the kitchen, he removed her trash from underneath the sink and set it down on the kitchen floor in plain sight so he wouldn't forget it when he left. Then he returned to the living room, removed his white lab suit, put it in the trash bag, but left on his gloves and booties.

He put on his sweatshirt, pulled the drawstring tight, so only his eyes and nose were exposed. He picked up his duffel and trash bag and headed for the kitchen, where he met up with the third bag, picked it up and continued toward her laundry room where he punched in a code, resetting her system, allowing him just enough time to walk out the back door.

Once outside, he inserted a key into a deadbolt style locking device and relocked the door. Then he dropped her trash from under her sink into her trash container beside the garage and walked back down her driveway in the direction of his car.

He still had that funny feeling someone was watching him. He picked up speed. Trotting across the street to his car, he took a quick look around, but saw no one. He opened the trunk and tossed the two bags inside. Then he got into his car, started the engine, removed his gloves and booties, and put them in his glove compartment. Now, finally, he was beginning to feel more alone. He put the car in gear and slowly drove away.

As his taillights disappeared, so did everything around her.

Chapter 6

Ella wasn't sure where she was. But wherever she was—if it even was a place at all—was pitch black. Not a speck of light or sound. She thought she was floating, but she wasn't sure. There was no way to get her bearings while lost in the void. She was just there, waiting to find out what would happen next.

Ella's wait was short. Off in the distance, she saw a hint of light, no larger than a pinhead. And then the light came rushing at her faster than anything she could have possibly imagined … filling the empty space. At the same time the light overtook her, she felt like she'd been dunked in a pool of ice water.

Ella suddenly sat up and took a deep breath. As she did, a white sheet that had covered her fell into her lap. She didn't have a stitch of clothes on underneath. She raised the sheet again to cover her body. That's when she noticed the tag attached to her big toe and knew exactly where she was. She was back at the hospital in Marina Del Rey … in the morgue. But she wasn't dead.

She jumped up from the stainless-steel table. Wrapping the white sheet around her, she headed for a set of double doors, hoping to find someone who could point her back to the emergency room.

Once through the double doors, Ella found herself in an empty corridor. She decided to set out on her own, but which way should she go; to the right or to the left? She decided to go left. But after taking two steps, she heard a voice inside her head say, *you're heading in the wrong direction.* She turned around and went the other way.

Before long, she came to a cross corridor. On the wall were directional signs. ICU was to the right. Maternity was on the second floor. Radiology and the emergency room were straight ahead. The cafeteria was to the left. She remembered how hungry she was but continued walking toward the ER.

As Ella entered, she recognized the woman sitting behind the reception desk. "Tori West, at the *Hairem* on Washington Boulevard in Playa Del Rey."

"Excuse me," said the receptionist.

"When the nurse told you the woman with the blonde hair in Room 10A just flat lined, you said, 'That's too bad. I wanted to find out where she got her hair done.' Since I was walking by, I thought I'd give you that information."

"But you were—"

"Dead," Ella said. "Yes, I was, wasn't I?"

The receptionist stared in awe, completely dumfounded.

"Do you know where Dr. Henderson is?" Ella

asked. "I woke up in a room down the hall ... the morgue."

"Uh, stay right here. I'll page him." The receptionist keyed the microphone on the intercom. "Dr. Henderson, please report to the receptionist desk as soon as possible." She repeated the message hurriedly. The woman offered Ella a chair, who took a seat.

Several minutes passed by without either of the two women speaking. The receptionist didn't know what to say, she was still in shock.

Dr. Henderson rounded the corner and saw Ella sitting beside the receptionist. He took a double take. At first, he didn't believe what he was seeing. It couldn't be the same woman who passed away in Room 10A. His team had worked on her for ten minutes, but she showed no signs of life. The closer he got, the more he realized it was Ella Martin. She started to stand up when she saw him, and he said, "Please Ms. Martin, stay seated."

Dr. Henderson called out to anyone who could hear him, asking for a gurney to be brought to the reception area. A new shift of nurses was now on duty and had no idea who Ella was or what had happened to her.

Ella said, "Please, Doctor, I don't need a gurney. I feel fine. What I need is something to eat. I'm famished."

"Okay, Ms. Martin, but only if I can put you in a wheelchair and wheel you down to the cafeteria myself. I'll take my dinner break now. I want to keep an eye on you and ask you a few questions." Ella agreed.

After putting on a gown, Ella sat down in a wheelchair and Dr. Henderson pushed her down to the cafeteria, where they went through the buffet line. He found a secluded table where they could talk.

Once settled, Ella looked into the doctor's beautiful blue eyes. "How long have you been married?"

He looked at her oddly. "Why?"

Ella said, "When you shocked me for the last time, you were thinking about the gift you were going to get your wife for your anniversary."

"Twelve years," he said. "What else did you hear while we were working on you?"

"You declared me dead at 7:01 p.m."

He didn't have her medical chart with him, but that sounded about right. He removed a notepad and pen from his breast pocket and jotted down, *time of death 7:01?*

She took a deep breath, looked at him, and smiled. "I don't know how much time you have, so I'll give you the condensed version." She told him about how she left her body, watched him perform CPR on her, and he called a Code Blue. About how, after a while, she was pulled away. That she went right through the wall and into the hallway, where she floated down toward the receptionist. She told him about the exchange between one of the nurses and the receptionist. About where she got her hair done.

Ella continued, how she went through the ceiling and visited the maternity ward. She mentioned the two babies by name, and how much each one weighed. She told him how she watched an old man in the oncology department die. How a golden mist filled the room and took a human form, how the doctor told the relatives that when someone is close to death, they can become delusional, and see things that aren't there as the brain shuts down. She said the doctor's nametag was Alexander. Dr. Alexander said something about endorphins, but she didn't understand what he was talking about. She said the old man wasn't delusional. He was talking to the spirit when he died, and she watched as his soul was taken away. They went up through the ceiling.

This wasn't the first time Dr. Henderson had heard of an out-of-body experience by a patient. He had many patients tell him of hearing voices and even seeing themselves lying on a gurney. But none of them could tell him any more than that. When she started talking about the two babies in the maternity ward, he decided it would be easy enough to check out her story. She could have simply walked upstairs and gotten that information by looking through the window before she met him in the receptionist area. He didn't think there was any way to prove whether she was telling him the truth or not. But witnessing the death of the old man might be more interesting. Obviously, she couldn't have been in the room with Dr. Alexander when the man died. He knew Dr. Alexander well. They lived in the same area of Brentwood and were members of the same country club. Tomorrow, he would give him a call and find out if the event Ella said she witnessed ever took place.

Ella looked at Dr. Henderson. "You're thinking

about checking all this out. Aren't you?"

"So, you have some psychic ability?"

"No, none! Not that I am aware of. But it's easy to figure that one out. You're taking notes and you look a little bewildered. If you think what I've told you so far is incredible, you haven't heard anything yet. So, sit back and buckle up. I don't want you to fall out of your chair."

Ella told the doctor how she left the hospital and traveled through space. How she communicated with the being of light. How the light form told her she would have to return to her body, even though she didn't want to. She gave a shortened version of the episode with the killer, and how she went back and forth between the hospital and the murder scene. She told him the dosage of epinephrine he called out for, and how many joules he used when he shocked her. How she returned to her body in the morgue. When she finished, she leaned back in her wheelchair and said, "What do you think?"

He looked at her, mouth agape. "I've never heard anything quite like that before." He asked her what she planned on doing with the information she gathered from her vision.

She said, "It was not a vision, Doctor. I was *there*! It was real! As real as you are sitting here with me." She told him she would start her own investigation, beginning in Colorado. She'd search for a town where Wildwood Road and Hidden Valley Drive crossed each other's path. That's where she would find the house where the murder took place.

Dr. Henderson said he would like to admit her

into the hospital for a couple of days. She reluctantly agreed, after telling him she first had to call a neighbor friend to take care of her cat. Then she said, "I would go with the black one if I were you!"

"What on earth are you talking about?" he asked.

"The color of the car you were trying to decide on when you were thinking about what to buy your wife for your anniversary. That's the one I'd pick. Call it a hunch."

~~~

When Dr. Henderson headed for a car dealership not far from the hospital, his thoughts were not on the anniversary gift he was planning on getting his wife. They were on Ella Martin, the woman he'd declared dead the night before. Everything he knew about death was now in question. She'd had no respiration or heartbeat. There was no response to direct light or painful stimuli. Yet somewhere there had to be a spark of life in her that was undetectable.

Last night, after his workload diminished, he decided to slip away to check out Ms. Martin's story.

He started his investigation on the second floor outside the maternity ward. He stood in the hallway but couldn't see anything through the observation window. The blinds were closed, making it impossible to see inside. He looked around, found the entrance, and used his identification card to get through security.

Once inside, he found the duty nurse, and asked

if he could see the babies' birth records. She brought out a registration book, which listed the name, date and time of birth, weight, length, and who the doctor was.

He glanced down at the names on the register until he found Tyrone Smith. He looked at the information following the name and noticed the weight — 9 pounds 3 ounces — exactly as Ms. Martin had said. Then he glanced down again at the name below Baby Smith and noticed it was Fredrick Moorehouse, at 6 pounds 10 ounces.

He asked the duty nurse if she'd seen a woman looking through the window around 7:00 p.m., or shortly after that, clothed in a white sheet. The nurse looked at him as if he'd lost his mind. "Heavens, no. The blinds were shut when I came on duty at 5:00 p.m., so no one could have seen the babies unless they were a relative, or in the mother's room shortly after she gave birth."

Chapter 7

Colorado Springs, Colorado

The dart missed the paper target by an inch. Joe scratched his head and wished he had a new photo of Bill Clinton to aim at. The old one was punched full of holes — to the point of being unrecognizable, which didn't make his partner any too happy, since he voted for Bill twice.

The two men were as different as night and day. Rusty Stubbs was Irish, short, and stout. He had thick red hair trimmed neatly on the sides. Joe Longhorn, on the other hand, was a full-blooded Indian, tall and lean. He wore his hair short, in a flattop, tight on the sides, military style. Rusty was a Democrat and Joe a Republican. Rusty was a gay man. Joe was straight as an arrow, married with two children.

While Rusty burned the candle at both ends, Joe was in bed and asleep by ten o'clock. Rusty wore his firearm in a shoulder holster on the left side of his chest. Joe carried his sidearm in a holster on his right hip — western style.

The telephone rang and Rusty picked it up before it had a chance to ring a second time. "Homicide, Rusty Stubbs speaking! May I help you?"

The caller on the other end said, "Mr. Stubbs, I'm not sure I have the right precinct or even the right city, so please bear with me. I'm calling from Westchester, California, a suburb of Los Angeles. I would like to know if you had a woman murdered last night, found sometime after 7 o'clock."

Rusty asked the caller to hold while he checked. He set his phone down and walked over to the homicide board, scanning it for any new entries. Then he went back to his cubicle and picked up his phone. "No, ma'am, we didn't. Why are you asking?"

There was a long pause on the other end of the line. Then the caller said, "If I told you the truth, you would think I am insane, so let me leave my name and telephone number. If you find a dead woman in a green house on Wildwood Road, please call me back. Her name might be Sandy. I may be able to help you with the case." She slowly pronounced her name, giving him ample time to write it down, and then did the same with her phone number.

Rusty jotted down the name and number and was just about to ask her another question when she hung up.

"Who was that?" Joe asked, peeking over his cubicle into Rusty's area.

"Ella Martin, probably another psychic." He

wadded up the paper that had her name and number on it and tossed it through a miniature six-inch hoop attached to the back of his wastepaper basket. And then he said, "That's another three-pointer."

"What did she say?" Joe asked.

"It doesn't matter," Rusty said. "Either it didn't happen, or it hasn't been reported yet. Anyway, she's out in California. I figured it's either a prank or another so-called psychic trying to get their name in the paper."

"If you were an Indian, you might feel a little different about people who have visions. My relatives used to tell me stories about their visions."

"Your relatives were probably smoking funny stuff in their peace pipe. That's the only reason why they saw things. When you're dead, you're dead! You're not floating in space or invisible to the naked eye. There's no such thing as a spirit or a soul. When you die, it's all over. That's a fact, Jack — *sayonara!*"

Rusty defied the misconception about gays believed by most heterosexual males. He had a Hulk Hogan handshake and could out-arm-wrestle anyone in the department. He was tough as nails; everyone knew it and respected him.

Joe walked over to the corkboard that held the pictures of ten murder victims: seven females and three males. Two of the males were gang members killed in a drive-by shooting. The other male victim had been stabbed in the back six times and dumped beside the interstate. Two of the female victims were shot to death, direct results of domestic violence. Both of those cases were placed on the solved side of the board. Another female victim was a transient found inside a large trash container with her throat cut from ear to ear in the seedy section of downtown. And then there were the other four female victims, all found beaten to death in their homes.

Rusty disappeared for a minute, and when he returned to his cubicle, he yelled over to Joe. "Do you want to go for a ride? The refrigerator is empty, and we're out of cereal."

~~~

The two detectives had barely walked through the front door of a local grocery store when they received a call from their department asking them to respond to a reported homicide not far from their location.

Rusty got behind the wheel while Joe rode shotgun.

Rusty parked their unmarked car on Hidden Valley Drive, well away from the crime scene and unable to disturb any evidence left in the driveway or out in the street. Too bad the first responder didn't follow the same procedure.

They got out of their car, crossed the street, and ducked under the barrier tape limiting access to Wildwood Road. They walked toward the homicide scene: three doors down, on the left-hand side of the street, in a green color house.

When they reached the house, they found a man and a woman sitting on the front porch. The woman was crying hysterically. She had her head buried in her hands, resting on her knees. The man beside her had an arm wrapped around her shoulder.

The two detectives approached the couple and identified themselves. Joe was wearing a black turtleneck sweater, black slacks, and dark gray Navy style pea coat, while Rusty wore a UCLA gold and blue sweater, colors of his alma mater, with dark pants and a deep blue ski jacket. It was their first week out of their summer wear, usually a suit and tie, and into something more suitable for the winter weather.

The man stood up, shook hands with the detectives, and introduced himself and his wife as the victim's parents.

According to the victim's father, they were expecting their daughter for dinner at their house the previous evening, but she never showed up. They were a close-knit family, so if she wasn't going to make it or if she was going to be late she would have called. He called her home, then her cell phone, but no one answered. This morning he tried again, but still no answer. Then his wife called her work phone, but all she got was her answering service. She left a message for her to call them back, but their daughter never did. That's when they decided to drive over to her house, to see if she was home.

When they first arrived at their daughter's house, they knocked on the front door. When no one answered, they tried to open it, but it was locked. They went to the back door, but it, too, was locked. The victim's father then peeked through the garage window and noticed her car parked inside.

With a spare key to the house and the code to disarm the alarm system, they let themselves in, disabled her alarm, and found their daughter on the living room floor and called the police.

~~~

One of the crime scene investigators gave each detective a pair of paper booties, medical gloves, and a dust mask to put on before allowing them entry.

Once inside, the smell of death was obvious — mask or no mask. Joe had been on the police force for seven years, four of which were in homicide. He was an ex-marine who saw combat during the first Gulf War and had seen many dead bodies before, but never got used to the smell. "Rusty," he said, "if I ever say to you, after we leave a crime scene, let's go get something to eat, I want you to put a bullet through my head. You got that!"

"Ditto!" said Rusty.

Rusty had joined the force right out of college, in homicide for fifteen. With twenty-five years on the job, he was the oldest and most seasoned detective in his precinct.

The scene looked familiar. Another woman found with the back of her head bashed in. No blood spatter. All five women had similar ligature marks on their ankles and wrists. Probably made by a single binding: a plastic tie drawn tight against the skin. All the women also had a sticky substance around their mouths, on their eyelids, and bridge of their noses. Forensics identified the material as a product found in duct tape.

The woman on the floor had brown hair, she was single, under the age of forty, and fully clothed — the same as the other four victims. There was no evidence of a break-in and nothing disturbed or missing that her parents could identify. The only thing they noticed out of the ordinary was the condition of the house. It was spotless. She didn't have a housekeeper, so they were a little surprised to find it in the shape it was in. This didn't surprise the two detectives. They'd heard it all before.

A profile was beginning to take shape. He was a clean freak. He went after women with brown hair who were in the same age bracket. He either knew something about alarm systems or he forced the information out of the women before killing them. He wore gloves. They were sure of that. None of the fingerprints taken from one crime scene matched any of those taken from another.

Joe recognized one of the crime scene investigators. "Hey, Bobbi, didn't you work the last case we had similar to this one. Over off Foothill?"

"Yes, I was in charge of that one."

"So, what's our victim's first name?" He'd met her parents, who never said her first name, only identified her as their daughter.

"Her name is Sandra, Sandra Brown. S. B. — like all the others."

Joe hadn't linked the initials together before. He looked over at his partner, who shrugged as if to say, *I don't know; how did we miss that?*

Joe turned to Rusty. "What did that woman from California say last week? What was her name?"

Rusty thought for a second, then got on his cell phone. When someone answered on the other end, he asked, "Hey, Pete, did the janitorial service ever empty our trash cans?"

There was a pause and then Pete said, "No. Why?"

"Don't worry about why. Just do me a favor and take the bag out of my trash can and put it on my desk."

"Okay," said Pete, "it's as good as done."

Rusty put his cell phone back in his pocket. Then he walked over to the dead woman's living room window and peeked out. From where he stood, he could see at least three news trucks setting up their equipment on the far side of the barrier tape.

He said, "I see the buzzards have arrived. This time, they're going to put two-and-two together and figure out that we've got a maniac on our hands — a serial killer."

Rusty was the spokesperson for the department. He decided to confront the reporters and give them just enough information to keep them happy without giving away the farm.

He walked down to the corner where they'd set up a live broadcast and spoke into the cluster of microphones. He knew most of the reporters and camera crew by name. He told them that he would make a statement but wouldn't answer any questions now.

In the past, he'd told the media the person or people who committed the crime left no obvious clues. CSI was checking for prints: shoe prints, tire prints, fingerprints, and blood spatter. All the typical stuff they look for at a crime scene. And that a statement would be forthcoming, when, or if any new information could be added. This time, he decided it was about time the public knew more. So he told them. The latest victim had died like four others in a similar fashion. He believed they were looking for a serial killer. The killer or killers were murdering women who were single, between thirty- and forty-years-old with dark brown or reddish-brown hair. All the murders occurred in the evening; usually on nights when the weather was bad. All the women had the same initials: S. B. What he didn't tell them was all the women had security alarm systems. Or that the killer or killers cleaned the entire house either before or after committing the crime. He didn't tell them the killer used zip ties to bind the victims' hands and feet, or that he covered their mouths and eyes with duct tape.

While Rusty spoke to the reporters, Joe gathered the rest of the information they needed to start a new investigation.

After Rusty had finished speaking to the media, he walked back to the victim's house. Bobbi, the CSI, was standing in the driveway smoking a cigarette, talking to Joe. She said that based on decomposition, the coroner estimated the victim's time of death to be somewhere between three and four days before discovery.

Rusty thought about the phone call he'd received on Friday from the woman in California. She'd told him the murder occurred on Thursday night. That would fall right in line with the coroner's preliminary report.

Joe said, "I'm finished inside; let's wrap it up. Bobbi will send us all they have as soon as they're done."

The killer was slick. He did his homework. He'd left no obvious evidence at the crime scene. Just like all the others. Rusty expected the same results this time — no real clues to his identity.

Chapter 8

When the detectives got back to their workplace, the department secretary met them at the door. Without saying a word, she said all she needed to say. She pointed toward a conference room with one index finger, while pretending to cut her throat with the other.

The news of a serial killer had spread through the department and the community like the atomic bomb dropped on Nagasaki.

Rusty and Joe strolled into the conference room and took seats alongside the other detectives in their department. Joe said, "What's all the mystery about?" before he noticed all eyes glued to a TV set in the corner with Rusty's face on the screen, speaking into half a dozen microphones.

But before anyone had a chance to answer, Captain Price came rushing in, confounded. "I just got off the phone with Mayor Wilson, who's upset with the comment you made to the news media."

Rusty said, "Which one?"

"Which one, what?"

"Which remark upset him?"

"The one about a serial killer. We don't know that for sure!"

"This one makes number five. I think we knew it was the same person after number three. Don't you, Captain? It's time we told the public the truth!"

"The mayor said if anyone should tell the public, it's him, not you!"

"Since I'm the designated PIO, I made that decision, hoping it might save a life. Not to get a few more votes at reelection time."

"Okay. What's this about initials? When did you figure out that this guy is killing women with the initials S. B.?

"The moment Bobbi over at CSI told us he was. That's when."

The other detectives started laughing.

"You two didn't figure it out on your own? She had to tell you? That's great! Maybe I should hire her!"

"That's not a bad idea," Joe said. "She's smart! Maybe she should run for mayor."

~~~

After the meeting was over, the two detectives returned to their cubicles. Rusty sat down and started fishing through the bag of trash on his desk. Joe dusted off a picture of his hero, Jack Webb, dressed up like Joe Friday, with a clear view of his badge — number 714.

Finally, after a couple of minutes of searching, Rusty located what he was looking for: a wadded-up piece of paper at the bottom of the trash bag. He removed it from the bag, ironed it out so it was legible, and read the information the woman from California had provided. She was right on the money. A dead body in a green house on Wildwood Road. She thought the victim's name was Sandy. Close enough. He didn't believe in psychics, but he had to admit he could not explain why she knew what she knew … unless she was there when the murder took place — an accomplice. Well, he would find all that out soon enough after he called her back. But first, he needed to make up a new case file, one with Sandra Brown's name on it, and place her picture on the homicide board next to four other women — all suspected victims of the same killer.

While Rusty worked on that, Joe called Sandra Brown's security alarm company. He wanted to know what time the system was disabled on the evening of November 15th. And what time it went back in service.

According to the security company, her system went down at 7:20:14 p.m. and went back on at 8:31:05 p.m. He now had a timeline, which fit in with what the woman in California had said.

After pinning her picture on the homicide board, Rusty went over to Joe's cubicle next to his and stuck in his head. "While I was being grilled by the media — giving my resignation speech — did you have a chance to speak with any of Ms. Brown's neighbors?"

"No."

"So now we'll have to go back and canvass the

neighborhood. See if we can find someone who might've caught a glimpse of the killer as he was either entering or leaving her property."

"Okay, when?"

"How about tomorrow? Today I'd like to focus my attention on our lady in California."

Because of his seniority, Rusty usually took the lead. He never told Joe what to do. He just offered a suggestion. 'Maybe we' always meant you ought to do this or that.

Rusty said, "Someone ought to get with that dimwit profiler we hired and fill him in on our latest victim. So far, he's told us our perpetrator is male, has a great dislike for women, and is calculating. Gee whiz, any five-year-old could come up with that. For God sake, the man has a Ph.D. in psychology. Don't you think he should be doing some psychoanalyzing? He's supposed to go to the crime scene and give us some insight into what makes a person tick. As far as I know, he's never been anywhere. He's gotten all his information from a newspaper clipping or one of the pictures posted on our homicide board."

Rusty returned to his cubicle, picked up his desk phone, and dialed the number on the wrinkled paper.

Ella was in her kitchen feeding Gizmo when her phone rang. She answered it with a cheerful, "Hello."

"Mrs. Martin?" Rusty asked.

"Ms. Martin," Ella replied.

"Ms. Martin, this is Detective Stubbs from the Colorado Springs Police Department, Homicide

Division." He gave her a second to let it soak in.

She was expecting a phone call from someone, so now she knew the location. Colorado Springs. "Hello, Detective Stubbs. You can call me Ella if you like," she spoke.

"Ella, on Friday of last week, you gave me some information that turned out to be accurate. This morning we found the body of a woman inside a house on Wildwood Road. The same street you'd mentioned during our short conversation. The woman was bludgeoned to death. Her name was Sandra Brown. I'd like to ask you a few questions about the D.B. if you don't mind."

"What is D.B.?"

"I'm sorry; it's short for a dead body."

"Okay, go right ahead, Detective."

"Can you tell me where you were when Sandra Brown died?"

"Yeah, sure," she said. "I was on a gurney in the emergency room at Marina Del Rey Hospital in California."

"What were you doing there?"

"I had an M.I. That's short for myocardial infarction — a heart attack!"

Rusty took notes as Ella spoke. "Can you verify that?"

"Yes, Detective, I can."

"Have you ever been inside Sandra Brown's house?"

"No! Not physically."

"Have you ever lived in Colorado?"

"No." Ella figured out why the detective was asking her the questions he was asking, so she decided to save him some time. "No, I've never met Sandra Brown, nor have I ever been in the state of Colorado."

"Can you describe Sandra Brown's house?"

"Yes," Ella told him. "The house was small. It was the third house down from the corner. It was light green with dark green trim. The garage was in the rear. It was not connected. She used the back door where her alarm system keypad was. Just inside the back door, to the right of her washer or dryer. That led into the kitchen. Her refrigerator and sink were on the left side, and there was a full wall of cabinets on the right."

Rusty couldn't believe her recall of details. He reached into his desk drawer and turned on a tape recorder, which was connected to his telephone. He didn't want to miss a thing. He asked her if he could record their conversation.

She said, "Go right ahead, I don't have anything to hide."

"Okay," he said. "Please continue."

"Okay! Let's see, where was I? After passing through the kitchen area, there was a dinette set off to the right. There was no dining room, per se, so it looked a little out of place. Directly in front was the living room with a large throw rug in the center. There was a fireplace on the wall to the left, or just to the right, if you enter through the front door. On the mantel was a small trophy of a female bowler and several pictures of people I assume were family members. And what looked like a tiny urn with the name 'Zoey' on it that said, 'All dogs go to Heaven.' On one side of the living room was a hallway that led to two bedrooms and a bathroom. The living room had a hardwood floor, while the two bedrooms were carpeted. The kitchen floor was linoleum. The throw rug was Oriental, with lots of green and red in it." Then she stopped and asked, "How am I doing?"

He remembered her saying she wasn't there physically, which meant she was either a psychic or lying through her teeth. He asked if there was anything he could check that would put her there inside the house the night of the crime.

She thought for a second. "Right before she was attacked, she set her purse down on top of her washer or dryer. It should still be there unless someone moved it since then. Also, there was an envelope on the dining room table addressed to Sandy Brown from someone named Joey. I didn't notice a postmark date because I wasn't looking. But it might be something she received recently. Will that do?"

"That'll help. Especially the purse."

She had a good idea what he was up to. But it didn't matter. She could prove where she was physically the night the woman died.

"Do you know the code to the alarm?"

"No, I was too far away to see."

He decided to continue with the same line of questioning. "Where were you standing?"

"I was standing, or floating, behind the man in the Pillsbury Doughboy suit."

Rusty nearly choked on his chewing gum. "Can

you repeat that?" he said.

"I was standing behind a little man in a white laboratory suit that reminded me of the Pillsbury Doughboy. All puffed out."

"Could you identify the man if you saw him again?"

"Of course," she said, "I was close enough to count the whiskers on his chin."

"Do you think you could work with a sketch artist to develop a composite drawing of our perpetrator?"

"Absolutely," she replied.

"How soon can you get here?"

"I can leave tomorrow if a flight is available."

"That will be great. I'll have our secretary make the arrangements and get back to you."

"Fine," she said. "I'm looking forward to meeting you, Detective Stubbs."

Rusty ended their conversation and turned off the tape recorder.

~~~

Joe had just finished describing their latest victim to Dr. Chateau. He told him how they'd come across the S. B. factor by sheer dumb luck.

Dr. Chateau said he'd already heard about it earlier in the day. That you couldn't miss it. It was all over the news.

Rusty came over to Joe. "I just finished talking with our psychic out in California. She's coming here to see us. I don't have anything else on my schedule, so do you want to run over to Sandra

Brown's street with me and talk to the neighbors today, rather than wait until tomorrow?"

"Yeah, sure, Joe said. "What did she say?"

"I'll fill you in on the way."

~~~

When Rusty and Joe left the station, it was late in the afternoon. After seeing their latest victim on the floor with her head bashed in, neither had eaten lunch. But now, hours had passed and the smell of death had finally left them. They decided to make a pit stop at a nearby donut shop on their way to Wildwood Road.

The moment he swung open the door and the wonderful bakery smell drifted past his nose, Joe thought it was like being in Heaven. At the same time, he started to wonder if it wasn't all a diabolical plot. He asked himself, *How come they always put a donut shop near a police station? It was like putting a liquor store in a low-income neighborhood.* He wondered, *maybe it was done to undermine the police department. Fattening up the officers so they couldn't run fast enough to catch their suspects in a foot pursuit.* He pondered the thought for a few seconds more, until his eyes locked on a huge bear-claw in the display case, erasing any predetermined notion that a conspiracy was involved.

Rusty didn't believe in conspiracy theories, unless, of course, it had George Bush's name on it. Then anything was possible. His mouth started watering the moment he spotted the chocolate covered éclair with the vanilla crème center.

After making their selections, they took their

treasures with them, expecting to eat on the road.

All the responding agencies were gone by the time Rusty turned the corner and drove his unmarked car down Wildwood Road. The only sign out of the ordinary was the tape still visible, crisscrossing the victim's front door.

They parked across the street from the dead woman's house. As they stepped out of the car, Joe said, "Why don't we start on her side?" He pointed off to his left.

"Sounds like a plan."

They crossed the street and walked down to the corner house. Rang the doorbell. Got no answer. Rusty left his calling card with a note on the back asking the resident to call him as soon as possible.

Then they went to the next house in line and did the same thing. Once again, no one answered. Rusty rang the bell a second time, and this time, they got a response. A light blinked on inside the house. The door opened a crack and a woman in her mid-to-late eighties peeked out at them.

Rusty thought how much she reminded him of Aunt Bee on *Mayberry U.S.A.*, an old television sitcom. He said who they were and why they were there. He asked if the woman was home on Thursday, the night her neighbor died.

She said she was usually in bed watching TV when Sandy got home. Sometimes she could hear her garage door open and close. But not on that night. The only thing she remembered was that it was snowing and she heard loud rock and roll music coming from next door. The music stopped a little after eight o'clock, about the time she turned off the television and went to sleep. Rusty handed her a business card and asked her to give him a call if she remembered anything else.

After they left Aunt Bee's house, they continued to the fourth, fifth and sixth house. They wanted to complete one side of the street before they went back to the station. But what they got was of little value. No one remembered seeing or hearing anything out of the ordinary the night their neighbor died, so they decided to call it an evening.

But before they reached their car, Rusty had a change of mind and wanted to take one last look inside the victim's house.

They entered the house through the front door, using a key supplied by the victim's parents. The alarm system had been turned off the moment they found out there was no one alive at the address to pay the bill.

Once inside, Joe turned on the dead woman's stereo and heard a tune he was familiar with: "Blue Eyes Crying in the Rain." Her stereo was set to a country western station. Not rock and roll. He looked around and found a handful of CDs, all country: Garth Brooks, Shania Twain.

Rusty found the envelope with the name Joey on it, last name unknown, right where Ella said it was on the dining room table. He put on a new pair of medical gloves and picked up the envelope. He slipped it, unopened, into his jacket pocket. Next, he walked over to the fireplace and removed the bowler's trophy from the mantel. The engraving read, 'Most Improved Bowler of the Year, 1999.' He replaced the trophy and picked up the urn named

'Zoey.'

He had one more area he wanted to check out — the dead woman's laundry room. He turned on the overhead light, and there it was, the purse, right where Ella Martin said he should find it, sitting on top of a white appliance.

Chapter 9

Jason Bradford was in his mother's basement, reading the front page of the *Gazette*. It was about time he made the headlines. But he didn't like the name they'd given him — the S. B. killer. It was too easy to turn around, and make it sound like bullshit. He shouted, "I'm not the B. S. killer. I'm the Cleaner!" Then, calming down, he read the rest of the article. Since he'd started cleaning houses, this was the first time his work received top billing. The other times, it was just a mention, only a paragraph or two usually found on one of the back pages.

He cut the article from the paper and put it in his scrapbook with all the other news clippings.

The plastic sheet he'd used with the woman on Wildwood Road was gone; he'd gotten rid of it in a landfill north of town. The bloody towels and the white lab suit were ashes in his mother's fireplace. There was no blood on the bat, not that he could see, but he couldn't afford to take a chance, so he did what he'd always done after each cleaning. He put the bat in a bucket of water mixed with bleach to draw out any blood that might be invisible to the naked eye. After a good soaking he would remove it from the bucket, let it dry, and lightly go over it with sandpaper before using it again.

Jason's mother, Sally, was upstairs making dinner. Widowed after her husband had accidentally shot himself while cleaning a shotgun, she still lived in the same house her boys grew up in. Prescott, Troy, and Ryan moved away years earlier. The only one left was Jason, who lived in an apartment a few miles west of her in Manitou Springs.

But his place was small and he liked to tinker with electronics, so his mother let him set up a workshop in her basement. She let him use the basement so she could cook him dinner and they could talk. Most of the time when he was there, he took his food down to the basement, so they didn't spend much time together. The first thing he did was put a padlock on the door to keep her out when he wasn't around. He also put a sliding bolt lock on the inside to keep her out while he was there, which didn't bother her because she didn't like going down there anyway. It was creepy. Dead animals were down there.

~~~

There were two rooms in the basement: a large unfinished family room, and a small bathroom containing a toilet and a sink. Exposed overhead plumbing ran from one end to the other. There was no heat in the basement except for the small plug-in heater Jason used to warm his feet.

Jason used his father's footlocker to store the remains of many dead animals he'd tortured and

killed over the years. He kept them as mementos —
a link back to his past.

Occasionally, he would take them out and
display them on his workbench.

He knew how each one of them died, and what
great fun he'd had watching them take their last
breaths.

~~~

Three laptop computers sat on his workbench,
all connected to the Internet. The computer screen
on the left displayed names and addresses of
customers for a company, EnterLock. The center
computer was running similar information on a
company called SafeSystems. The computer on the
right had the words CODEX INTERNATIONAL
moving across the screen repeatedly in big red
letters over a black background.

Jason had an MS degree in computer science.
He worked for a company that developed fire and
security monitoring software. EnterLock,
SafeSystems, and CODEX INTERNATIONAL all
used the same product he'd designed. He'd built a
back door into the system that only he knew about
to access the information any time he wanted. Once
he entered through the back door, he could go into a
client's accounts, which would give him all the
information about the user: The customer's name,
age, gender, and billing address. From there, he
could display the equipment they were paying for:
door and window contacts; motion detection; video
equipment; or fire detection.

The back door also allowed him to access the
client's activity log — alarm on-and-off mode, like

he was a console operator at the monitoring company. He saw what they saw, except he couldn't tap into the property owner's camera system if they had one.

Before he entered Sandra Brown's house, he'd hacked into SafeSystems and gotten all of her billing and monitoring information. He knew the time of day she left her house for work and when she returned. He'd entered the house on two prior occasions before *cleaning*. Her system was simple, door and window contacts only. He programmed a television remote control to send a signal to her monitoring panel inside the back door, which would disable it for thirty seconds. This gave him enough time to pick the lock on the door, enter the house, and punch in the code so he could disarm the system.

His first job while attending college was working nights for a lock and key company; little did he know how important that information would be later in his life.

Chapter 10

Detectives Stubbs and Longhorn entered the Colorado Springs airport and illegally parked their unmarked car in a no-parking zone used for passenger pick-up. They entered the building and checked the arrival schedule for Flight 114.

"Right on time," Joe said. They headed for the baggage claim area, where they had prearranged to meet Ella Martin. Their wait was short; Ella was the first one to walk through the passageway into the arrival area.

Ella recognized the two detectives from the description the secretary provided: one in his late forties, short and stocky with thick red hair; the other, in his mid-thirties, tall, good-looking with short brown hair. Obviously, the secretary was biased, being young and single and not interested in older gentlemen.

Rusty watched as the blonde-haired woman entered the baggage area, took a quick look around, and then headed straight for them. She fit the description she'd given him: 5 feet 5 inches tall and slightly overweight.

When she reached them, Rusty smiled, stuck out his hand and in his best Henry Morton Stanley voice, said, "Ms. Martin, I presume?"

"Yes, and you'd be Detective Stubbs?"

"Correct. And this is my partner in crime, Detective Joe Longhorn."

Joe asked how she spotted them so quickly. She replied, "Your secretary's description was right on. But what gave you away was the badge. The one clipped on your belt. I noticed that as soon as I saw the two of you standing here."

Rusty laughed. "Oh! I thought maybe there was a little mental-telepathy involved."

"No, not at all," she replied. "You two look like cops!"

Joe said, "I don't know if that's a compliment or not."

"It's a compliment," she said. "At least to my way of thinking."

Since it was early in the afternoon and none of them had had lunch, they decided to eat before leaving the airport. This would also give them a chance to get acquainted.

The conversation was mostly small talk: what Ella did for a living, where she grew up. It was the same for the two cops. Why did they get into homicide? They talked about Joe's ancestry and how his family migrated from Oklahoma to Colorado. Rusty and Joe were good at making a person feel at home.

After the three finished eating, they left the

airport and drove through the downtown section of Colorado Springs, heading toward police headquarters. It gave Rusty the opportunity to point out some of the notable landmarks. It also gave him time to explain how the police department in their city was put together in three sections: Administrative Service, Operations Support, and Patrol. Homicide was a part of the investigation department, which fell under Operations Support. Patrol was comprised of four areas: Falcon, Gold Hill, Sand Creek, and Stetson Hills.

A reservation had been made for Ella at the Broadmoor Hotel and Resort, just down the road from police headquarters. Joe asked if she wanted to check in at the hotel first and freshen up before they got involved in Sandra Brown's murder. She said, "No, the sooner you get this psycho off the street, the better I'll feel."

They drove past the front of the building where the two men worked. The building was modern, three stories, with a reddish-brown finish. In a small courtyard, in front of the entrance, an American flag flew at full mast. To the right of the main building was a parking garage; it was separate from the main building, yet attached in front by a single common wall, making it look as though it was all one building.

Rusty drove into the parking garage and parked in the stall marked Stubbs. Then the three walked over to the main building and entered through a side entrance. Once inside, they got on an elevator and took it up to the third floor, which housed all the departments under the Operations Support Bureau, including Metro Vice and Specialized Enforcement.

After exiting the elevator, they walked a short distance, and then entered a door, marked 'Investigations.'

Ella could see the entire layout. The left-hand side was an open area filled with five-foot-high cubicles, while the right-hand side had enclosed rooms with doors. The ones marked as interview rooms had sliding bolt locks on the outside. Understandably, they were there to keep the detainee from leaving the room.

As they passed by the department secretary's cubicle Detective Stubbs introduced Ella to her. The woman was young and attractive, with strawberry-colored hair and a small gold stud through her right nostril. She wasn't wearing a wedding ring. *Good guess*, Ella thought about her previous deduction. *Maybe the spirit or angel — or whatever it was — was right, and she was starting to develop an intuition that she'd never had before.*

Rusty escorted Ella into a small well-lit room with two couches facing each another. As she took a seat, Ella immediately thought, *this must be where they break the bad news to the relatives of a homicide victim*. A maple credenza was against the far wall. On top of the credenza was a large coffeemaker.

After Ella got comfortable, Joe asked her if he could get her anything to drink — coffee, tea, or water.

She said, "Coffee will do. Could you add a little color to it, maybe a scoop or a packet of creamer?"

As Joe got busy making a fresh pot of coffee,

Rusty stepped out of the room. He turned on the video camera to record their conversation and have something to refer to. Also, to see how she reacted to certain questions.

While he was gone, Ella asked Joe, "So, where's the room used to beat your suspects into submission?"

Joe turned around to face her, and as he did, he pointed back in the direction from which they had come. He said in a sinister German accent, mimicking *Hogan's Heroes* Sergeant Hans Schultz, "That would be in Interview Room number 1. Where we keep the shackles and the cattle prod!"

They were both laughing when Rusty walked back into the room. "Did I miss something?"

"No," Joe said, "just a little old-fashioned humor."

"Good, then let's move this along."

Joe handed Ella her coffee, and then sat down on the couch facing her.

When he thought she was ready, Rusty said, "For the record, Ella, please state your name, age, and social security number. After that, you can tell us what you know about the death of our homicide victim, Sandra Brown."

"Ella Mae Martin, age 54, social security number 569-74-2727. Where would you like me to start? Would you like the short version or the one with more details?"

Rusty paused for a moment and then said, "Let's start with the shortened version. Then we'll have a better understanding of the type of questions we should be asking you."

Ella started out by briefly mentioning her heartburn on Wednesday, the day before the murder. How it was still bothering her on Thursday before she went to work and continued to bother her the entire day. She left work early. On her way home, she made two stops: one to the post office to drop off mail, the other to a grocery store to pick up cat food. That shortly after she walked into the grocery store, she got dizzy and passed out.

Ella rapidly went through the paramedic's response and the transport to the hospital. She put herself in the emergency room talking to Dr. Henderson. She said the doctor wanted to admit her overnight for observation. And then, if all went as expected, she could go home the next day.

Ella had been building up for the next part of her story, which she knew would be hard for the two detectives to swallow. But since she knew of no other way to say it, she just said, "At this point, everything went black." She went on. "Then I sat up on the gurney, except my body was still lying there. I floated away, off toward the ceiling, maybe seven or eight feet away from my body. I could see a straight line on the EKG monitor and all the other pertinent information — blood pressure, pulse and so on — dropping to nothing."

The detectives listened intently. As quickly as she could, she pressed on. "I heard the doctor shout out 'Code Blue' and the room number '10A.' I saw everybody running around crazy, pumping on my chest, trying to bring me back to life. I didn't want to go back into my body, because my pain had disappeared and I felt great. No, not great; I felt fantastic. Better than I had ever felt in my entire life. I was watching and listening and then suddenly I was pulled away." She took a sip of coffee and continued.

"I left the room where my body was and floated down the corridor toward the receptionist area." She told them about the conversation she'd overheard between the receptionist and one of the nurses. How she traveled upward, through the ceiling, and saw the babies in the maternity ward and watched the old man die. And then, how she left the earth and traveled through space at light speed.

She described meeting the being of light that told her to go back because she hadn't completed her mission.

"What mission?" Rusty asked. That was the first time he'd interrupted her.

"I don't know! I asked the same question, but it wouldn't say. It just said, 'You'll know when it happens.' Anyway, the next thing I remember is standing or floating on or above the snow, right here, in a residential section of your city."

Ella knew the detectives looked forward to the next part. The part that describes what the killer looked like, how he committed the crime. She decided to provide more detail now.

"I knew the street name because I could see the sign lit up under the lamppost. I also knew I needed to focus my attention on the third house down." She said she watched the little man park his car and walk across the street. She tried to talk to him, but he couldn't hear her. He wore paper booties similar to what they wear in a hospital or a clean room. He carried a duffel bag and walked with his left leg pointing toward ten o'clock. When he got to the rear of the house, he took off his sweatshirt and put on a white lab suit with a built-in hood and booties, and a pair of medical gloves.

She hurried her speech. "He was around 5 feet 5 or 6 inches tall. He had dark brown medium length hair, trimmed short on the sides. He had a bushy mustache that covered his upper lip. I think it hid a deformity — a hair lip. He was around thirty to thirty-five-years-old. He had brown eyes, a small thin nose, high cheekbones, and probably weighed no more than 130 pounds, maybe less."

She brushed her blonde hair out of her eyes, took another sip of coffee, and continued.

"He was left-handed. I watched him remove a pack of cigarettes from his bag, take out a cigarette, tear off the filter. He put the filter in his bag and after smoking the cigarette, he squeezed the tobacco from the paper and put in in his bag."

"He field-stripped it," Joe said, "which means there's a military link somewhere. Please continue."

"He had a small bat, maybe twelve to fifteen inches long. I watched him wrap it in an Ace bandage. Then the woman came home and the little man hid behind a large hedge to the right of her back porch."

Rusty played back the crime scene in his head and remembered the hedge she was talking about.

"… After she parked her car in her garage, she did something with a remote control before unlocking the rear door and stepping inside. That's when he attacked her, using the little bat. He hit her once in the back of the head. She fell to the floor.

Then he restrained her hands and feet using two long plastic ties. Then he quickly went through her house closing all the blinds and curtains. He rolled up her throw rug and laid down a large white sheet of plastic, about the same size as her rug. After he placed her on the sheet, he removed a large CD player from his duffel bag."

"Boombox?" Joe asked.

"Yes, a boombox. Then he carried it, the boombox, into the kitchen and set it beside the sink and started playing one of the CDs he'd brought with him."

Joe momentarily interrupted her by asking, "What kind of music was he playing?"

"It was rock and roll."

"Are you sure of that?" Rusty interjected, remembering what the dead woman's next-door neighbor had said.

"Yes, I'm sure. It was the Rolling Stones." Then she said: "Let's see, where was I? Oh yeah! He took off his gloves and removed a drinking glass from a kitchen cabinet. He returned to the dining area where he'd left his duffel bag, opened it, and took out a bottle of wine. After popping the cork, he must've decided against using the glass, because he returned it to the shelf and found another one; this one was a wine glass. He poured himself a drink and set the bottle next to his CD player."

"It was at this point everything went black, and I heard a voice say, 'She's back.' When I opened my eyes, I was looking up at Dr. Henderson. I was back in the hospital. I remember thinking that I shouldn't be there. I was missing what was happening back in the house with the little man. But I wasn't in the hospital long before I returned. This time, there was no fooling around. I was instantly back, watching him as he finished washing her dishes.

"When he was done, he drank the rest of his wine. Put the wine glass in the soapy water, washed it, drained the sink. Then he put his gloves back on, rinsed the dishes, dried them, and put them away, including the wine glass. He put it back in the exact spot from where he got it. Then he wiped off her cabinets and counter top, everything he had touched when his gloves were off."

"Except for the water glass," Rusty said excitedly. "You said he put it away after he took off his gloves."

"That's right, except the water glass. I think I would check that for latent fingerprints." She laughed. "I guess I've been watching too many *CSI* shows on TV. I'm starting to pick up the lingo."

"Then what happened?" Rusty asked.

"Then they shocked me, and I was back in the hospital... again. Then here. Then there. Then here, again. But this time, something else happened. I brought the hospital with me. At least the audio part. I could hear every word the medical staff said back in the hospital where my body was, while my spirit form was in the house with the little man. It was kind of like being in two places at once. I followed him back through the house into the woman's bathroom, where he turned on the light and admired himself in the mirror. Then he said something crazy about the way her toilet paper hung on its holder. He found a new roll inside her vanity cabinet and replaced the old. Next, he sneezed and then sneezed again, grabbed a tissue, blew his nose, and was going to drop it into the toilet, but suddenly changed his mind. That's when I realized I had another new ability. I could read his mind. He was thinking about something his mother had told him: 'Don't put Kleenex in the toilet. It doesn't dissolve like toilet paper.' He put the tissue in the small trash can next to the commode."

The two detectives were astonished at what she said she could do. While Joe believed every word, Rusty was skeptical. He didn't believe in a spirit or a soul, so there had to be another explanation. He knew the government had once funded a project called Stargate. It was used to gather information about a distant or unseen target using extrasensory perception. If he remembered correctly, they called it remote viewing. But as far as he knew, the government had scrapped the idea years ago.

"… Then I heard a female voice with a Spanish accent say, 'I've got an IV,' and Dr. Henderson said, 'Give her one milligram of epinephrine.' Then I had that pain in my chest again and I was back in my body staring up at a bright light. But like before, it didn't last long, and I was back here.

~~~

"The killer was still in the bathroom when I returned. He was down on his hands and knees, scrubbing the tub and shower stall. Then he wiped off her mirror and vanity cabinet and headed down the hallway to a closet where he removed a dust mop. He went over her hardwood floors and vacuumed the carpeting in both of her bedrooms.

Then he hung up a blouse she'd left out on her unmade bed and made her bed.

"He returned to where the woman was and stood over her for a minute or two. She started fidgeting and I could hear her moaning through the tape."

"What tape?" Joe asked.

"The tape he placed over her eyes and mouth after he tied her hands and feet together. Didn't I mention that?"

"No," Joe said, "not that I recall. But that's okay. I would have eventually asked you about that anyway."

Rusty needed to hear that. That confirmed one thing they already knew; the killer had used tape, at least on the other four victims. They hadn't gotten back any of the forensics from the Sandra Brown crime scene yet. That would still be a few days away.

"What kind or tape did he use?" Joe probed.

"I don't know; what do you mean by that?"

"Was it Scotch tape, white medical tape, masking tape?"

"No, it was wide silver tape. Duct tape."

"Please continue," Rusty said.

"I remember he called her Sally. He called her that on at least one other occasion. He said something like, 'Go ahead, Sally. If it makes you feel better.' He was referring to her crying.

"Then he walked into the kitchen, got his boombox and bottle of wine, and carried them back to the dining area, where he set them down next to his duffel bag. He reached into the bag and removed half a dozen white folded towels and set them down on the plastic sheet next to the woman.

"He waited until the Stones finished and put a new CD in his player. After doing that, he carried the small bat over to where the woman was, straddled her and sat down on her hips.

"She must have realized something bad was about to happen because she started thrashing around. And as she wiggled underneath his weight, I had another new awareness. I could feel what he was feeling, not her squirming, but his excitement watching the terrified woman trying to escape. It was a rush ... like I've never experienced before.

"After she gave up her struggle, he removed the top towel from the stack and carefully placed it over the woman's head and said something I'll never forget. It was a line from a Toby Keith song. He said, 'Who's your daddy.' Then he picked up the bat. Removed the Ace bandage and hit her in the back of the head. And when he hit her, I was moved, not emotionally, but physically. I was now looking at the event as if I were him. Seeing it from his viewpoint. Feeling what he was feeling. And what he was feeling would be impossible for me to explain. In his mind, he was getting even for a lifetime of misery.

"He swung the bat again, hitting her a second time. This time knocking her out. He waited for her to regained consciousness. And while he waited, he noticed a spot of blood on the towel, so he placed a second towel over the first. Then once she was awake, he hit her three times in rapid succession. He checked for a pulse; she was still alive. He saw more blood and added a third towel, then gave her three more whacks. He checked for a pulse again. She still had one, but this time, she was barely alive.

"He knew she was far too weak to scream for help, so he removed the tape from her mouth. As he peeled away the tape, I watched the room fill with a beautiful golden mist. Then the mist took on a human form, just like what I'd witnessed in the hospital with the dying man. The spirit or angel or whatever it was—maybe the angel of death, although I don't recall seeing any wings — knelt down and whispered something in the woman's ear. And she said, "Thank you, Lord.""

"What did it say?" Joe asked enthusiastically.

"I don't know. I wasn't privy to anything the woman heard, felt, or thought. She wasn't important. I know that sounds callous, but it wasn't about her. It was about him. He was the reason I was there. She could have been anyone. She was going to die, and there was nothing I could do about it.

"After the little man heard what the woman said, he went crazy. He shouted, 'That's right, Sally! You'd better thank me!' Then he rambled on about cleaning a house, wearing a dress, and being locked up in a basement. None of which I understood. For some reason, I wasn't given that insight. I couldn't see the deep-rooted cause for his rage. I could only feel the emotion.

"It was then the angel — for lack of a better word — took the woman's hand and they floated upward through the ceiling and were gone.

"I remember feeling happy for her, knowing

that she was at peace, going where I'd already been.

"After they left, the man continued to ramble on, and it was then that I started seeing a face, but it wasn't the face of the dead woman on the floor. It was someone else. Someone who looked a lot like her. He started beating on her head like he was driving a six-inch nail into a two-by-four. Thank God the woman was already dead.

"I got the impression that this wasn't the first time he had done this."

Joe looked over at his partner. Neither one of them had mentioned to Ella that he was a serial killer.

She took another sip of coffee and cleared her throat.

Before she had a chance to continue, Rusty said to Joe, "We need to get the profiler off his ass and in here tomorrow. We also need to get a hold of our sketch artist; maybe Ella and Randy can come up with a good composite drawing of both our killer and the woman in his head he keeps killing."

Ella asked, "Do you want me to continue? There's not a whole lot more to tell you."

"Yes, I'm sorry for interrupting, but I had to say that before I forgot."

"It was about then that Dr. Henderson pronounced me dead. I heard him say, 'Let's call it.' I watched the nurse write down my time of death."

Ella continued, telling the detectives everything she could remember in detail. "I could now see what was happening at the hospital and back in the house at the same time."

She finished her coffee and caught her breath. "Once the little man was done cleaning up everything, he headed down the driveway toward his car parked across the street." She took in a deep breath. "I was right behind him all the way."

"Do you recall what make of car he had and did you notice the license number?"

"Yes and no," she said. "The car was white, maybe a Buick or an Oldsmobile. It was an older model, probably made in the late 1980s. I couldn't read the license plate. It was covered with snow. As soon as he left, I woke up in my own body. I was alone, lying on a stainless-steel table. In the hospital morgue."

Joe felt a cold chill run up his spine.

"I left the morgue and wandered around, trying to find my way back to the ER. Eventually, I did. I found the receptionist who paged Dr. Henderson. And I told him everything that had happened while I was out of my body. What I saw and what I heard. At first, I don't think he believed me. Until I told him what I couldn't have known — the time of my death and who recorded it."

"Did you tell him about witnessing a murder?" Rusty inquired.

"Yes, I did."

"Do you mind if I call Dr. Henderson to confirm your statement?"

"No, go right ahead. I would be disappointed if you didn't."

"Is there anything else you can think of that may be of some importance?" Joe asked.

She thought for a second and then said, "Yes, he lit his cigarette with a Zippo lighter. And he has a tattoo of a happy face on his right hand, between his thumb and index finger."

"Yes, I would say that was significant," Rusty remarked.

Rusty developed a long list of items to evaluate. He drew three columns on a sheet of paper. In the first column, he jotted down what the perpetrator looked like. In the second column, he wrote down what the killer used to commit the crime. In the third column, he wrote down a description of the car. Then he added a note at the bottom: the killer had special knowledge of security alarms.

Rusty ended the interview and left the room to turn off the recording equipment. When he returned, he asked Ella if they could pick her up around nine o'clock the following morning. They would bring in the sketch artist and the criminal profiler for her to work with. He said he would also like to take her to the crime scene, so they could reenact the event with her.

Chapter 11

Joe took one last bite of his glazed donut and drove the unmarked car under the canopy into the valet parking area of the hotel. Rusty flashed his badge at the parking attendant.

The Broadmoor Hotel and Resort was a large complex southwest of downtown in the shadow of Cheyenne Mountain. The resort covered 3,000 acres and consisted of two swimming pools, three outdoor hot tubs, one lap pool, fifty-four holes of golf, and six tennis courts. The hotel had over 700 luxurious guestrooms, with four different styles of décor to pick from. It also had eighteen restaurants, from elegant dining to a buffet style breakfast.

As the car rolled into the valet area Ella saw it and recognized Rusty. She headed for the lobby entrance and greeted him with a friendly, "Good morning, Detective Stubbs," when he opened the car door to step out.

"Well, good morning to you. You surprised me. How're the accommodations?"

"Wonderful," she said.

"Don't get too comfortable. We don't have a large budget to work with."

After she settled into the car, Rusty started giving her a brief history on the Broadmoor. How the owner, Spencer Penrose, built the hotel in 1916, possibly out of spite, after the Antlers management rebuked him for riding his horse into their bar.

They started out the day at Sandra Brown's house. Ella pointed out the house as soon as they turned the corner. The front door still had yellow crime scene tape crisscrossing the entrance. After exiting their car, Ella stood where she had been standing, or floating, when the little man walked across the street. She told the two detectives that he didn't park his vehicle directly across the street, but at a slight angle, catty-cornered from her location. Joe walked across the street and stopped when she told him he reached the spot where his car had been parked that night.

Rusty aimed his video camera at Joe and took some footage of him standing there with the address of the house behind him in clear view. Then Rusty swung his camera around and pointed it up the driveway as Ella retraced the little man's footsteps. He videotaped her reenactment … where he set down his duffel bag, how he jumped behind the hedge when the car drove up the driveway.

Then Ella played the woman's part, from the moment she pulled her car into the garage.

She walked up the back steps, pretending to carry groceries. Joe handed Ella a key, trying to keep it as real as possible. She methodically went through each step, setting her purse on top of the washer as soon as she got inside. Then she swung around and dashed back down the steps, turned to her left, and acted as though she was hiding behind the large hedge.

Then playing the part of the little man, she leaped out from behind the bush, ran up the back steps, and pretended to hit the woman in the back of her head.

Ella stopped for a second to catch her breath. "When the woman fell, everything in her grocery bag tumbled out onto the floor."

Rusty continued to videotape Ella's reenactment.

She stopped when she got to the part where the little man put the water glass back on the shelf. They were standing in the kitchen. She pointed at a cabinet on the opposite wall from the sink. "If you open that door, I'll point out the water glass he touched."

Wearing medical gloves, Joe swung open the door, and Ella pointed at one of three identical glasses lined up in the front row. "There, that one," she said, smiling.

Joe removed it from the shelf and placed it in an evidence bag, while Rusty continued to capture everything she said and did on tape.

Next, Ella pointed across the kitchen at the sink. "I was pulled away, back to the hospital, and shocked back to life." She carefully thought back. "When I returned, he had just finished washing her dishes. He put his gloves back on. Then he put her dishes away and returned the wine glass to the shelf.

"Next, I followed him through the house and into her bathroom." So that's what the three of them did, they walked through the woman's house, stepped around the chalk outline of her body, and went into her bathroom.

Rusty swung his camera around so he was looking into the tiny trash can where Ella had said the killer had disposed of the Kleenex during their interview. And there it was — a single tissue.

Joe reached down into the can and plucked it out. Then he slipped it into another evidence bag.

"About this time, I heard Dr. Henderson tell one of the nurses to give me one milligram of epinephrine. And when she did, I was back in the hospital.

"But once again, I wasn't there long before I was back here staring over his shoulder, watching him scrub the tub."

When they left the bathroom, Ella pointed out the closet where the man got the dust mop and vacuum. Rusty, Joe, and Ella momentarily visited the two bedrooms and returned to the dining area. Ella said, "It was about now that I spotted the envelope from Joey on the dining room table. But it's not here now."

Rusty said, "That's because after talking to you on the telephone, Joe and I came back here to look around and I found the letter you'd mentioned."

After he told her that, she took them through the killing, step-by-step. When she finished, she said, "Well, how'd I do?"

Rusty thought about everything she told them and it all added up. The reason the crime scene investigators couldn't find any fingerprints, shoe prints, or blood spatter was because he left none for them to find, at least none in any obvious places where a detective would normally look. But he knew the water glass was just circumstantial evidence; the fingerprints could have gotten there any time in the past. The tissue was a different story. That would shorten the timeline, figuring the woman emptied her bathroom trash basket at least weekly. Now that they had something to compare it with, what they really needed was to find his fingerprints or his DNA at one of the other locations. Then the time frame wouldn't matter that much.

Rusty said, "Well done. What you've described explains a lot."

"But you still don't believe me. Do you?"

"Let's just say … I'm skeptical. It's my nature. That's the business we're in."

"I understand. I would feel the same way if I were in your shoes. After all, you don't know me from Adam. Out of the blue, you get a phone call of a murder you know nothing about. And the caller tells you she was dead at the time she witnessed it. I can understand your disbelief. I have to admit, I was a little reluctant to believe it myself until you turned the corner and I recognized the house. Then I knew it was all real."

Ella picked up where she left off, demonstrating how the killer packed up, fiddled with the woman's alarm panel, then locked the back door using his own key.

Joe locked the back door and then they walked

down the steps into the back yard.

She pointed at a large trash container, next to the garage. "That's where he dumped the bag that he got from underneath the sink."

Joe made a note to get the forensics team to check out the container.

As they followed the driveway back toward their car, Ella said, "Do you remember me saying that he walked with his leg slightly twisted?"

"Yes," Rusty said.

"Well, it reminded me of Chester on *Gun Smoke*. Do you know who I'm talking about?"

They both nodded, which surprised Ella. She figured Rusty might know, but she didn't think Joe would.

Joe noticed her dubious look. "I like old Westerns. Especially the ones with the Indians in it."

On their way back to headquarters, Joe drove out of his way past two other crime scenes that they were blaming on Mr. Clean. He slowed down to a near crawl as they drove by, wanting to see if Ella would recognize either of the houses. Though it became conspicuous to her, she didn't, so he corrected his route and headed to the station.

Ella sat in the front passenger seat next to Joe and reflected on the events of the past week. One minute she was living her life in California, and the next she was working with two detectives on a murder case in Colorado.

In the back seat, Rusty reflected on the morning exercise. He learned a couple of things. One: the killer had a noticeable gait. Two: he knew alarm systems, something he had already surmised.

~~~

Back at headquarters, Ella was introduced to Randy, one of the nation's top sketch artists. Her work led to the capture of some of the most wanted criminals in U.S. history.

Ella followed Randy into a conference room, where she opened a briefcase and removed pencils of all kinds. She also removed photo albums of people with different facial features including big noses, little noses, round faces, square faces ... every type of face, hairstyle and color imaginable.

She explained how she worked. First, she would have Ella select a face: just the shell, the outer shape. She needed a starting point. Then she would add hair if Ella had seen the suspect's hair. After that, they would work on the eyes, nose, and mouth. When she finished explaining the process, she asked if Ella had any questions.

"Yes, only one; nowadays, don't they use computers to do this type of work?"

"I'm glad you asked," Randy said. "Some do. I don't. I'm old school. I think you get more detail, especially with shading, from a hand drawing." She asked, "Anything else before we start?"

"No, I don't think so," Ella said, "I'm ready."

"What gender was the perpetrator?"

"Male."

"Race?"

"Caucasian."

"What was his approximate age group? She

gave an example. "Was it ten to twenty, twenty to thirty?"

Ella got the picture. "Twenty-five to thirty-five."

Randy handed Ella two thin photo albums with approximately fifty faces in each. She said, "The last half of this one," she pointed to the top album, "has pictures of men twenty-five to thirty-years-old. The first half of the other has men from thirty to thirty-five-years-old. The reason why I ask you to identify age is that faces change over time. Cheeks sag, noses and earlobes get larger or longer. People wrinkle differently. They grow double chins. And so on. What I want you to do is to pick a shape, nothing more."

Ella found one within the first ten photographs that resembled the suspect. She looked at the others, but none of them got her attention. She put her finger on the photograph. "This one is real close, except he had a square chin."

Randy penciled in an outline from the photo Ella selected, changing the chin as she drew. "There," she said, "how's that?"

"That's good," she said. "That's real close."

"Okay, let's move on. Let's add some hair."

Ella was handed another photo album. She was surprised to see how many different hairstyles and colors she had to choose from. The styles assortment ran from a spike to a buzz cut, from a flattop to a Mohawk. There was a similar selection of colors, from burnt orange to chartreuse, every color of the spectrum.

She looked over at Randy. "There, that one,"

pointing at one of the photos. "His hair was medium length, dark brown. He wore it straight back, no part, real short on the sides."

"Good," Randy said. "Isn't this fun?" She drew in the hair.

Ella smiled but didn't say anything.

"Let's draw a line on his face, about where you think the center of the eyes were located." Randy drew a horizontal line across the paper, and asked, "How's that?"

"Too high," she said. "Drop it down just a little."

She erased the line and redrew it lower inside the oval outline.

"There, that's good," Ella said.

"Now, what kind of eyes did he have?" She handed Ella another album. "Were they small or large?"

"Small."

"Set far apart or close together?"

"They were close together."

"Did he squint, or were they wide open?"

"They were wide open but small. He had long lashes."

She was told what page to turn to in the album, and sure enough, all the photos on that particular page were of men with small, wide-open eyes, set close together.

Randy added the eyes Ella selected and over the course of two hours, they added a nose and mouth to the picture. Ella told Randy about the harelip or scar, and how he covered it with a large mustache. She also said he had a dimple in his chin, like Kirk Douglas, but not so deep. Randy added a few wrinkles here and there and followed Ella's instruction on shading, and that was that.

Ella looked at the finished product. She shook her head. "I can't believe it. It's as if he was standing right here in front of me."

"Okay," said Randy, "are you ready to work on a drawing of the woman you mentioned to the detectives?"

In the meantime, Joe was in another section of the building, handing Bobbi Bidwell the two items he'd brought back from Sandra Brown's house. Ms. Bidwell had been given the lead on the Mr. Clean case.

Rusty was in his cubicle with Dr. Joseph Chateau, the criminal psychologist and profiler. He gave the doctor a quick update on the latest murder and told him about the woman down the hall with Randy. He explained how he got the initial phone call before anyone was aware of the killing. But he didn't tell him anything more than that.

When Ella and Randy walked over to Rusty's cubicle, Ella was introduced to Dr. Chateau. Randy turned over the two sketches to Detective Stubbs, who immediately made copies and handed the one of the suspect to the doctor.

Rusty told Ella that Joe had taken the water glass over to forensics, so they could run a check through AFIS.

Ella said, "I should probably know what that stands for since I work for a law firm, but I don't remember. Could you help me out?"

"AFIS," Rusty said, "stands for Automated Fingerprint Identification System. It's a computer-generated program used by law enforcement agencies for criminal identification. It is biometric — using digital imaging technology to obtain, analyze, and store fingerprint data. In other words, if you have an arrest record, we should find you in the system. First, we'll run the prints through the criminal database because it's faster; it has fewer records to scan. If he has an arrest record, it should come up. If we don't get a hit, we'll send it through the civil database: the DMV. If he has a driver's license, his fingerprints and photograph should be on file."

It was early afternoon, and no one had eaten. Rusty asked the group if they were hungry. They all said, "Yes!" Rusty, Dr. Chateau, Randy, and Ella left the building and walked down the street to a local deli. Joe and Bobbi joined them a few minutes later.

~~~

After a brief and noneventful lunch, Ella returned to the conference room, this time with Dr. Chateau.

Rusty sat down at his desk, cleared his throat, and dialed the number on the back of the card Ella had given him. It immediately went to an answering service. Rusty left a message explaining who he was, and asked Dr. Henderson to please return his call. A few minutes later, they were talking on the phone. Rusty told Dr. Henderson he was working with a woman named Ella Martin, who claimed to be his patient.

Dr. Henderson corrected him. "Was. She was my patient while she was in the emergency room. Once she was admitted to the hospital, she became another doctor's concern."

"I'm calling to verify a story she told me while she was apparently under your care. What can you recall about the evening she was brought into the emergency room?"

"When I first saw Ella, she was in stable condition. I checked her vitals and she was okay. But because of her off-and-on chest pain and two blackouts, I decided to have her admitted for observation. And while I was getting her prepped, she suffered a heart attack."

"Do you remember what time that was?"

"No, not exactly. We have procedures we follow, but it can become chaotic inside the emergency room, especially when an event occurs while we're there. Anyway, she had no heart rhythm or respiration, so I started CPR. A portable defibrillator was brought in to stimulate her heart, shock treatment. At first, we had no success. We gave her drugs and got her back, at least for a little while. We lost her several more times. After about twenty minutes, we decided to stop all resuscitation. Her oxygen level had decreased significantly and her body temperature was starting to fall. We had nothing but a straight line.

Two doctors are required to make the determination to stop resuscitation. Based on our experience, Dr. Barnett felt that if we were able to resuscitate her, she would probably have irreversible brain damage. In my opinion, she met all of death's criteria. There were no vital signs at all. She had dilated pupils, indicating a lack of oxygen to the brain — hypoxia. We called the time of death at 7:01 p.m."

"Okay, Doctor, I'd like to confirm that we are talking about the same individual. Can you describe this person for me?"

"Yes, I happen to have a copy of her admittance record on my desk. According to her file, she was ..." he corrected himself by saying, "she is, Ella Martin, fifty-four-years-old. She's 5 feet 5 inches tall. Her weight is 130. My guess is she's closer to 140. I remember she had blonde hair, medium length. I'm sorry I don't recall her eye color. Blue, I think, but I could be wrong. That information is not in this form."

"It sounds like we're talking about the same person," Rusty said. "She called my office last Friday from California, asking if we had any information on a murder victim on Wildwood Road At the time of her phone call, the murder had not yet been reported. I asked her how she knew about the murder. She said I wouldn't believe her if she told me. To tell you the truth, Doctor, I thought she was a little wacko. You wouldn't believe how many calls we receive from people who claim to be psychics. So when she called, I wrote her off as another weirdo."

"Did Ella say she was psychic?"

"No, she didn't. But she didn't say she wasn't, either. I just figured she was, or thought she was. On Monday, we got a call from dispatch, asking us to respond to a house where a dead body was discovered. That dead body just so happened to be in the same house Ella had mentioned during my brief conversation with her. When I called her back, she told me several things about the murder that she couldn't possibly have known unless she was there. When I asked her where she was at the time of the murder, she said she was in the hospital, dead and she had an out-of-body experience. That's when she witnessed Sandra Brown's murder. When she woke up, she found herself in the hospital morgue. Is there anything you can remember that evening that might lend credence to her story?"

"Well, I can verify that she was declared dead and that her body was sent to our morgue. Sometime shortly after she was sent to the morgue, she experienced something known as the Lazarus Syndrome, which means that she went through a spontaneous resurrection. She was dead and then she came back to life. It's happened before. There's no scientific explanation for it, other than to call it a miracle.

"I've had several patients report leaving their body and watching medical procedures being performed on them. But none of them were ever able to convince me that it really took place, nor could they tell me what type of drugs were given or how much they received. Ella, on the other hand, knew exactly what took place. She knew who said what, and when they said it. I can honestly say she has profoundly changed my perspective on death. I don't know if we truly know what death is anymore. She relayed a conversation between the emergency room receptionist and one of our nurses, which checked out to be accurate. She said she visited the maternity ward and knew the names of two of the babies, one black and one white, and how much each one weighed. I discovered that the blinds had been closed and no unauthorized person had been inside. I checked the birth records, and Ella was right about the babies.

"Ella said she also witnessed the death of a patient on the third floor. She knew the name of the patient's doctor and how many people were in the room at the time of the man's death. I spoke to the doctor on duty that night, who confirmed that one of his patients had passed away and verified the number of relatives Ella had said were in the room." Dr. Henderson went further, repeating what Ella had heard the doctor say to the family.

"Dr. Henderson, if we catch the person responsible for this crime and if Ella Martin is instrumental in his capture, can I count on you to testify as an expert witness on her behalf at his trial? I can tell you the defense will love to get her in the hot seat. They will try to dismiss her as a psychic or crazy like a loon."

"Yes, I would be willing to testify. I can only tell you what I know, or what she told me. And I just told you everything I can think of that occurred that evening."

Rusty was just getting ready to say goodbye when Dr. Henderson asked, "Detective Stubbs, to satisfy my curiosity … was Ella's description of the murder at all close to what really happened?"

"At this time, I can't dispute anything she has stated. She recognized the house before I had a chance to point it out. She seemed to know the floor plan as if she had been there before. She worked with a sketch artist to produce a composite drawing of our suspect. Right now, that's all we have to go by. And that creates a problem, because our eyewitness, Ella Martin, was in another state on a gurney — dead — at the time she witnessed the murder. Do you see my dilemma?"

"Yes, I do," said Dr. Henderson. "May I suggest for your own information and peace of mind that you search 'NDE' on the Internet? That stands for Near Death Experience. I can tell you it sure opened my eyes. Maybe it will help you, too."

After thanking the doctor for his time and hanging up, Rusty sat quietly in his chair thinking about what the doctor had said. Ella's story to him was almost identical. Usually, when people make up something, they never tell the same story twice. What he wanted to hear, he heard.

~~~

Ella had an uneasy feeling about Dr. Chateau from the moment she first laid eyes on him. He was short, at only five feet five or five feet six inches tall, wearing Levis and an LSU sweatshirt. His jet-black hair was pulled straight back in a three-inch ponytail. He stared at her with dark, half-moon shadows under both eyes, as if he was trying to read her mind. When they shook hands, his was cold as ice.

She felt as though she was a threat to him. When they walked into the conference room, the tension grew, almost to the point where she thought the room might catch on fire.

They sat down and Dr. Chateau opened his laptop computer and smiled insincerely. He asked, "So you're psychic?" in a high pitch Cajun, Southern-Bayou French drawl.

"No," she insisted, "I'm not." It was quite obvious to Ella he had no use for psychics, and probably no use for anyone who had an opinion different from his. "I've never had a psychic experience. My understanding of a psychic is one who sees future events or someone who communicates with the dead as a mediator. I've never been able to do either one."

She guessed by the number of rings he wore that he was well off financially. He probably came from a wealthy family. One of those deeply entrenched in the community, a pillar of society. She envisioned an old southern mansion, in the heart of the bayou, with moss-shrouded trees covering the property.

"I'm sorry," he said. "Detective Stubbs told me you were in California at the time the event took place. That's all he said."

Ella noticed a diamond stud in one of his earlobes and a quarter-inch gold circle, resembling a 1960s peace sign, in the other.

Ella speedily took the doctor through what she had experienced the night of the murder. When she finished, he pulled out the copy of the composite drawing Ella and Randy had developed, and said, "I pictured him as being much older and larger than your vision of him. If he's the size that you claim he is, I'm not sure he could move the body that easily. I also see him as knowing these women personally."

"What women?" she asked.

"This is number five," he said.

"I don't know anything about other women."

"You said he called her Sally; is that correct?"

"Yes, that's right."

"As far as I know, none of the other women were named Sally. You said he complained about wearing a dress and being locked in a basement. Can you expound on that at all?"

Dr. Chateau had a bad habit of tapping his foot as he spoke, as if he were keeping in time with an invisible drummer.

"No. Not really. He just shouted that out. I have no idea what provoked him into saying what he said," she lied. She had a good idea that the victim's final comment, "Thank you, Lord," had something to do with his rage.

"None of the houses where the murders took place had basements."

"I don't know, Doctor. I'm only telling you what I saw and heard that evening, nothing more."

Dr. Château finished the interview with only a few notes on his computer. The notes were not on the incident itself, but on the woman sitting in the chair across from him. He'd jotted down his description of her and the word delusional with an exclamation point after the word. Underneath that he wrote 'Egotistic' in capital letters. After they shook hands, Ella went back to Rusty's cubicle.

Rusty asked, "How did the interview go?"

She shrugged her shoulders. "I don't know. He's a little different. He seemed more interested in me rather than your suspect." Rusty smiled, thinking, *What a jerk. We've been paying him good money, for what? We haven't solved a single crime based on his analysis.*

Rusty had one more thing he needed to finalize before letting Ella go. He asked if she wouldn't mind looking at a few photographs. Ella said she wouldn't, so Rusty produced five pictures. He laid them out on his desk and asked if she recognized any of them. The pictures were headshots given to the detectives by the relatives of the five victims. Ella only recognized one of the women pictured. She pointed, "There, that one! That's Sandra Brown!"

"You don't recognize any of the other faces?"

"No, should I?"

"No, probably not. The other women in the photographs are all dead, too. We believe they were murdered by the same person, the person who killed Sandra Brown. He has the same M.O., meaning *Modus Operandi,* a Latin term for a mode of operation."

Ella knew what the term meant, having worked for the law office of the three singers, Riedel, Darin, and Charles. She said, "You still think I'm a psychic. I'll say it again. I don't have any psychic ability, at least not that I'm presently aware of."

Rusty decided to move away from the subject and told her he'd spoken with Dr. Henderson, and that everything she'd said checked out. He also said that since he couldn't think of anything else she could add to the investigation, he could no longer continue paying her hotel bill beyond one more night. She said, "That's all right, I have to be back in Los Angeles tomorrow afternoon anyway.

Rusty yelled over to Joe. "Do you think we could drop Ella off at the hotel?"

Joe knew what Rusty meant by *we*. "Yeah! I can take her in a couple of minutes."

Joe had been sitting in his cubicle comparing telephone bills of all five victims. The only numbers that matched were from the cable company and the alarm company. Three of the victims used the same cable company while the other two were satellite subscribers. Two of the victims used Enterlock and two used SafeSystems for their security. Only one used a different alarm company, CODEX INTERNATIONAL. He was at a dead end.

On the way to the hotel, Joe said, "Give me a call tomorrow an hour or so before your flight and I'll pick you up and take you to the airport."

~~~

Over in Forensics, Bobbi sat at her desk, drinking a latte from a nearby Starbucks and staring at the latest forensics report. It looked identical to the last one, and the two before that. No matching fingerprints. No blood spatter. Nothing to compare.

Yet everything else was the same. Five women beaten to death. All in the same age bracket. All white. All single. All living alone. All of them roughly the same size — with brown hair.

Joe had stopped by earlier in the day and given her a glass and tissue to examine. When she asked him how they came about, he told her about the woman from California, and what she'd experienced while she was dead. It didn't seem crazy to her; it made perfect sense forensically, explaining why she could not find any matching fingerprints from the other crime scenes. And why there was no blood spatter.

Bobbi had worked for the police department for fifteen years, her first five as a uniformed officer working in the Patrol Bureau out of the Falcon Hills Division. After receiving a bachelor's degree in criminal justice, she moved to forensics. She continued her education and eventually received her master's.

She had a long history with Joe Longhorn. They were once high school sweethearts. She had never married. While she still held a place in her heart for Joe, she never let her true feelings get in the way of their friendship or business. She knew Joe's wife and children and liked them.

Bobbi was a true believer in the afterlife. She couldn't imagine that when the body died everything shut down. Why did people feel like they had been someplace before when they knew they'd never been there? How could one know who was on the other end of a telephone call before they'd picked it up to answer it? Especially when they hadn't heard from the other person in years? Was it just a coincidence that you thought of the words of a song and when you turned on the radio that particular song was playing? The numbers against that happening were astronomical. Yet there were always skeptics who dismissed everything that didn't fit their philosophy. If you asked ten scientists how the universe was created, you'd get ten different theories.

Bobbi knew Rusty had videotaped the

interview with Ella Martin, and Randy, their sketch artist, had developed a composite drawing of the suspect based on Ella's description. She decided she would mosey on up to investigations. Hand Joe her report. Tell him that she was personally running the prints from the glass through their identification system. The DNA would take longer, even if she put a priority on it. But her main purpose for going upstairs was to watch the video of the woman from California. She was once a devoted church-going Christian but had drifted away from the fold. She hoped to find it inspiring — spiritually.

Chapter 12

Even though she gained one hour on the flight, the trip home was long and slow for Ella. She missed Gizmo and her own bed. She stopped by her mail slot and picked up two days' worth of mail, mostly junk. When she entered the front door, Gizmo was there to greet her. He rubbed his head against her calf and meowed for attention.

She checked her phone messages. She had four. Two from work and two from doctors; Dr. Obi, her new cardiologist who wanted to change the date of her next appointment, and the other from Dr. Henderson. He left his cell phone number and said, "I hope your trip was enjoyable and stress free. Please call me after you settle back in."

Ella wrote down the number and headed into her bedroom.

After unpacking her bag, she stretched out on her bed, with Gizmo beside her, and thought about her trip to Colorado. The snow on the ground. The resort where she stayed and the detectives who met her at the airport. Overall a positive experience, except maybe her brief meeting with the doctor in the LSU sweatshirt. That wasn't so pleasant; that part she would like to forget.

She rolled over and removed her phone from its cradle and dialed the number she'd jotted down.

Chapter 13

Bobbi jumped up and down as a face with a narrow nose, small eyes, brown hair, and thick mustache appeared on her computer screen. The first time she ran his prints, she got nothing. That was through the criminal system. So she ran it through the Department of Motor Vehicles. And there he was. Plain as day.

The photograph was four years old, taken the last time he'd renewed his driver's license. But she would have recognized him anyway; time had not changed him that much. He still had the same thick mustache and hairstyle in the composite drawing that Rusty had given her. She made a copy of the information and took the stairwell up to the third floor.

The two detectives were eating lunch in one of the conference rooms that had a television set. Rusty was watching *All in the Family*, an old comedy sitcom from the seventies starring Carroll O'Connor. Rusty liked him in real life, but hated his portrayal of the bombastic, bigoted Archie Bunker.

He was much more aligned politically with Bunker's son-in-law, Meathead, played by Rob Reiner.

Joe was reading a science fiction novel that had a crashed flying saucer on the cover, entitled, *In the Beginning: Project Genesis.*

The door burst open and Bobbi Bidwell stood in the opening with a big grin on her face and both hands behind her back.

Joe looked over at Rusty. "She has something."

"Do we have to guess which hand, whatever you have is in?" Rusty asked.

"No," she replied. She stepped forward and set the DMV sheet on the conference table next to the drawing Randy had developed.

The two men stared in silence at both pieces of paper. Finally, Rusty said, "I think we ought to fire our so-called profiler and double Randy's salary. Don't you?"

"I'll second that notion," Joe said.

Bobbi said, "It's so close to the one Randy drew, we probably could have run her drawing through the facial recognition system."

"I think you're right," Rusty said, as he continued to compare the two faces looking up at him.

"I guess it's time we introduce ourselves to Mr. Bradford," Joe said. He folded over a page in the novel he was reading, so he wouldn't lose his place.

~~~

The detectives didn't have enough evidence to arrest Jason. But they did have enough probable cause to bring him in for questioning. They drove to the address listed on the driver license.

Joe rapped on the door.

After a few seconds, the door opened and a woman in her mid-fifties stood in the opening. The two detectives took a double take. They recognized her immediately from Randy's second composite drawing. Joe smiled and announced who they were and asked if Jason Bradford was there.

"No," said the woman, "he doesn't live here. Not anymore. I'm Sally Bradford, Jason's mother. Why are you interested in him?"

Joe told her they were investigating a homicide, and that Jason's car was spotted in the vicinity, at, or around the time of the incident. "We're just following up on some of the information we've collected. It doesn't mean he's involved, but he may have seen something that night that might help in our investigation.

"What night are you talking about?"

Rusty finally piped in. "Last Thursday, around eight o'clock."

"It couldn't have been Jason's car. He was here with me. He may not live here anymore, but he comes over every evening."

"Well, we would still like to talk with him. Can you give us his address?" asked Rusty.

"Sure," she said. "But it won't do you any good. Like I said, he was here. By the way, if you don't mind me asking, who died?"

Joe didn't elaborate. He simply said, "A woman named Sandra Brown."

Sally gave them Jason's address and said, "He should be home; his days off are Wednesday and Thursday." She also told them the name of the company he worked for.

When they got back in their car Joe said, "Well, I think we know who he was screaming at when he was beating Sandra Brown to death, don't we?"

~~~

On the way to Jason's apartment, the two detectives decided to make their usual stop at JohnnyMax donut shop. Joe asked the woman behind the counter, who he knew as Flo, for his usual. She reached in the glass enclosure and swiftly scooped up a fat glazed donut.

Rusty could not decide between two donuts: a custard éclair and a jelly-filled chocolate. He did a quick eeny, meeny, miny, moe, and picked the one with the jelly in it.

~~~

Jason was trimming his mustache when the phone rang. When he answered, his mother said, "Jason, two detectives are headed to your place."

"Why?" he asked.

"They said they were investigating a homicide that took place last Thursday evening and that someone reported seeing your car in the area."

"What did you tell them?"

"I told them you were at my house, so it couldn't have been your car."

He thanked her for the heads-up and finished trimming his mustache, then went into his living room and peeked through the mini-blinds. His timing was impeccable, because just as he lifted the single slat, a sedan drove up in front of his apartment with two people inside who looked like cops.

Rusty was driving. He parked behind a new black Mercedes and grabbed his clipboard from the backseat.

Jason watched the two men exit the car. One was chunky with red hair. The other was tall and muscular, reminding him of his father. The one with the clipboard acted as if he was in charge. He pointed toward Jason's apartment as he stepped up onto the curb. And when he did, Jason let go of the window blind and stepped back, hoping they didn't see him looking at them.

Rusty said to Joe, "Maybe he's not home. I don't see an old Buick or an Oldsmobile anywhere around."

Joe finished chewing the last of his glazed donut and then said, "Everything I see looks new. Or almost new."

Rusty rang the doorbell and waited for someone to answer. Jason waited, too. He stood on the inside, peeking through the peephole. When it looked like the men were getting ready to leave, he opened the door, rubbing his eyes, pretending like he just woke up. "May I help you?"

Rusty politely introduced himself and his partner and asked if they were speaking to Jason Bradford.

Jason nodded. "Yes. Why?"

"We are investigating a homicide that took place a few blocks away from here. On Wildwood

Road, just off the Hidden Valley Drive. May we come in and ask you a few questions?"

The first thing Joe noticed was a scar on his upper lip that disappeared into a thick brown mustache. The second was ... he spoke with no impediment. And his third observation, was the way the man stood — with his left foot asymmetric to his right. And last, when they shook hands he noticed the happy face tattoo on his right hand.

"Sure. I have nothing to hide," Jason joked as he stepped back, allowing the two men to enter.

Closing the door behind them, he pointed toward a couch. "Please, have a seat."

The detectives sat down on the couch while Jason sat in a nearby chair. Rusty took a quick look around and noticed a lone cigarette filter, no longer attached to a cigarette; it was in an ashtray on a nearby end table. Beside the ashtray was a Zippo lighter.

"Well, what can I do to help you two gentlemen?" Jason asked.

Rusty got right to the point. "Someone spotted your car last Thursday evening in a location not far from where the homicide took place. We wonder if you might've seen something that evening that would help in our investigation?"

Jason knew that was baloney. He was in the area all right, except he was driving his mother's car. She was sound asleep in the big recliner, like always, when he left the basement and snuck out the back door with his father's duffel bag. He was sure no one had seen him. It was snowing and visibility was at a minimum. Plus, he had his hood pulled over his head when he left the car and walked to the back of the house. No one could have recognized him.

He did his usual homework. He reviewed her billing information. There were no hidden cameras. What did they really have on him? He said, "Well, whoever told you that was wrong. I was at my mother's house all evening and nowhere near the two streets you mentioned. You can call my mother and she'll verify that."

"We've already spoken with your mother, and yes, she said you were there. But we still have to check it out. After all, a description of your car was reported in the area."

"What does my car look like, Detective Stubbs?"

"According to the description we were given, you were driving a late 1980s or early 1990s white Buick or Oldsmobile. Would that be correct?"

"No, that wouldn't. I drive a 2000 black Mercedes. So, Detective, what are we on here, some kind of fishing expedition?"

Rusty noticed the change in attitude and countered by saying, "The god's honest truth, Mr. Bradford, is ... you fit our suspect's description, right down to the happy face tattoo on your right hand."

Rusty knew the minute he said it he'd made a mistake. He shouldn't have let that information out.

Joe knew it, too ... and decided to intervene before Rusty said anything else he would regret. He stood up, stretched, and asked if he could use the bathroom.

Jason caught on but thought it was a ruse. The redheaded cop said something confidential and the taller cop pretended like the other had let something slip that he shouldn't have said. But he didn't believe it for a second. No one could have gotten that close to him that night without him seeing them. He did have the oddest feeling someone was watching him, but that proved to be without merit, because he'd checked every nook-and-cranny, and no one was in the house, except for him and Sally. He was sure of that. He decided to play the game. He pointed toward his bathroom. "Sure. It's down the hall. The first door on the right."

He figured the detective would probably be looking in his medicine cabinet to see if he was on any drugs. He was no addict. He didn't even like taking an aspirin. Drugs were for stupid people who couldn't face reality. People like that were just asking for trouble. He took no souvenirs, no mementos, and no keepsakes from any of the houses he'd cleaned. He was invisible. He was sure the redheaded cop was just blowing smoke. He said, "You have a witness, someone who could put me at the scene of your crime?"

Rusty decided he'd said enough. He didn't want to let the cat entirely out of the bag, so he said, "If you don't mind, Mr. Bradford, I'll ask the questions."

Jason pretended to be concerned and deliberately lowered his voice an octave. "I think I have the right to ask a few questions since you're accusing me of something I didn't do. Especially since I have an alibi."

While Rusty continued questioning Jason's

whereabouts the night of the murder, Joe looked through Jason's medicine cabinet and his dirty clothes hamper. He found nothing. He flushed the toilet, pretending as if he'd used it, and when he did, he noticed a half-dozen soiled tissues inside a tiny wastebasket beside the sink. He decided to take one and give it to B. B. to see if she could match it up with the one they found at Sandra Brown's house. He picked it up by what looked like an untarnished edge, wrapped it in a clean tissue and put it in his coat pocket. Then he washed his hands and left the bathroom to rejoin the other two men in the living room.

"Find anything of interest in there, Detective?" Jason asked as Joe took a seat beside his partner.

"No," Joe said.

"Well, if you two don't have anything else. I have a lot to do, so either arrest me or say goodbye."

Rusty said, "Just one more thing before we go. Can you tell me what you do for a living, and could you take a look at a few photographs and tell us if you see anyone you recognize?"

"That would be two. I'm a software engineer. And yes, I guess I could look at a few pictures."

Rusty handed Jason eight photographs. The first five were of the women they'd found beaten to death. They were family pictures given to them by close relatives. The other three photos were of Ella, Bobbi, and their secretary. Rusty watched Jason's eyes as he scanned the pictures. No reaction. He didn't even flinch, not even when he got to Ella's picture.

Jason recognized the first five photos, all of Sally. They made him mad, but he knew he couldn't show any emotion. After looking at them, he laid out the photos on the corner of his coffee table. "There. Maybe this one. I may have seen her before somewhere."

The picture he pointed at was the one of their secretary.

Rusty stood up, collected the photos, still irritated by Jason's last comment. "Don't leave town, Mr. Bradford. We may want to speak with you again."

When they left, Jason followed them as far as the front porch. He stood there, watching, until they got in their car, then went back into his apartment.

Joe looked at Rusty sitting behind the wheel. "Smart guy."

"Yeah, real smart; he knew we were coming. So, what did we learn?"

"Well, Ella was right about the tattoo and the way his left foot pointed in an odd direction," Joe said.

"She was also right about the lighter," Rusty said, "and the way he removed the filter from his cigarette."

Joe asked, "Then how could she be so wrong on the car?"

"Maybe she wasn't. Maybe he drove a friend's car. Take down the license number on that black Mercedes and we'll run it when we get back."

"Do you think we can get a judge to sign a search warrant on what little physical evidence we have?" Joe asked.

"I wouldn't say anything other than we found fingerprints of our suspect inside one of our murder victim's houses. Our suspect said he didn't recognize Sandra when we showed him a photo of her. So how did his fingerprints get there? Yeah, I think we can get a search warrant on that alone."

"Oh! By the way. While you were spilling your guts, giving away all our secrets, I picked up a used Kleenex from his bathroom trash container. When we get back I'll give it to Bobbi."

~~~

Joe had a huge task. He needed to convince a judge that they had probable cause to search Jason Thomas Bradford's property. He sat down and started drafting out an affidavit for a warrant. He wrote down Jason's full name and address. He wrote down the date and time they wanted to serve the search warrant. Next, he made a list of everything they were looking for, which included a duffel bag and all its contents, plastic trash bags and zip ties, handcuffs, and duct tape. Then he added a blunt object that could be used as a weapon and computers and other electronic equipment. When he finished, he took the information to their department secretary so she could turn it into a legal document, ready for a judge's signature.

With that in the works, Joe called Jason's place of employment, Emerson Electronics, and was put on hold. While waiting for a live person to come on the line, Joe listened to a recording telling him all about the company, how long they'd been in business and what they made. Finally, someone answered. Joe said who he was and what he wanted — information about one of their employees. He was transferred to a supervisor, someone authorized to give out that information.

That person was Dr. Henry Swanson, a high-level manager over the company's fire and security software product line. He was also Jason Bradford's immediate supervisor.

When asked about Jason, Dr. Swanson said Jason was his most gifted employee. Jason was a computer programmer, but he was much more than that. He was the brain inside the machine; the wizard behind the curtain. The one who made it all come together — the designer of their product. If it wasn't for Jason, he told Joe, their stock would be in the toilet.

"Say … he's not involved in anything bad, is he? Like hacking into a government-run computer — the Internal Revenue Service?" he asked jokingly.

"No, nothing like that," Joe said. But what Dr. Swanson said gave Joe an opening. A crack he could enter without giving away the farm. He said, "The reason I'm calling is because Mr. Bradford lives a few blocks away from where a crime took place. His car was spotted in the area around the time of the incident. And the person who committed the crime knew something about home security systems."

"Oh!" said Dr. Swanson. "Then you knew what Jason's occupation was … before I put him on a pedestal."

"No, not exactly," said Joe. "I found out where

he worked through his mother. He told me he was a software engineer. I found your company in the yellow pages and decided to call. I had no idea what work he was in, only that he worked on computers. I'm sure it's probably only a coincidence that the person we're looking for and Jason both know alarm systems. I guess you could say he was in the wrong place at the wrong time. If it weren't for his car, he wouldn't be on our radar at all. But since someone spotted it, we have no choice but to follow up on the information."

"I see," Swanson said.

"So, since I have you on the line, maybe you could share some of your knowledge with me."

Dr. Swanson said, "I'd be more than happy to provide you with as much information as possible. Go ahead and ask whatever you would like to know."

"All right. I'll do just that," said Joe. "Do you think Mr. Bradford has the expertise to disarm a house without setting off the alarm?"

"Well, that depends on who designed it. If we did, then the answer is no. Not even Jason could avoid setting it off. He would need an access code. But if it were anyone else's system, yes, most likely he could. You see, most alarm companies provide the user with a touch pad box, mounted somewhere near the area they wish to enter. That box can be hacked. Our software, however, requires the use of a handheld remote control given to the user so only he or she has access to it. It would be impossible for a burglar to break in without setting off the alarm, unless somehow he or she got their hands on the remote control."

"You mean like stealing a woman's purse? Then he might have the remote control and the woman's home address."

"Exactly," Dr. Swanson said.

Joe then asked, "Do you know if EnterLock, SafeSystems, or CODEX INTERNATIONAL use your software?"

"Why yes," said Swanson. "All three use our technology."

"Then wouldn't Mr. Bradford have access to all the entry codes? Couldn't he dig into your records and find that information?"

"No. We don't have that information. That's created on the users' end. It's the last step before the monitoring company activates the system. The user must create a unique password using a combination of random numbers and letters. Once it's programmed into the remote control and the semi-smart panel inside the house, then the system is turned on. The only person who knows the user's password is the user and a few bonded employees working at the monitoring company with the right clearance; that's it. So, to answer your question whether my employee, Mr. Bradford, could access a house that had one of our software packages installed, the answer is no. I don't think so."

Joe thanked the doctor for the information and said goodbye.

~~~

Rusty was working on a new whiteboard devoted to their last homicide victim, Sandra Brown. Under the word 'suspect,' he had Jason's full name in large capital letters. Under transportation, he wrote, 'white Buick or Oldsmobile' with an addendum, 'black Mercedes,' followed by a question mark. He was about to add the suspect's description when Joe walked up and handed him the affidavit.

"Let me know if I've missed anything," Joe said.

Rusty scanned the document. "No. It looks good. That should do it."

As he handed it back to Joe, Joe told him all about his conversation with Jason's supervisor, Dr. Swanson, then told Rusty he was leaving work a couple of hours early. He had dinner reservations at the Blue Dolphin and wanted to get there, eat, and leave before the band started to play and his wife forced him out on the dance floor.

Rusty returned to the whiteboard and added, 'Computer Programmer' under the word occupation.

~~~

Joe left headquarters in the pouring rain. It was his wife's birthday and he had a dozen red roses waiting for him at a nearby flower shop. He figured even with the rain, he had plenty of time to pick up the flowers and his two daughters from school, drive home, jump in the shower, dress, walk the girls next door to the babysitter's house and still get to the restaurant on time.

Joe was six years older than his wife, who just turned thirty-two. April stood four feet eleven with dark brown hair and a shapely figure. Her field of expertise was health care. She had a business degree and managed the billing department at Penrose Hospital. The girls took after their mother, both short and good-looking, at least in Joe's mind. They had a dog named Dog. The dog took after Joe, big and muscular. The dog was a Bullmastiff, and the girls rode him around the house like a horse.

After tipping the waiter five bucks for a secluded table in a corner of the restaurant, Joe decided to tell his wife about the case they were working on while they waited for dinner to arrive. Not because he enjoyed talking about work, he didn't. But because April fit the description the killer was attracted to: short with dark hair. So far, the killer hadn't gone after anyone who was married or had an animal in the house, and all the women had the same initials: S. B. Who was to say that wouldn't change. Maybe he would start going after older women or young girls just to throw them off — especially if Jason was doing the killing — now that he knew they were on to him.

Joe told April they were sure they knew who their killer was. They had him backed into a corner. It was just a matter of time. He also told her all about their star witness but said not to mention it to anyone, at least not until after the case went to trial.

After a lovely candlelight dinner — with no dancing involved — they went home to an empty house, except for the dog, who they shut out of the bedroom, while they made love. It was the first time in a long time that they were truly alone. They could make as much noise as they wanted to without the fear of little ears wondering what Mom and Dad were doing.

Chapter 14

As Sally walked the short block to the bus stop, she thought about the two detectives and wondered how their meeting went with Jason. She hadn't spoken to her son since she warned him they were on their way over to his place. And last night, she was alone. He didn't bother to stop by for dinner like he usually did.

She knew he couldn't have committed the murder the detectives were talking about, because he was at her house, down in the basement ... all evening. He even woke her up before he left, just to say he was leaving. And that was about eleven o'clock, if she recalled. Plus, she knew he couldn't have done it anyway. It wasn't in him. He wouldn't hurt a fly.

And then she rethought that thought, remembering why she didn't like going down into the basement, because of the bones in the box.

She knew how rough it was for him when his father died. He took it harder than anyone else, even though Jack wasn't always that kind to Jason. He still loved his father and moped around for weeks after his death.

After Jack passed, the twenty-five-thousand-dollar life insurance policy quickly disappeared, leaving her no choice but to go back to work full-time to support the family. She did the only thing she knew how to do: either pick up a dust rag or carry a tray as a waitress in a restaurant. The days of playing tambourine in a band died with the hippie generation.

Sally hadn't changed much over the years. She was still attractive. After Jack's untimely death, she went into a state of depression, which took nearly a year for her to get over. After she had recovered, she tried dating a few times, but it never worked out. Men don't like an already-made family, let alone one with four boys in it.

Soon after she started back to work, the two older boys, Prescott and Troy, moved out. They both followed their father's line of work and joined the military and at the end of each month, they sent home a little of their paychecks to help out.

Prescott and Troy were now married and doing well. They remained in the service and moved up in rank. One was a major and the other a captain. Ryan moved around a lot. He was in sales, and she never knew where he was from one moment to the next; he was the hardest to keep track of. Ryan usually called her on Christmas once a year.

Jason was the last to leave. He moved out on his birthday almost four years ago, and he was the only one she still saw regularly. She was proud of him for his accomplishments. Mostly, because of all the obstacles he had to overcome growing up. Jack always said he would never amount to anything. He was wrong. Out of the four boys, Jason was the most successful. No, he wasn't the president of a company or owner of a business, but he had a steady income and money in the bank.

But now all that was history; a lot of water had passed under the bridge since then. Then it was Jason who helped her out. Thank God for Jason, her savior. If it weren't for him, she'd be on food stamps.

To save money, Sally had quit driving her car. She parked it in the garage where it stayed unregistered and undriven for five years. Jason started it weekly and add gas when it got low.

Sally knew how difficult life was for Jason growing up. Born with a harelip and small bones made him an easy target for other children to go after. And go after him, they did … unmercifully teasing him and making him feel like a freak.

To make matters worse, shortly before his father died, Jason fractured his leg in two places below the knee. It was summertime and he was out rabbit hunting with his father when Jason tripped over a rock. Jack didn't want to take him to the hospital, so he tried to set it himself. But when infection set in, he had no choice. He took him to the doctor. Because of the long wait before seeing a doctor, it never healed correctly.

When he walked, his leg was stiff and slightly twisted, a tad out of alignment, which gave him another mountain to climb. It was good that he was a male instead of a female, Sally thought. When he was old enough, he grew a mustache, which helped cover the scar … not entirely, but enough to get by. Enough where he no longer felt self-conscious.

~~~

When Sally got to work everyone was talking about the S. B. killer. One of her regulars, who was sitting in a booth, read the latest article in the newspaper out loud, including the description of the killer's victims. One of the waitresses thought she'd be funny by saying, "Hey, Sally, you're next," and laughed. Sally didn't see the humor in it and gave her a disapproving look.

~~~

After the detectives left his apartment, Jason sat around the rest of the day, trying to figure out how anyone could have recognized him driving his mother's car. He always filled it using a gas can. It was never out of the garage, unless of course, he was cleaning someone's house. And on those nights, the weather was always bad; they were purposely picked so no one would be out on the street to see what he looked like. He always wore a sweatshirt with the hood pulled up, so only his eyes, nose, and mouth were visible. So how and who could have spotted him? They couldn't have tracked him down using the license plate. The car would come back to the registered owner: his mother, if it showed up at all. The tags had expired.

He didn't like the cops, especially the shorter of the two. What was his name again? *Stubbs. Detective Stubbs.* He must have been the brains between the two. It was obvious the big guy wanted to look around the apartment, so he let him look.

Not a lot. Just a little peek in the bathroom to satisfy his curiosity. He kept his cleaning supplies at his mother's house; there was nothing they could possibly find here at his apartment. He had been so careful not to slip up. But there they were, knocking on his door. Asking him questions about the houses he had cleaned, showing him all those pictures of Sally.

He got a little information out of the chubby one when he deliberately irritated him. Asking if he was on a fishing expedition, got him upset enough to tell him there was a witness. Someone had seen his tattoo. But he didn't believe that for one minute. No one had gotten that close to him. Still, they had to have something or else they wouldn't have come around asking questions. But what possibly could have given him away? Whatever it was, it wasn't enough for them to arrest him right there on the spot.

He thought back, remembering all the houses he'd cleaned. Yes, he had made mistakes. Probably too many, but he got better as time passed. The first time he got Sally, he was slow running up the steps. She turned and saw his face.

The second time, he got in too big of a hurry and rushed Sally before she had a chance to unlock the door. It was a good thing she'd inserted the key in the lock before she went down.

He didn't use zip ties the first two times. He used twelve-gauge coated wire. But the wire had a tendency to cut into the skin, so he fixed that problem by switching over to a ¼ inch wide plastic tie.

The third time was a charm. It went down smooth as silk, not a wrinkle or a crimp in anything he did that evening. That was a confidence builder. That's also the night he spotted the wine in her refrigerator and decided to celebrate. While she was lying on the floor, he turned on her stereo and put his foot on her back like he was the conquering son who had just slayed a dragon. He drank straight out of the bottle, toasting her death. From then on, he decided to bring his own wine and music. Something to get him into the right mood. That's why he brought along the Rolling Stones and a little Bob Seger. It helped fire him up and reminded him of his father laying a stick to his backside down in the basement when his mother was away cleaning houses. His father was a big fan of the Rolling Stones and liked to play their music while beating him. He would crank up the music so the neighbors couldn't hear his son scream.

~~~

Joe spent the whole next morning trying to find a judge willing put his name on the warrant based on the evidence they had. He finally had to settle with Judge Jonathan Webster, a senior officer of the court who was, in fact, so senior that he was accused of sleeping through most of his hearings. He never questioned anything on the affidavit; in fact, he barely even looked at it. He mumbled something unrecognizable to Joe as he hacked up some phlegm, nodded, and signed his name.

Once Joe had the signed document back in hand, he called Jason at Emerson Electronics. Jason wasn't happy when Joe told him he had a search warrant, signed by a judge, giving him the authority to search his place for evidence related to Sandra Brown's murder.

"Who's Sandra Brown?" Jason asked inquisitively, even though he knew her true identity.

"She's one of our latest homicide victims."

"What evidence are you searching for?"

Joe rattled off the items listed on the paperwork.

Jason smiled, knowing he had none of the items mentioned, at least not at the apartment. But still, he wondered why they were looking for a duffel bag, unless their witness saw him through a window removing the duffel bag from the trunk of his mother's car. This would also explain why they were looking for the driver of a white Oldsmobile or a Buick. But that wouldn't explain why they had their eye on him. There was something more to it. He was sure of that. But *what?* That was the million-dollar question.

Had he left his fingerprints in Sally's house? If so, when? He thought back, trying to recall where he might've slipped up, when he touched something without his gloves on. He remembered taking them off, several times, but was always careful, wiping everything clean afterward. So where did he go wrong? Then he thought, what difference did it make? His fingerprints only proved that he was in the house sometime in the past. Nothing more.

~~~

After Joe got off the phone with Jason, he and Rusty left headquarters. They wanted to make sure they had got to Jason's place before he had a chance to hide any of the evidence listed on the warrant.

When Jason arrived home, the two detectives were standing on his front porch. And they weren't alone. They brought along three uniformed cops to help in their search. As soon as Jason stepped up on his front porch Joe handed him the warrant.

Jason quickly scanned the document. As he read, he noticed someone had added his car, garage, and storage unit to the list; three locations Longhorn had failed to mention over the phone. Once satisfied the document was legal, he unlocked the door and let them in.

After entering, Jason walked over to his couch and sat down. He watched with curiosity as the five men huddled in a circle, going over their game plan of who would search where and for what. Then they split up and went in different directions.

Rusty started his search in the kitchen area. First, he opened up the cupboards; not finding anything of importance, he moved over to the refrigerator. As soon as he opened the right leaf of the French-styled doors, he saw a bottle of red wine and knew it wasn't on his list. He couldn't remember if Ella had mentioned the color of the wine or the brand of the bottle the killer was drinking the night of Sandra Brown's death, so he closed the door and moved to the hallway closet.

Joe was in the bedroom going through Jason's dresser. Everything neat as a pin. Nothing out of order. Dark socks in one drawer, mixed colors in another, and white socks and white T-shirts in still another. Joe moved over to the bed. He lifted the mattress and peeked underneath; nothing. He looked under the box spring and found four rifles. Two were single shot .22s, one a 16-gauge shotgun and another, a .300 Savage deer rifle; all had belonged to Jason's father. Next, he slid back the mirrored closet door. Inside he found nothing, except once again, everything in an orderly matter. On the left side Jason hung his suits, lined up by color from light to dark; the center area was filled with white starched work shirts. On the right was a combination of pants, mostly jeans; farther to the right hung several sweatshirts and a full jogging outfit. His shoes were on the floor, lined up like soldiers: some so shiny, Joe thought, they might burn his eyes if he stared at them too long. *More military influence*, he thought.

Joe walked out of the bedroom and into the living room area where he joined Rusty and the three uniform officers. He shrugged his shoulders to show that he hadn't found anything.

Jason sat smirking, knowing they came up empty.

The five men huddled again. This time they spoke in a whisper, so Jason couldn't hear their conversation. Then Rusty turned to face the man on the couch. He said, "Mr. Bradford, we found four rifles underneath your bed. How come they're all loaded?"

Jason recited what his father once told him. "'You never know when someone may break into your place. You got to be ready.' I didn't see that on your search warrant?"

"It wasn't," Rusty replied. "I just thought I'd ask." Then he said, "Do you have a private parking garage? If so, can you take us to it and let us look around?"

"Yes, I do. But I seldom use it for parking unless I can't find a place on the street."

The six men walked outside together and down to Jason's parking unit. Jason lifted the door and unlocked an overhead storage cabinet. "Have at it."

Everything was neat, like the apartment. Boxes were stacked neatly one on top of the other, all marked according to their contents. One of the uniform officers climbed into the unit and started handing them out. Jason left and soon returned with some masking tape. After they had inspected each box, Jason resealed it.

When they finished with the garage, Joe asked if they could look inside his car. And Jason asked, "Do I have a choice?"

And Joe said, "No, I guess not. It's on the search warrant."

Jason led them back to the front of his building, where he normally parked. Then he opened the trunk and the side passenger door, so they could look inside.

In the trunk, they found a laptop computer, the only item they found so far listed on the search warrant. They removed the spare tire and looked in the well. But nothing was there. Joe got in the driver's seat and dug through the center console. He found an empty CD jacket from an album called *Flashpoint*, recorded during a live concert of the Rolling Stones. He reached over and pushed the eject button on the compact disc player, ejecting the Stones' music. He put the disc back in its jacket and put it in an evidence bag. The detectives thanked Jason for his time and said if they found nothing of interest, they would return his computer in a few days.

Jason stood on the sidewalk and waved as the officers drove away. He wanted to give them a one-finger salute but decided against it; he didn't want to antagonize them. He just wanted them to disappear. They got his computer. They wouldn't find anything of value; it was his work computer. They also got his Stones CD. *Why would they take that?* He thought, *I'd better get that back; that's the one with all their big hits on it.*

"So, what did we learn here today? Rusty asked. He made a U-turn and drove back down the street in front of Jason's place, just in time to see Jason's front door close.

Joe shrugged his shoulders. "Not much. Only that he's a neat freak. And that he likes the Rolling Stones. I guess we'll have to go back to the drawing board if we don't find anything on his computer. Say ... do you want to make a quick stop at the donut shop, pick up something to snack on?"

"Yeah, sure, why not. I'm not starting my diet until mañana."

Chapter 15

When Ella returned Dr. Henderson's call, she found out that he had gotten in touch with Dr. Alexander, who confirmed everything she'd said happened the night his patient died, right down to his statement about endorphins. He told her the two of them had discussed the idea of her sharing her experience with a group of doctors in a monthly forum that he hosted.

The thought of standing up in front of an audience, speaking to a bunch of doctors who probably thought the same way Dr. Alexander did intrigued her. She was no public speaker, but she thought she could pull it off because she was the one who experienced it. It was coming straight from her heart. She didn't need to write anything down. No preparation necessary; what happened, happened. She would remember every intricate detail. The only thing that concerned her was how much she could reveal. She picked up the phone and dialed Detective Stubbs' number.

When he answered, she identified herself and

said, "I'm sorry for bothering you, but Dr. Henderson and Dr. Alexander, the cancer patient's doctor, would like me to speak at one of their monthly forums about my experience. I thought maybe I should ask you before I say something that I shouldn't."

"Well, thanks for consulting with me first. As far as I'm concerned, you can say anything you wish … except what you saw here. Please leave the homicide out."

"That's what I thought you'd say."

Rusty added, "We haven't arrested him yet, so he doesn't know our eyewitness wasn't here physically."

Ella chirped in. "Oh, but I was. Maybe not in the flesh, but I was there."

"I know," said Rusty, "but try telling that to a jury and see what happens. They deal in facts, tangible evidence, not an unproven theory."

"That so-called unproven theory — as you call it — has been around since the beginning of time."

Ella knew he was right, she knew it all along. She knew it wasn't going to be easy convincing anyone what happened to her after she died. But she was sure she'd done just that. She convinced Dr. Henderson, and from what she heard, she may have also convinced Dr. Alexander — or at least, had him rethink his thoughts on dying.

Rusty veered off the subject of death and instead focused on the killer, "We identified the fingerprints on the water glass, but he didn't have an arrest record, so it took us a little longer to find him.

"The only part that differs from what you saw is that he doesn't own a white Buick or Oldsmobile. He owns a black Mercedes-Benz. Other than that, everything you said was right on the money. The picture Randy drew looks just like him. And the second one looks like his mother."

"Oh good," she said. "But I don't understand why the car was different. Maybe he wasn't driving his car. Maybe it belonged to someone else."

"That's possible. He's a real smart guy. He works with computers and knows a lot about alarm systems. I'll try to keep you informed as we go along. And good luck on your speaking engagement."

Ella thanked him and said goodbye.

After hanging up, she went into the bedroom and started digging through her closet, looking for a buried filing cabinet. Once found, she removed a folder with her personal finances in it and carried it back to the kitchen, where she set it on her table. Then she sat down with a fresh cup of coffee and a cat that wanted her attention.

She opened the folder and stared at the contents. The top sheet was the deed to her townhouse — all bought and paid for. After her husband had passed, she sold their house in Long Beach and moved to Westchester, California to be closer to work.

She got out the calculator and started crunching numbers. She calculated what her pension plan would be worth if she were to leave work now. Then she added in her 401k, her late husband's life insurance policy, and her savings. And when she finished, she couldn't believe her eyes. She went through the figures a second time to make sure she hadn't made a mistake. When she finished, she sat back in her chair and smiled. She had way more than she needed to survive. In fact, she could live well … if that's what she wanted to do. She had no children to support — only a hungry cat. She didn't want to retire and sit around the house. She wanted to work with the community. After her resurrection she had this new driving force — to help others who couldn't help themselves.

She picked up the phone and called the number Dr. Henderson had given her. Dr. Alexander answered on the second ring. He said he was happy to get a chance to talk with her over the phone and not through a medium. She wasn't sure if he was trying to be funny, making light of what happened, or if he still didn't believe in an afterlife.

"Well, Ella, have you made a decision yet?" Dr. Alexander asked.

"Yes, I have," she said. "I would love to speak at your conference. But I want you to know that I cannot talk about anything I witnessed in Colorado. In other words, it will only be those events that took place here in the hospital and my trip to …" she hesitated, "Heaven."

"That's fine. I suppose you have a gag order not to talk about the murder; is that right?" Dr. Henderson had told him the whole story from start to finish.

"Yeah, it's unofficial. The detective there asked me not to mention it until they've made an arrest."

"Fine," Dr. Alexander said. "The conference is

here at the hospital on Wednesday at 11:00 a.m. It includes lunch."

Ella said, "I'm going to be a little nervous. I've never been good at public speaking."

"That's understandable. Dr. Henderson will help you through it. He'll be there to interject and give his position on what he was doing while you were out of your body. You'll work as a team. Then, when you get to the part about my patient ... I'll step in and talk about what I saw when my patient died. You'll do just fine."

"Okay, Dr. Alexander, thanks. I'll see you Wednesday."

~~~

Rusty checked in with B. B. in Forensics. "What about our comparison. How long do you think it will take to match up the two tissues?"

"Not long. We don't have to run them through a data bank searching for a needle in a haystack. We already have the needle. It's just a matter of ... do they match."

"Well, call me as soon as you get the results."

"Oh, I will! You can count on that. Your name is at the top of my list."

~~~

Bobbi thought about her conversation with Rusty. If the two tissues came back with the same DNA on them, that meant that everything Ella said was true, which would shore up her belief in an afterlife.

She hadn't been over to the crime scene since the day they discovered the woman's body. Now she wanted to go back over there and walk through it, seeing it the way Ella had described it during her interview with Rusty and Joe.

Bobbi borrowed the key from Homicide and drove to the house on Wildwood Road. She stood where she thought Ella might've stood the night of the murder. She stared at the street sign, picturing it lit up under an overhead street lamp. Then she walked to the third house from the corner, the green one with the dark green trim; Sandra Brown's house. She momentarily stopped and imagined a white car driving up to the curb on the opposite side of the street. She pictured a small man dressed in Levis, wearing a hooded sweatshirt, get out of the car and open his trunk. Then she pictured him carrying a duffel bag as he crossed the street and walked right past her.

Bobbi followed the invisible man into the back yard. Everything Ella said went through her head. How he dressed in the white lab suit. What he looked like. How he removed the filter from his cigarette. The tattoo between his thumb and forefinger, and the little bat he held in his hand, as he crouched behind the hedge, waiting for the woman to open her back door.

She pictured the back door opening and the woman stepping inside as the little man came flying out from behind the bush, leaping up on the porch and striking her in the head.

Bobbi unlocked the back door and entered. Once inside, she pretended to step around an invisible body on the floor, and then made her way through the rest of the house, imagining the killer closing blinds and shutting curtains. She pictured him tying up the woman, moving her body, drinking wine, washing dishes in the sink, and then walking into the bathroom. She went into the bathroom and stared at herself in the mirror as if she were the killer. Then she saw the new roll of toilet paper on the spool and pictured him blowing his nose and tossing the tissue in the small trash can on the floor.

After that, Bobbi walked back into the living room and looked down at the white chalk marks on the rug where they found the woman's body. She closed her eyes and tried to imagine the little man sitting on top of the woman, beating her to death. She felt satisfied once she thought she had relived the sequence of events leading up to and through the woman's death the way Ella had described it in the interview. And there was no need to fantasize any longer. She had seen all she needed to see.

She relocked the door and returned to her car.

As she rounded the corner at Wildwood Road onto Hidden Valley Drive on her way back to her office, she passed by a black Mercedes-Benz as it turned onto Wildwood Road. She got a quick look at the driver, just a passing glance, and thought he looked familiar, but from where she didn't know. He was wearing a baseball cap and dark sunglasses.

Bobbi had been dating a pathologist who worked for the Medical Examiner's office, but lately, they weren't getting along. He wanted to get married, and she wasn't sure she was in love with him. They were two opposites. He was a bookworm and she was athletic; she loved hunting and fishing, bike riding, backpacking, football. He, on the other hand, was more intellectual; he loved reading, going to operas, cooking fancy dishes, and discussing politics that they seldom agreed on. She wished she could find someone like Joe Longhorn again. It was her fault for their breakup. *Oh well*, she thought, *I can't continue to dwell on the past.*

When she got back to her office, she decided to call her lab to see if they had matched up the two tissues. When one of her techs answered, she found out the person working on it had an emergency at home and had to leave work early. So nothing got done.

~~~

Jason left work early. He'd told his supervisor, Dr. Swanson, that he wasn't feeling well. He lied. He had an ulterior motive. He needed to get back into Sally's house. Walk the floor, see if he could remember where he might've slipped up, touched something that he hadn't wiped clean.

As he turned the corner onto Wildwood Road, he recognized a woman in a city car turning onto Hidden Valley Drive. He remembered her from a week or so earlier, when he saw her standing in front of Sally's house talking to a cop. That was shortly after they discovered her body — before it made the headlines. He had been milling around, watching from behind the barrier tape, wearing the same black cap and dark sunglasses he wore today. When he turned the corner, the woman glared at him as if she knew who he was … giving him a long look. Maybe she recognized him as one of the looky-loos — one of Sally's neighbors.

He drove up and down the street three times before eventually parking his car on the same side where Sally had lived when she was alive. He waited, watching the house for an hour before deciding to go inside.

Jason got out of his car and walked briskly toward her house. He pulled the brim of the cap down, so if someone looked out their window, they wouldn't get a good look at his face. He brought along the remote control he'd preprogrammed with her password in it and used when he'd entered her house before, in case her alarm was still active.

He rushed down the driveway and ducked behind the back of her house, did a quick look around, and rethought what he had done that night. He remembered dumping one of the plastic bags in the trash can beside the garage on his way out. He walked over and looked inside. It was still there. There was nothing in that bag that could possibly give him away. Then he stepped up on the porch and peeked through the window in the door. It was light enough inside to see the alarm panel mounted on the wall next to the washer and dryer. Not seeing a power light lit, he used his key and unlocked the back door. Then he opened it and stepped inside.

Once inside, he retraced his footsteps, thinking about what he did, in the order he did it. When he was wearing his gloves and when he wasn't. When he got to the part where he entered the bathroom, he couldn't remember if he'd taken off his gloves when he changed out the toilet paper roll. He remembered wiping off the chrome holder later when he knew he was wearing gloves, but he wasn't sure if he'd wiped off the sprocket. He didn't think so.

Then he thought, *man this is ridiculous. Getting all worked up ... for what. No one in their right mind would worry about something so trivial. And no investigator would waste their time looking for fingerprints on it. But still, there must be something.* Then he remembered blowing his nose and getting rid of the Kleenex in the small trash can beside the toilet. He peeked in, but it was empty. *Did I empty that or did someone else remove it from the basket?* He didn't remember emptying it. If he had, then it should have gone into the bag with the zip ties and used tape.

He quickly walked the rest of the house and decided he'd worn gloves when he'd touched everything else. He relocked the back door, hurried back to his car, started his engine and slowly drove away toward his mother's house.

~~~

It was time to get rid of everything he could think of that might connect him to the killings.

His mother was at work, which was good, because he didn't want to see her ugly face anyway.

He unlocked the door to the basement, turned on the light at the top of the stairs, and slowly took the steps down into his workshop.

Once at the bottom, Jason kicked the bucket he used to clean the little bat in, sending it flying across the room, wetting the wall and the floor. He cursed when he realized what he'd done. It didn't call for that. Now he'd have to clean up the mess.

He was still mad at himself, not knowing for sure if he'd emptied the basket with the tissue in it. That would probably haunt him until they arrested him — if they arrested him. Or the whole idea would simply fade from the picture.

He could tell himself it was no big deal, but he knew deep down inside it might be. It might make the difference between a life-or-death sentence. If they could prove he was there when Sally died, then he was dead meat.

After mopping up the mess and wiping off the wall, Jason looked around the room, trying to decide what he needed to get rid of and what he didn't. Unfortunately, not much would remain. He would take the three computers back to his apartment. There was no need to think the two detectives would return to his place and rummage around through his stuff a second time if they didn't find anything of interest the first go-round.

He unplugged the computing equipment and carried it up the stairs and out to his car. He decided to leave the lock-and key-making apparatus. It was cumbersome and too expensive to get rid of. He would have to get rid of his faithful lock pick, though, in case it had any microscopic particles on it belonging to one of the other houses he'd cleaned.

The scrapbook would have to go. That could cook his goose. A few years down the road, he could find the information at the library, print it out, and make a new scrapbook. He didn't want to use the metal drum in the back yard that sat idle for well over fifteen years. He was afraid someone would report seeing the smoke and turn him in for creating an environmental hazard — the unauthorized burning of waste. Instead, he went upstairs and lit a fire in the fireplace.

Once the fire was raging, he threw the scrapbook and little bat into the flames and closed the screen.

Jason went back down into the basement and opened the cabinet underneath his bench, where he kept most of his cleaning equipment: Tyvek lab suits, shoe coverings, Nitrile medical gloves, duct tape, plastic bags, zip ties—the whole shebang—everything except for the white towels. He kept them on a shelf in the bathroom. He scooped up what he could squeeze into his late father's duffel bag, dragged it up the stairs and out to his car. What he didn't get on the first trip, he got on the second.

When he thought he'd gotten it all, he went back up, turned out the light, and locked the basement door. He decided to get rid of the evidence in the fireplace, though there wasn't much of it left. Mostly ashes. He swept them into a pile and poured them into a bucket. Then he took the bucket out to the large metal drum out back and dumped it inside.

Afterward, he remembered the gloves and booties he'd stashed in the glove compartment of his mother's car, so he went and got them.

Finally, it was time to go.

~~~

Jason took the main highway toward Pikes Peak, through Manitou Springs, through Cascade, into Woodland Park. All the while, his thoughts keep drifting back to that little basket in Sally's house. The one he wasn't sure if he'd emptied. He kept telling himself it didn't matter. But it did. It mattered a lot.

In Woodland Park, he took a side road that led to a golf course. There he threw his lock-picking tools into a small pond by the eighth hole.

On the way back to Colorado Springs, he stopped at a hardware store and picked up a can of black spray paint. Then he drove to the city dump on the outskirts of town where he found a secluded area — not a soul in sight.

There he partially emptied his duffel bag, first getting rid of his lab suits, mixing them in with all the other garbage.

He drove to a new location inside the dump where he got rid of his booties and gloves. Then he moved to the far side of the dump where he scattered the zip ties and tape. And last, he took his father's duffel bag out of the trunk and sprayed black paint over his father's name. He watched the name disappear and started feeling better. It was like erasing an old memory. A bad-old memory. As the last letter in the name Bradford vanished, he said, "Good riddance. I hope it's hot down there!" Then he took out a utility knife and sliced up the bag so no one could use it.

As Jason drove out of the dump, he was feeling good. Better than he had in a while. He'd taken care of everything, except for that one little thing he couldn't do anything about. So he decided to enjoy the ride back to town. He inserted another Rolling Stones CD into his player, an album called *Aftermath*. This album was not his favorite. The police had his favorite. A few seconds later, Mick Jagger's voice came through the speakers, singing the words to, "Paint It Black." Jason grinned when he heard it, and thought, *how fitting is that?*

Chapter 16

Rusty left his office and headed for the other side of town for an appointment with a new doctor. He was a little apprehensive about going. He already canceled the first appointment he'd made and was now thinking about doing it again.

As Rusty drove, he kept saying to himself: *You're all right; you don't have to do this.* But this time, the steering wheel was not cooperating. It wouldn't let him turn around and drive home. Deep down inside, he knew he desperately needed the help of a professional.

He pulled into the parking structure and immediately found a spot. He took the elevator to the eleventh floor. The waiting room was empty; a lone woman in her mid-thirties worked a crossword puzzle on the other side of a counter. As he walked through the door, she turned her head to greet their new patient. "Mr. Stubbs?"

"Yes," he said, as she handed him a thousand forms to fill out. Twenty minutes later, the doctor stuck his head into the waiting room. "Mr. Stubbs, please follow me."

Rusty stood up and followed the doctor down a short hallway decorated in degrees. He had a Ph.D. in psychiatry from Harvard Medical School and another from UCLA, Rusty's college. *Smart guy,* Rusty thought.

At the end of the hall, they entered a room designed to make clients feel at ease. The room was bright, painted in a warm yellow. The doctor introduced himself as Dr. Barnard Wasserman and asked Rusty to have a seat on a couch that faced a gas-burning fireplace. Rusty took a seat and the doctor sat in a chair off to one side. The furniture was modern, but not too modern. The couch rested on a beautiful Prussian rug, woven from gold, brown, and red thread, all meant to do one thing: take the patient's mind off his problems. *And that it did*, Rusty thought.

Dr. Wasserman asked, "Are you comfortable? Is there anything I can get for you to drink, Mr. Stubbs, before we start? I have coffee, bottled water, or wine if you wish."

Rusty said, "Maalox! Do you have any Maalox?"

The doctor laughed. "I see you have a sense of humor, Mr. Stubbs. That's a good sign." Then he looked down at his paperwork. "According to the information you've provided, you're a homicide detective."

"Yes," Rusty said. "You can call me Rusty if you like, Dr. Wasserman."

"And you can call me Barney, if you like, Rusty."

Rusty thought of another ploy to make one feel comfortable. He had a quick daydream of the doctor dressed in a German officer's uniform standing in a cold interrogation room, saying, 'we have ways to make you talk, Mr. Stubbs.' As quickly as the thought came to him, it disappeared.

"I'm going to guess that your work would be incredibly stressful. Would that be correct?"

"Yes, it is. I've been doing it for a long time, fifteen years."

"What can I help you with, Rusty?"

"I don't know if you can." He hesitated. "Lately I've been having suicidal thoughts."

"How would you go about it, if you were to kill yourself?"

"Well, first, I'd make sure I had all my paperwork in order, who was to get what. Then I would leave a note on my front door so my partner wouldn't walk in unexpectedly and find me behind the shower curtain in the bathtub with a hole in my head. That's how I would do it."

"Okay, Rusty, tell me a little about yourself. Are you normally a happy person? When did you start having this feeling that life wasn't worth living?

"Yes, normally I'm a cheerful guy. I started having these feelings about a year ago."

"I see you've checked off single. Have you ever been married?"

"No, I've never been married. I've been gay from as far back as I can remember."

"Do they know that at work?"

"Yes, they know I'm gay. They've known it almost from the start, a few years after I started working on patrol."

"Do they tease you about it?"

"Yes, they tease me."

"Does that trouble you?"

"No, it doesn't bother me. Not anymore." Rusty felt as though the table had turned. He was no longer the interrogator. He was the interrogated.

The session lasted a little more than one hour. Dr. Wasserman thought he'd learned a lot about Detective Stubbs. He knew he wasn't one of those people who acted irrationally.

He knew Rusty wouldn't spontaneously put a gun to his head or jump out in front of a car. He'd leave a note. He didn't want to make a mess. This showed a consideration for other people. He was comfortable in his own skin — with his homosexuality; at least, he tried to leave that impression. The doctor didn't feel Rusty was in any immediate danger since he'd taken the time to sit down and share his thoughts.

While the doctor evaluated Rusty, Rusty evaluated the doctor. He thought, *sharp dresser.* The doctor wore a dark brown pinstripe suit with a matching vest. He wasn't wearing his coat, which also made him feel more relaxed and his light pink long-sleeve dress shirt, with his shirtsleeves rolled up, was another trick to make him feel at home. He was in his early sixties and didn't wear a wedding ring. He was of medium height and build, and looked in good shape, probably an avid runner.

Dr. Wasserman looked and acted like one of his

all-time favorite actors, Paul Newman. He wore rectangular-shaped, gold-framed reading glasses that sat low on his nose, which he looked over the top as he talked.

"Are you a religious man, Rusty?" The doctor asked. He knew that most religions frowned upon the act of suicide.

Rusty wasn't in a big hurry to answer that question. The doctor noticed his reluctance. "Is that a difficult question?"

"Today yes, yesterday no," Rusty replied. "If you would have asked me that question a week ago, you might have gotten a different answer. No, I'm not religious. But I'm having second thoughts about whether there's a creator, a supreme being, a higher power guiding us."

"Would you like to talk about that?"

Rusty knew the doctor couldn't ethically repeat their conversation, so it didn't matter. He decided he didn't want to go into it at this time, so he said, "No, not now. Maybe next time. It's a long story."

"Okay." Dr. Wasserman jotted down something on his notepad. "Why don't we call an end to this session, and I'll see you in, let's say, two weeks. How does that sound?"

"Okay, Dr. Wasserman. Thank you. I think you've already got me feeling more at ease with myself."

"Good, that's what I'm here for. If you need to talk, please feel free to call anytime, night or day." He handed Rusty a business card with his work and home phone numbers on it.

~~~

After leaving the doctor's office, Rusty was in a cheerful mood. He couldn't remember the last time he'd felt like this. Not that he was cured. He knew he wasn't. But he was feeling a whole lot more like his old self. When he got in his car, he donned his happy hat: a bright red baseball cap with the words 'Old Fart' written on it and headed for home.

Over the past few months, he had been out of control, doing things that he normally wouldn't do. Eating too much, for one thing. He even stopped taking his Glock home, afraid he might do the unthinkable — putting a bullet in his head — ending it all.

Maybe now, just maybe, there was a spark of hope. Maybe this new doctor could figure out what was ailing him.

~~~

Halfway home, Rusty had an epiphany. What if the DNA found in the tissue Joe illegally took out of Jason's trash actually matched the one at the victim's house? A sharp lawyer would most likely ask where they got the tissue and if it was on their search warrant. Rusty suddenly changed course and headed for Jason's apartment.

Once there, he parked in the alley behind Jason's place, not far from a community dumpster. He wasn't waiting for Jason to dump his trash, but to see if that was possible, and if he could set up surveillance for a later date. And lo and behold, as if it was a miracle from Heaven (though he didn't believe in Heaven), who came marching down a pathway between two apartment buildings carrying a white plastic trash bag and heading toward the trash receptacle, but the devil himself, Jason Thomas Bradford.

Rusty reached into his glove box and removed his video camera and started recording Jason a few feet from the container.

After Jason returned to his apartment, Rusty went to the trash container. The lid was up, and as luck would have it, the only white trash bag in sight was the one Jason deposited seconds earlier.

Rusty continued to record the whole event, not allowing a break in the action from the moment he first turned on the camera. He wanted to make sure no one would accuse him of planting evidence. Still recording, he opened the bag to show what was inside. And there was material he could use to get Jason's DNA, mostly cigarette butts. But there was also an occasional crumpled Kleenex, mixed in with the usual stuff found in a trash bag.

After putting it in his trunk, Rusty turned off his camera and got back in the driver's seat. By now, he was feeling even better than he had when he first left his doctor's office. Everything was falling into place. Maybe there was a God in Heaven after all.

Chapter 17

Ella had followed her doctor's advice by taking two weeks off to rest and recuperate. What rest, she thought as she stood behind a curtain waiting to hear Dr. Henderson invite her onto the stage.

Dr. Henderson looked relaxed standing behind a lectern going over his notes, getting ready to address a packed house. Not an empty seat in sight.

The room was banquet style. Ten dining tables, each with five chairs. Each table had a number.

None of the doctors in the audience knew what Dr. Henderson had planned for them. He was afraid if they knew they might not attend, so he kept it a secret between himself, Ella, and Dr. Alexander.

The doctors attending today's meeting were specialists in fields of medicine that dealt with death: Oncology, Cardiology, and Emergency Room care.

Dr. Henderson waited until everyone had taken a seat and the chatter had dropped off. Then he opened Pandora's Box when he projected the day's agenda on a large screen mounted on a wall behind him. He didn't have to wait long before he heard grumbling when the doctors got to the subject down the list: Lazarus Syndrome — spontaneous resurrection.

He addressed the audience. "You know me. I don't have to introduce myself. I've been doing this for a long time. And believe me, I wouldn't have invited you here today unless I thought I had something important to share.

"I'd like to get right into the heart of the matter. "On Thursday, a week and a half ago, while I was in charge of the ER, we received a female patient named Ella Martin. On arrival, her vitals were normal. She had been transported to our facility after passing out in a supermarket. The paramedics responded immediately. Her chief complaint then was chest pain, similar to that of heartburn. She'd been suffering from indigestion over a two-day period, and she had already passed out once earlier in the day. Neither she nor her parents had a history of heart disease. After checking her out, I decided to have her admitted for observation. Primarily," he hesitated, "because of the two fainting episodes. While prepping her, she went into a full arrest. We bagged her and started CPR within the first thirty seconds."

At this point, Dr. Henderson stopped talking and invited Ella to join him on the stage. She stepped out from behind the curtain and strolled across the stage dressed in a black pantsuit with low heel shoes.

As she walked toward Dr. Henderson, he said, "Ella works for Riedel, Darin, and Charles. The three singers' law firm," as if everyone knew who they were.

"Okay Ella, can you tell us what you experienced the moment you flat-lined?"

As she prepared to speak, she could hear the skeptics in the room whispering their disapproval. Both doctors had warned her beforehand that she might be met with some opposition, so she was prepared.

She started off by taking a step backward. "Before I died, I felt fine. Then suddenly everything started getting blurry. I saw double and the room started to spin. I felt this pressure in my chest and before I could tell the doctor about it, the pressure turned into a stabbing pain. It was much worse than the pain I had earlier in the day. Next thing I knew, I floated up toward the ceiling, where I had this bird's-eye view. I looked down and watched Dr. Henderson touch the side of my neck and yell out something like, 'V-fib, code blue, in Room 10A.'

"I could see right through the walls into adjoining rooms and watched as all the medical personnel dropped what they were doing and rushed into my room. One of the nurses wheeled in a cart with some equipment on it. At first, I didn't realize it was my body on the gurney. Then I heard Dr. Henderson call out my name, not once, but several times. Each time I answered, but he never looked up. That's when I realized it was me down below."

She took a deep breath and continued, "I watched Dr. Henderson leap up on the bed, straddle me, and start pumping on my chest. Then he got down, and one of the nurses cut open my hospital gown, exposing my chest. Another one of the nurses lubricated a set of paddles. I heard Dr. Henderson shout, 'clear' as he shocked me. But I didn't feel anything. Nothing at all."

At this point, Dr. Henderson interrupted Ella. "Everything she said happened exactly as she said it did."

He went back in time and picked up where she started: "I had been talking to her, but when I heard a familiar sound coming from the monitor, I looked over to see a horizontal line running across the screen. I checked the leads and they were all connected. I checked her pulse at her carotid and called a 'code blue.' Everyone on my staff did what they're trained to do when they hear that. When the crash cart arrived, I shocked her."

Then he looked back over at Ella. "Do you want to pick it up from here?"

Ella said, "As I watched, I realized I had no pain. I felt wonderful. I felt warm all over and my body took on this golden glow. I could see through myself; I didn't want to go back into my body. But then I thought if I'm dead, who will take care of my cat? Then I started drifting away. I had no choice; it was like I was a piece of metal drawn toward a magnet. I went through the wall and could see all the building material used to make it. Next thing I knew, I was out in the corridor traveling toward the receptionist desk. I heard a nurse tell the receptionist the woman in Room 10A just flat-lined. Then my body, soul, or spirit, whatever you want to call it, started moving again."

Ella took a sip of water and continued with her

story: "I went through the ceiling and the next thing I know I was in the hospital's nursery, staring at two newborns. One, a baby named Tyrone Smith. He weighed 9 pounds 3 ounces." Once again, she could hear some commotion coming from the crowded room of doctors, and without skipping a beat, she continued. "The other baby's name was Fredrick Moorehouse. He weighed 6 pounds 10 ounces. From there, I continued to travel upward into the Oncology Department. I was in the corridor outside Room 301. I didn't need to enter the room because I could see through the wall and hear everything that was said inside. An elderly man was lying on a bed, with people all around him. Dr. Alexander was also in the room."

At this point, Dr. Alexander borrowed Ella's microphone. "The patient Ella is talking about had lung cancer." He handed the microphone back to her.

"I watched Dr. Alexander check the man's vital signs and shake his head in a negative manner. I could see the old man talking to someone, but I didn't know who it was at the time. Then this golden mist filled the room and took a human form. The man in bed was ..." she hesitated, "talking to this form. I heard Dr. Alexander tell the relatives he was hallucinating, that it was just one of the signs when someone is near death. And then he said something about endorphins. I watched as the person in the bed continued to speak to ..." once again, she paused, "for lack of a better word, an angel." She heard several doctors grumbling among themselves, but she didn't let it get her down. "The angel bent down and whispered something in the man's ear. This I did not hear. Then it took him by the hand and kissed him on the forehead and they both left the room together, up, straight through the ceiling."

Dr. Alexander took the microphone from Ella once again. "I can't explain what Ella saw. But I can say that my patient died that evening and that I did say those things to the relatives. He was talking to someone or something, or at least he thought he was, right up to the point of death, but neither I nor the relatives saw or heard a thing." He gave back the microphone.

Ella looked to Dr. Henderson for guidance. "Should I continue?"

"Yes, but don't spend much time on the next part. You can talk more about that if you're asked to during the Q and A period."

"After the man died I continued to travel upward, through the ceiling and into space. I could see the cars on the street down below getting smaller as I got farther away. As I continued to rise, I watched the sun come up over the Pacific, but the sun wasn't really coming up. I was getting farther from Earth and seeing it from a different viewpoint. Soon Earth became basketball sized, then a baseball and then a small marble. I was traveling faster and faster until the stars became blurred lines in the sky. At some point, I saw a fixed-point of light that started to grow in size and intensity. It was by far the brightest light I could see. And I was drawn toward it. I had no control of where I was going. Soon I began to slow down. I stopped in front of the light and I felt like I was a part of the light, like I was reconnecting. Like I'd been away and now I was back as one. Inside the light was a human form. What I mean by that is, it had arms and legs and was similar in size. It emitted a light source brighter than any star. It should have burned my eyes, but it didn't."

She decided to skip most of what happened in Heaven and brought herself back down to Earth. "I was there for what seem like hours or days or perhaps a lifetime. I don't know. I had no real concept of time. Eventually, the being of light spoke to me and told me I hadn't finished my purpose on Earth and I had to go back. I didn't want to. I argued with it, but I had no choice. My descent was instantaneous. Just like that. I was there, wherever there was, and then I was back on Earth again."

Dr. Henderson interrupted Ella again. "There's a lot more to her story than you'll hear here today. To save time, I've asked her to shorten it. Also, a part of her story is missing. She's under a gag order not to talk about it. I'm sure as time goes by, you'll know the whole story." There was more chatter among the doctors as Dr. Henderson stepped back, giving Ella the floor again.

"When I returned to Earth, I didn't enter my body right away. I'm not allowed to talk about this time. What I can say is that all my senses were heightened to a degree I never imagined possible. I'm sure I could have heard a pin drop a mile away and my eyesight was better than that of a hawk. When I reentered my body, the first time, the pain was horrible. I opened my eyes to a bright overhead light and saw Dr. Henderson's pretty blue eyes staring down at me."

Some of the audience thought the remark was

funny and started laughing, while others weren't so kind.

Dr. Henderson reentered the conversation. "I saw Ella open her eyes and I said, 'Welcome back.' She didn't respond orally because by now we had intubated her with an endotracheal tube. We didn't have her long and she rearrested." He stepped away again, letting Ella take over.

"I was back where I was before. But this time, it was different, because now I could hear voices from the hospital room and I could see things taking place in another realm. I heard a female voice with a heavy Spanish accent say, 'I've got an IV.' And then I heard Dr. Henderson say, 'Give her 1 milligram of epinephrine IV push.' Whatever that meant. For a short time I was back in my own body, but not for long."

Dr. Henderson stepped up again. "The female's voice she said she heard came from Rita Moreno, no relation to the actress. She's one of several PAs working in the ER. She was not part of the original response team. She came in much later, after Ella had already arrested the second time." He stepped back, giving Ella space.

"And then I was gone again, in another realm, out of my body, back to where I was before. Back to the place I can't talk about. This time I wasn't gone long, before I could see, not just hear what was going on in the hospital room. It was like watching a split screen on a television set. Seeing two separate events taking place at the same time. I remember watching Dr. Henderson and heard him say, 'Let's call it.' I continued to watch as a nurse with freckles wrote down 7:01 p.m. And then I was gone again — this time for good. The hospital room faded away and I was back in the other place."

It was obvious that without telling them where the other place was, all the coming and going was beginning to confuse the audience. She decided to end it by saying, "This time I was out of my body a lot longer. And when I returned, I didn't wake up in the hospital room like before. I woke up in the morgue."

She took a deep breath. "I got up off the metal table and walked around the hospital until I found the ER and Dr. Henderson. I sat down with him and told him everything I told you ... and more."

Dr. Henderson retook the floor. "I hope all this moving back and forth from one place to another — in and out of body — didn't turn you off. But what happened in this other realm ... that neither she nor I can talk about, was as real to her as what happened here at the hospital. So, before I go any further, how 'bout we give Ella a big hand for sharing her experience. This is her first time in front of an audience of this size. I know how difficult it has been to try to explain it, especially to a hostile audience. What I mean by hostile is that most of you will walk away from here today still not convinced it was more than a chemical reaction. But maybe, just maybe, some of you might question what you were taught in medical school. Maybe they were wrong. Maybe there is more to life than just death? I think what's important here is that we examine the facts. Separate them from the unknown. What's verifiable and what isn't."

Half the audience stood and applauded while the other half remained seated. Dr. Henderson spoke again.

"After seeing Ella in the receptionist area, I couldn't believe my eyes. Everything Ella explained matched the facts of what happened and when and was confirmed by the appropriate parties.

"Okay, let's open this forum up for discussion. You can either raise your hand and I'll call on you, or you can write your question down on a piece of paper we've provided. You don't have to write down your name if you don't want to. Just hand it to one of our aides as they come to your table."

The first question came from the back of the room. Dr. Henderson said, "Yes, table number 8, Dr. Westdale. For the benefit of the new attendees, Dr. Westdale is a cardiologist."

Dr. Westdale was an experienced transplant surgeon in his mid-sixties. "I've heard all this before. Maybe not so graphic, but it's certainly not new. A well-known surgeon did a good job at debunking the out-of-body experience. Before operating on a patient, he put a sign on top of the sheet near the foot of the bed that read, 'YOU'RE DEAD.' But none of his patients who said they'd had an out-of-body experience remembered seeing it. So, Dr. Henderson, are you telling us that you're willing to stick your neck into the noose and say for a fact that what this woman said is true?"

"Yes." Dr. Henderson said without any hesitation. "I'm willing to confirm what I know. I know what drug I gave and the dosage. I'm willing to stick my neck out and say I called her death at 7:01 p.m. and told a nurse, who recorded the time of death. Yes, I'm willing to go out on a limb and say that and more. I confirmed the statement with the nurse who supposedly told the receptionist the woman in Room 10A had flat lined."

Ella stood on stage staring out at the audience, wondering what in the world she was doing there. She was getting a sample of what was to come. The first question out of the box was questioning the truth of her statement. If she thought this was bad, she could hardly imagine what would happen when they asked her to testify against the psychopath in Colorado.

Dr. Henderson took one of the pieces of paper collected by an aide and started reading it. "Ella, did you see any of your relatives? Did you see God? Is there a Hell? Is there a Heaven? Did you go through a life review? I see the writer didn't leave us a name. Okay Ella, do you want to take a shot at any of these questions?"

"Yes, I saw all my relatives on the other side, but not physically. I saw them during my life's review. I was shown every event that had ever taken place, from the moment of my birth to the instant of my death. I saw myself being born. And I watched myself die. During my life's review, I never felt as though I was being judged; if I was being judged, it was I who was doing the judging. Is there a God? Absolutely. I asked if I could see God, and I was told that everything you see is God, including yourself. When you die, you cannot reconnect or reunite," she used a music analogy, by saying, "until you learn how to sing in harmony with one another.

"This brings up the subject of Hell. As far as my understanding goes, Hell is where you go to lose your negativity, anything that keeps you from singing in unison. Heaven, yes, I believe there is a Heaven. I believe I got only a quick glimpse of it. I saw what I thought Heaven should look like. It looked exactly like I'd pictured it. But perhaps that's what Heaven is all about; it is what you want it to be. I hope I answered your questions satisfactorily."

Dr. Henderson pointed to one of the front row tables. "Table number two." An oncologist from Santa Monica Hospital stood up and introduced himself and asked, "Ella, before this event took place, would you say you were a religious person? And if not, what label would you have placed on yourself?"

"I grew up in a religious family, though we were not regular church attendees, and went only occasionally. Over the years, I guess you could say I strayed. I started believing less and less. I would have considered myself an agnostic before, but now I'd have to say I know the truth. You, on the other hand, don't know the truth, unless you've had a similar experience. You can only have faith or believe there's a Heaven or something beyond this reality. I no longer have to have faith. Because I've been there."

A third of the audience stood up and applauded her tenacity. The other two-thirds sat somber in their seats, still not knowing what to make of the whole event. Ella started feeling more and more confident and comfortable as time went on. She understood the doubt. She, herself, had been a doubter, but not to the point of complete disbelief.

For the next hour, she answered questions. Dr.

Henderson and Dr. Alexander were so impressed with the way she handled the crowd, they wanted her to speak again at another forum. Dr. Alexander also had something else in mind. He envisioned Ella speaking in front of a different audience, not an assembly of doctors, but a gathering of hospice patients, setting their minds at ease by erasing their fear of death.

Ella thanked the doctors for inviting her to speak at their forum and as a parting comment, she looked out at the crowd. "I have no fear of death. In fact, I welcome it. Remember, we made the decision to come here in the first place. It was our own free will, so make the most of it. As Dr. Martin Luther King once said, 'He's allowed me to go up to the mountain. And I've looked over. And I've seen the Promised Land.'" She quoted him out of context; he wasn't referring to Heaven. But it didn't matter, everyone understood what she meant. And as the forum came to a close, an overwhelming majority stood up and applauded the three as they walked off the stage.

Chapter 18

Rusty sat in a corner booth at Sal's Diner talking to a man he'd just met an hour earlier up the street at Cosmos. Cosmos was a nightclub off the beaten path in one of the rougher sections of town, next door to an adult bookstore.

The man wore a wedding ring on his right hand, but his left hand told the real story. A white ring of skin was visible on the finger next to his pinky, a clear sign of deception. He'd probably removed the ring minutes before they met and put it on the other hand. The man called himself Jim — Jim Smith — but Rusty figured it was an alias. He could spot a phony a mile away.

Rusty wondered if this was the guy's first time out. Probably, he thought, or else he would have picked a better spot for an encounter. The man had a large vocabulary and dressed well — far too good to hang around a sleazy club like Cosmos. Unless, of course, it was an act, a ruse, part of the game meant to seem like he was naïve, a first-timer.

Sal's Diner wasn't known for its finger-licking-good chicken. More often than not, it was referred to as 'Salmonella Sal's' for its 'C' rating by the Health Department. This had been Rusty's home away from home. Over the years, he'd spent many hours staring out the big picture window watching the activity on the street corner where the dealers sold crack, the main drug of choice in this neighborhood.

Early in the evening Rusty had been on the clock pulling a double shift. He sat at the bar in Cosmos watching all the patrons come and go until he saw someone staring at him. The man was tall, good-looking, had blue eyes, in his late twenties or early thirties. He stared back. They exchanged glances for several seconds, and then the man walked over and sat down on the empty stool next to him.

He asked if he could buy Rusty a drink, who said, "Sure, why not." Rusty was on a stakeout looking for a homosexual impersonator, one who had an appetite for robbing and beating up gay men. His latest victim succumbed to the many injuries he had suffered without regaining consciousness. The only description they had of this vicious predator was that he was tall with blue eyes.

After they had some of Sal's finest, the man asked if Rusty wanted some company for the rest of the evening.

Rusty said, "Yes, that would be nice." The detective excused himself for a minute to use the restroom. Once inside, he washed his face with cold water, stepped into an empty stall, where he double-checked his Glock and called the precinct for backup at his house. The killers *Modus Operandi* was to attack the victims inside their houses or apartments — never on the street where there might be a potential witness.

Rusty walked back to the table, opened his wallet, and pulled out a stack of bills. He made sure his new friend had a good look as he thumbed through the big bills on top until he found something more suitable in size to leave at the table — two twenties and a ten. That covered dinner and a tip. He spread them out on the table like a deck of cards, and they both left the restaurant together.

Outside, Rusty wrote down his address and asked the man to follow him. He took the scenic route home, making sure his fellow officers would have plenty of time to arrive before he did. They would communicate by cell phone; he would place it where it couldn't be seen, but where it could be heard from anywhere in the house. If this were their guy, at some point, Rusty would yell Geronimo, one of Joe's favorite words.

As the evening progressed, Mr. Smith asked Rusty if he wanted to get more comfortable. Rusty thought maybe this was it. He went into the bedroom where he put his Glock under his pillow and changed into some blood-red silk pajamas.

While Rusty was sprucing up, the man got up off the couch and walked over to the front door. A key was in the dead bolt. He turned the key, engaging the bolt, and put the key in his pocket. He didn't want Rusty running out trying to escape if things didn't go as planned.

Then he looked around to see what good old Rusty had of value. And he had a lot, he thought. It was going to be easy pickings. He would wait until they got in bed, then he would simply overpower the man, tie him up, and ransack the house. As he strolled around making a mental list of the items he wanted to take, he noticed a cell phone with the lid open, resting on a shelf. It looked like it was turned on. He decided to be a nice guy, save the battery for good old Rusty. He turned off the power and closed the lid.

When Rusty came out of the bedroom dressed like Santa Claus in his bright red PJs, Mr. Smith almost burst out laughing, but he didn't. He held it inside and thought, *Oh man, this is going to be fun.*

Rusty asked Mr. Smith if he'd like a glass of wine, a little something to relax him; he said he did. Rusty made them both a drink and then headed for the bedroom. Rusty crawled under the covers on the left side of the bed. He reached back and slipped his arm under his pillow and got a good grip on his Glock. There was just enough illumination coming from the night-light so he could see a punch coming, if this was the man Rusty thought he might be.

Rusty watched as the man undressed. The night-light cast a large shadow of the man on the opposite wall, making him look like a monster, a hunchback. Then he slowly peeled back the covers and crawled into bed. He mounted Rusty, riding him high on his waist, making it difficult for Rusty to defend himself. The man held one of Rusty's arms down with one hand and then swung at Rusty with his other fist.

Rusty saw the punch coming and yelled, "Geronimo," as he raised his free arm trying to block the punch.

His attempt was somewhat futile, but not entirely. He prevented a direct blow to his nose and cheekbone, turning it into a glancing shot against his temple and ear, which hurt like hell.

The house was quiet, no storm troopers coming through the front door. *Where's Tonto*? Rusty wondered as he repeated the words that were supposed to save him. He yelled "Geronimo!" three more times in quick succession, but still no response from the gladiators. He wasn't so lucky blocking the next punch; a left to the right eye stunned him momentarily. When he regained his wits enough to swing the Glock, he hit the man on the side of his head, knocking him off the bed, with Rusty coming down on top. The night-light was inches away, giving Rusty a good look at the man's face. The man looked terrified, as if he'd been taken completely by surprise. Rusty screamed out Geronimo several more times, but still no one responded. Then he looked the man straight in the eye. "How does it feel when the roles are reversed?"

The man on the bottom struggled hard and was soon able to overpower Rusty. He pinned him to the hardwood floor and tried to remove the gun from Rusty's hand. Rusty decided the only way he was going to get any help was by discharging his weapon. He pulled the trigger and heard the man scream out in pain as the bullet found the man's big toe.

Joe heard the shot and tried to open the door, but it was locked. He kicked it a few times before the hardware let go. His team rushed in and found Rusty sitting on top of the man, with the barrel of his gun resting nicely against the man's forehead.

Joe looked down at Rusty. "Good work, Kemosabe."

Rusty looked over his shoulder at Joe. "Where the hell were you guys? I called out Geronimo at least six times, maybe more."

"Geronimo? I thought the secret break down the door word was 'Hi-yo Silver?'"

Rusty watched the paramedics roll Mr. Smith out through the broken front door, his foot bandaged and his wrists restrained to the side rails with leather straps.

~~~

Bobbi called Joe to give him the good news. But first, she wanted to congratulate him on successfully capturing the 'Eastside Mugger.' When he answered, Bobbi said, "I heard you caught the 'Gay Basher' last night. It was all over the news this morning."

"It's not me you should be congratulating, it's Rusty — he's the one with the black eye and fat lip. He set up the whole sting operation, which almost turned into Little Bighorn."

Bobbi was used to Joe's metaphors to explain a situation. This one was simple to figure out. It meant the operation nearly went bad.

"Our mugger, Perry Bloodworth — that's his real name — did a few unexpected things to screw up our response, which could have cost us dearly. We could be putting a white sheet over Rusty, like Lincoln, instead of slapping him on the back and telling him what a good job he did. He was lucky to only receive a few bruises. Mr. Bloodworth, on the other hand, wasn't so lucky. More than likely, he'll be hobbling through the chow line at our lovely rehabilitation center for the next twenty years."

Bobbi beamed with excitement. "Well, anyway, the reason I called is to give you some good news. I tried to get in touch with Rusty, but his line was busy. He wanted to be the first one to know. You know that Kleenex with the snot on it, the one you confiscated from Mr. Bradford's apartment?"

"Yes ..."

"Well, it just so happens to match the one you plucked out of Sandra Brown's trash can. That should tighten our timeline, don't you think?"

Joe was thrilled with the news and knew Rusty would be, too. They'd gotten lucky the night before; now maybe they'd be able to get Mr. Bloodworth a roommate, someone he could snuggle up to. Someone to keep him warm on a cold night in his prison cell.

"That's wonderful. I'm sure that will relieve some of Rusty's pain. We still need to find some more evidence. We haven't checked his mother's house yet. The DNA will help secure another search warrant." He thanked Bobbi for the good news and was about to hang up when she said, "Oh, I almost forgot, here's some more ammunition for you. The laptop computer you gave us had some interesting information on it. Mr. Bradford had searched MapQuest and got directions to Sandra Brown's house. The starting point was from 123 Eucalyptus Avenue."

"That's Bradford's mother's house!" Joe

exclaimed. Once again, he thanked B. B. for the information and finally said goodbye.

Joe heard Rusty hang up the phone in the cubicle next to his and said, "Yo, Adrian," in his best Sly Stallone voice. "I just got off the line with Miss Twiggy, our favorite CSI. She got a DNA match to our prime suspect." Miss Twiggy was not a degrading name to Joe or to Bobbi. She had once referred to her as Miss Twiggy, because she was tall and thin, and once she'd modeled for a teen magazine.

Rusty looked over the partition with his one good eye and gave Joe a half smile with the unswollen side of his mouth.

Joe said, "Hey man, you look like crap. Why don't you take the rest of the day off — call in a locksmith? Put another bullet in your shirt pocket." It was an inside joke between them referencing Deputy Barney Fife on the *Andy Griffith Show.* Andy gave Barney a single bullet and told him not to put it in his gun, but to keep it in his shirt pocket so it wouldn't accidentally go off and blow a hole in his foot or someone else's.

"Very funny, but your advice is a little late. I've already repaired the door and replaced the bullet."

Joe told Rusty what Bobbi found on Jason's computer. "Maybe our Mr. Bradford is hiding what we're looking for over at his mother's house?"

"Yeah, maybe. Let's get another search warrant, this time for her place. Draft something up that includes her entire property, then give it to Sleepy."

~~~

It was late in the afternoon when Joe sat down on the edge of Mary Jean Hathaway's desk with the affidavit. Joe knew he had to go through her first to get to Judge Webster. Mary Jean was a widow in her early forties on the prowl, looking for a new partner. Someone she could have fun with, someone like Joe Longhorn. She knew Joe was married but didn't care. She liked the big Indian and called him Chief.

She asked Joe what she could do for him, hoping the question might lead somewhere. Joe said he needed to pick up another search warrant. They wanted to serve it first thing in the morning and wanted to know if the judge was available.

She said, "I don't know. Let me wake him up and ask him." Everyone knew the history of Judge Webster. They both laughed as Mary Jean reached for the phone. Judge Webster answered right away and had Joe step into his office. Joe noticed the telltale red mark on his forehead from where he had probably been resting his head on the desk.

Joe was in and out in a flash. The judge signed the warrant without asking any questions. Mary Jean watched the big Indian as he exited the outer office.

When Joe got back to his office, Rusty was sitting in a conference room with a bag of popcorn watching an interview between Perry Bloodworth and one of the other detectives. Rusty was afraid if he was doing the interview, he might load that single bullet into his gun and pull the trigger. They'd booked Mr. Bloodworth the night before on an aggravated assault charge. The detectives were hoping to get a confession out of him. One of his victims, still in the hospital recovering from his injuries, identified Mr. Bloodworth from a mug shot taken shortly after his arrest. They were waiting to compare results of skin tissue taken from under the bed of the fingernails of another of his victims, one who wasn't so lucky, before they could charge him with murder.

The detective doing the interview asked Mr. Bloodworth if he would take a polygraph test and give him a sample of his DNA. Mr. Bloodworth immediately declined the offer and asked for a court-appointed attorney. The detective told him he could decline the polygraph but would have no choice on the DNA sample.

Joe walked into the conference room holding up the warrant. "First thing in the morning."

"What did you have to do for Mary Jean?"

"Nothing," Joe said. "I just gave her my best smile and wore my tightest Levi's."

"That's all it took?"

"That's it," he joked.

Chapter 19

The house was small, two bedrooms and a bath, with an unfinished basement. It had an unattached garage behind the house, invisible from the street. The house was on a large corner lot. The side yard was surrounded by a six-foot tall, sun-bleached redwood fence.

Rusty could see smoke coming from the chimney as he parked in front of the house at 123 Eucalyptus Avenue. Less than thirty seconds later, two more cars parked behind his. The second one belonged to Bobbi Bidwell and the third belonged to patrol, with three rookie police officers fresh out of the academy. The new police officers were on a training exercise. They were there to help in the search. Their instructions were to look, point, but don't touch unless told to do so.

The newbies waited in their patrol car, while Rusty, Joe, and B. B. walked up to the front door.

Rusty rang the bell and Joe held the warrant.

It took Sally a minute or two before she found

her slippers and answered the door.

Sally recognized the two men immediately, but not the third person.

Rusty said, "Good morning," before Sally had a chance to say a word. Then he introduced Bobbi Bidwell and told Sally why they were there, and what they were looking for.

Sally looked at Rusty's black eye and swollen lip but didn't say anything. Joe handed her the warrant and asked if they could step inside.

She stepped back, allowing them room to enter. "I have nothing to hide. Look all you want, but I expect you to leave my place the way you found it. Not all tore up."

Bobbi went back outside to where the rookies were. She sent one of them to the house to help Rusty and Joe, while the other two went with her to search the property outside.

The side yard was knee-deep in weeds, making it difficult to spot anything unless you were standing on top of it. Rather than spend much time looking for a needle in a haystack, they moved on to what they could see.

The first thing Bobbi noticed was the picnic table. She could tell it hadn't been used in years, most of its green paint gone, worn away by weather and time. She didn't know that where she was standing, another CSI once stood, staring down at a dead body, the co-owner of the property.

Next, she looked around and saw a large metal drum, so she walked over to it, removed the lid, and peeked inside. The drum, like the bench, hadn't been used in years, at least not for its intended purpose as a burn barrel. The city no longer allowed it. But she saw that a fresh layer of ash was recently added.

She picked up a dead branch that had fallen from one of the many trees in the woman's back yard and stuck it in the ol' burn barrel, poking around. On her third stab, she hit something hard. She put on a pair of medical gloves and turned the drum on its side. Then she got down on her hands and knees and started digging through the ash until she found what she'd hit with the tree limb. It was a round piece of steel, six inches long and nearly one inch thick. It was partly attached to a piece of burnt wood — species unknown. She set it aside and continued to stir up the gray matter.

Soon she found the remains of what looked like the corner of a book. She could see the binding, but there wasn't much of anything else left. She put it in an evidence bag with the other item she'd collected. Then she stood the barrel back up and continued her search of the back yard.

Joe and Rusty combed through most of the house without finding anything listed on their warrant. The two men stopped when they got to a padlocked door. They asked Sally why it was locked. She said, "It goes down to the basement. Jason is the only one who goes down there. I haven't been down there in years."

"I guess you don't have a key for it?" Joe asked.

"That's right, I don't."

"Then we're going to have to cut the lock," Rusty said.

"Oh no, you're not!" she said. "Jason will kill me if I allow you to go down there." When she realized what she'd said and how it sounded, she said, "I don't mean that literally. I just meant to say that he'd be upset, really mad."

"Mrs. Bradford, maybe you don't understand. The piece of paper we handed you is a search warrant. It allows us to look anywhere listed on the paper, and on this particular warrant it includes the entire property," Rusty said staunchly while Joe examined the lock.

Rusty handed his car keys to a third officer, who'd been following them around the house. "I have bolt cutters in the trunk of my car; could you go get them for me?" The young woman was more than happy to help. So far, all she'd done was watch. She took the keys and left. Two minutes later she was back with the bolt cutters.

As Joe cut the lock, Sally picked up her telephone, and a couple of seconds later, Joe and Rusty heard Sally respond to questions from someone on the other end of the line. "No, I told them I didn't have the key. Yes, I told them they couldn't cut the lock, and they told me the warrant allowed them to look anywhere."

She walked into another room so Rusty and Joe couldn't hear her. After a minute or so, she was back standing right behind them as Joe opened the door and started down the stairs. Two steps in, he spotted the light switch, turned it on, and continued to descend.

When they got to the foot of the stairs, Joe noticed another light — a fluorescent fixture —

hanging over a workbench. He walked over and turned it on.

They had a good look at what was down there, which wasn't much. The workbench had a piece of equipment on top used for making keys. The rest of the bench was empty. Clean as a whistle, like it had never been used.

The room was cold and damp and there was a strong odor of mildew and bleach. Sally followed the threesome around the room, watching them like a hawk.

Rusty noticed a bucket lying on its side up against a wall. He walked over and picked it up. Then he raised it to his nose and took a whiff. "It smells like bleach."

Joe found a green footlocker with the name Sgt. Bradford stenciled on top. The SGT was ex'd out and PVT was added below it.

Joe flipped open the two latches on the front and raised the lid. The upper section held a tray designed for toiletry articles. It now held the remains of a dozen small lifeless creatures: animals, reptiles, butterflies with their wings clipped. A fossilized frog, frozen in time, with its ribs showing through its shrunken hide. Joe didn't recognize some of the other creatures but guessed they might be rodents.

Rusty knew they couldn't legally take the footlocker into custody. But there was nothing stopping him from taking a few pictures of its contents. Maybe the pictures would open a window into the killer's psyche. He handed the young officer his car keys and asked her, once again, to return to his car ... this time to get his camera from the glove compartment. When she returned, Rusty took pictures from several different angles close enough to make out what was on the top shelf inside the footlocker.

Joe removed the drop-in shelf to get a view of the lower half. There were more creatures, larger animals, some with obvious injuries, a cat with a nail through its head. A small dog or puppy with its paws nailed to a board. A sickening sight, causing Sally to turn her head away. She had known about the creatures and quit going down there years ago.

Then Rusty noticed something else in the lower portion of the box, something that didn't belong: a Davy Crockett watch. It was out of place. Rusty took more pictures, then took photographs of the entire basement, including the bucket and the key-making equipment.

When they finished searching the basement, they walked back upstairs, empty-handed. Nothing to show for their effort except some photographs that had little to do with their case.

When they reached the top landing in the main part the house, Rusty asked Sally about seeing Jason on the evening of Sandra Brown's death. "Can you tell me again, Mrs. Bradford, about what time your son arrived here on Thursday the week before last?"

"It was early. I know that because he was down in the basement while I was cooking dinner. It was sometime before five o'clock."

"What time did you see him leave?"

"Now that I'm sure of, because he woke me up

at 11:00 p.m., so I could go to bed."

"You say he woke you up. Where were you?"

"I was in the recliner," she pointed, "right there in the living room, watching TV. I know what time it was because the show *Law and Order* was just going off the air."

Rusty jotted down what Sally said, word for word. He knew how important her statement might be later. He thanked her and the three of them walked out to meet Bobbi's team.

Bobbi was just about to enter the garage when Rusty, Joe, and the third rookie joined them. The garage was small, designed to look like a barn. Only one car could fit inside. It had double doors that swung outward. The lock was a stick through a hasp. When she swung the doors open, they smiled at one another. Inside was a late eighties white sedan.

Joe said, "Checkmate."

"Well, I don't know if I would go that far," said Rusty. "It's no slam dunk. But it can't hurt our case; especially since we now know he has no one to verify his whereabouts between, let's say, 6:00 and 11:00 p.m.

"We need to go back to Sandra Brown's street and find someone who remembers seeing a white car that looks like this one. The last time we were there, we hadn't talked with any of the neighbors who live on the opposite side of the street."

Bobbi showed the detectives the piece of wood as well as the steel rod with the material that resembled a book cover she'd recovered from the drum. The detectives looked at each other and smiled. Joe said, "Bingo. When it rains it pours, doesn't it?"

"Yes, it sure does. I think it's time that I call Ella back. Update her on the case, let her know about the car. That should make her happy."

Rusty took pictures of the car and noticed the Buick was spotless. It looked as if it had just come out of a car wash. They got a key from Sally and opened the trunk; it was empty. Joe removed the spare tire so they could look underneath, but nothing was there to see.

Before leaving, the team took one last stroll around the back yard, wading through the tall grass, searching for anything that might help their case. They found nothing except an old broken archer's arrow and a tennis shoe.

Rusty decided to end their search. Yet the day hadn't been without merit. They had discovered a few things they weren't expecting, like the piece of wood and steel rod. There was no way it had any DNA on it now, not after it was set on fire. But the car was a different story — a much bigger deal.

Now all they had to do was to find someone, other than Ella, who could put Jason in the driver's seat. And their other discovery, finding out that Jason didn't have an alibi after all ... that was priceless.

Rusty wished he had Sally on tape saying what she said, rather than her words written down on paper.

They all got back in their cars and as Rusty pulled away from the curb, Joe noticed Sally looking out her window watching them leave.

Chapter 20

The two men, both wearing white shorts, sat on a bench off to one side of the indoor tennis court at the Broadmoor Country Club. It was their normal weekly get together. A time to relax, bang a few balls around, and talk a little shop. They were both practicing psychiatrists. They'd once been more than just friends but that had faded with time. Now their meeting was just a way to stay in touch and enjoy a morning away from the office.

Dr. Joseph Stern looked over at his friend and said, "Did you watch the news last night?"

"No. Why?" replied Dr. Wasserman.

"They caught the guy the media dubbed 'The Gay Basher' or 'Eastside Mugger.' They're crediting a Detective Stubbs with the collar. He looked like he'd been hit by a train."

Barney thought of Rusty and said, "That's too bad. But it's good he nabbed this guy before he hurt anyone else. I knew one of his victims." He wondered if he should mention it to Rusty at their next session.

~~~

Ella sat at her computer arranging a bulleted list of talking points for her next speaking engagement. She'd learned a lot from her first performance in front of a live audience. Now she had a good idea what to expect, the questions they would ask, and she wanted to sharpen her responses. She had the coming weekend to decide if she would retire or continue to work for the law firm. She didn't want to leave, but at the same time, she did. She had this growing obsession to help others who couldn't help themselves. She'd worked out the numbers and nothing prevented her from leaving. The question was, would she be able to keep herself busy? She was not one to sit around with nothing to do. Maybe she could volunteer her time, work at a hospital as a candy striper — an old candy striper.

Ella sat back in her chair and thought about the redheaded detective. And as he came to mind, the phone rang. She was surprised to hear his voice on the other end, but not completely shocked. She'd been experiencing more and more of these unusual episodes. Sometimes she could guess the next commercial on TV, or what someone would say before they said it. It all started with Dr. Henderson and his anniversary gift; she didn't know why she knew what he was thinking, but she did. And when she was answering questions at the doctors' forum, she knew some of the questions before they were asked.

Rusty asked Ella how she was doing and if she'd gone back to work yet. She said she was good, that she hadn't returned to work and wasn't sure she even wanted to. She told him about the other speaking opportunities the doctors had suggested.

After the small talk, he said, "The main reason I called is to update you on our progress. We searched our suspect's property and found directions for Sandra Brown's house on his computer. We also found used tissue in his bathroom that matched the DNA on the one found in Sandra Brown's house." He skipped over the Rollin' Stone CD found in the suspect's car and the cigarette filter in the ashtray. He wanted to get to the part that he knew had bothered her — why the car didn't match the one belonging to the killer. He said, "We got another search warrant that allowed us to search his mother's property. Her name is Sally."

Ella interrupted him. "That's what he called Sandra Brown the night he beat her to death. He called her Sally."

Rusty thought for a second and realized she was right. She had told him that during her interview and reenactment of the crime. For some reason, it had slipped his mind. Joe's, too. Was Jason killing his mother or just someone with the same first name? He didn't know the answer to that question. That would be up to a psychiatrist to figure out. He said, "So while we were searching her property, guess what we found?"

"What?"

"A white 1988 Buick Regal. We found it in her garage. She doesn't drive it. It's no longer registered. Hasn't been for years. Now all we need to do is find someone, other than you, who can remember seeing that car on Sandra Brown's street the night she died. What I want you to do is to think back. Do you remember seeing anyone who might've spotted the car? Someone walking down the street or driving by. Maybe someone who stepped out on their porch or peeked out their window?"

Ella thought back to that night. No one was on the street except her until the little man drove up, parked his car, and walked across the street. But now that she thought back, a woman was looking out her front window.

"Yes, I do remember seeing someone. After the killer drove up, an elderly woman was staring out her window. She had snow-white hair and brown eyes. I don't know what she saw or how long she was there because that's when I focused all my attention on the little man. Her house is not directly across the street from the victim's, but diagonal to the left. It's green, with a screened-in front porch. You can't miss it."

Rusty was once again astounded by Ella's recall. He remembered the green house she was talking about. It was behind Joe in the video he'd filmed with Ella there. Joe had walked over and stood in the spot where Ella stated the killer parked that night.

"Good," Rusty said. "We haven't finished interviewing all of Ms. Brown's neighbors. We're going back later today. We'll put the woman who lives in the green house at the top of our list."

Rusty couldn't think of anything else to tell her

that she didn't already know, except for the CD, cigarette filter, and possibly the discovery of the bat. Those things he would keep to himself for now. Over the years, he'd learned to hold back some information. With nothing else to say, he said, "Thank you for your help. I'll call you again in a week or so."

After saying goodbye, Ella thought about their conversation. She knew there was something he was holding back, not telling her. Unlike her first experience with Dr. Henderson, reading his mind the way she did, she found herself unable to do that with Rusty; it was as if there was a wall between them. All she knew was that he wasn't telling her everything he knew. But why? Was it just Rusty's way of doing things? She didn't know the answer to those questions or if it would make any difference if she did.

There was one thing she did know. That at some time during their conversation, she'd made up her mind to retire. She didn't have to wait any longer to decide. She picked up her phone again and dialed the law firm where she worked.

~~~

Rusty sat in his cubicle, working on a list of questions he planned on asking Jason Bradford once they brought him in for questioning. He knew Mr. Bradford was a smart cookie and would probably have an attorney with him. His list comprised of known facts and suspected acts leading to the death of Sandra Brown. Under known facts he had fingerprint evidence, DNA, and computer data. Under suspected acts he had blunt object (bat found in the drum), transportation (white car), eyewitness (neighbor) maybe?

After completing his questionnaire, Rusty asked Joe if he wanted to go for a ride over to Wildwood Road, so they could finish talking to the rest of the dead woman's neighbors.

Joe said, "Sure, I'll grab the reins and meet you in the corral."

~~~

By the time they got to the green house on the opposite side of the street from where Sandra Brown had lived, it was early evening. Rusty rang the doorbell outside the screened-in porch. Ten seconds later he pushed the buzzer again, but still no one responded. Through one of the windows he could see a light on in the house and he could hear an old familiar tune coming from a TV set. The sound was turned way up. Rusty figured the person inside was hard-of-hearing, and that's why she hadn't heard the doorbell.

Joe said, "I can get the bullhorn if you like or fire my six-shooter into the air. That should get the person's attention."

Rusty knew Joe was kidding, but said anyway, "No. I don't think that'll be necessary. Let's try a softer approach."

"Like what?"

"Like continuing to ring the bell until someone answers."

After Rusty pushed the button several more times, the front door opened a crack … just enough for the woman inside to see the two men standing on her front doorstep.

When Rusty saw her, he said in a loud voice, "Ma'am, we're with the police department. Can we speak with you in private, so we're not screaming back and forth?"

She squinted at the two men and then said, "Just a minute." She disappeared for a few seconds and returned wearing a thick pair of eyeglasses. She took another look through the crack at the two men. Then she unfastened her security chain, opened the door, and walked out on the veranda. "You can't be too careful anymore, officers, especially with what happened to Sandy across the street." She took a closer look at the men and their badges, and then lifted the latch on her screen door, allowing them access.

Once inside, she led them into her living room, pointed at her couch, and took a chair a few feet away. Then she picked up her TV remote control and turned off *Happy Days*. Once it was quiet, she asked what she could do for them.

Rusty got right down to business, asking, "Were you home the night your neighbor died?"

"Yes, I was."

"Do you remember seeing or hearing anything unusual?"

"Like what?"

"Like loud music playing. Or an unfamiliar car parked in front of your house."

She thought back. "I don't remember hearing any loud music. I'm a little hard-of-hearing. But now that you mention it, I do remember seeing a car parked in front of my house. I looked out my window to see if it had stopped snowing. That's when I saw a car pull up to the curb."

"Did you see the driver?"

"Yes, I saw the driver get out of the car and open the trunk."

"Could you tell if the driver was a male or a female?"

"Heavens, no. The driver wore a hood. I couldn't see a face."

"What did the driver do after opening the trunk?"

"The person removed a big bag."

"Then what?"

"Then I closed my curtain and went back to doing what I was doing before I looked out my window."

"And what was that?"

"I was reading a book. Hemingway. *The Old Man and the Sea.*"

Joe said, "I know that one. Anthony Quinn. That's the one with the big fish, right?"

"Yes, that's the one," the woman smiled at Joe, glad to know that someone younger knew who Hemingway was, even though it was the movie he remembered and not the book.

Rusty pointed toward a large picture window to the left of her front door. "Was it through that window you saw the car?"

She turned around in her chair and followed his finger. "Yes, it was."

Rusty stood up and walked over to the window and asked, "Were the blinds closed or open before you looked out?"

"They were open."

Joe took notes while Rusty continued to ask the woman questions.

"Was the porch light on or off?"

She thought for a second. "On; does that matter?"

"Maybe." Rusty peeked outside, staring at their unmarked car, trying to see how much he could make out with the porch light on. He knew if it went to court — which he was sure it would — it would be one of the details the defense would focus on.

He found the porch light switch to the left of the front door and turned it off. Then he walked back over to the window and looked out a second time.

Now the only illumination available was from a quarter moon and the street corner lamppost.

He said to Joe, "I can make out more features on our car with the porch light on."

Joe jotted down that information.

When Rusty returned to the couch, he said, "So you were wearing your reading glasses when you looked outside?" It was a statement and a question rolled into one.

"Yes. But they're not just for close-up, they're also for distance."

"Bifocals."

"No," she said, proudly, "trifocals."

"Progressive lens."

"Yes."

"So now we come down to the sixty-four-thousand-dollar question. Can you describe the car for me? Color, make, model, or year?"

"Lord, no. I don't know much about cars. I haven't driven one in ages."

"Well tell me what you do know. What color was the car?"

"White, the car was white," she said.

"Are you sure? Could it have been tan or another light color?"

"No, I'm sure it was white."

"Positive?"

"Positive."

Rusty: "Good. Now let's get down to the age of the car. Was it a new car or an older car?"

"It wasn't new," she said. "I'm sure of that. It was an older car. We … my late husband and I, once owned one with a similar body style."

Rusty decided it was time to show her a few pictures of cars and see if she could pick out one like the one Sally Bradford had in her garage.

He handed the woman a handful of pictures. She looked at all of them and then handed him back the stack. "No, I don't see that car here."

Rusty realized right away that he'd made a mistake. He was expecting her to know more about cars than she knew. All the cars in the pictures were taken from the front, back or at an angle. But none from the view that she had seen when she looked out her window.

He decided to end the interview. He'd come back in a day or two with more photos, taken from the angle and at roughly the same distance as what she saw that night.

~~~

The coffee was hot to the touch and the donuts were fresh, right out of the fryer. Joe had made a quick pit stop at the donut shop on his way into work. He'd gotten there before the construction crew working down the street could clean them out.

Rusty was already in his office, making some last-minute changes to his questionnaire. He wanted to see Sandra Brown's killer behind bars before the weekend started.

Joe volunteered to put together a new set of photos to give to Mrs. Moore, the woman who lived across the street from Sandra Brown.

Joe handed Rusty a chocolate éclair from his goodie bag and then headed for his cubicle.

After eating a bear claw, Joe settled in behind his computer and activated their automobile description database. He searched for a 1988 Buick Regal. A second later, a full page popped up with every angle imaginable. He picked the one closest to what Mrs. Moore would have seen the night of the murder. Next, he selected white from a color chart. He double-clicked the image and like magic, a single white Buick Regal filled the screen. He clicked on the image and shrank it down to the size Mrs. Moore would have seen through her window. He printed out the image, along with several other vintage cars, using the same technique. Soon he had a whole array of pictures from the correct angle and distance for her to view.

Joe called Mrs. Moore and asked if he could

stop by with more pictures of automobiles. She said she would be available and asked him to ring the doorbell just one time so she would know it was him.

Joe grabbed the photo folder he had just put together. "Cross your fingers," he said to Rusty and walked out the door.

~~~

It was twenty-four degrees outside and Joe had just returned from Mrs. Moore's house. He stood with his back up against a small portable heater he kept in his office.

Rusty knew Joe was back. He could hear him on the other side of the partition complaining about how cold it was outside. He asked, "How did it go? Was she able to identify the car?"

"Yes, she picked out the Buick right away, even before she finished looking at all the pictures."

Rusty stood up and gave his partner a high-five over the top of the partition. Then he said, "If everything goes as I expect, Mr. Bradford will be in the slammer before this day is through."

~~~

Jason stood in the street beside his car, scraped the ice off his windows as the defroster went to work on the inside.

He was in a bad mood. His mother had told him the two detectives had brought along a whole slew of cops to search her property. They combed through the weeds in the back yard and dumped over the big burn barrel. She said they were down in the basement for a long time taking pictures of the room and the contents of his father's footlocker.

They also went out to her garage and had her open the trunk of her car. They even took a few pictures of her car.

Jason asked her if they had quizzed her again about him being at her house the night the woman died. She said yes, repeating what she had told the detectives.

He kicked the tire of his car and screamed, "You crazy bitch!" as he thought about what his mother said. She destroyed his alibi. He got into the driver's seat and closed the door, fuming, when his cell phone rang. "Hello," he said in an angry voice.

"Hello, Mr. Bradford, this is Detective Stubbs from Homicide."

Jason froze. "Yes, Detective, what can I do for you?" he asked, in the nicest voice he could muster up.

"Well, Jason, you don't mind if I call you that, do you? Do you remember the last time I saw you, I said we might want to talk with you again? Well, that time has come. Would you be willing to sit down with us and answer a few questions?"

"You can't do it over the phone?"

"No, Mr. Bradford, I think we may need a more formal setting."

"Then you won't mind if I bring along my attorney, would you?"

"No! In fact, I think it would be a good idea."

"When?"

"How about this afternoon?"

"What time?"

"Whenever you're available."

"Okay, I'll have my lawyer call you back to schedule a time."

"Good. I'll be patiently waiting to hear from him."

Jason didn't like the tone in his voice, how he emphasized 'patiently,' sarcastically mockingly him. After hanging up, he muttered, "Patiently, my ass. I'll bet you'll be sitting on the edge of your seat with bated breath, waiting for my attorney to call."

~~~

The D.A. was a slick politician. In the third year of his second term, he was looking for a way to move up another rung on the achievement ladder, perhaps as the next state attorney general. Timing was everything in his line of work. You couldn't get there sitting on your duff. You had to be proactive. Rattle a few doors and sometimes ruffle a few feathers. He was good at ruffling feathers. He was well liked by his peers, but not so much among his subordinates. They knew what drove the man who sat behind the desk in the D.A.'s office. It was power.

District Attorney Tucker Collins paced back and forth waiting for Detective Stubbs to walk through his door. Stubbs was the lead detective on the S. B. serial killer case who'd said he thought he had enough evidence to make an arrest. But first, he wanted to go over what he had before charging their suspect.

Tucker knew some but not all the particulars. He'd heard a rumor that they had an eyewitness, but that's all it was, as far as he knew: a rumor. If it were true, they could put another mark on their side of the board. And that's all that really mattered; it was a game of numbers. How many convictions did he have compared to non-convictions? Successfully prosecuting a serial killer would enhance his marketability considerably.

When Rusty walked into the D.A.s outer office, the secretary took a double take, but didn't say a word about his appearance. Rusty said, "Hi, Carol, how are you?"

"I'm fine," she said. "He's waiting for you. I'll let him know you're here."

Rusty sat down in one to the armchairs against the wall by the entrance. He listened to a one-sided conversation.

"Tucker, Detective Stubbs is here." There was a short pause and then, "Yes sir, I'll send him right in." Rusty stood and walked through the right leaf of the large oak double doors.

Once inside, District Attorney Collins said, "You look like crap. I hope you feel better than you look, Detective Stubbs. What does the other guy look like?"

"He looks better than I do, except for the missing toe on his left foot."

"Did you see anyone in medical? Did they take x-rays?"

"No, I'm all right. Just a few bruises. That's all."

"I heard Sergeant Johnson is retiring. Are you thinking about taking his place? My guess is you'd be a shoo-in for the job if you want it."

"No, no. I don't think I want all that

aggravation."

"Okay, Detective, that's up to you. Anyway, I'd like to thank you for the fine work you and your team did a couple of nights ago."

"It's just part of the job, sir."

"Have a seat, Rusty; let's discuss the S. B. case."

Rusty handed the D.A. a copy of the report. "As you already know, we collected fingerprints and DNA of our prime suspect from the crime scene. We have a witness who saw a vehicle resembling our suspect's mother's car parked across the street from our murder victim's house on the night she died. Our suspect's mother is his alibi, which has some holes in it. We served a search warrant for his apartment and car. And guess what?" He didn't wait for an answer. "On the computer we found were driving direction to the victim's house from his mother's house. We got another warrant for her property. At his mother's house, we were able to retrieve a charred small section of wood; we think it could have been used as the murder weapon."

"Is that it, Detective?"

"That's pretty much it."

"What about the rumor I heard that you have an actual eyewitness? Is there any truth to that?"

"Yes, and no," Rusty said. He proceeded to tell the district attorney the story from the moment Ella Martin called until she sat down and gave the interview. Then he pulled out a small tape recorder, set it down on the D.A.'s desk, and played the interview in its entirety. When the tape was finished, he dug into his folder and removed the composite drawing Randy had created, along with a DMV photo of their suspect, Jason Bradford, and handed them to the district attorney.

The DA stared at the two pictures as Rusty continued with the story.

Tucker wasn't happy with the evidence they had. Without Ella, all it was … was circumstantial. If they could find Ms. Brown's DNA on the bat or on anything belonging to Mr. Bradford, then they had a prosecutable case. Right now, they had nothing putting him at the scene at the actual time of the murder. If the woman who saw the car got the license number or saw the killer's face, that might have been enough. He knew bringing Ella into the mix would turn the whole thing into a media circus. All the nuts would come out once she got on the stand, whether her testimony was true or not.

Rusty sat quietly waiting for Tucker to decide what to do. Finally, he said, "Okay, Detective, you got the ball. I'll let you run with it, but don't throw any Hail Mary passes. If you don't have anything, don't make it into something it's not. If you can get a confession, great, if not, let him walk for now. We can keep an eye on him; see where he goes, tap his phone. Who's his attorney? Do you know?"

"No, I don't."

Rusty stood up and collected his tape record and evidence folder.

As he turned to leave, Tucker said, "Take care of that eye, Detective Stubbs, and if you need to get a hold of me for any reason, call me on my cell phone. You can get the number from Carol."

Chapter 21

At 2:00 p.m., the odd couple walked through the door. Mr. Bradford was too short to recognize over the five-foot partition, unlike his attorney, John Preston, who resembled the character, Ichabod Crane, from the Sleepy Hollow legend. In fact, he reminded people so much of this character that his peers called him Icky behind his back. He walked with a long gait and talked with a slow Southern drawl. But he was no slouch in a court of law. He knew how to work the room.

Rusty saw the taller man and walked over to where the two were standing. He shook hands with both men, like two fighters touching gloves before doing combat. "Are you here today to represent Mr. Bradford?"

"That would be correct, Detective."

"Let me take you into our interview room." They walked down a hallway to the second room on the right. Rusty patted down Jason for weapons before entering. He asked if he could get either of the men something to drink, giving them a choice between coffee or a soft drink from a vending machine. Both men declined the offer.

Joe turned down the thermostat to interview room number two and joined the other three men at the small rectangular table. The table was bolted to the floor to prevent the interviewee from trashing the room. An eyebolt protruded from the floor underneath the table to secure a detainee in place with handcuffs or shackles if the detainee had a violent nature.

The first thing out of Rusty's mouth was an explanation of the meeting. He said, "We're here today to let you know we have enough evidence to arrest Mr. Bradford for the murder of Sandra Brown. And we are giving your client the opportunity to hear that evidence and see if he can explain any of it. Joe, do you want to do the honors and mirandize Mr. Bradford before we start?" Rusty turned on the video camera to record the session.

"You have the right to remain silent. Anything you say can and will be used against you in a court of law. You have the right to have an attorney present during questioning. If you cannot ..." He finished up with, "Do you understand these rights?"

Jason looked over at his attorney, who nodded in an affirmative matter. He turned his head back toward the detective. "Yes."

Attorney John Preston looked at the two detectives. "Turn over your down card, Detective. Let's see what you got."

Rusty said, "We lifted your client's fingerprints from a glass inside our victim's house. We also found his DNA on a tissue in a trash can in her bathroom. We have a witness that saw a car matching the description of your client's mother's car parked on the street where the victim lived the night of the crime."

"What does the car have to do with my client?" asked the tall attorney.

"It gives him the opportunity. You see your client has no alibi for that evening."

Jason's attorney looked at his client. "Is that correct?"

"No," Jason said, "that's not correct! My mother can confirm my presence in her house during the time in question."

"Is that true, Detective?" asked Preston.

"No, that's not correct, Counselor."

Rusty explained what Jason's mother had said, that she had been asleep and he had to wake her to go to bed. "That," he said, "leaves him without an alibi. As far as the car is concerned, he had the opportunity to use it during the time the crime was committed. His mother no longer drives it. According to your client's mother, the only person who takes care of it and drives it is her son, Mr. Bradford."

Perspiration began to build on Jason's forehead, even though the room temperature had dropped below sixty degrees.

Joe left the room and a few minutes returned with a cup of coffee.

"You got anything else?" Mr. Preston asked.

"We have in our custody a computer that belongs to your client. And on his computer is

MapQuest with directions to our victim's house. The starting point begins at Mr. Bradford's mother's house. This may only be coincidental, but I think a jury might find it interesting. Don't you, Counselor?"

Jason was surprised. He couldn't figure out how they could possibly have put together all that information, especially in such a short period of time. He'd forgotten that he used that particular computer to look up Sandra Brown's address.

"Our victim, Ms. Brown, had the back of her skull bashed in. According to the pathologist, the damage was caused by a blunt instrument. From inside a large burn barrel in Mrs. Bradford's back yard, we retrieved the remains of what appears to be a small bat. There's not much left of it, but I think there's enough to figure out what it once was."

Since Rusty didn't know what the other item was B. B. found, he didn't mention it. Nor did he say a word about their eyewitness, Ella Martin. She would be his ace in the hole. His closer, if he had nothing else to fall back on.

Rusty looked down at his questionnaire. "So, tell me, Mr. Bradford, why does your computer have directions to Sandra Brown's house on it? And why would we find your fingerprints and DNA inside her house?"

Jason was no dummy. Before he'd ever cleaned his first house, he'd thought about the "what ifs." What if they, the police, caught him in the act. What if he was seen leaving the property? What if he left fingerprints or bodily fluids that he missed while cleaning up? What would he use as an excuse? He responded, "Well, I guess you got me. I broke into her house on a Tuesday, two days before she died. I intended to steal jewelry, but once I got inside, I got cold feet. I had a change of heart. I left without taking anything. I didn't kill her. I couldn't kill anyone. I drove my own car to her residence, not my mother's." He knew if they could put him in that car, he was dead meat.

Rusty watched Mr. Bradford slowly transform from a cocky Mr. Hyde into a meek and mild-mannered Dr. Jekyll as he confessed to breaking and entering. Jason asked for a glass of water and wiped sweat from his forehead with the sleeve of his jacket. A sudden twitching occurred in his eyelid and increased in intensity with each word he spoke. He began squirming in his seat like a nervous child caught in a lie, or maybe the hemorrhoid cream he was using had stopped working. Rusty thought the former was more likely.

"Can you explain the bat in the big drum?" Rusty asked as he checked off number three on his questionnaire.

"Sure, you may not like the answer, but the bat has been around since I was a child. You can ask my mother. It used to belong to my brother, Troy. I was cleaning out the basement the other day and found it, so I decided to get rid of it. That's it; nothing mysterious about it. The bat was used to kill fish. It had a steel bar inside."

Jason didn't know if they had found the steel bar or not; he didn't think it would hurt to tell them about it, and if he had to take a polygraph, then so be it. He wouldn't have to lie. Unless, of course, they asked him if he'd ever used it to kill anyone.

"How did you get into Ms. Brown's house?"

"I disabled her alarm system. Then I picked her back-door lock."

"How did you disable the alarm?"

"As you know I work for a company that designs security software. I'm the creator of that software. I designed a backdoor that would allow me to access the database, no matter who bought the product. So I went into my system, got Ms. Brown's address and entry code. Then I programmed a TV remote control to do the same thing that her remote does. I momentarily shut down her system, picked her back-door lock, entered and disabled her system. It was just that simple."

"What did you do with the remote and the lock picking equipment?"

"I got rid of them somewhere halfway up Pikes Peak. It was dark at the time, so I have no idea where they might be."

He lied. The remote had more than one code programmed in it from several of the other houses he'd cleaned. He certainly didn't want to give away that information. That would cook his goose. He was rolling the dice, placing all his chips on the table. They didn't have the other computers with all the women's names on it, so they could only put him in the one house. And unless they had an eyewitness, they couldn't prove he committed the murder.

Rusty knew what was happening. He'd been down the same road many times before. Jason was feeding him, giving up little information. He was trying to take the fall for a lesser crime.

Rusty was surprised that Jason's attorney let him cut his own throat. They must have gotten together and worked out a strategy. This maneuver would certainly put Mr. Bradford in stripes for at least the weekend until he was arraigned on Monday morning.

"Where's the beef?" Jason's attorney asked. "So far, I haven't heard anything that places my client inside your murder victim's house at the time of the homicide."

He was right and Rusty knew it. Without Ella all they had was circumstantial evidence. Was it enough? Probably not.

The detectives decided to leave the little man with his attorney. They stepped out of the room and walked back to the big conference room where they could view the two men on close circuit television. The attorney knew the game and told his client to keep his mouth shut. Rusty said to Joe, "We can arrest him for breaking and entering. They'll probably give him a slap on the wrist; after all, he has no criminal history. He never took anything that we know of from any of the victims. We can't put him in any of the other houses, so Sandra Brown's place is all we have."

Rusty removed his cell phone from his pocket and punched in the number Carol had written down on the back of Tucker Collins' business card. After a few seconds, the DA answered. The detective passed on Jason's excuse used in the interrogation about being there days before Sandra was murdered, but not being there on the day she died. "He said, he broke into her house intending to steal something, but got cold feet and left without taking anything."

Tucker wasn't surprised by what Rusty told him. "Go ahead," he said, "charge him with breaking and entering and murder one."

The two detectives walked back to the interview room.

"What's the judgment, Detective Stubbs?" Ichabod asked. "Are you arresting my client or not?" He knew they couldn't just let him go.

"We're arresting and charging your client with breaking and entering, a crime he has already admitted to. We believe that crime took place during the commission of a more serious crime, for which he was there in the first place. We are charging your client, Counselor, with premeditated murder. A charge that the district attorney's office believes is valid." Rusty didn't tell him that they suspected his client was involved in several other murders.

The tall man started laughing. "You'll never make that stick, Detective." Then, as Joe handcuffed Jason, he turned and faced his client. "You'll be locked up over the weekend until your arraignment Monday morning. There's nothing I can do about it until we go before a judge."

Joe handed Jason over to a uniformed officer who escorted him out the back door of the building and into an awaiting van.

~~~

Jason was dressed in an orange jumpsuit. His watch, ring, and shoelaces were taken from him during booking. He'd had a horrible weekend. He was put in a cell with four other men, one of whom threw feces on him. Thank God the poop thrower was finally removed from his cell and placed in solitary confinement; he couldn't sleep. Another cellmate wanted to be his boyfriend for the weekend, but the man got bailed out before anything actually happened.

At 9:00 a.m., Monday morning, Jason heard his cell door open and sat up on his bunk. Two armed guards stood outside his cell; one of them said, "Rise and shine. It's time to see the judge." By now there were only two men left in the cell, him and a Mr. Bloodworth. They were shackled together at their ankles and separately handcuffed. They were escorted outside the building to a waiting van that took them around the corner to the courthouse.

They entered the building through a side door and were led down a long hallway into a bulletproof glass enclosure overlooking the courtroom filled with family members and attorneys for the jailed defendants. The bulletproof enclosure was more for the prisoners' protection than it was for the courtroom personnel.

Once inside the enclosure, the shackles on Jason's ankle was removed, along with one of his wrist handcuffs, which was then fastened to a brass rail that ran the entire length of the enclosure. Then he sat down on a bench alongside Mr. Bloodworth for the proceedings to begin. While waiting, he looked out into the crowded courtroom and found his attorney standing in a far back corner talking with his mother.

He didn't have to wait long before the court was called to order as Judge Wilson entered the room. She stood 4' 11" in heels, with a small build and wore large lens glasses. She was in her mid-fifties, Jason guessed; she reminded him of Judge Judy, the television personality who ruled her roost with an iron fist, except Judge Wilson was black.

All the defendants were being held on felony charges without bail until a preliminary hearing could be set for them; a small technicality that his attorney had failed to mention. This would prevent his release for another day or two.

Mr. Bloodworth was the first out of the box. He was being charged with assault on a police officer, robbery, and manslaughter. The judge explained the possible penalties for each crime. Mr. Bloodworth's court-appointed attorney instructed him to answer 'not guilty' to all charges. A preliminary hearing date was set and Mr. Bloodworth was led back to the holding area.

Jason was the last detainee to go before the judge. His attorney pleaded for him, "*Nolo contendere* on charge one, breaking and entering; not guilty on charge two, capital murder." The judge set a hearing date for the following day at 2:00 p.m. Then Jason was marched off with the other men back to the van and the short ride around the corner to the city jail.

~~~

On Tuesday at 2:00 p.m., the courtroom was almost empty. The only other defendant was a woman in her late teens charged with child abuse. She had a court-appointed attorney standing beside her as the judge set a trial date. The woman had no money to post bail, so she would remain locked up until her next court appearance.

Jason sat with his attorney on one side of the

courtroom staring at Stubbs, who sat on the opposite side with someone Jason had never seen before. Jason leaned over and whispered in his attorney's ear, "Who's that with Detective Stubbs?"

His attorney whispered back, "That's the prosecutor, Assistant District Attorney Raymond White. He's a first-class knucklehead. But he's good in a courtroom, so I'll have to be better."

The DA asked the judge to set bail at $500,000. Ichabod countered, "That's ridiculous. My client has never been in trouble before. He's never even had a parking infraction. $50,000 would be more appropriate, judge. He's lived here all his life; he's no threat to run or a threat to the community."

The judge reduced bail to $200,000. Sally would have to put up her house as collateral. Jason's attorney asked for a trial date to be set sometime in the following year. The judge looked down at her calendar and selected a date of June 1st, 2002. Both attorneys agreed to the proposed date. Jason was once again carted off to jail, where he remained overnight until Sally formally signed all the paperwork.

Chapter 22

The New Year came and went. The killings abruptly stopped, and Jason was back at his job. His lawyer was positive he would beat the murder charge and would not serve any time for the breaking and entering. He would probably have to do some community service, that's all.

Ella was happily retired, speaking at centers for seniors and nursing homes whenever she could. Seeing the relief on their faces after telling them about her journey to Heaven was enough to keep her going. When she wasn't doing that, she served food at one of the many homeless shelters in Los Angeles.

Occasionally, Dr. Henderson brought her back to be scrutinized by a new batch of doctors fresh out of medical school.

Rusty and Joe continued to work on the S. B. case, trying to tie Jason to any of the other four murders, but were unable to make a direct link. Shortly after Jason was released on bail, they received a phone call from the local dump operator, who said he'd found a white sheet of plastic and some tie wraps. Rusty and Joe went out to the dump site. They took some photographs and picked up the material to send over to Forensics for examination. No fingerprints were found on the sheet. Only a single hair was discovered trapped in the locking mechanism of one of the tie wraps. Unfortunately, the weather had degraded the DNA, making it impossible to identify the owner.

District Attorney Collins notified Ella that she might have to testify. He didn't want to put her on the stand, but they might have no choice. Without her testimony, they had nothing but circumstantial evidence against Bradford. No one could put him at the scene of the crime at the time of the murder except for her. Having worked for Riedel, Darin, and Charles, she knew her credibility would be on the line. The defense would try to paint her as some type of nutcase.

Bobbi was promoted to night shift supervisor and was now spending more time in her office than out at a crime scene. She was seeing a new man, a musician who played classical guitar, and taught music at a junior college.

Jason's attorney applied for a change in venue because of the publicity of the case. Sandra Brown was reported to be the victim of a serial killer the media dubbed the S. B. killer. This fact was never established. No evidence was ever collected to definitely link her to the serial killings, only the similarities, of which there were many. 'A mere coincidence,' according to the defense, that she had the same initials as the other women. He wanted to distance his client from any linkage.

The media was given a gag order prohibiting them from connecting the two cases together. The presiding judge, Judge Bartholome Jenkins, known as B. J., denied a change of venue and ordered the trial to commence as scheduled.

Chapter 23

Jason sat expressionless in his chair at the defense table on the left side of the courtroom. His attorney, Mr. Preston, sat to his right to prevent as much eye contact as possible between his client and the potential jurors.

As required, the prosecution notified the defense in advance that an eyewitness might take the stand during the trial. The defense attorney took the opportunity to review all the evidence against his client during Discovery. Mr. Preston watched the video recording of Ella Martin's interview. He heard her doctor's comments about what occurred that night. He knew that saying something happened and proving it were different. Proving it beyond a reasonable doubt would be difficult, no matter how good the prosecutor was.

As the judge entered the room, the bailiff called the court to order. Fifty prospective jurors listened carefully as the judge read the case to them, after which twelve jurors were selected to go through *voir dire*.

The first prospective juror was a pimply-face young man in his early twenties named Travis Smith. The first question came from the prosecuting attorney. "Mr. Smith, what do you do for a living?"

"I'm a truck driver," the man replied.

"What kind of truck driver? Are you a big rig, a long-haul driver?"

"No, no, I'm a delivery driver."

"Whom do you work for?"

"At the present time, I'm unemployed."

"How long have you been out of work?"

"Six months, this time."

"Are you married?"

"No, I'm divorced."

"Do you have any children?"

"Yes. Two."

"Who supports your children?"

"Their mother."

"What does she do for a living?"

"Nothing, she watches the children."

"So, I presume she's living off the State?"

"Off the state of what?" Mr. Smith asked.

"I presume she's on welfare, living off the taxpayers. Is that correct?"

"Yes, I guess so."

The prosecutor asked several more questions and then turned it over to the defense.

Mr. Preston looked the juror square in the eye and asked, "Mr. Smith, have you ever been arrested?"

"Yes."

"What for?"

"Which time?"

"Well, why don't you start with the first time and then bring us up to date?"

"The first time was for breaking and entering. I broke into my neighbor's house. I had a drug addiction and needed some money for a fix."

Mr. Preston had a change of heart and decided not to go through all the felonies and misdemeanors the man committed. He interrupted him with a revised question. "How many times have you been incarcerated?" he asked, figuring it would shorten his response.

"In what?"

"Behind bars?"

The man sat back in his chair and thought; he started counting on his fingers but didn't have enough hands to finish his count.

The defense attorney interrupted again. "Never mind, Mr. Smith. I have only one more question for you. What do you do during the day when you're not working?"

"I play *Assault* on my computer."

"What's *Assault*?"

"It's a video game where you see how many people you can kill or maim without getting caught. The more people you assault, the higher the score."

"Okay, thank you, Mr. Smith," said Mr. Preston.

The court called out the name of the person to

Mr. Smith's left, Timothy Barry, who identified his occupation as accountant. As with the prior prospective juror, the prosecutor went through a litany of questions and was satisfied with Mr. Barry's answers. He turned the floor over to the defense.

The defense attorney said, "Mr. Barry, you've heard the charges brought against my client, Mr. Bradford. What do you think of those charges?" The defense was trying to find out if the potential juror had any preconceived ideas of his client's innocence or guilt.

Mr. Barry looked out at the crowded courtroom. "Well, to tell you the truth, I don't think he would have gotten this far in the system if he wasn't guilty."

The defense attorney had no other questions for the accountant. Over the next hour and a half, five more probable jurors entered the jury box: one firefighter, two in the medical profession, one housewife, and one health inspector. It was close to lunch, so the judge called a two-hour recess and ordered all the potential jurors, both in and out of the box, not to discuss the case.

After lunch the jury selection continued. The next person questioned was Imogene Olson, a retired garment worker. She was a widow with ten grandchildren and lived with her daughter's family.

The prosecutor quizzed her on several different facets of the trial. He told her the case could go on for quite some time. He asked if selected, could she make it through the trial? She coughed up some phlegm and spit into a Kleenex before answering.

"Yes, I think I could make it through." The two attorneys had their doubts.

The defense attorney took the floor. He turned to the woman in the jury box. "My client is accused of premeditated murder. Do you know what that means?" He didn't wait for an answer but answered for her. "It means if convicted, Mr. Bradford could receive the death penalty. Could you vote guilty, knowing that he may be put to death?"

She looked over at the man seated at the defense table. He looked clean-cut, small, weak. He didn't look like the type who could hurt a fly, let alone another human. He looked back at her with the saddest, most pathetic look he could muster. She held her hand out in front of her, pointed her thumb toward the ceiling, and then turned it over as if she were in the Colosseum sentencing a gladiator to death. At the same time, she said, "In a heartbeat."

The attorneys were stunned. Jason's attorney was expecting a simple yes. After all, it was a capital case. It was the way the person responded that would decide whether he or she remained in the jury box for the entirety of the trial.

The next person questioned was an out-of-work actor. He was good looking, articulate, and loved the camera, which is where he focused his response rather than to the attorney asking the questions. His name was Joel Whitehead. The prosecuting attorney asked if he had a stage name.

"Yes, my stage name is Galore."

"Is that a first or last name?"

"Both, it's the only one I go by."

"What type of movies do you make?"

"What do you mean, by what type of movies do I make?"

"Are they comedy? Are they adventure? Are they romance?"

"They're all the above, but I would classify them as loveee ..." he said slowly, letting it roll off his tongue, as he stared into the camera's eye.

"Have you ever played the victim of a crime?"

"No, never."

"Have you ever played the perpetrator of a crime, a killer or a burglar?"

"Yes, many times."

"Are there any notable films that we might be familiar with?"

"It depends on your taste. My most memorable film was a remake of *Debbie Does Dallas*."

"Oh; you're in the porn business?"

"I'm in the love business," he glanced over at the camera again, "but I'm trying to break into the more commercial side of the business; it's not that easy to get work over there."

"Okay, thank you, Mr. Whitehead." He turned toward the judge. "I have no further questions."

By 4:00 p.m., they had questioned nine of the potential jurors in the box. The judge called an end to the session. "The court is adjourned until tomorrow. Everyone in the jury pool and those sitting on the panel must be back at 9:00 a.m."

~~~

B. J. was in his mid-fifties, a man of average height and a runner's build who always wore a colorful bow tie with his black robe.

He was elected to the bench in 1990 after a short but memorable career as a prosecuting attorney. He had two boys attending law school, one in his last year, and the other in his second year. His wife was a corporate attorney for an aerospace firm located in Boulder. He was an avid golfer and triathlon participant, once an alternate on the United States Olympic Marathon team. Unfortunately, he never got the chance to participate; a draft notice ended his lifelong dream.

The morning started out as a normal day. Several reporters were seated a couple of rows behind the jury pool. The judge recognized them by their faces but didn't know their names or the news outlets they worked for. He watched as the defense attorney towered over the oak railing asking the jury panel questions; with his height, he might seem clumsy, but he was as agile as a praying mantis on a leaf. The judge was a friend of both Mr. Preston and Mr. White, although he knew the two lawyers didn't get along. They were enemies inside the courtroom. He figured it was their nature, both fierce competitors, opponents jousting with each other.

Mr. White was at the top of the list for the D.A.'s position, and almost everyone expected him to be sitting in that seat as soon as Tucker left. If you were the defendant, Mr. White was the last person you wanted to see on the other side of the aisle. He had a ninety-five percent conviction rate.

It was time for the chess match to begin again, the battle for dominance over the jury panel to see which side would have the advantage when the trial began. This was as important as any statement the attorneys could make during the trial. Some attorneys hired consultants to help pick the jury. It was a game, and both were good at finding that one juror who would tilt the scale in their favor. But winning for the defense didn't always mean your client got off the hook and walked away scot-free; sometimes it meant a hung jury or accepting a lesser sentence in the penalty phase. For the prosecution, it made little difference; it was a win if the defendant paid a price for the crime.

The prosecution went first. Mr. White stood up and walked over to the jury box. "Mr. Smith, you are excused." The defense drew a line through his name, as the bailiff read another name from the prospective jurors' list. The prosecutor turned next to a tall man in his late thirties. "Mr. Cliff can you tell us your occupation and a little bit about yourself?"

"I'm a doctor of emergency medicine. I'm thirty-five-years-old. I'm married and have one child who is six-years-old."

"When you say emergency medicine, can you tell the court exactly what that means?"

"It means I'm an emergency room physician. I treat the sick and injured."

"I'm surprised to see you here today. I didn't think they took people in certain professions, yours being one of them."

"I'm on a three-month sabbatical. I needed some time with my family. The emergency room can be long, stressful work that can put a strain on a relationship. When I received the jury summons, I decided to participate, you know, do my part to serve the community."

The prosecutor asked a few more questions and turned it over to the defense.

The big attorney took several large strides over to the jury box and gripped the railing that separated him from the jurors. He looked directly into the doctor's eyes. "I suppose you've seen it all. Haven't you, Doctor?" The doctor looked at the attorney, not sure if he was asking a question or making a statement, so he waited. The tall attorney clasped his hands behind his back, paced the floor back and forth in front of the jury box, and then said, "I guess many of your patients are the victims of violence: beatings, stabbings, shootings, everything imaginable. Is that right, Doctor?"

"Yes, we deal with all the ones you mentioned, unfortunately, way too often."

It was obvious to the prosecutor where the defense was going with his line of questioning. He wanted to show the doctor could not be fair. He'd seen far too much violence over the years in the ER; it had to rub off on him. He had to feel the pain of the victim and hatred for the offender. The doctor would not be one of the twelve selected.

The defense attorney asked Dr. Cliff a few more questions, mainly for the audience's amusement; no one could say he didn't give him a fair shake, even though he'd made up his mind way before the questioning ever began. He finally said, "Thank you, Dr. Cliff." He turned his attention toward the judge. "I'm finished with this gentleman."

The judge nodded toward at the prosecutor.

The prosecutor stood and faced the twelve people in the jury box. "Mr. Barry, you are excused."

The bailiff was a large black man. He stood 6' 3" and weighed 300 pounds. He'd once played center for a pro team in the NFL. He kept in shape by working out daily and could still bench press over 350 pounds. His courtroom friends called him The Enforcer. His biceps bulged as he held up the paper containing the list of names of the jury pool. He scanned down to the name following Dr. Cliff and read it aloud. "Mr. Howard Kennedy, please take the empty seat in the jury box."

A small angular man in his early thirties rose from a chair and marched across the hardwood floor toward the box dressed in western apparel. He wore a white shirt with a green band of flowers that orbited his upper torso and a bolo style necktie, and his blue jeans were held up by a belt that had the word 'Stud' engraved on the buckle. Wearing cowboy boots, his legs were bowed as if he'd just stepped down from a saddle. When he walked, he had a noticeable limp because of an arthritic hip. He carried a Starbucks coffee cup in one hand and a leather trench coat with a rabbit-fur collar draped over his other arm. He worked his way down the row of seats to the vacated seat.

The judge turned the floor over to the defense attorney, who asked him to state his name and occupation.

"My name is Howard 'Rowdy' Kennedy," he said with great expectations of an oncoming applause, as if it was a household name; not a peep was heard. The slight man had a handlebar mustache — heavily waxed; he also had a large lump on the right side of his cheek, inside his mouth.

The defense attorney looked at him. "Are you chewing tobacco, Mr. Kennedy?"

He spit it out into a cup. "No, not anymore."

"Thank you. Mr. Kennedy, during your career, have you ever had an injury to your head, let's say a concussion or perhaps a fractured skull?"

"Both. I've had both. A mean old boy named Melvin split my head wide open. Don't let the name fool you, this bull had testicles the size of a boxcar." A roar of laughter came from the back of the courtroom. The judge pounded his gavel against the round sounding block to call the court back to order. The little man in western wear continued where he left off. "He could really kick some butt. I was on him for six whole seconds," he said with pride. "That was the longest six seconds of my life. I remember hitting the ground and then the sound of thunder as Melvin stomped on my head. I've been knocked out cold more times than I can count on my fingers." He held up both hand in front of him so all could see.

The judge raised his eyebrows and looked directly at the bull rider over the top of his small square frame glasses. He reminded those in the jury box that they were in a court of law, and that everything they said was recorded.

When it was Ichabod's turn, he asked the cowboy several more questions. Then he took four strides, moving his lanky 6'9" frame from the jury box back to the defense table, where he turned his head to face the judge. "I have no further questions."

The prosecutor took the floor again. "Mr. Kennedy, may I call you Rowdy?"

"Yes. Please do."

"Rowdy, has anyone in your family been the victim of a vicious crime, an attack where they were defenseless?"

"Only me."

"How's that, Sir?"

"You remember the bull I was telling you about, well, I was defenseless against him."

The judge was almost ready to pull his hair out, what little hair he had left. He wondered if Ringling Brothers was in town, or if the summonses got lost in the mail and went to a local mental institution.

After the prosecutor finished his questioning of the cowboy, the defense had the floor again

The tall man stared at the jury. "Mrs. Olson, you are dismissed." She stood up with a dejected look, hacked up more phlegm, and spit into a Kleenex as she made her way from the jury box and out of the courtroom.

The bailiff read the next name on his dwindling list of potential jurors. A man strolled across the courtroom floor and made his way into the jury box. The defense attorney asked the man to state his name and occupation.

"My name is Hector Gonzales and I am a letter carrier." The man was short. He had a dark complexion, a combination of heritage and time in the sun.

"Are you also referred to as a mail carrier, mailman, or postal worker?"

"That would be correct."

"When people use the term "going postal," does that make you mad?"

"No, it doesn't. I can empathize with them. There're way too many people in my profession who have flipped out. They need to do a better job of screening these folks before they hire them."

"While delivering mail have you ever met up with a vicious animal?"

"Many times," he said, wiping his forehead with the sleeve of his shirt.

"Did one of these animals ever bite you?"

"Yes, twice before."

"So you know what it's like to be frightened?"

"Absolutely!"

"While delivering mail were you ever accosted by a robber, someone who wanted either your mail or your personal belongings?"

"Yes, twice. Once I was pistol-whipped by a man who wanted my wallet. And another time by two armed men who wanted all the mail on my delivery truck."

"I'll bet that scared you."

"Yes, it was a trying time. One that I don't like remembering. After that incident, I started packing a gun." His voice began to break up and rose to a higher pitch. He wiped more sweat from his brow. "I volunteered to see a psychiatrist and after a short period of time, I was back to normal."

"Do you still carry a gun?"

"Oh no, I got rid of that a long ago. No one knew I had it; if they did, I could have lost my job."

The defense attorney asked several more questions and then turned it over to the prosecution. The prosecutor quizzed the mail carrier for several more minutes, and then said to the judge, "I'm finished with my examination."

After three days of selection, the two attorneys agreed on the twelve members who would serve on the jury panel. They decided on one substitute schoolteacher, two self-described homemakers, one bull rider, one sanitation engineer, one health inspector, and two medical professionals not involved in emergency room care. They also selected one mail carrier, one out-of-work economist, one actor, one college student who was out on summer break, and one professional golfer.

Chapter 24

It was pouring rain outside the courthouse as the media, jurors, and relatives of both the victim and the accused filed through the courtroom door and were shown where to sit, courtesy of the bailiff, Mr. Jones, 'The Enforcer.' Jason Thomas Bradford sat alone at the defense table. His attorney, Mr. Preston, was in a deep conversation with the court reporter.

After making sure the relatives were in their rightful place, the bailiff checked the identification cards of the press and pointed out an area preselected for them to sit. The remaining seats were up for grabs, given to anyone who wanted to watch.

Sandra Brown's parents sat several rows back on the prosecution's side of the courtroom. The couple owned a small farm, ten miles north of Colorado Springs. Sandra was their only child. Mr. Brown was a big man who looked uncomfortable dressed in something other than bib overhauls. His dark brown, medium length hair was combed straight back and held in place using some form of greasy substance. A touch of gray was beginning to show at each temple. Mr. Brown towered over his wife, who, from behind, looked like a child sitting beside him. She wore black and looked as though she'd just come from a funeral. Motionless next to her husband, she stared off into space, as if she were somewhere else, far away.

On the opposite side of the courtroom sat Jason's mother, a petite woman in her fifties. She dressed provocatively, her hemline well above her knees. Her low-cut blouse showed more cleavage than appropriate for the setting.

A deputy assigned to the trial counted the bodies using a clicker as each person entered the large courtroom. A sign above the entrance door read: seating capacity 200. Maximum occupancy 225.

At 10:15 a.m., the bailiff closed the doors and took his place near the judge's bench.

Seconds later, the judge entered the courtroom and the bailiff said, "All rise. Hear ye, hear ye..." He stated the district and introduced Judge Jenkins.

Judge Jenkins said, "You may be seated."

The judge looked at the court reporter, who gave him the nod. He then turned his attention toward the jury box and issued the prefatory instruction to the jury. "Ladies and gentlemen of the jury. You have been selected and sworn in as the jury to try this case: The State of Colorado versus Jason Thomas Bradford. This is a criminal case. Mr. Bradford is charged with murder in the first degree. The definition of the elements of murder in the first degree will be explained to you later. It is your solemn responsibility to determine if the State has proved its accusation beyond a reasonable doubt against Mr. Bradford. Your verdict must be based solely on the evidence, or lack of evidence, and the law."

As he continued to read the instructions to the jury, Jason stared at the judge.

The judge went on to explain how a trial is conducted.

"At the beginning of the trial, the attorneys will have an opportunity to make an opening statement if they wish. The opening statement gives the attorneys a chance to tell you what evidence they believe will be presented during the trial. What the lawyers say is not evidence, and you are not to consider it as such." He completed the jury instructions and looked over at the prosecuting attorney. "Mr. White, would you like to make an opening statement?"

Tucker Collins sat next to prosecuting attorney Assistant DA White. Collins wasn't there to work the case or to give advice; he was there to make sure he got some face time in front of the camera.

White stood and faced the jury. He made eye contact with each and every panel member before speaking. He was dressed in a blue form-fitting Giorgio Armani designer suit with matching vest. He wore a patriotic tie with the colors in the American flag. He stood 6 feet tall. If you didn't know better, he easily could have been mistaken for Arnold Schwarzenegger. The resemblance was uncanny, both in facial and in physical appearance.

He hung his jacket on the back of his chair and

then walked toward the jury box. In most cases, strutting around without a jacket showing off his physique worked to his advantage, but occasionally it went against him, especially with men.

Mr. White turned and faced the crowded courtroom. He focused his attention on the back of the courtroom, then scanned each and every seat row by row until he had made brief eye contact with every person in the room. Once he felt he had their complete attention, he refocused his attention on the juror box. He was now ready to begin.

He kept his hands out of his pockets, a mistake so often made by many litigators. He used his hands as a tool, a form of expression, and raised and lowered his voice in modulation, knowing a monotone voice was boring and could easily lose their attention.

Mr. White smiled at a pretty young student in the back row of the jury box. "Ladies and gentleman of the jury, I'd like to start by thanking you for your time and attention in this case. As the judge said, an opening statement is a preview of what the evidence will show during this trial. Now, what will the evidence show?" He placed a stack of two-by-three-foot Styrofoam boards on an easel. Each board was marked with an exhibit number. Each of the boards had an enlarged photograph glued to it. He stepped back. "You'll see that on November 15th, 2001, the defendant, Jason Bradford, drove his mother's car to Sandra Brown's residence." He pointed to a photo on the easel marked exhibit number one, which consisted of a white 1988 Buick Regal. He continued, "He hid behind a hedge beside her back door and waited until Sandra returned home from work. After she opened the back door, he, the defendant, viciously attacked Ms. Brown hitting her in the back of her head with a small lead weighted bat." He removed exhibit number one from the easel, which now displayed exhibit number two showing two separate photographs: the upper one displayed a new, intact bat, while the lower photo showed what had been removed from the defendant's mother's burn barrel.

Mr. White pointed to the one on top. "This bat is called the Thumper. It's used primarily for checking tire pressure on large trucks or as a fishing tool to knock out the angler's catch so the fish can be removed from the hook. We've labeled each section of the bat so you know what we're talking about when we use certain terms as the knob or grip." He read the words out loud for the benefit of the people in the audience who might not be able to see them from a distance: knob, grip, barrel, end cap. Then he pointed to the photograph in the lower half of the Styrofoam board. "As you can plainly see, there are similarities, but the two bats are not identical. They were manufactured years apart." The bat on the bottom was badly charred. The only part recognizable was a little bit of the knob, part of the handle and the lead core that was no longer intact.

"The evidence will show that Mr. Bradford did not enter the residence at 111 Wildwood Road to commit a robbery for personal gain, but that he went there with murder in mind. Premeditation, that's what the evidence will show." He raised a hand to his chin, rubbed his face, and paused, as if in deep thought. Finally, he said, "During the trial, we, the prosecution, will take you on a journey through the rear door of the victim's house. Once inside, based on the evidence collected at the scene, we will reenact the crime the way in which we theorize it happened the night Ms. Brown was brutally taken from us."

Mr. Brown wiped a tear from his eye as the DA continued to speak. His wife showed no emotion whatsoever, still staring off into space.

Mr. White removed exhibit number two from the easel, revealing exhibit number three, which also displayed two photographs: one in the upper section, and one in the lower. The upper section showed a picture of Mick Jagger and the Rolling Stones taken from one of their many album covers. The lower was similar, but of a different group, Bob Seger and the Silver Bullet Band.

Mr. White refocused his attention on the jury, this time looking directly into the actor's eyes. "After knocking the victim unconscious, the defendant played the rock and roll music he brought with him. We know this because the next-door-neighbor heard that type of music, turned up loud, coming from the victim's house the night she died. She said Sandra never listened to anything other than country western. Our witness, not the next-door-neighbor, will say that the music was by the Rolling Stones and Bob Seger." He decided not to give any details about Ella Martin and how she fit into the picture, at least not yet. He went on, "We did not find any evidence that she, our victim, owned either of these albums or listened to that type of music. No rock and roll albums or CDs were found in the victim's house and her two sources of music — a stereo and a radio — were both tuned to the same country western station."

The picture he painted was like reading the dust jacket of a bestselling novel, just giving an overview. The detail would come out during the trial. He turned to face the spectators, raised his hand, and pointed his index finger at the defendant. "The defendant may look like your boy next door or a friend, but don't let his looks fool you. He is a danger to the community. He's a calculating, vicious killer who premeditated and executed, with malice, the murder of Sandra Brown, a loving lady in the prime of her life. After all the evidence is presented, you will have a chance to discuss the evidence and come to a conclusion; that conclusion will end in a verdict of either guilty or not guilty. We, the prosecution, believe there can be only one conclusion; that conclusion is guilty as charged."

Mr. White thanked the jury for listening. Then he walked back to the prosecutors' table and sat down next to his boss, DA Collins.

Judge Jenkins looked in the direction of the defense table. "Mr. Preston, do you have an opening statement?"

"Yes." Mr. Preston got up out of his chair and stood next to the defendant. He wore a light brown tweed suit with a cream-colored shirt and brown tie. His shoes were dark brown, size sixteen. He smiled a toothy grin, showing all of his cosmetically enhanced white teeth. As he thanked the jury for the opportunity to counter in his opening statement, he started. "Smoke and mirrors. That's what this is all about. Not all things are what they appear to be. When the judge read the indictment against my client, I saw the look of horror on all of your faces and I understand that. The crime my client, Mr. Bradford, is accused of committing is a despicable, horrendous crime; what could be worse than killing a helpless woman in the sanctuary of her own home? A place one should feel safe in." The method was slow and deliberate. "I want you to know that this man," he put his hand on the accused's shoulder, "did not commit this crime. He is being blamed for something he did not do. My client is innocent. The evidence against him is circumstantial; it could be any one of you. *You* could be sitting where my client is sitting. The prosecutor is throwing stuff against the wall, hoping something will stick."

He took a drink of water and continued. "If I were a betting man, I'd bet that I could find at least ten other cars here in Colorado Springs that match the one spotted near the crime scene. The prosecutor's eyewitness did not get a license number. And the witness, according to the statement I read, said she could not identify the driver. Didn't know if the person driving the car was male or female. Well, folks, that's pretty ambiguous, isn't it? Certainly too vague to put my client behind the wheel. And as far as the bat goes, I'm sure all of you have found something around the house from when you were younger that you no longer use, so you decided to get rid of it by throwing it away or burning it in your fireplace. That's what we have here, nothing more. A toy bat that once belonged to his brother, Troy. If my client is guilty, the only thing he's guilty of is bad timing. The point is, ladies and gentleman of the jury, you have to prove that the bat was used during the commission of a crime. Not that it *could have* been. *May have* been." He circled the room between the defendant's table and the jury box three times during his opening statement.

Then he stopped and focused his attention toward the economist who was about his age. "Do any of you own an album, cassette, or compact disc by the Rolling Stones? Can I see a show of hands?" The economist raised his hand, and so did the student. "What about Bob Seger? Does anyone own any Bob Seger music?" The cowboy raised his hand, which surprised the attorney. "The reason I ask is, once again, you see, you could be sitting over there," he pointed toward the defense table. "It's called circumstantial evidence. Who can say that the killer didn't just turn on the stereo and tune in a rock station?"

He made a final trip around the room and came to rest beside his client. He closed his statement by saying, "If you have a witness, the witness should be tangible, physical, solid, concrete, a real person, a person of substance, not someone dreaming of being in another place seeing visions, things that are not real. Psychics are not eyewitnesses." No one had the slightest idea what he was talking about. But he had their attention, and that's what was important to him. He knew if the prosecutor brought in his eyewitness, sparks would fly. He wanted to plant a seed, something subliminal. Something lost in their subconscious that would be recalled when the right time came.

He finished the way he started. "Let me repeat. My client did not commit the crime for which he's being accused. There is no physical evidence that can put him in the same room as the victim at the *time* of her death." He emphasized the word time.

He turned to face the judge. "That completes my opening statement."

B. J. gazed down at his watch and slammed the gavel against the sounding block. "Let's break for lunch." He warned the jury not to talk about the case, and to return promptly at 1:00 p.m. sharp.

Chapter 25

Rusty sat next to Bobbi Bidwell, cleaning his glasses, one row in front of the victim's parents. He was expecting to take the stand and testify after Bobbi.

The first witness called by the prosecution was a patrol officer named Smit, who was the first to arrive on the scene. He took the stand and was sworn in. Attorney White asked him, "What did you observe when you first arrived on the scene, Officer Smit?"

"On my arrival, I noticed the victim's parents sitting on the front porch."

"What were they doing?"

"They were crying and waiting for me."

"What did they say on your arrival?"

"They said they found their daughter dead in the house."

"Did they say how they got inside the house?"

"Yes, they said they had a key and the code to

the alarm. They let themselves in after not being able to contact her by phone."

"Did you enter the house?"

"Yes."

"By the front door or back?"

"I entered the house through the back door."

"What did you see after entering?"

"I saw the victim lying face down on an area rug in her living room."

"Did you touch the victim?"

"No. It was obvious she was dead."

White showed the patrol officer a photograph of the crime scene. "Does this picture represent what you saw?"

"Yes, to my recollection … that's exactly the way she was lying on the floor when I first saw her."

The prosecutor asked the patrol officer several more nonessential questions and then passed him over to the defense for cross-examination.

Mr. Preston had only one question for the witness. "How did you notify your department of the death?"

"I called it in to Dispatch."

"Was that by telephone?"

"No, I used my radio."

"Thank you, Officer Smit. I have no further questions for this witness, Your Honor."

Bobbi Bidwell took Officer Smit's place on the stand.

Attorney White asked, "What was your

position at the time of Ms. Brown's death?"

"I was the lead daytime Crime Scene Investigator."

"What is your position now?"

"Nightshift Supervisor."

He asked several more questions about her education just to clarify her qualifications, then pressed on.

"Was the scene secured when you arrived?"

"Yes, all the way to the street."

"What was the first thing you did?"

"I shut down the entire block to through traffic."

"What was the purpose in that?"

"To preserve any evidence that may be on the street."

"Did you find any?"

"No, we didn't. It was snowing the night of the crime and any tracks that were there were long gone by Monday, four days later."

For the next half hour, she was grilled on her procedure. Finally, the defense got a chance to cross-examine.

Attorney Preston spoke. "You told the prosecutor that you dusted for fingerprints throughout the house, which included the doorknobs and door handles. Where else did you dust for prints?"

"We dusted the kitchen sink, refrigerator, dining room table," she went on, and on.

"Did you dust the stereo system?"

"No, we didn't."

"Why not?"

"You can't dust everywhere. At the time, we had no reason to suspect there might be fingerprints other than the victim's on it."

"Did you recover any latent fingerprints belonging to my client on that day?"

"No. Not on that day."

"When did you recover his prints?"

"Several days later."

"What made you go back to collect more fingerprints?"

"I didn't. Detective Longhorn gave me a glass and a Kleenex to process. He told me they both came from the victim's house."

"What did you find?"

"I found several good fingerprints on the glass. And some unknown DNA on the tissue that did not belong to the victim."

"That's interesting."

The prosecutor knew what was happening. The defense attorney was setting up his case. He was trying to show the evidence against his client was planted, and so far, he was doing a good job.

"What about the DNA evidence. You said you didn't know who it belonged to. How did you link my client to the tissue?"

"About a week later, Detective Longhorn gave me another tissue to examine. He said it came from Mr. Bradford's bathroom trash can."

"Do you know if he had a warrant that would

allow him to collect DNA samples from my client's living quarters?"

"I don't know. You'd have to ask him that. I didn't see the warrant. I'm not sure what was on it and what wasn't."

The defense asked some technical questions about how the testing was done for both latent fingerprints and DNA. Then he said he had no more questions but would like to have the right to recall the witness later.

The judge granted him the recall right and dismissed the witness.

Next, the prosecutor called Detective Reginald Stubbs to the stand.

The judge knew this was going to be a real barnburner. Attorney Preston and Detective Stubbs had gone head-to-head before. The detective was not intimidated by the verbal gymnastics of the lanky attorney. He was educated and could hold his own.

He was sworn in by the bailiff and turned over to the prosecution.

"How long have you worked for the Police Department, Detective Stubbs?" asked Prosecutor White.

"Twenty-five years."

"Of those twenty-five years, how many were in Homicide?"

"Fifteen years."

"So, you've seen many dead bodies?"

"Yes, you could say that." He knew the prosecutor was not going to eat him alive; it was the defense that would draw blood.

"Do you remember when and where you were when you first heard about the body found on Wildwood Road?"

Rusty looked down at his notes. "Yes, it was on Monday morning, at 10:00 a.m., November 19th, 2001. I was with my partner in a market buying groceries for the department."

"Who notified you?"

"Dispatch. Dispatch called us."

"When you went to the address, what was the first thing you noticed?"

"I noticed the entire street closed off."

"So where did you park?"

"We parked on Hidden Valley Drive — the main street that intersects Wildwood Road — and walked down to the crime scene."

"Were you the first detectives on the scene?"

"We were the first and only detectives on the scene. We were the ones assigned to the case."

"Was the house broken into?"

"No, it didn't appear to be."

"Was the house in disarray? Did it look like someone had burglarized it?"

"No. The house was spotless. Neat as a pin. Not a thing out of place."

The defense attorney objected to the witness adding more to his "No" answer. The judge scolded Rusty and reminded him not to volunteer any additional information unless asked to do so.

Score one for the defense, Rusty thought.

"When you saw the body, was it bound in any way?

Following the judge's instruction, Rusty answered, "No."

"Did the body have any marks on it that would lead you to believe she'd been restrained?"

"Yes," Rusty said.

"What type of restraints do you think were used to restrain the victim?"

"Based on my experience, the ligature marks found on the victim would be similar to that of cable ties or heavy zip ties."

The prosecutor realized right away that they were in deep trouble. Attorney White decided they needed Ella Martin now. Otherwise, the case was going to get real confusing, and he didn't want to lose control.

Rather than being at a disadvantage and letting the defense bring Ella into the conversation, he decided to take a chance by asking, "What made you think CSI might find physical evidence on two items Detective Longhorn gave Investigator Bidwell?"

"This came about during an interview with a potential witness."

"Who was this potential witness?"

"Ella Martin."

"What did she say during the interview?"

"She said I should look for fingerprints on a glass inside the kitchen cabinet and DNA on the tissue in the victim's bathroom trash can."

"What made you believe the words of this

person?"

"Because of the accuracy of the information she'd provided me with during our first and second telephone conversations."

"When did that conversation take place?"

"The first time I talked to Ella Martin was on Friday, the day after the murder of Sandra Brown."

"What did she say?"

"She asked if we had a report of a homicide on Wildwood Road."

"What did you tell her?"

"I told her no, we had no newly reported homicides."

"What did you think?"

"I thought she was crazy. I asked her where she got that information. She said I wouldn't believe her if she told me. She left her name and number."

"What did you do with the information?"

"I threw it in the trash can …"

People in the crowded courtroom began to mutter among themselves. The judge banged the gavel against the sound block to regain order.

The defense was busy jotting down rebuttal notes.

"… On Monday, after visiting the crime scene, I … *we* … my partner and I, remembered the telephone conversation I had with the woman in California. I had one of the other detectives back at the precinct save the contents of my trash can. When we returned to the station, I called her number. During that conversation, she told me other things about the crime scene that only a person who was there would know."

"Did she identify herself as a psychic, clairvoyant, mystic, soothsayer, seer, prophet, mind reader, telepathic, fortune-teller, visionary, or just intuitive?"

"None of those."

"Did you ask her again where she got her information?"

"Yes," Rusty replied.

"And what did she say?"

"May I play the tape-recorded version, so it's not considered hearsay?"

"You recorded the conversation?"

"Yes."

"Did she know you were recording her?"

"Yes."

The defense attorney knew about the tape. He had a chance to listen to it during Discovery. He had a list of questions already prepared for Detective Stubbs and Ella Martin whenever they took the stand.

The two attorneys gathered at the judge's bench and discussed whether they would allow the tape-recorded conversation between Detective Stubbs and the so-called eyewitness, Ella Martin, at this stage of the trial. They decided not only to allow the tape-recorded conversation, but also the in-person interview the detectives had with Ella at the Colorado Springs police headquarters. The attorneys also agreed that they would allow each other the opportunity to stop the tape to ask the witness questions.

Mr. White directed his attention back to Detective Stubbs. "Before we play the audio recording, was there anything else said that we should know about before we start playing the tape?"

"Yes."

"Can you explain?"

"Yes, I asked her where she was when Sandra Brown died. She said she was on a gurney in an emergency room at a local hospital in California, having a heart attack."

The courtroom erupted in hundreds of confused voices whispering among one another from the spectators' seats. The judge beat the gavel against the sound block once again trying to regain order.

He continued, "I asked her if she could prove it. She said yes. I asked her if she had ever lived in Colorado and if she could give me a description of Sandra Brown's house. She said she had never been to Colorado and then went into great detail describing the house, both interior and exterior. That's when I decided I wanted to get it down on tape."

"From what she told you, how close was her depiction?"

"One hundred percent."

"Okay, start the tape; this is exhibit number ..." he looked down at the exhibit list, "five."

When the tape started, Ella's voice could be heard.

Rusty asked, 'Is there anything I can check that would put you inside the house the night of the crime?'

"Stop," the defense attorney said. He stood up and walked over to the stand where Detective Stubbs sat. He put one hand on his back, Napoleon fashion, and with the other he touched his chin, paused for a second, and then said, "Why did you ask her that question?"

"To tell you the truth, I still didn't believe some of the things she had told me, so I was trying to link her to the crime."

"What didn't you believe?"

"I had a hard time believing she saw all this while in the emergency room of a hospital many of hundreds of miles away. I was hoping to trip her up."

"Turn the tape back on."

The tape conversation picked up where it left off, with Ella's describing the victim setting down her purse, and the letter from Joey on the dining room table.

"Stop. Did you find the purse and the letter, and if so, was the letter sent by someone named Joey?"

"Yes, the purse was right where she said it would be." Rusty took a sip of water. "Joey is a friend, living in New York."

The bailiff pressed the start button and Rusty was asking, 'Do you know the code to the alarm?'

'No, I was too far away when he turned it off.'

'Where were you standing?'

'I was standing, or floating, behind the man in

the Pillsbury Doughboy suit.'

The crowded courtroom burst into laughter. Judge Jenkins pounded the gavel and shouted, "Order, order, order in the courtroom."

The tape continued playing through the turmoil, so the bailiff rewound the tape to just after Ella's statement had caused the commotion. Then he started it again.

'Can you repeat that?'

'I was standing behind a little man in a white laboratory suit that reminded me of the Pillsbury Doughboy. All puffed out.'

"Stop," said the prosecuting attorney. He stood and approached the witness stand. He stopped several yards away, turned and faced the jury box. "What were you thinking after her doughboy comment?"

"I thought I needed to see her in person."

"Why? Would that make a difference?"

"Oh yes, after you've done this type of work for a while, you can tell when someone is telling you the truth and when someone is telling you a lie."

"Can you clarify?"

"Yes. For example, if a person refuses to make eye contact, that's a good indication he or she may not be telling you the truth. Sweating profusely or appearing overly nervous may indicate lying. Stuttering or tapping their foot may signal deception. I'm not a psychologist and I don't claim to be, but I can usually tell when someone is not telling me the truth, especially during a face-to-face interview."

The attorney had the bailiff restart the tape.

'Could you identify the man if you saw him again?'

'Of course,' she said, 'I was close enough to count the whiskers on his chin.'

'Do you think you could work with a sketch artist to develop a composite drawing of our perpetrator?'

'Absolutely.'

'How soon could you get here?'

'I could leave tomorrow if a flight is available.'

'That would be great. I'll have our secretary make the arrangements and get back in touch with you.'

'Fine. I'm looking forward to meeting you, Detective Stubbs.'

Rusty said to the bailiff, "That's all of the telephone conversation. You can stop the tape."

The judge looked down at his watch and decided it was a good time to adjourn. He banged his gavel. "We will resume tomorrow at 9:00 a.m. Court is adjourned."

Chapter 26

I got to the courtroom early and found my place two rows behind Sally Jo Bradford, Jason's mother. She and Jason's attorney were whispering back and forth. I tried to hear what they said, but all I picked up were a couple of words: "basement" and "bones." Detective Reginald Stubbs and his partner, Detective Joe Longhorn, sat in the first row on the plaintiff side of the courtroom. Sitting between them was a woman in her mid-fifties with blonde hair.

I had studied art as an elective in high school for several years and was good enough to get a job during summer break working in a Denver mall doing colored pencil portraits. This was my first time reporting from inside a courtroom. The first day of the trial, there were four of us; today, there were eight. News travels fast and news of Ella Martin, the psychic, taking the stand, brought in news organizations from all over the state. Most of the media were outside with cameras waiting to get a picture of her as she left the courthouse.

I wasn't sure if Ella was the one seated between Detective Stubbs and his partner. But if it was, I didn't want to miss the opportunity to draw the two or three of them together, even if it was from behind and at a slight angle.

On a couple of occasions, I thought she actually noticed me. She looked over her shoulder in my direction and I thought our eyes locked on each other for just a brief second — it may have been my imagination. I drew as fast as I could. When I was done, I was quite impressed with the results, especially after not having used my artistic skill in a long time.

The gavel hit the sound block and the trial was in its second day.

The first person called to the stand was Detective Stubbs. A second tape was introduced as evidence. This tape consisted of both audio and video, with added text running across the bottom of the screen for the hearing impaired. The video showed a picture of the witness, Ella Martin, sitting on a small couch on the opposite side of the room from the two detectives. I was right. The woman I drew in my picture was Ella Martin.

Before playing the video, the tall attorney had the bailiff pause it so he could ask Detective Stubbs a few questions about his interrogation technique. Then the bailiff turned the video back on and the two attorneys decided to let it play in its entirety without asking Stubbs any more questions.

The second tape started out with Ella Martin stating her name, age, and social security number. For the next hour, I watched the videotape and listened to Ella tell the detectives how she died, went to Heaven, and returned to Earth. How she witnessed the murder of Sandra Brown. She went through every detail. What the killer looked like, where he hid behind the house, how he attacked the woman from behind. And how he eventually beat her to death.

I noticed Jason's mother head drop down, as if she were praying. But I don't think she was. I think she was embarrassed. I was sure that most of the people in the courtroom had no idea who she was. Or that her name was Sally.

The tape continued with Ella describing the angel spirit she witnessed and how it whispered something in the victim's ear.

When Ella said the woman responded, 'Thank you, Lord,' I heard someone cry out, "Thank you, Lord. Thank you. Thank you! Thank you for taking my daughter." I knew who it was; it was Sandra Brown's father. Sandra Brown's mother didn't say a word, she remained silent, sitting beside her husband, staring off into space.

Ella spoke again, describing the final moments of the woman's life in gruesome detail.

I looked around the courtroom in search of a dry eye but had a hard time spotting one.

Then Ella added, 'I got the impression that this wasn't the first time he had done this.'

"Stop the tape!" the defense attorney shouted. The bailiff stopped the tape. "Objection, may I have that entire last line stricken from the testimony, starting where she says, 'I got the impression …'"

"Sustained," said the judge.

They waited for the court reporter to make a correction, then the judge nodded to the defense attorney.

"Go ahead. Play the tape," said Mr. Preston.

The tape ended with Detective Longhorn asking if Ella could remember anything else of importance.

When she mentioned that the man lit his cigarette with a Zippo lighter and had a tattoo of a happy face on his right hand between his thumb and index finger, I watched Jason suddenly place his right hand in his lap out of the jury's view.

Jason sat in his chair staring at the woman in the video. He was numb from the information the mid-aged woman fed the detectives. He wondered how she could possibly be so correct. He hadn't seen anyone in the street and or the back yard, although he remembered having the oddest feeling when he reached the woman's driveway. And a couple of times inside the house he thought he was being watched. He wondered what else she knew. *Did she know what he did with his cleaning supplies?*

When the taped interview was over the judge looked at his watch and decided it was a good time to break for lunch and said court was adjourned.

~~~

After lunch, the bailiff called Detective Stubbs back to the witness stand and reminded him that he was still under oath.

The defense attorney started out the afternoon session by asking Rusty, "After interviewing Ms. Martin, what did you do?"

"We drove to the victim's house."

"Why?"

"So Ella could walk us through what she said she saw the night of the crime. If we had done the walk-through before the interview, she could have made it up as she went along. This way, if she saw what she said she saw, the narrative should remain the same as what she said in the interview. Plus, we needed to know which glass he supposedly touched."

"I see. You have it all on videotape?"

"Yes."

Mr. White looked at the bailiff. "Could you play exhibit number fourteen."

The video began with Detective Joe Longhorn standing in the street where the white car had parked, according to Ella Martin. Behind him was a green house with a screened-in porch, the address of the house in plain view.

The camera followed Detective Longhorn and Ella up the driveway to the back yard as she reenacted what happened in the order in which it happened. She pointed out where the little man sat down his duffel bag and how he dashed behind the hedge when the car drove up the driveway. She played the woman's part until she was knocked unconscious and then played the part of the killer, doing everything he did the night of the crime. The tape showed her stop and point at a kitchen cabinet where she said the man put the water glass he touched.

The courtroom watched as the detective swung open the door and Ella pointed at one of three identical glasses lined up in the front row. Detective Longhorn put the glass in an evidence bag, and then the tape continued following Ella through the house to the bathroom.

The camera showed her mimic the man looking in the mirror and then shifted, showing the tissue holder she pointed at and the small trash can on the floor beside the commode. Next, it showed Joe reach in and remove a lone tissue at the bottom of the can.

Not a peep was uttered during the entire viewing.

When the tape ran out, the prosecuting attorney said, "The tape explains everything, you, the men and women of the jury need to know. I have only a couple of questions for the witness.

"Did you check with Ms. Martin's employer to find out if she was of sound mind, not subject to exaggerate or make up stories?"

"Yes. I did. Not exactly in those terms, but close. Her boss said she was an upstanding citizen who wouldn't deliberately say something that wasn't true."

"How about her doctor; did you talk with him to corroborate her statement?"

"Yes, I did."

The prosecutor had no further questions for the detective and asked for the right to recall the witness later.

The judge adjusted his green bow tie and said, "Granted." Then he looked over at Mr. Preston. "Would the defense like to cross-examine?"

The defense attorney didn't care what was on the tape. He'd seen it during Discovery. As far as he was concerned it was all complete nonsense and could be easily dismissed as fantasy. To prove his client did what he was accused of doing, the prosecution would have to prove that their witness left her body, and later returned, otherwise it was all theory, speculation. He didn't believe in ghosts, except for the ones who showed up on his doorstep Halloween night; if you couldn't prove there was such a thing, then it didn't exist.

The defense decided it was a good time to clear up a few things before they went any further. Jason's attorney stood up and put his hand on his client's shoulder. "When you rummaged through my client's apartment, did you have a search warrant?"

"Yes."

"What did it say you could look for?"

Rusty knew the question was coming at some time during the trial, so he brought a copy of the search warrant with him. He opened a folder, found the warrant and begin reading out loud, 'Duffel bag and whatever is inside, handcuffs, duct tape, a blunt object, computers, and other electronic equipment.'

"Is that all? Of all the items on your list, was there anything that you removed from my client's property? Anything of importance?"

"Well, that all depends on what you consider important."

"Yes or no, Detective? Did you remove anything from his residence?"

"No, we didn't remove anything from his

residence, but we did find two items listed on the warrant in his vehicle."

"Let me make sure I have this right. You didn't remove anything from his apartment. Is that correct?"

"Yes, not that I recall."

"Well then, let me refresh your memory. Does a tissue ring a bell? According to what I read during Discovery, your partner removed a tissue — illegally obtained, mind you — from my client's bathroom trash can without his permission or knowledge. And had it analyzed, tested to see if it matched a tissue found at the victim's house. Does that sound familiar?"

"Why yes, now that you mention it. It had slipped my mind."

"Yes, I'm sure it did. And wasn't that link the reason you arrested my client? Because of the similarity."

"Yes, but there was no likeness; it was an identical match."

"Possibly planted there by your partner."

"But later I took care of that issue … I …"

"Not now, Detective. We'll go over that in a minute. Let's just finish with the search warrant served at my client's place. What else did you take?"

"We found a Rolling Stones CD in his car and a computer. That's it."

"Okay, let's move on. You said you took care of the issue. What issue?"

"The *tissue*, issue."

"Explain?"

"After we had got back positive results, I realized the way we got the tissue from Mr. Bradford's place might cause a problem. I decided to go to his place to see if I could stake out the rear of his apartment, where the trash receptacle is found, and possibly catch him dumping a bag."

"And—"

"And while I was there checking it out, he happened to come out of his apartment with a white trash bag and tossed it in the dumpster. I caught it all on video."

"Is that tape available?"

"Yes."

"Can we play it?"

Detective Stubbs handed it to the bailiff, who put it in a player and pressed the start button.

The tape showed the detective catching Jason midway between his apartment and the trash container. Then it showed Jason throwing a white trash bag into the large receptacle, his bag — the only white bag in view — rested on top of all the others, never out of the camera's sight.

The camera remained running and continued to record Jason leave the dumpster and return to his apartment. Then it captured Detective Stubbs leave his car and walk to the dumpster. It showed his hand reach in and remove the bag, never losing sight of it. Then, it showed him fumble around with one hand trying to open the bag. Finally, it showed him open it up showing the contents, which included many cigarette filters and crumpled up Kleenex.

The tape showed the detective pick up the bag and put it in the trunk of his car. Then the camera went dead.

The tall, lanky attorney knew all about the tape. He'd watched it and read about it in Detective Stubbs' report. He also knew the detective had come from an unidentified doctor's office before driving over to his client's apartment. So he asked, "Where were you coming from when you decided to visit Mr. Bradford's place?"

"I'd just left my doctor's office. Nothing planned. It was a spur-of-the-moment thing."

"What kind of doctor were you seeing?"

Detective Stubbs frowned when he heard the question.

The prosecutor jumped to his feet. "Objection!"

The tall attorney knew he'd hit a nerve.

"I'll allow it," said the judge. He turned to the detective. "Answer the question."

"What difference does that make?"

"I'm asking the questions, Mr. Stubbs, not you!"

Rusty looked at the judge for help but got none. He answered, "Psychiatrist."

Mr. Preston knew he'd just struck gold. He asked, "For what reason?"

Rusty said, "I don't think I have to answer that question since my therapist wouldn't have to tell you why he was treating me!"

"So be it," said Jason's attorney. He got more out of it than he'd expected. Now the jury would wonder why he wouldn't answer the question, what he was afraid of or hiding. The attorney knew that sometimes the littlest things could play on a juror's mind.

"Okay, let's move on a smidgen to the next step in your investigation. To the time when you served a search warrant at my client's mother's house. Do you remember that? Or has that somehow slipped your mind?"

"Yes, of course I remember it."

"What were you looking for at Mrs. Bradford's house?"

"The same items we were looking for at her son's place, except we added a generic white car, model and year not identified on the warrant."

"How many people did you invite to help ransack Mrs. Bradford's residence?"

Rusty didn't like the way the angular attorney described what they did, but knew it was all part of the show to vilify the police, to make them look like the bad guys as often as the defense could.

"Can you name them, so we know who they were?"

"Detective Joe Longhorn, Crime Scene Investigator Bobbi Bidwell, and three police officers just out of the academy." He scanned down his notes. "Smith, Jones, and Watson."

"That's just great. You had three rookies with you digging through her stuff."

"No, they were there strictly as observers. They could look, but not touch."

"What did you find?"

"We recovered a small bat, similar to what Ms.

Martin said she saw the killer use to beat the victim to death."

He held up exhibit number two. "Are you talking about this?" He pointed at the photograph in the lower portion of the picture. "That looks like it might have been a bat at one time?"

"Yes," Rusty said, not sure where the attorney was taking him.

"Where did you find the bat?"

"Ms. Bidwell found it in a burn barrel in the back yard."

He walked over to the jury box and stared at the cowboy. "Do you remember what I told you during my opening statement? About having something you no longer found useful and deciding to throw it away. And if you recall I said if no DNA was found on the bat, then you had nothing to base your case on." He turned away from the jury box and faced Detective Stubbs. "Did you find any DNA on the bat?"

"No, we didn't."

The lanky attorney put exhibit number two underneath his arm and wrung his hands together as if to say, *Okay, now that we're done with that!*

Then he lumbered over to the easel and set exhibit number two back on its stand. "So, what's next? What else did you find, Detective?"

"We found a car that matched the description of a vehicle seen at the crime scene."

"Are you talking about your so-called eyewitness? Or are you talking about the elderly woman who wears glasses and lives across the street from the victim's house?"

"Both."

"Let's see." Mr. Preston pulled out a copy of the courtroom transcripts, recorded from the previous day. "May I approach?" he asked the judge as he carried it in his hands like an open book.

"Yes, granted."

The attorney handed Stubbs the transcript. "Detective, will you read for the court, the last paragraph on the right-hand side of the page, where it starts out: 'The car was white.'"

Detective Stubbs started reading, "'The car was white, maybe a Buick or an Oldsmobile. It was an older model, probably late 1980s. I couldn't read the license plate. It was completely covered with snow.'"

"Okay, you can stop now. Is this," he held up exhibit number one, "the exact picture of the car parked in the garage at Mr. Bradford's mother's house?"

"No."

"Why not?"

"Because we didn't have an ignition key to move the car out of the garage; we couldn't get a good photo of the car from the angle we had available. So we blew up a photo of a similar car, the same make, model, year, white, with the same pin striping."

The defense attorney turned to face the jury and asked, "Do you remember when I told you if I were a betting man I'd bet that I could find at least ten other cars here in Colorado Springs that matched the one spotted near the crime scene?" He turned to face the detective again. "Let's see, you have a witness who saw a white car. Wasn't sure if it was a Buick or an Oldsmobile, but she knew it was an older model, probably late 1980s. Let's dissect that word, Detective."

The angular attorney pulled out a thesaurus, thumbed through the text until he found what he was looking for and read, "'Probably,' 'almost certainly,' 'most likely,' 'in all probability,' 'perhaps,' 'maybe,' 'possibly.' I don't hear anything that resembles the words 'definitely,' 'absolutely,' 'positively,' 'unquestionably,' 'without a doubt,' or 'undeniably.' Do you, Detective?"

Stubbs didn't answer because it wasn't really a question. The defense attorney was grandstanding for the jury. He'd gotten his point across. They didn't have proof the car in the garage at Sally Bradford's house was the same car seen at the scene of the crime.

The defense attorney shook his head. "I have no further questions to ask Detective Stubbs now, Your Honor."

Stubbs returned to the front row seats where the other witnesses were waiting to take the witness stand.

The prosecutor called his next witness. Ella Martin took the stand. She was wearing a blue business suit and was ready for anything the two attorneys could throw at her. She was sworn in, smiled for the camera, and felt right at home answering questions about her out-of-body experience.

"Please state your name for the court."

"Ella Mae Martin."

"How old are you, and what do you do for a living?"

"I'm fifty-five and retired."

"When did you retire?"

"I retired December of last year."

"What kind of work did you do?"

"I was a legal secretary for a large law firm." She went through some of her duties at the request of the prosecuting attorney.

"What do you do now to keep yourself busy?"

"I donate most of my time to the poor. Three days a week I serve food at a mission in downtown Los Angeles. I also spend time at several nursing homes. And occasionally I participate in seminars sponsored by doctors at different hospitals."

"When you say you participate, what are you asked to do?"

"Lecture. I'm asked to share an out-of-body experience I had after suffering a heart attack."

"How much are you paid for your..." he hesitated, trying to find the right word, "... involvement?"

"Nothing. I do it free-of-charge."

"Have you ever been offered anything monetarily?"

"Yes."

"Are you independently wealthy?"

She laughed. "I should say not. I have enough

to get by. That's all."

The prosecutor wanted to make sure everyone in the courtroom understood she was not speaking at these conferences for personal gain.

"When you talk about your out-of-body experience, do you usually include witnessing a murder?"

"No, I leave that part out."

"Why?"

"Because Detective Stubbs asked me not to talk about it."

"No one knows about it back in California?"

"My doctors, Dr. Henderson and Dr. Alexander, are the only ones I've told. I told Dr. Henderson what happened shortly after I reentered my body."

"Objection," said the defense attorney. "Pure speculation; she doesn't know she left her body. That's only an assumption made by her."

"Overruled," said the judge. "I'm going to allow her to continue. If I didn't, she might as will take a seat, because it's all speculation."

"Okay, Ella, would you tell the court the whole story, starting the day before the murder when you first started having indigestion?"

Ella was allowed to go through her story without an interruption.

The prosecutor wanted the jury to hear the whole story without him butting in with confusing questions. The defense didn't care about the witness; he just wanted to put some doubt in the minds of the jury before she had even begun, to discredit her testimony. It was nothing personal. It was his job and he was good at planting doubt. His expert witnesses all had Ph.D.s.

After telling her story, the court recessed until early afternoon without a single question asked by either attorney.

Chapter 27

Outside during recess, a good number of people gathered on the courthouse steps. A few carried signs; one read, THERE IS NO GOD. Twenty feet away, two more people held up signs; one message read, GOD IS LOVE and the other, EVERYONE GOES TO HEAVEN.

When the trial resumed, I noticed someone seated in one of the chairs reserved for witnesses. He was a small, good-looking man, probably in his late fifties or early sixties, with blue eyes and silver hair. He reminded me of one of my English professors.

The prosecution called its first expert witness. The man with the blue eyes and silver hair stood up and took a seat to the left of the judge. His name was Dr. Melvin Slocum.

After being sworn in, Mr. White asked the doctor to give a brief description of his work. He smiled, and with a voice soft yet full of life, he said, "I'm a psychiatrist. For the past twenty years, my work has focused primarily on people who claim to have had a near-death-experience, known as an NDE. I have authored seven books on the topic of near-death and have written many articles for scientific and medical study. I have interviewed more than four thousand people who have claimed to have experienced this phenomenon. My research has led me to believe there are nine common features to the near-death-experience."

"Where were you while our witness, Ella Martin was describing her near-death-experience?"

"I was on the road somewhere between here and Denver."

"So, you know nothing about her testimony? Her experience? Would that be correct?"

"Correct."

"Would you please explain to the court the similarities in the near-death experience?"

"Certainly. Some people hear a buzzing or ringing tone in their ears. Those who advance beyond the auditory noise may feel great pain that is suddenly relieved as soon as they separate from their body. They sometimes talk about seeing a medical team working on them. Some speak of being in a spiritual body — a living, glowing, energy field. Next, they may feel the sensation of leaving Earth by either floating away or traveling through a tunnel or tube at an amazing rate of speed. In either case, they eventually come to a complete halt. Some say they meet with an old friend or relative that had passed on."

Dr. Slocum stopped briefly and took a sip of water. Then he smiled and continued. "If they go beyond this point, they usually talk about meeting a being of light. Some call the being of light an angel. Others say it is Jesus they meet on the other side. Many of those who get this far go through a life review of everything they have ever done."

I don't know if it was a coincidence, or if it was something the doctor said, but suddenly the judge shifted in his chair and reached for a tissue to sponge his forehead, causing enough disturbance for the doctor to pause until he was done.

Then the judge looked at the doctor. "Sorry! You can continue."

"They see themselves from birth to death, every act, good and bad. They don't feel as if they are judged. Afterward, they feel that love is the only important thing in life. Last, most are told they must return to their body. Sometimes they are given a choice to stay or return. After returning to their bodies, most of these folks spend the rest of their lives either devoting their time to the church or helping others less fortunate than themselves."

I watched the expression on each face in the jury box as the doctor spoke about the similarities. He mentioned more than nine. I couldn't help but think they must have noticed the parallel between what the doctor said and what Ella Martin described in her NDE. They were almost indistinguishable, except I don't recall Ella ever saying she heard a ringing or buzzing in her ears.

"Doctor, are you a religious man?" Mr. White asked.

"No. Not really."

"What does 'not really' mean?"

"It means I don't attend a church or belong to

any particular religious organization. I am not a believer or unbeliever. I would consider myself an agnostic."

"Can you, for the jury's benefit, define the word agnostic?"

"Sure. An agnostic is a person who believes there can be no proof of the existence of God but does not deny the possibility that God exists. Agnostic means unknown."

"Dr. Slocum, what would it take for you to believe that an NDE actually occurred?"

"If the experiencer described events occurring elsewhere in a place far removed from the physical body of the experiencer, I would consider that to be proof. The only evidence we have to suggest that an out-of-the-body, OBE, has ever occurred is from remote viewing, and the person doing the viewing is in no way dead during the experience."

"What If I told you one of my witnesses had such an experience?" The attorney went through a quick narration of Ella Martin's near-death-experience for Dr. Slocum.

"Well, if it's verifiable, if this event actually occurred, then I would say it's in a class of its own. I would love to hear the whole story in its entirety where I could ask the experiencer questions."

"Thank you, Dr. Slocum. I have no further questions," said Attorney White.

The defense attorney saw an opening, a mistake made by the prosecution, and decided not to let the opportunity go to waste. He stood up and began his cross-examination. "Dr. Slocum, the prosecution just finished telling an incredible tale. One, in fact, if true, might prove the existence of an afterlife. Surely this would be the most important scientific discovery of all time. Would you agree with that statement, Dr. Slocum?"

"Yes, I suppose I would."

"More important than finding a cure for cancer?"

"Yes, more important than finding a cure for cancer."

"I was told as a kid, if it's too good to be true, it probably isn't. You said you studied four thousand cases of people who claimed to have experienced an NDE. None of those cases even come close to this woman's statement, do they, Doctor?"

"No, they don't."

"I have no more questions for this witness."

Next in line was a neurosurgeon named Dr. William Jobe.

"Dr. Jobe, would you consider yourself one of the leading neurosurgeons in hypothermic cardiac arrest?" asked Mr. White.

"Yes."

"Would you mind giving a brief description on the procedure?"

"No, I wouldn't. The procedure is usually performed on patients who have a basilar artery aneurysm in their brain. We reduce the patient's body temperature to 60 degrees. The heartbeat and breathing stop. All brain-wave activity ceases to exist. We drain the blood out of the head. The patient is now considered dead or in standstill. After we remove the aneurysm, we restore life to the body."

"Thank you, Doctor. How long is the patient in "standstill?"

"The procedure itself usually requires roughly thirty minutes to complete. That's how long the patient is in standstill."

"Worst case, how long could the patient last in this condition?"

"I don't know, we've never gone beyond one hour, so I can't tell you how long anyone could survive."

"You recently performed this operation on a patient who experienced an NDE. Is that true?"

"Yes."

"Can you describe for the court what she told you after recovering from surgery?"

"Yes, she said while I was cutting through her skull, she felt herself 'pop' and she was outside her body, hovering above the operating table. She said she watched for a while. She described the tool I use perfectly. She said it sounded like an electric toothbrush."

The doctor removed a tool connected to a flexible steel cord from a black case. "This is the tool she was describing." He plugged it into an adjustable speed foot switch and then into an outlet hidden behind the witness stand. He pushed down on the switch and the saw began to move in a reciprocating, back-and-forth manner. The faster the blade moved, the more it sounded like a toothbrush.

"What else did she describe that was accurate?"

"She mentioned seeing the monitors registering

no life and hearing some of the conversation taking place between the doctors and staff."

"How many people are on your team when you perform this procedure?"

"Usually two brain surgeons, a cardiac surgery team, three anesthesiologists, and as many as a dozen nurses and technicians. It's a crowded environment."

"How long have you been performing this procedure?"

"I think the first time I performed this procedure was 1990."

"You have many years of experience?"

"Yes."

"I have no other questions for this witness, Your Honor."

The defense attorney stood and faced the jury box. "That's all fine and dandy, but it doesn't prove that it happened. While the good doctor was relating his patient's story, I went on the Internet and pulled up a picture of a tool that looks a lot like the apparatus the doctor showed you."

He walked back to the defense table and picked up a piece of paper he'd printed out. He asked the judge if he could approach the witness stand. The judge granted the request. He carried the paper over to where the witness sat and handed him the picture he'd just printed. Then he said, "Doctor, is this the same instrument, or is it used for the same purpose as the instrument you demonstrated for the jury?"

"Actually, it's a newer version. The one I showed the jury was the same model I used during the operation that I performed on the patient who'd experienced the NDE."

"Before you perform the surgery, do you explain the procedure thoroughly to the patient?

"Yes, of course!"

"Could they go on the Internet and find out all about it on their own?"

"Yes, that information is available. I sometimes encourage my patients to do just that. Their own research, so they know all there is to know about the procedure before we begin."

"So then, it's possible the patient knew what the tool looked like before you started the surgery?"

"Yes, it's possible."

"Thank you, Dr. Jobe; I have no more questions for this witness."

I thought the rebuttal went well. It was obvious that the tall defense attorney was trying to instill some doubt into the minds of the jurors.

The prosecuting attorney decided he had no choice but to bring forth the witness who had experienced the NDE. She was smart; maybe she could salvage some of the harm already done.

Her name was Gloria Stern. She was tall, thin with red-brown hair, worn long over her shoulder. She was in her early forties and had light freckles covering her nose and cheekbone area. She described herself as an English teacher who liked to write poetry. She said she was married and had two teenage daughters.

Attorney White started his direct by asking, "Did you know what the tool looked like to open your head before the surgery?"

She replied, "Heavens, no. That would have scared the daylights out of me. The only information I had before the surgery was how long the procedure would take and what to expect afterward during recovery."

"Dr. Jobe did not talk about your adventure while he was on the witness stand. Only that you told him you had an out-of-body experience. He said you described the tool he used during the surgery. He also said you overheard some of their conversation while sedated. Can you tell the people in the courtroom what you remember when you were out of your body?"

"Sure. First, I 'popped' out of my body and floated around the room. Then I was looking over the doctor's shoulder. I was always under the impression all my hair would be cut off before surgery but it wasn't. Only some of it! I asked the doctor in recovery *why* they didn't cut it all off. He was surprised that I knew what my head looked like because I was sedated when they removed my hair. It was gone only on one side of my head and when I woke up in recovery, my head was bandaged. Also, during surgery I heard one of the nurses complaining about the size of my veins. I should have warned them that they were small before my surgery, but I didn't ..."

She took a sip of water and continued with her story. "I soon got bored of watching the surgery and felt compelled to leave. I was drawn away, slowly at first, then I began to pick up speed. I went through this shaft or tunnel and at the far end, I could see a speck of light. The light was bright.

Brighter that anything I'd ever seen before, but it didn't hurt my eyes. Soon I was aware of other light forms. Not the same as the speck that seemed to grow brighter the closer I got, but these other light forms were taking a human shape. Soon they were recognizable. I knew all of them. They were my relatives and friends who had already passed over. One relative in particular surprised me. It was my Uncle Pete. We were never close. I didn't know that he had died. I later confirmed that with his mother who is still alive …"

She took another sip of water and brushed her hair back away from her eye. Then she continued, "… I wanted to stay. But I was told I couldn't. I felt wonderful. I didn't want to leave. My uncle took me by the hand and led me back through the tunnel, back to the hospital, and told me to get back into my body. My body looked terrible; it was a bluish color and looked dead. I guess it looked dead because I was dead. My uncle gave me a push and I returned to my body. It felt like jumping into ice water. The next thing I remember was waking up in recovery."

The prosecutor had no more questions for the witness and turned the floor over to the defense, who declined to cross-examine. The prosecutor then recalled Dr. Jobe to the stand. "Dr. Jobe, is there a clinical test that can determine brain death?"

"Yes. There are three different methods we use to determine brain death. First, a standard electroencephalogram, or EEG, measures brain wave activity. A 'flat' EEG indicates a non-functioning cerebral cortex or the outer portion of the cerebrum. Second, we can measure brain-stem viability, the same way we did during Gloria's surgery. We evoked auditory potentials (clicks) using ear speakers. An absence of these potentials indicates a non-functioning brain stem. And third, the documentation of no blood flow to the brain."

"How many of those did your patient meet during her surgery?"

"All three. Her electroencephalogram was silent; her brain-stem response was nonexistent, with no blood flowing through her brain. Still, in this state, she experienced something, something we in the medical field do not know how to measure."

The judge excused the doctor, who took his seat next to his former patient, Gloria Stern. Then the prosecuting attorney went through a parade of witnesses, all who claimed to have had out-of-body experiences. One of these was of particular interest. The person was male. He was in his late forties. He was undergoing a quadruple bypass at the time of his NDE. He later reported to his surgeon that he'd watched him place his hands under his armpits and flap his elbows like a duck getting out of the water. The man had thick gauze pads taped over his eyes during the entire operation. His doctor confirmed the elbow flapping took place. It was a way for him to relax, and nothing that his staff or medical team ever talked about.

The defense attorney did not cross-examine any of the witnesses. He had his own expert witnesses waiting to take the stand.

The court was adjourned for the remainder the day.

I watched as Ella Martin left the courtroom. The crowd outside had grown into the hundreds …

all wanting to get a good look at the woman who said she'd crossed over. Detective Stubbs led her down the courthouse steps and into a waiting police car.

Chapter 28

It was about now that I decided Jason wasn't the only one on trial. I hadn't heard his name mentioned since early the day before. A religious belief was on trial: a belief in an afterlife. A belief that does not rest on logical proof or material evidence.

The prosecution was trying to prove that a person could leave his or her body, travel to a distant place, and return with full memory of the event. So far, the experts who testified for the prosecution did a good job showing the similarities between those who claimed to have had an out-of-body experience. But me … the skeptic … I needed more than someone telling me they visited the other side, I needed tangible proof.

Day three of the trial began with the prosecutor calling yet another expert to testify. His name was Dr. Leo Mann, and like all the others, he had a Ph.D. after his name. He'd published a report based on a study he'd done on whether religion played a role in what a near-death experiencer saw while out-of-body.

The prosecutor asked Dr. Mann if he could explain the results of his study to the jury.

"Yes, of course. First off, what I did was to place the experiencer into a group according to his or her belief. The groups consisted of five categories: Christian; non-Christian but religious; new age advocates; agnostics, and atheists."

"And the results?" asked White.

"First let's look at the five groups as a whole," he said. He began reading a long list of variables he'd found in his study: "Those feeling overwhelming love: 69 percent. Mental telepathy: 65 percent. Life reviews: 62 percent. God: 56 percent. Ecstasy: 56 percent. Unlimited knowledge: 46 percent. Afterlife/different levels: 46 percent. Told not ready: 46 percent. Shown the future: 44 percent. Tunnel: 42 percent. Jesus: 37 percent. Forgotten knowledge: 31 percent. Fear: 27 percent. Homecoming: 21 percent. Told of past lives: 21 percent. Hell: 19 percent. City of Lights: 17 percent. Temple of Knowledge: 13 percent. Spirits among the living: 10 percent. Suicide: 6 percent. And the Devil: 0 percent.

"Then I looked at each group independently and the results amazed me. I hypothesized I would see a wide swing between religious believers and nonbelievers, but I was wrong, there wasn't. They all went through a similar experience.

"Seventy-five percent of the Christians said they felt an overwhelming love. Interestingly enough, 75 percent of the atheists responded in the same manner. The lowest percentage was the new age advocates with 60 percent."

He quickly went through mental telepathy: "The new age folks scored the highest percentage here, with 80 percent. The lowest was the agnostics, with 50 percent. Next, he gave his statistics on God, ecstasy, unlimited knowledge, afterlife levels, etc., until he went through all the elements.

When he finished, the prosecuting attorney thanked him for his time and turned the floor over to the defense for cross-examination.

Jason's attorney asked the expert witness if he would repeat two of the elements. "Doctor, could you please repeat your findings for unlimited knowledge and seeing the future?"

"Yes, sure. As a whole, 49 percent said they experienced unlimited knowledge, while 44 percent said they got to look into the future."

"So, if I were to ask someone in your test group who scored higher on either one of the aforementioned categories, would he or she be able to tell me the winning numbers in the next state lottery or the winning horse in the fifth race at Arapahoe Park on Friday?"

"No, of course not. They only said they had the ability while they were out of their body."

"Thank you, Dr. Mann. I have no further questions."

More came and more went until the morning session was over. The afternoon started out with the prosecution calling Sally Jo Bradford to the stand. She wore a blue dress with high heels. Her hair was short, cut in the latest style. She looked ten years younger than her age.

I drew fast, catching her and the judge in the

same sketch. She smiled, the camera liked her face; she didn't seem the least bit nervous. Her son sat looking down at the defense table. He didn't appear too eager to make eye contact with her. The prosecutor asked if she could recall the day the two detectives served the search warrant. She smiled again, looked over at her son, and nodded.

The prosecutor said, "For the record, Mrs. Bradford, you need to say either yes or no. The court reporter needs a verbal response. A physical response is not entered into our documentation."

"Yes. I remember."

"Thank you. What do you remember telling Detective Stubbs when he asked you what time Jason arrived at your house on the night Sandra Brown died?"

"I don't recall."

"Here, let me refresh your memory." He asked the judge if he could approach. The judge granted his request, and the prosecuting attorney handed the witness a copy of Rusty's report.

"Here, the top paragraph on the right-hand side of the page. You see where it says, 'It was early. I know that because he was down in the basement while I was cooking dinner. It was some time before five o'clock.'"

"Yes, I said that."

"Do you recall your response when he asked, 'What time did you see him leave?'"

She looked down at the report. "I didn't, but I do now." She read from Detective Stubbs's report: 'Now that I'm absolutely sure of because he woke me up at 11:00 p.m., so I could go to bed.'"

The courtroom burst out in laughter at her comment. Judge Jenkins beat his gavel against the sound block trying to reestablish order in the court.

After the courtroom quieted down, the prosecutor said, "Is that what you said?"

"Yes."

"Next, he asked, 'Where were you?' Is that right?"

"Yes, I guess so."

"Would you please read your response out loud for the court?"

"Yes." She read, 'I was in the big recliner, right there in the living room, watching TV. I know what time it was because Jason woke me up at the end of *Law and Order* so I could go to bed. Just like he always does. So he had to have been here.'"

"Was that your statement?"

"Yes, I think that's correct."

"So, exactly when was the last time you saw Jason on the night in question before he woke you up to go to bed?"

"Let's see. It would have been when he came upstairs to get his food. Sometime around 5:30 p.m."

"That was the last time?"

"Yes. I guess so."

"I have no further questions, Your Honor."

The tall defense attorney stood. "Mrs. Bradford, are you sure you said what the detective said you said?"

"Well, I'm not absolutely sure; after all, it was

over six months ago. But I don't think the detective would lie about it, do you?"

"I have no further questions."

Bobbi Bidwell was recalled to the stand by the prosecution. On redirect the prosecuting attorney asked, "Ms. Bidwell, please tell the court how you came across Mr. Bradford's laptop computer."

"Yes. I got it from Detective Stubbs."

"Do you know where he got it from?"

"Yes. He seized it during a search of the defendant's property."

"Was it taken from his living space or elsewhere?"

"I believe it was found in the trunk of his car."

"Did you find anything of importance on it?"

"Yes."

"What was that?"

"We recovered a map to the victim's house."

"Where did the directions originate from? From what address to what address?"

"The starting point was Mrs. Bradford's home and ended at the victim's house. I'm sorry, I don't recall either address."

The well-dressed attorney turned the floor back over to the defense attorney.

"Ms. Bidwell, is there a possibility that one of the detectives could have looked that information up on the computer before they gave it to you?"

"Yes, I guess so."

"Do you know when that information was originally searched?"

"No, I don't. But I could get —"

"Thank you, Ms. Bidwell. I have no further questions, Your Honor."

It was getting late in the afternoon, but the prosecution wanted to get one more witness on the stand before they adjourned for the day. Mr. White called Mrs. Moore to the stand. She was short, overweight, in her seventies, wearing a dress from the late 50s era. She seemed a little bewildered as she waddled to the stand and the bailiff swore her in.

The prosecutor smiled, realizing she was overwhelmed by the process. He asked her if she was comfortable, or if he could get her anything before they started.

"Water," she said. "May I have a glass of water?"

He had the bailiff pour her a glass, and once he thought she was relaxed, he began his examination. "Mrs. Moore, I want you to think back, back to the night Ms. Brown was murdered. What were you doing on that particular night?"

"I was at home watching television."

"Was anyone with you?"

"No, I was alone."

"What did you see on that night?"

"I saw a white car parked in front of my house."

"Did you see anyone get out of that vehicle?"

"Yes, I saw a person wearing a hooded jacket or sweatshirt."

"What did the person do?"

"Opened the trunk and removed a large bag."

Mr. White held up a gym bag. "Like this?"

"No. Much bigger!"

He held up a duffel bag and asked, "Was it more like this?"

The defense attorney yelled, "Objection; he's leading the witness."

"Sustained," ruled the judge.

The prosecutor put the two bags side by side and said, "Which one of these two bags looks more like the bag you saw the person remove from the car?"

"It looked like the one that's the larger of the two."

"He held up the duffel bag. "This one?"

"Yes. It looked a lot like that one."

The prosecutor held up a photo marked exhibit number one. "Would this picture be a good representation of the car you saw on that evening?"

"Yes."

The prosecutor had no other questions for Mrs. Moore and turned it over to the defense.

"Mrs. Moore, what time of the evening was it when you saw a white car parked in front of your house?"

"It was sometime after 7:00 p.m."

"So, it was dark out? Is that correct?"

"Yes, it was dark out."

"Why did you look out the window?"

"I wanted to see if it was still snowing."

"Was it?"

"Yes."

"After the car parked and the person got out, could you see if the person was a male or a female?"

"I couldn't tell if it was a man or women. I couldn't see their face."

"Was the person tall or short?"

She looked at the defendant. "Short."

"So there was a good chance the person you saw was a woman?"

"Maybe. I don't know."

"Right, you don't know!"

"Could you be mistaken about the car?"

"Oh no, I'm sure about the car."

He handed her six photographs of different automobiles. "Of these six pictures, which car looks like the one you saw that night?"

She studied the photos carefully before answering. Then held up one and said, "I believe this one."

All the photos shown to her were from a different angle from what she would have seen that evening. The photo she identified was a silver Oldsmobile, 1989, with no pin striping.

He held up the photo of the Oldsmobile. "Please note that Mrs. Moore identified a silver 1989 Oldsmobile Cutlass. He held up another photo. "This is a picture of a 1988 Buick Regal. This picture she did not identify. The car in this picture is identical to the one parked in the defendant's mother's garage, except for the color. The one in this picture is blue."

"Mrs. Moore, in Detective Stubbs' report you said you were wearing your glasses on that evening; is that correct?"

"Yes, that's correct."

"When was the last time you had your eyes examined?"

"Oh, it's been awhile, probably about five years."

The defense attorney, with the help of his assistant, wanted to give Mrs. Moore an eye examination. The prosecutor objected to the test but was overruled.

The defense attorney's assistant walked to the back of the courtroom and held up a 5" x 6" card. On the card was a large three-inch letter 'E.' The defense attorney asked, "Mrs. Moore can you read the letter on the card my assistant is holding up in the back of the courtroom?"

She studied the card for a few second and then said, "It looks like an 'F' or 'E' or maybe an eight."

"Thank you, Mrs. Moore. I have no further questions."

Chapter 29

After court had adjourned for the day, Rusty sat staring at the flames leaping from the fake log inside the gas-burning fireplace at Dr. Wasserman's office. The doctor had asked Rusty questions about his past, starting with his childhood and working his way toward the present. Each month Rusty revealed a little more. Over the past couple of years, Rusty had been the patient of eight specialists in various fields of medicine. He'd gone through a series of tests: blood test, CT scans, MRIs; they looked up one end and down the other, to no avail. Dr. Wasserman prodded Rusty for more information, which was like pulling teeth. He asked Rusty if he could give him an example of his symptoms.

"Sure," he said, "but I don't know what good that would do; you're not a medical doctor.

"That's where you're wrong. I am a medical doctor. But the part of the body that I treat is not captured by x-ray or CT scan. It's invisible. The mind can create symptoms that are real. What I do is to treat the mind, hoping it will cure the body.

And since no one can find anything physically wrong with you, let's look somewhere else. Inside your head."

"Well, it started several years ago, shortly before I turned forty-eight. I started having pain on my right side; it didn't go away. Then I started having pain in my feet, in my armpit area, heartburn, headaches, and so on. It kept spreading until I couldn't take anymore. All the tests came back normal except the colon exam. My doctor told me I had IBS, Irritable Bowel Syndrome. He wrote me out a prescription for medication, but the pills didn't do much good."

The doctor watched as Rusty cleaned his glasses for the third time in less than ten minutes. He remembered their first meeting; he'd noticed the habit then, too, but not to this extent. He thought Rusty was getting better, but now he wasn't so sure. Rusty had been his patient for a little over six months. Usually, he had a good idea after six months how to treat a patient. Rusty was a hard nut to crack. He didn't like giving out information.

"Rusty, I'd like to tell you a little story about a friend of mine. His name is Berberack. Mr. Berberack had just turned forty when everything started going south, or downhill. It could have happened at thirty or maybe fifty. But for him, the turning point was age forty. We all face it at one time or another. A wrinkle here, a wrinkle there, and soon we start thinking death is just around the corner. Anyway, he was a lot like you. He'd seen a bunch of specialists, but no one could find a thing wrong with him. Many of the symptoms he described were the same as yours. It doesn't have to be about life expectancy. For Mr. Berberack, it was a combination: his father had died at an early age from a heart attack; and he, the young Berberack, had just lost his job after twenty years of employment. It was the only job he'd ever worked. Sometimes it's just an accumulation of little things that messes with the nervous system, causing it to go out of whack. The point I'm trying to make is, if they can't find anything wrong with you physically, maybe nothing's wrong with you physically. Maybe something's bothering you emotionally, mentally. You have a stressful job, and I'll bet no matter how hard you try, the job goes home with you. I want you to give it some thought. Next time you're in your car, look and see if you're squeezing the steering wheel. If so, relax. I call this illness the Berberack Syndrome.

"Do you remember our first meeting when I asked if you believed in God and you said you would have said no a week earlier? Are you ready to take on that subject?"

The doctor knew from what he had read in the newspaper and seen on late-night television that Rusty Stubbs was the lead detective in the murder trial of Mr. Jason Bradford. The media had turned it into a circus. He didn't know all the details, but enough to know the star witness was not present in a physical form when she supposedly witnessed the crime. The two men had not discussed the trial. Dr. Wasserman did not believe or disbelieve in the Hereafter. He was smart enough not to give his opinion on the subject. But he knew enough about the mind to know that he knew little. He did know the mind could make a person sick; he also knew the mind could cure terminal diseases, although most doctors would never admit it, saying it was simply a misdiagnosis.

"Well, it all started with a phone call three days before we found the body of Ms. Brown ..."

Rusty was the doctor's last patient. He told Dr. Wasserman the whole story, all two hours of it. When he finished, the doctor asked, "So, what do you think; was she telling you the truth?"

Rusty replied, "I believe she told me what she believes. I don't believe she was lying." It was the first time Rusty had discussed the case with anyone outside work. "Everything she said that I could verify ... was proven true."

It was getting late, so Rusty said goodbye. Dr. Wasserman made a note in his Rusty Stubbs' file: neurotic, hypochondriac, obsessive-compulsive, depressed. At the end of their session, he still didn't know what Rusty thought about a higher power, whether he'd changed his mind.

After leaving Dr. Wasserman's office, Rusty drove home and on his way, he started thinking about some of the things the doctor had said. He remembered the doctor saying: *the next time you're driving in your car, look to see if you're squeezing the steering wheel.* So he did. And he was. He was squeezing the wheel so tight his knuckles whitened, a death grip on the wheel. Consequently, he relaxed his hands and instantly started feeling better. Maybe his doctor was right — maybe all his symptoms were his own creation.

Chapter 30

As I walked up the courthouse steps on the fourth day of the trial, I had to fight my way through a carnival of characters. By now the crowd had tripled in size and had split into two groups: those who thought Ella Martin was a saint, and those who thought she was a liar. A charlatan. The Devil in disguise. Some in the religious community had even taken a position on the atheist side of the steps saying she was a fraud. Further, that she shouldn't be allowed to testify. They were the people who believed you weren't allowed to see the other side until after you took your last breath of air — for the final time.

~~~

The trial opened with the prosecution calling Dr. Henderson to the stand. After giving a brief description of what he did for a living and where he worked, the prosecuting attorney asked Dr. Henderson if he recalled the evening of November 15th, 2001.

"Yes," he said, "that was the evening I met Ella

Martin in the emergency room."

"Why was she there?"

"She had collapsed inside a supermarket and was unconscious when the paramedics reached her."

"What was her condition when you first examined her?"

"All her vital signs were normal, but after still complaining of a little discomfort, I decided to admit her overnight for observation."

"Doctor, can you describe for the court what happened next."

"Yes, to make it simple: Her heart stopped pumping and started fibrillating, which means a rapid, irregular twitching of the muscle fibers. It can be caused by heart disease such as coronary artery disease, by drugs, or by electrocution. If fibrillation occurs in the lower chambers, the ventricles of the heart, it can cause cardiac arrest, which will rapidly lead to death because the heart is now pumping little or no blood through the circulatory system. I called out a 'Code Blue' and gave a room number. While waiting for the entire team to arrive I started CPR. Sometimes we can restore normal heart contractions by using electrical shock; we use a machine called a cardiac defibrillator to deliver this electric shock."

I drew fast while he spoke. My tape recorder ran silently in my breast pocket as his words flowed into the small microphone clipped to my collar. Later, in my hotel room, I would have to decipher what I could for my column. Spruce it up a little bit. After all, it didn't have to be verbatim.

"... I continued to give her CPR until we shocked her. After shocking her, we got her back for a minute or so, then we lost her again. One of my staff established an IV and gave her one milligram of epinephrine. This brought her back again, but not for long."

"How much time had passed from when you first started giving CPR until the first time you got her back?"

"I don't know, probably ten to fifteen minutes. It's always a little hard to tell how long something takes, because everyone has a job to do, and they're busy."

"What else do you remember?"

"This went on for some time. We worked on her for about forty minutes, altogether, and the last twenty minutes, we had nothing, just a straight line. She had dilated pupils, anoxia, no oxygen to the brain. Another doctor, Dr. Barnett, and I decided it was time to end it. I was afraid if we got her back, she would have irreversible brain damage. She met all the criteria for brain death, so I said, 'Let's call it.' The time of death was 7:01 p.m.

"All the tubing was removed and Ella was wheeled down to the morgue. Around thirty minutes later I was paged to report to the receptionist desk inside the ER. As I rounded the corner toward the receptionist desk, I saw Ella sitting there. At first, I didn't realize who it was until I got right up on her. I tried to get her to lie on a gurney, but she didn't want to, so we compromised and she sat in a wheelchair. She hadn't eaten anything since before she arrived at the hospital and was hungry, so I wheeled her down to the cafeteria. While she ate, she told me what she had experienced."

"She told you she had an out-of-body experience?"

"Yes."

"Did that surprise you?"

"Not necessarily. Over the years, I've had a few people tell me that."

"Was there anything different with what Ms. Martin described?"

"Yes, she told me things I knew had occurred that she couldn't possibly know."

"Like what?"

Dr. Henderson described the conversation Ella told him she had overheard between the nurse and the receptionist, which he confirmed. Then he picked up the pace, quickly going through what Ella had told him after she'd left the emergency room.

The lanky attorney scribbled notes as the doctor spoke. I drew a picture of him and his client from behind, sitting at the defense table.

Prosecutor White wrapped up his questioning of Dr. Henderson by asking, "So, Dr. Henderson, what do you think? Do you believe Ms. Martin's story?"

"Objection," said the defense attorney. "It would only be speculation on the doctor's part. It's not up to the doctor to decide whether it's true or not. It's up to the jury."

~~~

After lunch, the defense got its chance to call their first witness, Dr. Henry Swanson, Jason's work supervisor. He was in his fifties. He had short silver-white hair with a bald spot on the back of his head, which, from a distance, reminded me of a yarmulke. He was of average height and weight, dressed in a gray business suit, and looked like a typical businessperson.

Mr. Preston started out by asking questions about the company Dr. Swanson worked for. What product they made, how long he had worked there, and how many years he'd been in a supervisory position. The defense was trying to show the man had experience working with employees and could make an honest evaluation of a person's character.

He was the manager of a company that sold software for fire and security alarm systems for five years and was being promoted to director, one step away from vice president.

"Mr. Swanson, what kind of employee is the defendant, Jason Bradford?" Before Mr. Swanson had a chance to answer, the tall attorney asked, "What I mean by that is," he hesitated, "is he reliable? Is he knowledgeable? Does he make good decisions?"

"Jason is by far my top employee. He has worked for the company for nearly ten years. He hardly ever takes any time off. He's a senior software engineer. He's reliable, responsible, and the most dedicated employee I've ever had the privileged to supervise." The man painted a wonderful picture of Jason.

The defense turned the floor over to the prosecution.

Mr. White now had the opportunity to establish

two points. One: that Jason had the knowledge and ability to disable Sandra Brown's alarm. And two: that Jason made a good living working as a software engineer. There was no reason for him to break into a house and burglarize it.

"Dr. Swanson, could Jason disarm my security alarm without entering my house?"

"Yes."

"How would he go about doing that?"

Dr. Swanson told the court how easy it would be for someone with knowledge, especially someone who created the program, to make a remote control that could shut off the main panel inside the house. "The hard part," he said, "would be getting the information you needed to program the remote. But yes, it's possible."

The attorney didn't want to get into specifics; he just wanted Dr. Swanson to say it was possible."

"Do you know how much money Mr. Bradford makes annually?"

"Yes. Let me see. I should have that information right here in front of me somewhere." Dr. Swanson fumbled through a folder full of paperwork and then replied, "Here it is. He grosses ninety thousand a year. He's our highest paid software developer."

The defense attorney knew there was a risk in putting Jason's supervisor on the stand. He had weighed the damages before he called him. He needed someone who would give his client a good character reference. That, Dr. Swanson had successfully done.

The prosecution continued with the same line

of questioning. "Dr. Swanson, do you know if your employee, Mr. Bradford, is a gambler?"

"No, I don't think so."

"Have you ever seen the circulation of a World Series baseball pool inside your place of work?"

"Yes, I have."

"Have you ever seen Mr. Bradford's name on that pool?"

"No. Not that I recall."

"Have you ever seen Mr. Bradford with a lottery ticket or a horse racing form?"

"No sir."

"Would you call Mr. Bradford a big spender? Does he dress flashy? Or does he spend money on material items?"

"No. Not that I'm aware of."

Mr. White thought he got his message across to the jury that Jason was not hurting for money.

Several more character witnesses testified on Jason's behalf. None of the witnesses had any knowledge of Jason being hard up for money and all reported him as having good character.

Chapter 31

On day five things heated up. The defense called their first expert witness, Abigail Silverstein, a married woman with three grown children. The bailiff swore her in and she took a seat beside the judge.

Attorney Preston asked her to state her name and occupation, and why she considered herself an expert in her field of work. She said she was a cardiologist and a doctor of internal medicine. She claimed to have helped set the standards for the way cardiopulmonary resuscitation was performed today.

Mr. Preston started his questioning by asking, "Mrs. Silverstein, how long have you been on the committee overseeing this important medical procedure?"

"I've been a member for more than five years."

"So you would be in a position where you may have heard stories from other doctors about patients who have experienced this out-of-body phenomenon?"

"Yes, I suppose you could say that."

"What do you think is happening to the patient that would cause an out-of-body event?"

"First, let me say I don't believe the event takes place when the patient is dead. I heard Dr. Henderson describe how he watched Ms. Martin arrest. He immediately started CPR, which in my mind means that she, Ms. Martin, was only oxygen deficient for a matter of seconds. My guess is that he or one of his staff worked on her the whole time until they declared her dead. During the down periods, when they stopped CPR to give an electrical shock or drugs, the monitoring equipment would have registered no activity."

"So, let me see if I have this right. What you're saying is, you don't believe that Ms. Martin was ever dead ... not until all life support had ended. You believe the whole time she was in the emergency room she was alive. As long as they were performing CPR, perfusion was taking place. Is that correct?"

"Basically, yes. She never was clinically dead, until all CPR stopped. Then perhaps cerebral anoxia caused her near-death experience."

"So, should I also assume that if perfusion, or blood flowing to the brain is taking place, the patient may be able to hear voices at the same time in the room or nearby vicinity? Is that possible?"

"Yes, that's possible."

The defense attorney turned the floor over to the prosecution for cross-examination.

Mr. White took a deep breath and flexed his

chest muscles causing his vest buttons to almost pop. He turned to face Dr. Silverstein. "Is there any reason to believe that a person's auditory ability would improve during periods when they are receiving less oxygen to the brain?"

"No. I don't believe that would be the case."

"So, let's say someone is down a hallway in a secluded area conversing with another person one hundred feet away. There's no reason to believe that an unconscious person could hear that conversation any better because of their unconscious state, is there?"

"No."

"If Ms. Martin said she heard a conversation taking place between two people outside the immediate area at a distance beyond the normal hearing range, what would your response be, Doctor?"

"I would say there was a likely explanation for that, but I don't know all the facts. Maybe the conversation didn't take place where they said it took place; maybe it was outside in the hallway within hearing range."

"If Ms. Martin said she had her NDE while the medical team was performing CPR and it continued long after CPR had stopped, what would your response be?"

"I would say she was mistaken. Confused about the time and sequence of events."

"If she knew the time of her death, and who recorded it, what would you say?"

She had no response to that question.

"Dr. Henderson had testified that before stopping CPR on Ms. Martin, he conferred with another doctor. They did a physical examination, one including no response to pain. She had fixed and dilated pupils, steady gaze, lack of reflexive blinking to stimulation, and no spontaneous respirations."

The prosecuting attorney ended his cross-examination of the witness and turned the floor over to the defense.

The next person called to the stand was a woman who identified herself as a skeptic. Her background was in psychiatry and she had written several books and many articles trying to debunk the whole life-after-death experience as mental illness or hallucination. She was in her mid-sixties, of average height and weight. She had a one-inch wide snow-white streak of hair that originated in the left temple area and wrapped around her head, fading somewhere behind her back into her ponytail. She spoke in an I-know-everything, just-ask-me, manner.

I thought Mr. Preston needed her testimony badly. Even though according to the present outcomes it was a coin toss on whose side was winning.

The woman's name was Shannon, Dr. Shannon Knightowl, all one word, spelled with a 'K.' I had an odd feeling she could be trouble. Trouble for one of the attorneys, though which one I wasn't sure. She told the court she was an Arizona Indian, but didn't mention any specific tribe, and had half a dozen turquoise wristbands covering her forearm. Her dress was old style, tie-dye, dating back to the

Woodstock era. I checked to make sure I had enough tape to cover the session.

Dr. Shannon started out by talking about Ketamine. How she had used it in college and how she was an expert on mind-altering drugs like LSD, hashish, and peyote. Then the questioning drifted toward one of the articles she'd written on death and dying.

"So, Doctor," Attorney Preston asked, "would you say your research on the subject of life-after-death was from a nonbiased, neutral position?"

"Certainly, I had no prejudice one way or the other, especially when I started out."

"Doctor, in one of your articles you suggest there are two theories or hypotheses to the near-death experience. One: the dying brain. Two: the spirit separating from the body at the moment of death. Between the two, which theory do you support?"

"I would have to support the only logical one, the dying brain hypothesis."

"You're not a supporter of the spirit or soul leaving the body after death?"

"To me, that is all a bunch of foolishness. My ancestors were into all that nonsense. They took drugs for only one reason, and that was to get high. Clear or critical-thinking people believe in the dying brain hypothesis."

"Can you name some of these critical thinkers? I don't mean necessarily by name, but by occupation?"

"Sure, those in academia who've studied the phenomena believe in the dying brain hypothesis.

They're the people who make up the scientific community: physicists, cosmologists, psychologists, chemists, and microbiologists, to mention only a few."

Jason's attorney finished his questioning and turned the floor back to the prosecution.

Attorney White turned to face the jury panel. "I don't know why we're going down this road again. We covered all this information before." He made a quarter turn to his left and stared at the woman on the witness stand. He thought for a second and then asked, "How long has humanity been interested in the afterlife, Dr. Knightowl?"

"I suppose you could follow it back to when they first painted symbols on a cave wall."

"So, the spirit theory has been around a lot longer than the dying brain theory?"

"Yes, you could say that. But as our brain continued to develop, so did our way of thinking. We started relying on science instead of the local shaman for advice. We discovered the world was not flat, but round, and the earth was not the center of the universe. We invented the wheel when we realized the only rocks that rolled were the Rollin' Stones."

She chuckled at her comment as if she was having fun answering the questions. "With time, science had replaced many of our ancestors' beliefs. After a certain age, we stop believing in Santa Claus, the Easter Bunny, the Tooth Fairy, and we move on. We grow up!"

"Do you believe in UFOs, Doctor?"

"Of course not! I have yet to see any evidence

that would lead me to believe that UFOs are real. Most clearheaded people do not believe in UFOs."

"You realize, Doctor, that more people believe in UFOs than don't?"

She laughed. "Yes, I know."

"Do you believe in the big bang theory?"

"Yes, it's the only theory that makes any sense."

"So, let me see if I got this right, Doctor. You believe the universe was so dense that it was packed into a particle smaller than an atom. For some unknown reason, the particle goes KABOOOM through rapid inflation we call the big bang, expanding to softball size in less than a trillionth of a second. This is now the beginning of time. In less than a second, this hot soup of electrons, quarks, and other particles start to cool, allowing quarks to clump into protons and neutrons. The charged electrons and protons prevent light from shining; the universe is a hot fog. After a few hundred thousand years go by, the electrons combine with protons and neutrons to form atoms made up of mostly hydrogen and helium: light is now visible. A billion or so years later, gravity causes hydrogen and helium gas to coalesce to form the giant clouds that will eventually become galaxies—smaller clumps of gas collapse to form the first stars. This brings us up to present time. Gravity causes galaxies to cluster and stars to start dying out."

She sat in the witness chair, dumbfounded. She didn't know Prosecutor White was an amateur astronomer. Mr. White had studied the heavens with his telescope for years.

"Would you say that Einstein and Hawkings were clear thinkers, Doctor?"

"Yes, one was, the other is." She made a point to correct the counselor on his tense. "Einstein is dead. Hawkings is still alive!"

"What would you say if I quoted someone by saying, 'Science without religion is lame, religion without science is blind'?"

"I would say that was a childish statement. At least the first half."

"How about, 'If the facts don't fit the theory, change the facts'?"

"I would ask if the quote came from the well-known philosopher, Yogi Berra. It sounds like something he might say!"

"For your information, Doctor, Albert Einstein, one of your clear thinkers, is responsible for both of the aforementioned quotes. Who, by the way, never said he didn't believe in God. He was smart enough to say he didn't know. He was an agnostic on the subject. So, Doctor, to sum up, you believe the mind, or consciousness, and the brain are one and the same. When one dies, so does the other. Would that be correct?"

"Yes."

"Thank you, Dr. Knightowl. I have no further questions for this witness."

Score one for the prosecution, I thought.

Chapter 32

After three weeks of testimony, the attorneys were ready to give their closing statements. Following protocol, the prosecution would go first.

Mr. White stood and walked over to address the jury panel. He thanked the men and women for their participation. Pacing the floor back and forth the length of the jury box several times before speaking, he finally turned and looked at the cowboy. "I'm going to draw you a map. And we're going to take a road trip. On this map, I'll place dots. Above each dot, I'll write a city name. Each city will represent a piece of evidence. Let's see where we end after we've traveled the length of the map and linked all the dots together."

He walked over to the easel and shuffled some of the exhibits around, placing them in a new order, with number twenty-two on the stand facing the jury. The exhibit was a picture of a laptop computer. Mr. White pointed to the exhibit. "Let's start our trip right here at Jason's computer. Jason laid out his journey in advance. He typed the directions from his mother's house to Sandra Brown's home into a map search website. Let's call his mother's house, his starting point, New York City. Why would he start his trip here? I'll tell you why. Because he wanted to use her car. He waited until after his mother fell asleep, as she has stated, thinking this would give him an alibi. Then he drove his mother's car to Ms. Brown's house, where he parked across the street in front of Mrs. Moore's house. That puts us in Columbus, Ohio. Mrs. Moore looked out her picture window to see if it was snowing and saw a small person get out of the car parked in front of her house, in a car that looked exactly like the one the defendant's mother owns."

Mr. White poured himself a glass of water from the sterling silver water container sitting on top of the prosecutor's table and continued his closing statement.

"Mr. Bradford exited the car, his mother's car, and removed a duffel bag from his trunk. We know this because Mrs. Moore identified the bag as being large. Jason then crossed the street and waited in Ms. Brown's back yard until she returned home. After Ms. Brown entered her house, he struck her and knocked her unconscious. The apparatus used was a small leaded bat, around fifteen inches long." He put the exhibit with the burnt bat up on the easel. "That puts us in Indianapolis. Jason secured the woman's hands behind her back with plastic zip ties. He moved her furniture and laid down a sheet of white plastic in the center of her living room floor. He used a white sheet so he could see if there was any blood spatter on it."

He took another sip of water. "This should

place us in or around Kansas City, Missouri. Jason removed a water glass from a cabinet and then put it back. We know this because his fingerprints were on a glass inside Sandra Brown's kitchen cabinet. He played rock and roll music in a compact disc player that he brought with him. We know this because the neighbor and our eyewitness reported hearing the music that evening. Our eyewitness identified this music as being the Rolling Stones. She also reported hearing two of the songs played that evening as: "Sympathy for the Devil" and "Satisfaction." A CD album call *Flashpoint* was recovered from the defendant's car. Both songs were on that particular CD. The defendant washed the victim's dishes and scrubbed her bathtub, and according to our eyewitness, he changed out her toilet paper roll. That, my friends, puts us in Denver, Colorado."

Then he said, "This is where the defendant made a fatal mistake. Mr. Bradford blew his nose on a Kleenex and discarded it into the victim's bathroom trash container. We know that as a fact, because we found it and had it tested. That puts us in Las Vegas, Nevada. Jason then went back into the living room and beat Sandra Brown to death. Afterward, he cleaned up the area, removing her bindings, the towels, and the white sheet of plastic, putting them all back into his duffel bag. He reset her alarm, then locked up the house using a key he'd made with his key cutting equipment, which was found in the basement of his mother's home. Finally, he drove back to his mother's house, parked the car in her garage, and woke her up before driving home. That puts us in Los Angeles, our final destination."

"We believe Mr. Bradford put the small bat in a bucket of bleach to dilute the blood. A few days later, when he got wind *we* were interested in talking to him, he burned the bat in his mother's fireplace and dumped the remains in the burn barrel in her back yard. That's around the same time we believe he got rid of everything else, taking it to the city dump."

He walked back over to the jury box, put his elbows on the rail and clasped his hand together. He stared at the jury panel, wondering what their thoughts were. After a few seconds, he said, "That completes our road trip to hell. As you can plainly see, it's not hard to imagine how we got from point A to point B.

"As far as Ella Martin, our eyewitness, she's not on trial here. Although I believe that if she were, we proved beyond a reasonable doubt there *is* life after death. That ends my closing statement."

Once again, he thanked the jury panel for their service.

Attorney Preston stood next to his client with a hand on Jason's shoulder in a comforting gesture. He turned to face the jury box.

His eyes scanned the jury panel one by one, looking into each person's eyes, trying to read his or her mind. He wondered who was in his corner and who was in the prosecutor's. His eyes locked on the college student. She would be a problem; she would be the one most likely to be on the other side, the one he needed to work on the most.

After thanking the jury for their participation,

he walked back to the easel and put up exhibit number one, the white Buick Regal. "Do you remember when we discussed the car supposedly parked in front of Mrs. Moore's house the night of the murder? And do you remember how I told you that it might resemble a car that looked like my client's mother's car? The car Mrs. Moore picked out of my photo display was a different make and model. It was also a different color. And do you recall that she could not read the three-inch letter on the five-by-six-inch card my assistant held up in the back of the courtroom? Well … this is not evidence. It is not even circumstantial evidence. If she could identify the car, because she wrote down the license number, that would be evidence. Or if she guessed the make, model, color, and year of the car correctly, then you might give that some consideration. But as I demonstrated, she could not do any of that. What we have now is nothing.

"So," he said, using an old Johnny Cochran analogy, "if the glove doesn't fit, you must acquit. What I see are many holes in that fictional road map the prosecution was trying to draw; so many, you could slice it and put it on a ham sandwich."

He put his big hands on the railing that separated the jury box from the rest of the courtroom. "The bat, the tiny bat had no hair particles or DNA evidence found on it. There's no reason to place that bat at the scene of the crime. No ties, no plastic sheet, no duffel bag, no white towels; no evidence, other than a couple of fingerprints that my client has admitted to."

I noticed the attorney didn't mention the Kleenex found inside the house with his client's

DNA on it. Nor did he mention the computer or the compact disc. He looked over at the defendant. "Please look at my client. Do you believe Mr. Bradford is strong enough to pick up or drag a person twenty or thirty feet as Ms. Martin, our invisible eyewitness, has stated?"

He directed his attention back to Ella Martin and articulated, "I know you'd like to believe in the Hereafter. So would I. But as my expert witnesses have testified, there is no reason to believe that life continues after death. No proof. Show me the evidence! Did anyone see Ms. Martin that night during her escapade here? No! No one saw her here, did they? She mentioned how my client killed Sandra Brown, but none of the items used in the killing were found, according to testimony by CSI and the detectives assigned to the case. Nothing they could link to Mr. Bradford."

He walked back to where his client was sitting and stood beside the little man. He once again placed his hand on Jason's shoulder. "This man's life is at stake. As I mentioned in my opening statement, if you have a witness, the witness should be tangible, physical, solid, concrete, a real person, a person of substance, not someone dreaming of being in another place, seeing visions, things that are not real. Psychics are not eyewitnesses. My client did not do this horrendous crime he has been accused of committing: he is an innocent man. You, the jury, have the responsibility to weigh the evidence presented during the trial and decide whether it meets the requirements outlined in the law. To convict Mr. Bradford of this crime, the evidence must show beyond a reasonable doubt that he is guilty. I say the evidence does not support a guilty verdict. With that, I rest my case." With that, he sat down.

Mr. White stood once again and walked back over to the jury box. In the prosecution's rebuttal, he reinforced his position on several key points including the fingerprint and the Kleenex, and then took a parting shot at one of the defense's expert witnesses, Mrs. Knightowl, by saying, "I would rather have a smart person judging me than someone well-educated."

Judge Jenkins hit the sound block one time with his gavel, regaining control over his courtroom. The judge turned toward the jury box and instructed the jurors on how to apply the law to the evidence noted at trial. He had the bailiff hand each juror a booklet with tips on how to organize themselves. The booklets also included how to consider the evidence and how to reach a verdict. He also gave them guidelines to follow. He said they should respect each other's opinions and to listen to all points of view. They should be fair and give everyone a chance to speak. If he or she wanted to change his or her mind, he or she could. Do not bully anyone into changing his or her mind. Don't rush into a verdict. Take their time: the people involved in the case deserve thoughtful deliberation.

After the judge's instructions, the jury left the courtroom and headed to the jury room to begin their deliberation.

Chapter 33

The twelve jurors sat around the large, egg-shaped, mahogany table in the deliberation room. The chairs were comfortable, made of brown leather with high backs and deep bucket seats, able to swivel and rock at the same time. Two large coffee pots sat on top of a credenza against the wall farthest from the door. In the middle of the conference table sat a stack of legal-sized yellow notepads and a small basket full of pencils.

Once comfortable, the cowboy spoke first. "Okay, who's going to run this rodeo?" They went around the table asking for a volunteer. When no one offered to take the job, they took a vote and selected the economist as the presiding juror. He accepted the nomination and decided to see where they stood on the case before starting their deliberation. Each juror received a sheet of paper and was asked to write guilty or not guilty and to give a brief statement if they wished to explain their reasoning behind their decision. Once they had their thoughts in writing, they folded the papers and placed them in the basket in the center of the table.

The recently selected jury foreman opened each folded paper and read its contents out loud. There were many interesting opinions. The last one he read, said, 'Not guilty,' with the following statement: 'There's a difference between dead, mostly dead, partly dead, slightly dead, somewhat dead and dead, dead. When you're any of those others, you have a chance of coming back. When you're dead, dead, that's when your relatives fish through your wallet and go out on the town to celebrate their newfound wealth.'

Everyone looked around the room wondering who the philosopher was among them.

The jury foreman tallied up the guilty and not guilty votes to see which way the panel was leaning. It was a dead heat. Six voted guilty and six voted not guilty. Next, he laid out the trial transcripts on the table and asked if anyone wanted to volunteer to read the trial information transcribed by the courtroom stenographer. One of the housewives volunteered for the job.

The foreman asked for another volunteer to take notes during the reading of the transcripts so they could go back over the more important points. The notetaker's name was Emma, Emma Shine, and she wanted everyone to call her "M" like the letter. She was another self-described homemaker who had once won a national spelling bee.

The jury foreman, Dylan Morrow, was tall and thin, with wavy brown hair, graying at the temples. He wore spectacles and said he had been an economics instructor at the University of Colorado in Colorado Springs, but had recently lost his job because he didn't have tenure. He blamed the Internet bubble and the downturn in the economy for his unemployment.

Dylan walked over to the whiteboard and in the center at the top, he wrote 'EVIDENCE' in large capital letters. Then he asked the reader to read from the first page of the transcripts. They all listened closely as the woman covered the material.

Jane, the reader, was in her late sixties and had a marvelous voice. She read as if it was coming from the original testifier's mouth, often varying her pitch in modulation, and making her voice more pleasing to listen to. At the end of every paragraph, she paused, allowing comment from the panel. While she read, 'M' wrote down key points on her notepad as Dylan worked the whiteboard.

The reader started with the phone call from Ella Martin to Detective Stubbs. Dylan wrote down all the things that Ella knew that she shouldn't have, like where the murder took place and the victim's name. The panel meticulously combed through the evidence, allowing each juror a chance to voice his or her opinion. By the end of the day, the whiteboard was completely covered.

By the end of the fifth day of deliberation, the jury had reached a unanimous decision and notified the bailiff, who, in turn, had them sign the verdict form. The form was then turned over to the judge for review.

~~~

Rusty was cleaning his glasses when he received a phone call from Carol, the district attorney's secretary. She told him a verdict was in and he needed to get his butt over to the courthouse if he wanted to be there when they read it.

The judge entered the courtroom and the jury took their seats in the jury box. The bailiff called the court to order as Judge Jenkins stepped up onto the platform and sat down. He beat his gavel twice and asked if the jury had reached a verdict.

"Yes," the jury foreman, Mr. Morrow said, and handed the court clerk the documentation.

Judge Jenkins asked the clerk to read the verdict.

"We, the jury, find the defendant, Jason Thomas Bradford, not guilty as charged of first-degree premeditated murder. We, the jury, find the defendant guilty of murder in the second-degree. We, the jury, find the defendant guilty of assault during the commission of a crime."

The clerk continued to read the verdict on all the charges against Mr. Bradford and then, after a quick sentencing hearing, Judge Jenkins delivered the punishment.

Twenty-four years — the maximum for the crime. Then he immediately reduced the sentence to eighteen years, because Jason had no prior criminal history. He had a stellar work record and had been a pillar of the community for years. All these things the judge had considered before giving out the sentence.

Jason lowered his head, disillusioned to say the least. He was hoping for community service. Mr. Brown, the victim's father, put his hands over his eyes, bowed his head, and began to cry. He thought the sentence was far too lenient; he was hoping for the same sentence his daughter had received: death!

Mrs. Brown sat stoic, staring at the ceiling as if she wasn't there.

The trial was over. Jason was put in handcuffs and taken away. Attorney Preston wasn't happy, but he had accomplished one thing: his client didn't get the death penalty. He hugged Sally Bradford, Jason's mother, and said, "Don't worry; I'll file an appeal immediately."

Attorney White was not happy with the verdict or the sentencing, but there was nothing he could do. He looked over at Rusty and shrugged his shoulders.

I don't know if I was surprised by the verdict. It could have gone either way. The people sitting behind the prosecution table thought Jason got off easy and should have received a much harsher sentence, while those sitting on the opposite side of the courtroom, behind the defendant, thought he got a raw deal and should have gone free.

After hearing both verdict and sentence, everyone slowly filed out of the courthouse and gathered in front of the building. The media was there, including me, taking as many pictures as possible, trying to get that one good shot of someone crying or laughing that would make my article. The two attorneys were there, answering questions for the five o'clock news hour. The DA made sure he got his face in front of the camera, even though he had not said one word during the trial. He didn't lose the case. Jason was going to jail for a long time.

I sat on one of the steps long after everyone else had packed up and left. I wondered what the impact of the verdict would be; would it change anyone's opinion on the life after death subject? Mine had not, although when I thought about it, I would have to say sure, a few people had changed their minds. One for sure was Dr. Henderson and probably Dr. Alexander. And then I thought of all the medical staff where Henderson worked. Some of them must have changed their minds, too.

I headed back to my car for the one-hour drive home. Back to Denver to complete what I thought would be my last article on Jason Thomas Bradford. How wrong I was!

Chapter 34

Five years later

Rusty relaxed on his boat sipping on a Southern-styled Mint Julep while his partner rubbed sunscreen on his neck and shoulders. The boat was a thirty-eight-foot cabin cruiser — bought new two years earlier — the day after he retired. Stenciled across the stern, in large blue letters, was the name of the craft: HEAVEN.

Two big red and white feathered jigs trailed behind the boat some 100 yards away, waiting for a bite from a large Tarpon. The two men were fishing in the waters off the Florida Keys in the Gulf of Mexico.

Two days had gone by without a single bite from one of the big silver fish, but it didn't matter. The water was calm, the sky was clear, and both men had retired.

~~~

Back in Colorado Springs, Joe Longhorn lay on his side on top of a flattened cardboard box. Resting his head on a pillow of rolled-up newspaper, he slyly surveyed the area around him, one hand clutching a half pint of Sunny Brook whiskey. He was north of Memorial Park, across the street from a baseball diamond, in an alley with little foot traffic, in the heart of one of the city's highest crime areas. He hadn't shaved in a couple of weeks. His long hair was in a ponytail, braided down his back. Wearing faded Levis well-worn around the knees, his upper body was clad in a tattered old Pea coat that had clearly spent time on the street. Joe had given a homeless man ten dollars for the use of the jacket and said he would return it before the weather got cold again. He held his revolver tight in his free hand, hidden under the leaf of his jacket as he waited for the entity the media had called the 'Torch.'

The Torch had a nasty habit of setting bums on fire. His prey had all been Indians. His rampage had lasted for three weeks so far, and there was no reason to believe he would quit anytime soon.

It was shortly after 2:00 p.m., the most active time for the Torch. He'd lit six men on fire: four dead; one in critical condition with burns over 60 percent of his body; another in less critical condition, with burns only to his upper chest. This man was lucky to have survived the attack.

Joe heard whispering, voices off in the distance. In a flash, he saw two pairs of men's shoes standing directly in front of him: one in tennis shoes, the other in cowboy boots with steel-tipped toes. Joe couldn't see their faces. The voice coming from the one he thought was wearing the tennis shoes said, "Check this guy out. I wonder what he would look like as a human match?"

"I don't know," said the other one. "Would you like to find out?"

Joe tightened his grip on his revolver, ready to respond. He heard what sounded like a cap unscrew from a container. Then the man dressed in tennis shoes poured gasoline on his legs while the other man lit a match. Joe removed his hand from underneath the Pea coat and pulled the trigger, hitting the man holding the gas can square in the chest. The man with the can flew backward, spilling gas on himself and on his partner, who was still holding the match. Joe rolled off the flattened sheet of cardboard and watched as the two men went up in flames.

The one who took the bullet was dead before he hit the ground. The other man screamed for help, but there was nothing Joe could do. For a brief second, he thought about shooting the man, putting him out of his misery, but then he would have to explain why he did it — *more paperwork* — so he decided against it and watched him burn. *Poetic justice*, he thought.

Then he turned on his radio and called for help.

~~~

Rusty heard some chatter over the radio and went inside to turn up the volume. He fine-tuned the static out of the radio just in time to hear a woman's voice say, "… We're happy to announce that Jason Bradford, a man doing time in a Colorado prison for a murder he committed back in 2001, has confessed his involvement in six other murders: four women, his father, and a childhood friend."

The woman continued: "All the killings took place in the Colorado Springs area of Colorado. The case first gained national attention because of the media hype surrounding the star witness, a woman who said she witnessed the murder during an out-of-body experience while she lay dead in a California hospital after suffering a massive heart attack."

Rusty turned the volume dial two more clicks and flipped the switch so the sound went through the outside speakers. He ran out onto the rear deck. "I knew it. I knew he was responsible for those others killings."

His partner said, "Whoa, slow down. He? Who's he? Who are you talking about?"

"Do you remember the guy we suspected of being the S. B. killer? That's what the media called him. We, Joe and I, had a different nickname for him. His name was Bradford, Jason Bradford. We never could provide it, but he was our main suspect in four other murders identical to the one he was eventually convicted of. After his arrest for killing Sandra Brown, the body count dropped to zero. This case put my department on the map.

"Do you remember when I told you the story? It was a little while after I first started seeing you as a patient. You asked me if I believed in a higher power — God. I never gave you a definitive answer then. But I believed the woman in the case, Ella Martin, couldn't possibly have known what she knew unless she was there and had witnessed the killing firsthand. I believe she was my savior; the one who prevented me from killing myself, not you, Barney. But your treatment helped. It convinced me that all my symptoms were self-made. What did you call it, the Berberack Syndrome?"

"Yes, that's right," said Barnard Wasserman.

The retired therapist squeezed Rusty's arm, smiled, and took a long sip from his Pina Colada. They leaned back in their comfortable fishing chairs and watched a pod of whales breaking the water some 100 hundred yards off to the east. Rusty removed a cell phone from his white shorts and punched in a number.

~~~

Joe stood by the pumper truck, nude, except for the blanket wrapped around him. He'd just gone through a decontamination cycle to wash off the gasoline that had soaked through his jeans and onto his skin. He had removed his fake ponytail and was talking to the captain from Fire Station number 23 when he heard his cell phone ring. He walked over to where his gas-soaked clothes lay on the ground and fished through his pocket. "Hello," he said.

"Hey, what's up, Tonto?" said the voice on the other end of the line.

"Who's this?" Joe asked. "Rusty …?"

"That's correct."

"So, how's Heaven?"

"Wonderful, we're floating in 200 feet of water off the Keys. Did you hear the good news? Jason confessed to being the S. B. killer. He also said he was responsible for his father's death and that of a classmate."

"You're kidding, right?"

"I kid you not! There was a condition in his

confession. For him to confess, they had to promise him the death penalty."

"Bless his heart," Joe said sarcastically. "Ella must have influenced his decision!"

"Yeah, maybe, I don't know. He did admit that everything she'd said during the trial was true."

They talked for a few minutes and then Rusty said goodbye. He sounded happy, Joe thought. That was good. But he missed having someone to poke fun at. He missed the morning trips to the donut shop and his partner's indecisiveness. But most of all, Joe missed the friendship that had developed between them over the years.

Joe turned to face a reporter, who asked, "How does it feel having to watch a man burn to death, Detective?"

Joe had replaced Rusty as a spokesperson for the department after his retirement; he now knew how it felt having to say something that wasn't necessarily true. Now he had to mind his Ps and Qs. He looked into the eye of the camera. "It was terrible, but there was nothing I could do." Joe had his fingers crossed behind his back. "The man I shot had just poured gasoline on me and I was afraid, afraid the match would ignite the fumes coming off me." This was a boldface lie. He hadn't given that any thought at all.

Chapter 35

I was sitting in my car eating a peanut butter and jelly sandwich when I heard the news over the radio that Jason had confessed to six more murders. At first, I couldn't believe my ears. That wasn't the Jason I remembered from inside the courtroom. I hadn't heard his name mentioned in years. If it weren't for Ella Martin, I wouldn't have remembered him at all. I was even more surprised when I heard the reporter say he had demanded the death penalty. My brain started racing; *could I find something worthwhile to write again?*

I wondered what I could do. And then I remembered that reporters sometimes got the opportunity to witness an execution. Chances were small, but it was possible. So, a week after hearing the news, I filled out all the proper paperwork and waited. Like all government agencies, the process was slow. Three weeks came and went without a word. I forgot about it, figuring I wasn't one of the lucky ones. Then one day, months later, I picked up my mail and noticed a letter addressed to me from the Colorado State Attorney General's Office. The letter was standard. A form letter with my name and twenty-nine other witnesses said I was selected by a panel of prison board members to witness the execution scheduled for November 20th, 2007 at 12:00 a.m.

I jumped up and down and thanked the good Lord for my luck. Then I wondered why I did that because I didn't believe in the 'good Lord.' I was in dire straits. I needed some work. Fewer and fewer of my articles were in the paper. It seemed like a terrible way to make a buck, watching someone suffer while you gained monetarily from the experience, but I was literally one paycheck away from the soup line.

I looked down the list of attendees and recognized three of my colleagues: competitors, people in my same line of work. Most of the names I didn't know; I figured they must have been relatives of the victims. I was surprised to read the last name on the list: Ella Martin. I wondered why she was going. She had been his enemy, the one responsible for his captivity. If it wasn't for her, who knows how many more bodies would have made it to the city morgue?

~~~

The weather was bad the night of the execution. I left my apartment three hours in advance to make sure I would arrive on time. As I drove the snowy highway between Denver and Canon City, I asked myself again why Ella Martin's name was on the witness list. It had haunted me for weeks. I was so intrigued by the mystery I just had to find out. I planned on asking her for an interview after the execution.

Well, as you know now, the evening came and went and I got my interview with Ella Martin. I had seven hours of tape to comb through to decide what to write, how to put it into words where it would all make sense. I decided to start at the end. Well, not exactly at the end, there was still more to the story that I hadn't imagined. Ella had said the being of light told her she had to return, that she hadn't completed her mission or met her soul mates. That was plural, not singular. The being of light had mentioned three. I figured Jason was one of them, but who were the other two?

~~~

When I got home, I listened to my taped interview with Ella Martin again — all seven hours — trying to decide where to start. Ella wanted me to write something that would lessen the fear people have of death. That death is not the end. But since I didn't believe in the afterlife I was completely lost. Maybe if I started by interviewing the people Ella had mentioned, like the warden, I'd have a better idea of how to proceed.

After spending the next two weeks tracking down the people on Ella's 'must talk to' list to interview, I received the sad news that she had died. But the news of her death didn't change my willingness to finish what I'd set out to do — complete a book about life after death and Ella's trip to Heaven — whether I believed it or not.

It was several months into the new year before I was able to arrange meetings with all the people I needed to interview, including a few who weren't on Ella's list: Jason's mother, for one.

We scheduled a meeting at her place of work. It was shortly after 1:00 p.m., when the lunch crowd had thinned to only a couple of patrons.

When I entered the diner, Sally immediately recognized me from the night of the execution and from all those days I sat behind her at the trial. We sat in a booth in a secluded section, where our conversation was more private. The only ears that could possibly hear us were those belonging to another waitress who repeatedly strolled by our booth until Mrs. Bradford introduced me to her. She told her I was a journalist who was interested in writing a book about her son.

Sally was wearing a blue and white knee length western styled dress, the standard uniform for where she worked. She had great legs for a woman of her age. Her hair was combed back in a long ponytail with a fancy clip holding it together. She had long red fingernails and wore more makeup than necessary.

I took out my trusty tape recorder and placed it in the center of the table. The first question was a tough one to ask and for her to answer. I said, "Mrs. Bradford, can you tell me why you would go and watch your son's execution? Did he invite you?"

She looked at me oddly. "I was there on his birthday, the day he was born. I was sure as hell going to be there on the day he died, if possible. I was the only one he could depend on to support him in his time of need."

That answer seemed funny to me; the way I remembered it, Jason didn't even acknowledge her presence. It was Ella he mentioned in his going away speech, not his mother.

After only a few minutes I realized she was in complete denial. She dismissed Jason's confession as pure fantasy. She put the blame on the authorities, that somehow he was coerced into saying those terrible things. She also blamed Ella Martin. "That damn woman poisoned his mind, got him believing he would go to Heaven if he confessed."

I asked about his friend, the boy who lived on the other side of Miller's Bridge. Did she believe he killed him?

She said, "Of course not. Why would he do that? He was the only friend Jason had."

"What about his father; do you believe he killed his own father?"

"No, he couldn't have done that! He loved his father. He moped around for weeks after his death. Sometimes his father could be mean; I mean he wasn't always nice to Jason, especially when he drank. But sometimes he treated him good. One time when I was at work, Jack took Jason rabbit hunting in the woods. Jason tripped over a rock and broke his leg. Jack carried Jason on his back for over a mile to get back to civilization. Back to where our car was. That's how much he loved his son. No, I don't believe for one minute he killed his friend or had anything to do with his father's death. Jason was a good boy."

I asked her about the footlocker in the basement and Jason's bone collection. It was a subject only briefly mentioned by the detective during the trial. I could see her unwillingness to talk about it, so I decided to change the subject by asking her to tell me about her childhood, how she met Jack Bradford, and Jason's early days. When she finished, I thanked her for her time and said I would send her a book if it ever got published.

~~~

The cowboy had shaved off his handlebar mustache since the last time I saw him sitting in the jury box. Other than that, he hadn't changed at all. The economist sat to the right of the cowboy.

Rowdy wore his trench coat. The same one he held during the trial. The cowboy was easy to find. I simply searched famous bull riders on my computer and his name popped up close to the top. He had just captured first place at a bull-riding event at the Silver Spurs Rodeo with a mark of 89. I wondered if it was only a coincidence, but they listed his last ride as lasting 8 seconds on a bull named Melvin.

Dylan Morrow was back working at the university, but was afraid he might soon be looking for work again because of a new recession looming on the horizon.

The ground was still damp from an early morning rain and the temperature was in the low-forties. A mother pushed her child in a swing at the playground twenty yards away from where we were sitting. I pushed the red record button on my cassette recorder and set it down in the center of the park bench.

I asked how they felt about their second-degree murder verdict, knowing now that he was responsible for the S. B. killings.

Rowdy answered first. "There was no mention at the trial that Jason was a suspect in those murders, so we couldn't even consider it."

"Tell me about the trial," I said. "Was the decision an easy one to reach?"

"No, it wasn't easy at all," Dylan said. "We were split 50-50 before we read the transcripts and went through all the evidence."

Rowdy spat tobacco into an empty paper coffee cup. "We added up all the solid evidence against Mr. Bradford, which was substantial. We had fingerprints, DNA. We knew he used his computer to get directions to the victim's house from his mother's place. We also had an overwhelming amount of circumstantial evidence pointing at him."

Dylan butted in. "After two days of reviewing the evidence, we believed Ella was telling us what happened that night. It all made sense. But rather than convict him on the original charge, first-degree, premeditation, we went with the lesser charge, because her story wasn't provable, no matter how much sense it made. But without Ella's testimony, we couldn't prove that Jason had planned the killing in advance."

Rowdy jumped back into the conversation. "I knew he was guilty when Ella identified the Rolling Stones music he was playing, being that later the two detectives found a Stones compact disc in his car with the same two songs on it that she said he'd played that night. What were the chances of that happening?"

I asked if anyone's opinion had changed about life after death.

Dylan responded, "Yes, at least, one: mine. I was a nonbeliever, but now I've changed my mind and my whole outlook on life. I owe that to Ella Martin."

"What about you, Rowdy?"

"Me! I've always been a believer."

I thanked the two gentlemen for their time and put away my recorder.

Chapter 36

My windshield wipers kept time with the music as I drove my car into the parking lot at Canon Prison. I'd spent the night in a Motel 6 a couple of miles up the road. The last time I was here was on the night Jason Bradford died. Now, fortunately, because of my novel, I had the opportunity to return. I was following up on what Ella Martin had recommended the last and only time we met. I was going there to meet with Father Jess Angel, a resident lifer who'd spent the past twenty years behind bars and was a good friend of Jason until his death.

We met in the visitation area. He was a big man with tattoos up and down his arms. It was hard to find a patch of skin without ink. When we shook hands, he almost crushed my fingers. His forearms bulged from lifting weights. He smiled and asked what he could do for me.

I told him I was writing a book about Jason Thomas Bradford's life, which didn't impress him. In fact, the mood suddenly soured until I mentioned

I was writing it at Ella Martin's request. At that point, the conversation changed dramatically. He showed me his teeth, or what he had left of them, and asked, "You're friends with Ella Martin?"

"No, not really," I said. "I met her only one time, the night Jason died." I told him I was a reporter and had followed Jason's trial from its inception. I went to his execution to get information on the pros and cons of the death penalty. I also wanted to know *why* Ella Martin attended the execution, since she'd played a big part in his imprisonment. I told him how I had interviewed her after Jason's execution. Sometime during that interview I changed direction and decided to write about Jason and his newfound belief in an afterlife, that Jason was only part of the story and not the whole story. He looked at me with interest and asked me what I would like to know.

"First off, I'd like to know about you. What did you do to get here?"

"I grew up poor south of the border and entered the country with my parents. We were migrant workers, working in orchards from state to state. At twelve, I started picking fruit with my parents. At fourteen, I ran away. I made it to Houston, where I lived on the street. At fifteen, a Mexican street gang recruited me. I earned my keep by mugging old people. At seventeen, I was arrested for simple assault; I tried to steal a female undercover officer's purse. Over the next couple of years, I was arrested four or five more times. One night, while committing a home invasion with my friends, things went bad: they had a sixteen-year-old daughter, and one of my friends decided to mess with her. She pulled off his mask and got a good look at him, so I stabbed her. Then I decided we had to take care of her parents, so I killed them, too. One of my friends started bragging about being there when the killings took place; a week later, we were busted. To save themselves, they gave me up."

"How much time are you serving?"

"I'm doing life."

"After five years, I was running my cell block. After another ten, I was running the prison — at least as far as the Mexican Mafia is concerned. That was until I met Jason; he had a great effect on me. He'd been here a little over a year. He was one of those people you never noticed, quiet, kept to himself, a loner. One day he said he started thinking about the woman who helped put him behind bars and how everything she said he did was the truth. He started wondering if there could be an afterlife. He wasn't religious, but then one day out of the blue, he got a phone call from Ella Martin. She wanted to know if she could come to visit him. More out of curiosity than not, he said yes. But he didn't want to talk about the trial. He wanted to know what she saw when she was in Heaven.

"Shortly after their first meeting he decided to confess to killing Sandra Brown. He wanted to do it in front of as many of the inmates as possible. He asked the prison chaplain if he could speak at one of their Sunday church services. One Sunday Jason stood up on the stage and told the audience the whole story. Not so much what he did, but all about Ella Martin and what she said she saw while she was dead. It wasn't about him; he was more interested in telling the inmates about an afterlife;

that he knew it had to be true because no one could have seen what the dead woman claimed to have witnessed that night unless she was there."

"What did you think when you heard what he had to say?"

The big man stood up, moved his legs as if he was trying to bring back circulation, and sat back down. "I wasn't there. Not yet."

"A few days after his confession, everybody wanted to hear the story. So Jason repeated it, not once, but many more times, until everyone who wanted to hear it had heard it. The crowd became too large for the room where we hold church services, so they set it up outside in the yard. The number of stabbings and beatings dropped off. The only ones still occurring were between the new inmates, young punks who think they're immortal; us older cons know better. Like when someone caught W.C. Fields reading the Bible on his deathbed, said: 'You don't believe in God!' To that, he supposedly responded, 'No. But just in case I'm wrong, I'm looking for a loophole.'"

"I was one of the slowpokes, one of the last to admit that he might have something I needed to hear. Eventually, I heard what he had to say and from that day on my life was never the same."

I thought, *this guy seems much brighter than I would have expected for a convict who'd murdered three people.* So I asked, "You seem," I hesitated, searching for the right word, "more ..."

He interrupted me. "... intelligent than you'd expected."

"No offense. But yes, more intelligent."

"You can thank Jason for that. After I heard Jason speak, I wanted to learn more. But I wasn't well schooled; I could hardly read. So he worked with me. He taught me how to read, he taught many of us how to read and write, and more important, how to think. The warden let him tutor us. I took and passed the GED on my first try. I started reading everything I could get my hands on. I read the Bible, not once, but three times, looking for that loophole. And guess what? W.C. Fields may not have found it, but I did. It was right there, written in plain English. For me, it couldn't be any more obvious than it was. The words stood out like they were written in bold print.

Ella got a glimpse of Heaven. For those of us who don't get that opportunity, there's the Bible. I believe it's an accurate accounting of life's history. I don't mean you have to take it word-for-word; it was written by man. It's like the difference between a photograph and a painting. No matter how good the artist is, he can't duplicate the photograph. It's his interpretation, but it doesn't change the meaning. It's still identifiable."

~~~

The warden allowed me to tape the conversation with Father Jess Angel so there wouldn't be any inaccuracies. I was originally scheduled to interview the warden first, but there was a death in his family and he had to cancel.

Because of the scheduling change, my interview with Father Angel was brief; he had a prior commitment. But one thing stuck with me when he noticed me looking at his hands and he said, "Life is a contradiction."

He had the word 'LOVE' tattooed on the fingers of his right hand, just below the knuckles, in large capital letters. The left had the word 'HATE' inked in.

"Excuse me," I said.

He repeated, "Life is a contradiction: Love, hate, good, bad, yin and yang. I'm hoping there's no contradiction in the afterlife. Ella said Hell is a place you go to get rid of negativity. I'm hoping that that's all it is. Jason gave up his life to pay for his sins. I believe changing the minds and attitude of the souls still here on earth is my life's purpose. Life is short and we may not be able to make up for our past deeds, but we can try. We are all looking for that loophole — that back door."

I said my goodbye to Father Angel, thanking him for his time. I wished him continued success in bringing new members into his flock. I still wasn't a believer in the hereafter, but I did believe in rehabilitation, and if it took religion to bring about that rehabilitation, so be it, as long as it kept a person from committing a crime.

I drove back to the hotel where I was staying and started transcribing the recording of my conversation with Father Angel. I would be going back in the morning to visit another convict named James 'One-eye' Williams. He'd been and still was a member of a notorious black street gang.

~~~

Williams was a weight lifter. He looked at me out of his one good eye — the one that moved around in its socket. The other eye stayed fixed, staring at my forehead. He had a neck the size of my waistline and his hair was braided in dreadlocks. He looked at me with puzzling eyes or eye as he sat down on the blue bench across from me in the visiting area.

Clearly, Williams was not informed about our little get-together, which I thought had been arranged by the warden before he left on emergency leave.

I introduced myself and said, "You weren't expecting me?"

"No, should I have been?"

"Yes," I said," I was hoping you were. Yesterday I spent a delightful hour with Father Jess Angel. I was hoping to do the same with you today."

"Why?" he asked.

I quickly recited the same spiel as the day before when I talked with Jess Angel.

Then Williams said, "What would you like to know?"

"Can you tell me why you're here? And how much time you're doing?" I asked.

He brushed a braid off his shoulder. "I had a troubled past. I spent a couple of years locked up in juvenile detention. My father was dead, the results of a drug deal gone bad. My mother turned to prostitution to make up for the lost money after his death. While in juvenile hall, I met a couple of gang-bangers. After my release, I joined up with them. That was a big mistake." Then he looked around the room and whispered, "You can't be too careful. The walls have ears, you know.

"Not long after my release, my mother hooked up with a pimp named Leroy, who liked to beat his 'moneymaker.' One night, after doing speed with some friends of mine I came home and caught him working her over; I told him to leave her alone. He told me to shut up or he would do same to me. That was the last thing Leroy ever said. I pulled out my gun and put a bullet right between his eyes ... I got twenty years for that."

"How did you meet Jason?"

"Like everyone else. I met him at a church service. I went there to hear him speak. When I first arrived here, he was already well known. Doing his thing, telling everyone who wanted to hear it that there was an afterlife. He believed in it so much that once he thought he'd done all he could to spread the word, he confessed to all the other murders he'd committed. He believed that was the only way he could save his soul — redemption: that he had to give up his life to atone for his sins. That maybe by dying, the relatives of the murdered victims could move on."

"Then what happened?"

"Once he got moved over to Death Row, he was no longer allowed to speak to the other prisoners. The warden allowed Ella to take the stage to speak on Jason's behalf, which was even better, 'cuz now we could hear all about Heaven straight from the horse's mouth."

~~~

I ran out of tape, so I stopped him in midsentence and reloaded another cassette.

"... She allowed the inmates to ask questions.

She only said what she thought she knew or her interpretation of what she thought she saw. She seemed sincere. There was nothing phony about her.

"The day after Jason's death, she met with Father Angel, Whitey, and me to say goodbye."

"Who's Whitey?" I asked."

"You haven't met him?"

"No. I haven't."

"You should; he runs the Aryan Brotherhood. His life has changed more than anyone else's, as far as I know."

"I'll see if they will let me see him." I made myself a note.

I said goodbye and Williams returned to his cell. I asked the main guard in the visiting area if it was possible for me to interview James Whitmore, a.k.a. 'Whitey' before the day was over. He said it was possible if he wanted to talk and told me to come back to the main entrance after lunch.

~~~

I found the same Denny's where Ella and I had eaten shortly after Jason was put to death. I even sat in the same booth.

As I munched on a big cheeseburger, I thought back to that early morning. I remembered wondering what that special bond was between Jason and Ella when he gave her a thumbs-up sign during the execution. She showed her approval by giving it back. The warden had even wiped a tear from his eye before the executioner started dispensing the drugs. At the time, I knew I was missing something, but I didn't know what.

Now it was all starting to make sense. They loved Jason, not for what he was, but for what he gave them. He gave the warden a new prison. The inmates stopped warring against one another. Drugs were a thing of the past. The inmates did their time and when they left, few returned. What Jason gave to so many of the inmates was a lifeline, a buoy to hang onto in a sea of hopelessness, something to keep them afloat. Ella knew if I did my research, I would eventually find all this out. I wondered what Whitey could add to the story.

~~~

At two o'clock in the afternoon, I was brought back into the visiting area where I waited for Whitey to come through the door. I tried to picture him. What would he look like? Since he had such a high-ranking position in one of the most notorious white prison gangs in the nation, I guessed he would probably look like the other two men I'd met. I expected him to be big, another weight lifter, with tattoos, maybe a swastika on top of a bald head.

To my surprise, a small man in his mid-sixties rolled through the door in a wheelchair. His eyes were pink. He was an albino. I understood immediately how he got his nickname. He had no tattoos, and a head of white hair at an average length. When he smiled, he displayed a perfect set of teeth. He saw me and said, "I thought you might have forgotten all about me?"

"No," I said. He was on Death Row and had let all his appeals evaporate. He, like Jason, was ready to die. He was there for killing a black man and his wife over a property dispute. Whitey wanted the property for a low-income housing project he was working on, but the black man didn't want to sell his land. When the man refused to sell, Whitey hired a couple of out-of-state thugs to rough him up, to scare him a little. The man fought back, and one of the men Whitey hired killed him. To get rid of any potential witnesses, they killed his wife, too, who happened to be there at the time. After a month-long investigation, the police traced the crime back to the instigator, Whitey.

We shook hands and he proceeded to tell me his involvement with Jason Bradford and Ella Martin. He said he didn't meet Jason until after they moved him to Death Row. Before his conviction, James 'Whitey' Whitmore had been a big-time attorney in the Denver area; Jason eventually ended up in the cell next to him, giving them plenty of time to talk. He said he didn't see the complete transformation of Jason but saw enough to know he continued to evolve until the day he died.

Whitey wheeled his chair closer and looked me straight in the eyes. "Jason said when he was beating the last woman to death, he had the strangest feeling someone was watching, standing behind him, looking over his shoulder. Before the woman died, she said, 'Thank you, Lord.' He said he thought she was talking to him, but what she said didn't make any sense. Later, Ella told him the woman was talking to an angel, or some other angelic figure, that took her soul the moment she died." Whitey smiled again. "This movement is spreading, you know. I would like to give Jason some of the credit, but I can't. If it weren't for Ella,

Jason would never have confessed; he'd probably be out on the street today, killing more people. I don't know when it will end or if it will end. I certainly won't be around to see it. I'm scheduled to die next month. I hope Father Angel and One-eye Williams can keep it afloat. They were allowed to tape all of Ella's sessions for future use."

I asked how he got in the wheelchair. He said, "Oh, I can walk, I'm not completely disabled. I have a degenerating disc disease. I'll be dead before it completely disables me."

Chapter 37

The warden was next on my list. We met in his office and shortly after sitting down, I looked around the room and noticed several photographs on the walls of him shaking hands with people I didn't recognize. Then I noticed two photos of people I did recognize. One was a picture of the warden and Ella Martin standing side-by-side. The other was of Jason Bradford and Ella together.

The warden's name was Alford J. Bottoms. He'd been in the prison system for nearly twenty years, working his way up the totem pole from a guard's position. Everyone I talked with respected the man, especially the people who worked for him. He was a little overweight, medium height, with a little gray, evenly spread, throughout his hair.

He followed my eyes and watched as they locked onto a photograph inside a picture frame on his desk. The picture was of him when he was a little younger, with a boy about five-years-old and a nice-looking blonde-haired woman.

He said, "The woman in the picture was my

wife. She was the reason I had to postpone our appointment the other day. I don't know why people get cancer, but they do, and she died. My son, the boy in that picture, also died, a long time ago. He died the day I took that picture, my birthday. I've always felt responsible for his death. We had an argument; he wanted to buy me a present, but I told him not to spend his money. He got me something anyway and tried to give it to me. I scolded him and he got upset, running out of the house. A minute or two later, we heard the screeching of automobile tires. Both he and his dog were hit by a car and died instantly."

He reached into his desk drawer and removed a tissue from a small box that was next to an unopened envelope addressed to him from Ella Martin. He pushed the drawer closed and lightly dabbed at his eye, blotting out a tear. "The last time I saw Ella, she was sitting right where you are and she looked like she'd seen a ghost. I asked her what was wrong, but she avoided the question."

He continued, "When Jason first arrived here, he wasn't any different from the other prisoners. He claimed to be innocent, just like all the rest. You know there are no guilty men here! They're all innocent! Wrongly convicted of a crime they didn't commit or railroaded by the justice system.

"One day he had a visitor. The visitor just so happened to be the person who testified against him at his trial. Now, all our inmates go through a psychological evaluation shortly after they arrive. According to his evaluation, he didn't like women. So, it was a little unusual when he allowed this woman to visit him. Then she started seeing him regularly, every month or so. No one could understand why. Before long, he asked our prison chaplain if he could speak at one of his church services, that he had something important to say. The chaplain asked me if it was all right. I said yes, as long as I knew what he was going to say; I didn't want him starting a riot, saying something inappropriate. You'd be surprised at what just a few misunderstood words can do around here. He told me he wanted to confess; take responsibility for what he'd done. But more important, he wanted to tell the audience about an afterlife, so I talked it over with our resident psychiatrist, and we decided to let him speak. After he did, the response was astounding. Word got around. Soon all the inmates lined up, wanting to hear what he had to say."

I asked the warden if he believed in an afterlife.

He took a long look at me and smiled. "I guess I should. What I mean by that is, after seeing many lost souls change direction here inside this prison, I should believe, but I'm sorry to say, I don't. My boy died. He was only six-years-old. He was a good boy! My wife died a horrible death at only thirty-eight. If there's a God, why didn't he protect them? Why were they allowed to die? They were good people!"

I couldn't answer the questions. We shook hands and I thanked him for arranging the interviews with the inmates and his staff.

~~~

The prison psychiatrist was the last person on my Ella Martin must-talk-to list. And once again, how I imagined what the person would look like was wrong. I expected to meet someone who looked like Einstein and talked like Sigmund Freud. Or maybe an old hippie with an earring and long gray hair.

I was escorted down a long corridor, the same corridor I'd walked the night Jason died. We passed under the sign pointing out the way to A and B block and continued until we reached a steel door marked, INFIRMARY. Once inside, we walked around a large open area, short cubicles on the left, walled offices on the right. As we circled the perimeter, I was surprised to see so many specialists in one setting: doctors of internal medicine, cardiologists, oncologists, respiratory experts, and so on.

The name Ramona Johnson was painted on the clouded wired glass window outside the last office, with a long row of acronyms explaining her expertise.

A secretary sitting at a desk in the foyer area gave me a warm smile. "You can go in. Dr. Johnson is expecting you." She pressed a button releasing the locking mechanism on the doctor's door, reminding me of where I was. I pushed open the door and was pleasantly surprised to find a woman in her mid-thirties sitting behind a large oak desk. She was small boned. Her hair was blonde, worn short in the latest style. She dressed plainly and wore little if any makeup; I figured she was instructed not to dress provocatively, or maybe it was by her own accord. Dr. Johnson smiled, stood, and held out a hand.

The office was small and busy, but not cluttered. Dr. Johnson had one wall dedicated to her education with certificates covering nearly the entire wall. The one that stood out the most was one with big letters from the American Board of Psychiatry and Neurology. Another was from a three-year residency program. I tried to read some of the others, but there were so many they were beginning to look like wallpaper.

She noticed me looking at her pedigree. "My position is simple. I'm allowed to diagnose and treat patients with mental, emotional, and behavioral disorders." She made it sound way too easy; I liked that, nothing egotistical.

Dr. Johnson had two photographs on her desk. I recognized both; they were the same ones that Warden Bottoms had on display in his office, except larger. I decided, once again, to reverse my presentation. I said I was there at Ella Martin's request, to which she immediately responded in a positive manner. I told her I was writing a book about life after death and needed to know more about Jason Thomas Bradford. What made him tick? Why did he do what he did — kill all those people?

Dr. Johnson looked serious, touched her chin as if contemplating her next move in a chess match. She said, "I don't normally give out that information. But because you said Ella wanted you to write something on the subject of life after death, and because Jason was a big part of her life, I'll break my own rule and give you whatever information you need. I think he would have liked that."

Walking over to a filing cabinet, she bent down and removed a two-inch thick folder. I watched as she moved; she was graceful. She had a strange effect on me … something I couldn't put my finger on. She sat back down behind her desk and opened his file. Looking up from the paperwork, she said, "Jason was the most interesting and most complex person I've ever met."

I asked if I could tape our session. After nodding yes, I turned on my recording device.

"I can still recall the first time I met him," she said. "He was a strange little man. He didn't look like he could hurt a fly, he was so frail. He sat where you're sitting but wouldn't look me in the eye. He stared at his feet or at the wall behind me but wouldn't look directly at me."

She asked if I would like some coffee or tea. I declined, so she continued where she left off.

"He was smart. Incredibly smart! I couldn't tell if he was leading me on or not, at least not at first. It was difficult getting him to talk. He held everything deep inside. I remember his trial, being absorbed in the controversy as much as anyone. I read everything the press printed. Then, when he was convicted, I knew he would come here. We have three psychiatrists on site; I'm the most senior. I made sure I was the one to do the original work-up on him."

Dr. Johnson wore a small cross on a fine link chain around her neck. A picture of Jesus Christ hung on the wall behind her. She wore no wedding ring, which caught my attention.

"One day a year or so after Jason arrived, I got a phone call from the warden. He said he'd talked to a woman named Ella Martin, who wanted to come visit Jason. He asked me what I thought. Her name sounded vaguely familiar, but I couldn't remember from where. At first, I didn't think it was a good idea, but then, after thinking about it, I decided it might do him some good. I was surprised when he so willingly met with her. He must have thought long and hard about the night of the murder and had a few questions to ask her."

She took a deep breath, as if she were a boxer getting a second wind and continued. "After their first meeting, I sat down with him to find out how things went. I couldn't believe the transformation. I'd worked with him for a little over a year, and gotten nowhere; she, on the other hand, spent a couple of hours with him and he became a changed man. He told me he committed the murder that night, which was something he'd always denied before, and that the crime went down exactly as she'd stated during the trial. He also told me he felt her presence in the house while he was committing the murder but didn't understand what it was. It was just an odd feeling, he said, like someone was there … watching."

She paused as the machine shut itself off. She waited until I put in a fresh cassette.

Picking up where she left off, she said, "From that moment on they met regularly, once every month or two. He even started corresponding with her through the mail. One day the warden asked me what I thought about Jason confessing in front of a group of prisoners at a Sunday church service. At first, I thought it was a bad idea. I was afraid the other prisoners might make fun of him, put him back inside that shell. But after giving it some thought, I changed my mind. We decided to let him speak."

She knew I knew what happened, so she didn't repeat Jason's confession. Instead, she elaborated, "Jason surprised me. He knew he had to be good or the inmates would crucify him — pardon the expression. He told the story starting with Ella Martin and her untimely death. How she went to Heaven, while he was working his way into Hell. I have yet to hear another speech by any actor, politician, or preacher that comes even close to what Jason delivered that Sunday. I don't know if he sat in his cell practicing it or not. But he told the story with passion, straight from the heart. When he finished, no one said a word. That was the end of the service. Everyone just got up and left. I saw several grown men wiping their eyes with their shirtsleeves. It was unbelievable, something to behold. From then on, he was a regular. Unlike a preacher who changes his sermon from week to week, Jason told the same story, time after time. Nobody complained. That's the reason they were there, to hear what he had to say about life after death."

It was getting close to lunch, so I asked her if I could take her out to a nearby restaurant. She said yes, and we ended the interview.

~~~

Dr. Johnson picked out the place to eat. It was nice, and not beyond my budget. The name of the restaurant was Pepe's Italian Cuisine and was located inside a new mall. We sat in a booth, her on one side, me on the other. I watched as she combed her fingers through her hair. I asked if she had ever thought about going into her own practice.

"Yes," she said, "when I first started out, but after a couple of years, I changed my mind. You can't imagine the experience you get from working in a penal institution. Every day is Halloween. You never know what personality you'll find hidden underneath the mask until you remove it, and sometimes when you do, you find there is more than one."

She asked me if I was married, and I said I wasn't. I said, "Maybe someday; I just haven't met the right person yet."

"Me too!" she exclaimed unexpectedly.

The conversation drifted more in my direction with her asking me about my line of work. Did I like being a journalist? Did I find it creative? Was this my first book? Did I believe in an afterlife? I said, "Yes, I like writing. I believe it is creative and yes, it is my first attempt at writing a book."

She looked at me. "That leaves one question unanswered."

I smiled back. "Ella asked me if I was religious. I told her I wasn't, that I considered myself a devout atheist. I asked her if it made any difference. She said, yes, that I would look at things in a skeptical matter. To answer that question requires more investigation. I'm not ready to give my opinion yet." I looked at her. "Do you believe in an afterlife?"

"Yes. I can answer that without any hesitation. I, too, was once skeptical, but not anymore. Jason knew the truth and couldn't hide from it. If you saw Canon Prison before Jason started speaking and what it's like today, there's no comparison. I was here; I watched it happen. I can't give you a scientific explanation. I don't have one. It's just a feeling. When you've seen people, hundreds of people, change overnight, people who could take your life just because you looked at them in a way they thought offensive, it has to be a miracle."

We finished our lunch with small talk: where we grew up, what type of music we enjoyed, and then drove back to the prison.

~~~

She laid out a couple of cassettes on her desk and directed her attention toward me.

"After Jason confessed to all the other murders he'd committed, I had a lot of questions. We sat down and I picked his brain. Jason wasn't the type of person you could put in a box and say he was the way he was because of a certain mental disorder. He wasn't antisocial, although he may have started out that way. He wasn't a textbook sociopath, even though you might be able to check off several boxes in that category. And he wasn't necessary a psychopath either. Psychopaths are usually born that way, and they hardly ever learn from their mistakes.

"I believe Jason would have turned out normal if he had different parents. One of my staff doctors said he thought Jason had multiple personalities: DID. Dissociative Identity Disorder. But that's not true either. Jason was always himself. He was never anyone else. He may have been influenced by his parents; his father was the trophy hunter, his mother the cleaning woman. That may have played a part in how he went about it. Tracking down the women, cleaning their houses. The driving force was revenge. He wanted to kill them both. His father, for the physical abuse he had endured over the years. His mother for pretending that she didn't know the abuse was taking place.

"He was successful in killing his father, which ended the physical abuse. But the thought that his mother let it happen all those years when she might've stopped it, kept eating away at him. He could have ended it by killing her, but that was too easy. He wanted her to suffer like he had when he was growing up. He got pleasure out of killing her over and over again, pretending the women were her. The women he found looked like his mother when she was younger, and they had similar names or initials. It's not unusual. It happens all the time. A kid in a schoolyard is abused by a bully, so in turn, he or she abuses someone else weaker, which makes them feel better. The abused become the abusers."

~~~

She started her tape machine. She could be heard asking Jason to go back in time as far as he could remember.

Jason said the earliest he could recall was just before he started kindergarten. He had three brothers, all older. His father was in the Army at Fort Carson. His mother cleaned houses during the day and took him with her when she worked. His father paid little attention to him; he played ball and other games with his brothers, but Jason was rarely included.

'After I started school my mother took on a second job as a waitress, so I didn't see her much. That was the worst time in my life. I was a bed wetter, which made my father furious. I had to wear a diaper when I went to bed and wet the bed until the age of eight. My father would wait until Sally, my mother, went off to work and then would punish me by making me wear the wet diaper on top of my head. Sometimes I wore it for hours, until right before my mother came home. He told me to keep my mouth shut or I would pay the consequences, which meant he would take me down in the basement.'

'What do you mean, he would take you down in the basement? What happened down there?' Ramona asked.

'When he got real mad, he would take me down there and hit me with his belt. He would put on the Rolling Stones. He liked to beat me to the song "Satisfaction." He would keep in time with the beat.'

'Did he take the other boys down there?'

'No, never. I don't remember them ever getting punished for anything. Sometimes he would punish me for what they did.'

'Did you get along with your brothers?'

'Yes, most of the time.'

'Tell me more about the basement. Did anything else happen down there?'

'He took me down there and turned on the music, so my brothers and the neighbors wouldn't hear me screaming. While down there he made me wear a dress. It was a child's dress. He got it from one of his friends at work. My mother didn't know anything about it. When he hit me with his belt, he would say things like, "Sally, I'm gonna kill you."'

I felt a sudden chill run down my back as I recalled Ella telling me about the little man beating the woman to death inside the woman's house. I didn't know Jason, but I was starting to have some sympathy for him.

The tape continued to play.

'That's all,' he said.

'According to your confession, you stated you killed a neighbor. What happened?'

'That happened when I was ten-years-old. But before that, I started killing small creatures. First a bug; I used a magnifying glass on it, watched it pop! Then I did the same to a frog. It didn't pop. It just hopped away, so I nailed it to a board. I liked watching it squirm; it made me feel like I was in control. I had power over it. I hid it in the garage where no one would find it. Then I started killing rabbits and small rodents in my back yard. I used my slingshot and then my BB gun. I killed a couple of the neighbor's cats. That was fun because I knew, down deep inside, it was wrong. That's what made it interesting, the chance of getting caught.'

She stopped the tape briefly. "I let him talk. He was telling me everything I wanted to hear. How he started out with small creatures and worked his way up to the human, the ultimate prey." She turned the tape back on.

I was recording a tape of her tape, so when she turned off her machine, I was still recording our conversation. I would later replay it and rewrite it to fit in my book format.

Jason's voice continued through the audio: 'One day, when my friend, my only friend, and I were walking home from school, we stopped to play on the bridge, Miller's Bridge. We decided to walk the rail. I went first; I covered the span. I pretended to be a tightrope walker. I went from one side to the other without falling. We had done this many times before. My friend went next. His name was Robert, Robert Hall. When he got to the center where there was no place to grab onto, I gave him a little shove. He screamed and tried to catch the rail on his way down but missed. I looked around to make sure no one saw me. I was real scared, but I had this incredible feeling, something I can't explain. It was amazing. Better than a roller coaster ride. I looked down over the rail to see what happened to him. I thought he was still alive, but he wasn't moving. I ran down to the creek bed. There was only a trickle of water running. I reached down and removed his watch. He had this Davy Crockett watch I liked. After taking it, I ran home as fast as I could.'

I knew about his friend's death from his confession and the interview I had with his mother. Finally, it was starting to make sense. He kept the watch as a reminder, a trophy of his conquest.

'One day, about a year after Robert died, my dad took me down to the basement to punish me for something one of my brothers did. By this time, I was too big to get into the dress. He'd been drinking and I pulled away from him, and when I did, I tripped and fell on the concrete floor. He deliberately stepped on my leg to keep me from getting away, and when he did, he broke my tibia.

He didn't want my mother to know what had happened, so he said we went rabbit hunting and I tripped over a rock. It was days later that I saw a doctor, but by then, infection set in and it never healed right. That's why I walk with a limp and my foot is slightly asymmetric, pointing at ten o'clock.'

'And what about your father; what happened to him?'

'It was a Saturday and my mother was working. My father was in the back yard sitting on our picnic bench. He had gone hunting a few days earlier and was cleaning his rifles, something he always did within a few days afterward. I was inside the house, watching him from the kitchen window. I'd pictured the scene in my head a hundred times before; I played it over and over again. I knew his routine; he never varied. After he cleaned his shotgun, he loaded it, and sat it down on top on the bench with the barrel facing in his direction. It wasn't pointing directly at him, but off to his side. I saw my chance and took it. I went out and sat down on the bench on the opposite side. His shotgun lay there, just to my right. He was getting ready to clean his deer rifle. I picked up his shotgun and pointed it at his chest. He said, "Do you want to kill me? You little harelip bastard! Go ahead, pull the trigger!" So I did what he asked me to do. You should have seen the look of surprise on his face. That was priceless!'

'How did you make it look like an accident?'

'I was wearing gloves, thin latex gloves. I wore them when I did the dishes. That's what I was doing, washing the dishes before I went out to the back yard. I told you I had time to plan it. I broke off a dead branch from a nearby elm tree and wedged it in the tabletop between the redwood slats. I left only an inch or so sticking up. Then I placed his shotgun — trigger housing — over the protruding stub and pushed it forward. The gun had already fired, so I didn't have to worry about it going off again. Once the stub broke off, I left it lying on the table and placed the shotgun on the ground where I thought it would land after it had fired. It looked like an accident. It looked like he set the shotgun down over the stub and caught the trigger, causing it to fire. I even cried during the investigation. I think the investigator believed every word I said because I never heard anything more about it. After the funeral, I removed my collection from the garage and started putting them in his footlocker in the basement.'

Jason coughed and cleared his throat as Ramona asked him about the first woman he killed. He said, 'The first time was a disaster. I was way too slow going up the back steps. She turned around and saw my face. It didn't make any difference, because right from the start I planned on killing her. When she screamed, I put my hand over her mouth and hit her in the forehead, knocking her unconscious. This was before I realized I needed to wrap the pipe with cushioning material. The first two times I didn't use the bat. I used a metal pipe. I hit Stella, Stella Bigelow, the first woman, too hard, causing blood to fly everywhere. She reminded me the most of my mother. They looked a lot alike. It took me more than an hour to clean up the mess. That's when I decided to wrap the pipe.'

'And what about the second woman; do you remember her?'

'I remember them all. They all looked like Sally. The second woman's name was Sheila Blackburn. She was older than the others. She was somewhere between thirty-five and forty. I screwed up on that one, too. I got to her before she had a chance to open the second lock. That's when I decided to enter their houses on a trial run when they were at work. I was lucky I brought along the alarm code, otherwise, I would have had to kill her right there on the back porch. I used wire to tie Stella and Sheila up. Then I got this bright idea about using plastic ties.'

He then described how he killed number three and four without a hitch.

'Was there anything different the night you killed Sandra Brown?' Ramona asked.

'The night I killed Sandra Brown, I went to my mother's house early. We had dinner, separately. I ate down in the basement. I didn't want to see her ugly face. She did what she always does. She turned on her TV and reclined in the big green chair. When she's watching a movie she puts on earphones, so she can hear the sound better. That was never mentioned at the trial. I went upstairs around 6:30 p.m. I saw her wearing the earphones and knew she wouldn't hear me leave. I got into her car and drove to Sandra's house. I parked across the street and removed my cleaning supplies from the trunk. I carried them across the street in my father's big duffel bag. As soon as I reached the other side, I had an eerie feeling. Later, in the house, I had it again. Like someone was watching, but no one was there.'

'Was there any particular reason you picked out

the women you did?'

'Of course. I chose them because they all looked like my mother when she was young and pretended not to know my father was abusing me. She might say she never knew my father was abusing me, but I don't believe that for one minute. One day, I overheard my brother, Troy, tell my mother, shortly before my father's death, that he saw the two of us, my father and me, go down into the basement, and when we returned, he was carrying me. I couldn't walk.'

That was the end of the tape and the end of my interview with Dr. Ramona Johnson.

Chapter 38

Ramona and I married two weeks after we met. I moved into her house on the upper west side, not far from Canon Prison. Soon after our wedding, Ramona was pregnant and we were expecting a baby. The day after receiving the good news, I landed a job working for the local paper — *The Daily Record*. My work on the book slowed to a snail's pace, but I continued to plug away at it, even though I was running out of words. I'd been expecting a spectacular ending, but by now, nearly thirteen months later, it looked like that wasn't going to happen. After all my interviews and research, I still had this empty feeling there was more to the story: somewhere I was missing something, but what? I wondered.

On New Year's Day we were invited over to the neighbor's house to watch the Rose Bowl on their big screen TV. A little before kickoff, I was still in our office, sitting behind our desk, staring at an envelope addressed to me from Ella Martin. I'd received it shortly after her death. I wondered what she would think if she knew she was responsible for Ramona and me getting together.

Special instructions were written on the outside of the envelope:

Attention:
Do not open until after December 31, 2009

I had received it a couple of weeks after Jason was put to death. A little more than two years had passed and I was eager to find out what was inside. I anxiously cut open the sealed flap with my letter opener and peeked inside. I quickly removed the single piece of paper, laid it on my desk, and ironed out the folds. The first thing I noticed were the puffy white clouds on blue stationery. *Beautiful*, I thought. It was almost like they were moving across the paper. Then I noted the ray of light that shone through the clouds and lit up the handwritten words, neatly printed in the center of the paper. I noticed the date in the upper right-hand corner, just above the stamp. If I remembered correctly, she wrote it on the same day she died. December 1, 2007.

I couldn't believe what I was reading. The main body of the letter was made up of fourteen words, of which I will never forget.

Congratulations on the birth of your daughter!
And thanks for naming her after me!
P.S. Buy her a cello or any string instrument.
I have this funny feeling she'll play like an angel.
Say hello to Ramona for me, and tell her
Jimmy said it's okay to let go.
He's doing fine.

Then I remembered something Ella said on the tape I'd made. She asked the being of light if she would remember her experience, and it answered, 'You will remember it like you would a dream. Except that you will believe it was real. You will not remember any experience before your earthly voyage, only a sense of being somewhere else before. You will gradually become more in tune with the spiritual realm. You may call it instinct, intuition, or a sixth sense.'

My wife Ramona lost her younger brother, Jimmy, when he was fifteen. She'd always felt bad about not being there when he died.

Tears ran down my face and I finally understood why she'd picked me to tell the story. She wasn't here to save Jason; he was only the conduit. She was here for me — I had been a true nonbeliever. So had Detective Rusty Stubbs. But who was the third soul mate? I still didn't know the answer to that question.

~~~

It was almost time for the game to start, with kickoff just minutes away, and the three of us were making last-minute preparations. I was bundling up the baby for the short trek to the next-door neighbor's house.

Ramona read the letter from Ella and to my surprise, she was not the least bit surprised. She said she'd been a believer since Jason's transformation. But she was happy to hear about her brother; that made her day.

We were just starting to walk down the front porch steps when I heard the telephone ring. For some unknown reason, I felt compelled to answer it. I told Ramona to go ahead without me, that I'd be there in a couple of minutes.

I ran back into the house and picked up the phone in the office. I was surprised to hear a voice from the not-so-distance past. It was Alford Bottoms, the prison warden where Jason had been housed. He asked me if I had completed my book. I told him not yet, but I was getting there.

He started crying. "Do you remember asking me if I believed in an afterlife?"

I said, "Yes," and then asked, "Why?"

He told me that after his wife died, especially in recent months, he became extremely despondent to the point of having suicidal thoughts. This morning, he said he got up, sat down at his desk, and wrote a suicide note. He placed his revolver to his temple and was about to pull the trigger when the phone rang. He said he wasn't sure why, but he decided to answer it. When he did, no one answered back, but the line wasn't dead either. He thought he heard breathing, and then music, beautiful music playing way off in the background, barely audible … a symphony, like he'd never heard before. After he hung up, he felt compelled to open his desk drawer. When he did, he noticed a letter he'd received in the mail from Ella Martin shortly after Jason's execution. On the outside, it read:

Attention:

Do not open until after December 31st, 2009

He said he'd forgotten all about it. He asked if he could read it to me. I said, "Yes, please do!" I pressed down the button on the speakerphone, so I could lean back in my chair and relax. The letter started out, 'When you read this letter I will no longer be with you. You've been wondering why bad things happen to good people. God does not play favorites! It's all chance! Someone has to die; if not, where would God put all of us? We would be standing on top of one another's shoulders; we need to make room for a new soul. Occasionally, we get a second chance, especially if we were going in the wrong direction. Your son never felt anything. His soul left his body before he was hit by the car.'

I heard him blow his nose, and then he continued. 'When I had my out-of-body experience and went to Heaven, I met a young boy playing with a black Labrador Retriever. He told me to tell his daddy he was sorry for disobeying him and to look underneath the big rock. I didn't know what that meant or who his father was until I saw the picture in your office. I also knew that it was not the right time to tell you. When you read this, your wife will be here with him.'

He said his wife was diagnosed with cancer after Ella's death, not before. At the time she wrote the letter there was no way for her to know what would happen to his wife — unless she had help from above.

He spoke. "I ran into the back yard and found the big rock. The big rock was not large, except to a boy of six. It probably weighed no more than fifteen pounds. I turned it over and found a small box wrapped up in fancy paper. The paper and box were weathered, but still intact. I peeled back the once colorful paper and hurriedly opened the box. Inside was a Bible, my son's Bible. I turned the cover and read the inscription on its inside.

Happy Birthday Daddy
I love you,
Bradley

"I dropped to my knees and looked up at the sky. 'I love you, too, son.' Thank you, Ella!

"So, to answer your question, do I believe in an afterlife? Yes, I do!"

THE END

About the Author

Duke Woodrick was born in Santa Monica, California. He grew up in Venice, California, and now lives in Henderson, Nevada, with his wife, Marjorie. *A Matter of Faith* is his second published novel.

www.ingramcontent.com/pod-product-compliance
Lightning Source LLC
Chambersburg PA
CBHW071149250626
47159CB00001B/40